D0206377

DON'T LET GO

Michel Bussi

DON'T LET GO

*Translated from the French
by Sam Taylor*

Europa
editions

Europa Editions
214 West 29th Street
New York, N.Y. 10001
www.europaeditions.com
info@europaeditions.com

First published in French as *Ne lâche pas ma main* by Presses de la Cité,
a department of Place des Editeurs, Paris.
First published in English in 2017 by Weidenfeld & Nicolson, London

Copyright © Presses de la Cité, a department of Place des Editeurs 2013
First Publication 2018 by Europa Editions

Translation by Sam Taylor
Original title: *Ne lâche pas ma main*
English translation copyright © Sam Taylor 2017

Library of Congress Cataloging in Publication Data is available
ISBN 978-1-60945-453-1

Bussi, Michel
Don't Let Go

Book design and cover illustration by Emanuele Ragnisco
www.mekkanografici.com

Prepress by Grafica Punto Print – Rome

Printed in the USA

CONTENTS

For Chloé, 18 already

Fé lève lo mort . . .
("It is dangerous to bring back the past,"
a proverb from Réunion)

DON'T LET GO

SAINT-DENIS

Le Port

Boucan Canot

Saint-Benoît

Mafate   Salazie
                    Hell-Bourg

Saint-Gilles
La Saline-les-Bains

Piton des Neiges

Cilaos

Plaine
des Sables

Anse
des Cascades

Entre-Deux

Piton de la
Fournaise

Saint-Louis

Saint-Pierre

Cap Méchant

10 km

Réunion Island

PART ONE

1
A Few Wet Footprints
Saint-Gilles-les-Bains, Réunion Island

Friday, March 29, 2013, 3:01 P.M.

"I'm just going up to the room for a second."

Liane does not wait for a response, she simply tells her daughter and her husband, looking cheerful, radiant, as she moves away from the swimming pool.

Gabin, behind his bar, watches her with professional discretion. This week, Liane is by some distance the most beautiful woman in the Hotel Athena, yet she's not the type of tourist who normally catches his eye. Petite, very slender, almost no breasts, but there's something classy about her, a *je ne sais quoi*. Maybe it's her skin, still white with a bouquet of freckles starting to show on her lower back, just above her emerald and gold bikini bottoms. Or that sweet little rear, swaying gently as she walks, like green fruit in a treetop rocked by the wind. The woman walks barefoot across the lawn, seemingly without bending a single blade of grass. Gabin watches her go past the deckchairs until she reaches the patio, half hidden by a skinny palm tree. The last thing he saw—as he will tell Captain Purvi—was the woman discreetly removing her bikini top; the fleeting vision of a bare back, a white breast, the hint of a nipple, before she grabbed her large beach towel and wrapped it around her.

3:03 P.M.

Naivo, standing behind his mahogany desk in the reception area, returns Liane's smile as best he can.

"Hello, mademoiselle . . ."

She walks across the crowded lobby, passing between a stand displaying postcards and a clothes rail filled with *pareos* and flowery shirts. Her blonde hair drips onto the towel covering her breasts. Naivo finds this attractive: those strapless shoulders, white, unmarked. The woman walks slowly, careful not to slip because she's barefoot. This is not normally allowed, but Naivo is not there to upset the tourists. Water still trickles down the woman's legs. A second later, she has disappeared towards the lifts, and all that remains of her is a few puddles. Like Amélie Poulain when she bursts into tears, Naivo suddenly thinks. He doesn't know why. But that is what he will always think, afterwards. For hours, whole nights, tortured by his memories. The fact that the woman vanished into thin air, literally evaporated. But he won't dare tell the police that. It's not the kind of thing they would understand.

3:04 P.M.

The lift swallows Liane. Second floor. It goes up to paradise and opens to a stunning view, displayed through the large picture windows: the south-facing swimming pool and, beyond it, Ermitage Beach. Shaded by casuarina trees, the long golden crescent seems to stretch out forever, nibbled by the timid waves of the lagoon, which are calmed by the distant coral reef.

"Watch out, it's wet!" Eve-Marie shouts at the lift, before she even knows who is going to step out.

Eve-Marie pulls a face. It's that blonde from number 38. Barefoot, of course. The woman in the towel pretends to be all shy and embarrassed with the junior staff, just the right amount of hypocrisy. She walks on tiptoe, over to the side, a good meter away from the bucket and the mop, apologizing all the while.

"Never mind," grumbles Eve-Marie, clutching her broom. "Go on, I'll do it again once you've passed."

"I'm so sorry, really . . ."

Sure you are, Eve-Marie murmurs to herself.

The blonde wiggles her behind as she minces like a ballerina, afraid of slipping on the wet tiles. More like an ice skater than some little ballet dancer, Eve-Marie thinks. A triple axel in eighty-five-degree heat in the tropics, now that would be something! Watched by the cleaning lady, the pretty woman brings one last slide under control and stops in front of her apartment door, number 38. She puts the key in the lock, enters, disappears.

All that remains of her are a few wet footprints on the perfectly clean tiles. And even these are already vanishing, as if the cold tiles have sucked the rest of her in, leaving the feet until last. Like a sort of high-tech quicksand, Eve-Marie thinks. Standing alone in the vast glass-walled corridor, she sighs. She still has to dust the pictures on the walls, watercolors of Les Hauts, Réunion's craggy interior, small islets, the ancient forest; the most beautiful parts of the island where tourists never set foot. With the windows to clean and the corridor to wash, she has enough work to keep her busy all afternoon. Normally, after the siesta, she's left in peace up on her floor. Nobody comes back up; they're all out at the pool or the lagoon. All of them, except for the *katish*[1] . . .

Eve-Marie wonders whether she should bother mopping up the girl's footprints. She'll undoubtedly come back out in a few minutes wearing a new bikini top because she wasn't getting a good enough tan with the other one.

[1] "Pretty girl" in Réunion Creole.

2
WAVE GOODBYE

3:31 P.M.

Rodin's thing is taming the waves.

Using only his eyes.

And, contrary to what the drunks in the port at Saint-Gilles think, it is far from easy. It takes time. Patience. Cunning. It requires focus, a refusal to be distracted—by the sound of that car door slamming behind him, for example. Never look at the ground, always at the horizon.

The ocean is a crazy thing. Once, when he was young, Rodin went to a museum. Well, a sort of museum. In the north of France, near Paris, the house of some old guy who spent most of his day watching the reflection of the sun on the surface of a pond. Not even with waves, just water lilies. And this in a country where it's always cold, where the sky is so low you can almost touch it. It was the only time he ever left the island. It didn't make him want to do it again. In the museum next to the house there were some paintings—landscapes, sunsets, grey skies, a few of the sea. The most impressive ones were a good two meters wide and three meters tall. There was a crowd of people there, women mostly, old women, who seemed able to stand in front of a canvas for hours.

Strange.

The sound of another car door behind him. Using only his ears, he measures the direction and the distance; the car park by the port, thirty meters from the end of the pier where he sits on his rock. Probably a tourist who thinks he can capture the waves with his camera, like a fisherman who hopes to catch a fish just by standing in the water for a second. Idiots . . .

He thinks again about that bearded maniac. When it comes down to it, those painters are just like him really, trying to capture the light, waves, movement. But why burden yourself with canvases and paintbrushes? All you have to do is sit here, by the sea, and look. He is aware that some people on the island think he's mad to spend the whole day just staring at the horizon. But he's no madder than those old women standing in front of their paintings. In fact, he's less mad because he doesn't have to pay for the privilege. This view is free, a gift from the brilliant and generous painter who lives up there.

A muffled cry disturbs the silence behind him. A sort of groan. The tourist must be feeling ill . . .

Rodin does not turn around. To understand the sea, to fathom its rhythm, you must remain immobile. Barely even breathing. The waves are like nervous squirrels: one false move and they'll run away . . . The girl at the unemployment office asked him what kind of work he was looking for, his aptitudes, his plans, his skills. He told her he knew how to talk to the waves, to recognize and tame them, so to speak. He then asked the girl, quite seriously, what kind of job he could do with that. Something in research, perhaps? Something cultural? People are interested in bizarre things, after all. She had stared at him, wide-eyed, as if she thought he was making fun of her. She was pretty cute; he would have liked to bring her here to the pier and introduce her to the waves. He often does that with his great-nephews. They understand. Well, a bit.

Less and less, though.

The scream explodes behind him. It is not just a groan this time. It's clearly a cry for help.

Rodin turns around. The spell has been broken anyway; it would take him hours to enter into communion again.

His face turns pale.

He glimpses a car, a black 4x4. And a shadow too, stocky, almost wider than he is tall, dressed in a *kurta*, the person's face concealed by a strange khaki cap. A Malbar,[2] undoubtedly.

Rodin stutters. When he spends too much time with the waves, he has trouble finding his words. It takes him a moment to speak again.

"Excuse m . . . I wan . . ."

He cannot look away from the knife in the Malbar's hand, the red blade. He makes no move to defend himself. And really, the only thing he would have liked is to have had the time to turn back to the sea and say goodbye to the waves, the light, the horizon. He doesn't care about anything else. But the Malbar doesn't even give him the chance to do that.

Rodin sees the 4x4's open trunk. An arm, half-covered in a sheet, dangling from it. A . . .

Everything goes blurred.

One hand grips his shoulder while another stabs the knife into his heart.

---

[2] A non-Muslim inhabitant of Réunion, of Indian origin.

3
THE EMPTY ROOM

4:02 P.M.

The sun hangs above the swimming pool like a huge halogen bulb fastened there for eternity. The neat jungle of palm trees and octopus bushes, cloistered by three high teak walls, protects the enclosed space from even the faintest breath of wind. You can guess at the ocean's presence from the tropicbirds flying above, the cooling influence of the distant trade winds. But in the garden of the Hotel Athena, the heat beats down on the square of lawn and the few tourists escape it by diving into the chlorinated water then lying on the deckchairs lined up in shady corners.

"I'm going to see what Liane's doing."

Martial levers himself up from the pool with his arms. Gabin sees him approaching. Liane's husband isn't bad either, it has to be said, with his muscular legs, his six-pack, his broad shoulders. He looks like a PE teacher, or a fireman, or a soldier, one of those professions where you're paid to spend your days pumping iron. Perfectly tanned too, in contrast to his wife's milky skin. Less than a week they've been here, and already he looks like a Cafre[3] . . . The handsome Martial must have a drop of black blood, just the tiniest chromosome from a slave ancestor, a dormant pigment that only needs a bit of sunlight to allow it to percolate through, the way a single drop of Blue Curaçao can color a cocktail.

As the tourist moves towards the bar, Gabin watches the

[3] A person from Réunion of African original.

water running down his hairless chest. Martial and Liane Bellion make a beautiful couple, playing at lazing around in the tropics. Sexy and rich. Good for them, thinks Gabin. Win-win. The happiness of wealthy white lovers is fundamental to commerce in destinations that are supposedly paradise.

Their bizness . . .

Martial is standing in front of him.

"Gabin, has my wife come back down?"

"No, sorry, I haven't seen her . . ."

Gabin glances at the clock behind him. It is exactly an hour since Liane went upstairs. And one thing's for sure: if her sweet little ass had wandered back into his line of vision, he would have remembered. Martial turns around, and walks a few feet towards the bodies splashing around in the pool.

"Margaux, can you look after Sopha? I'm going to see what Liane's doing."

Gabin registers every detail of the scene with a precision he is not, at that moment, aware of. The exact time on the clock. The position of those around him, in the water, sitting on the edge of the pool, or lying back in deckchairs. The police will make him repeat his description ten times, sketching the scene just to be sure. Not once will he contradict himself.

Margaux, swimming lengths in the pool, barely even looks up. Margaux is half of another couple; the wife of Jacques, the lawyer who is sitting reading on his deckchair. Or sleeping.

"You know, Captain Purvi," Gabin will say apologetically, "it's hard to tell when they're wearing sunglasses . . ."

Margaux and Jacques Jourdain are a less glamorous couple than Liane and Martial, and at least ten years older. More annoying, too. He spends most of his time on the computer in the lobby, reading his emails, while she just swims from one end of the pool to the other. She swims for kilometers. Given that the pool is twelve meters long, that's a frightening number of lengths.

Worse than a tailless tenrec[4] caught under a crate by kids in Les Hauts. The Jourdains are bored shitless, even in the tropics. Gabin doesn't want to imagine what they must be like in Paris . . .

Sopha is Liane and Martial's daughter. Well, Sopha is what they call her; her real name is Josapha. In the pool, she whimpers as though she might actually sink, even with those Dora the Explorer water wings around her arms. Gabin spotted the little blonde girl's tyrannical temperament on the very first day, as if the kid had decided her sole duty during this holiday was to ruin it for her parents. She's gifted, or something like that. Barely six years old and already blasé. How many Parisian girls of her age have ever swum in eighty-five-degree water under the shade of casuarina trees, with fluorescent coral and clownfish slipping between their toes?

While Gabin pontificates to himself about this spoiled only child, Martial has slipped into the hotel.

4:05 P.M.

All Naivo can remember seeing is Martial Bellion's back as he stood in front of the lift. He must have been looking elsewhere when Bellion came through the lobby, or was immersed in his accounts. But it was definitely him, no doubt about it. Same swimming trunks, same back, same hair. It won't be easy to explain this to the police, but yes, it is perfectly possible to recognize a man from behind.

4:06 P.M.

"It's all right, go ahead, that bit's O.K. !" Eve-Marie shouts

[4] A small hedgehog native to the island.

at Martial, who hesitates at the sight of the spotlessly clean tiles. "It's dry!"

Through the immaculate windows on the second floor, Martial glances down at the hotel garden. Sopha is sitting at the edge of the pool, alone. Margaux looks up at her every three strokes. Martial sighs, then walks over towards number 38.

He knocks softly on the dark wooden door. He waits. Knocks again. After a few seconds, he turns around and explains to Eve-Marie, who has not said a word:

"My wife has the keys . . . I don't think she can hear me. I'm going to ask the guy at reception to open it for me . . ."

Eve-Marie shrugs. What does she care? The floor's dry now.

Martial returns a few moments later, flanked by Naivo, who plays Saint Peter with a massive bunch of keys chiming at his wrist. Eve-Marie rolls her eyes. It's like a carnival in her corridor this afternoon! Naivo is a methodical man: the first key he inserts in the lock opens the door to number 38.

Martial goes in. Naivo stands on the threshold, a meter behind him.

The room is empty.

Martial takes another step forward, disoriented.

"I don't understand. Liane should be here . . ."

Naivo puts a hand on the door frame. A shiver runs through his arm. Something is wrong here: he sensed it instantly. While Martial scans the room's few recesses, Naivo's eyes fix on every detail. The double bed, with the fuchsia duvet rolled in a ball. The scattered clothes. The cushions and the remote control on the carpet. The white glass vase knocked off the roble-wood shelf. All clues pointing to a violent domestic quarrel.

Or to a passionate fuck between consenting lovers, thinks Naivo, forcing himself to be more positive.

Frantic, Martial opens the bathroom door.

Nobody there.

Not in this room, or anywhere else. There is no balcony, no space under the bed in which she could hide, no cupboard with doors that close, only wooden shelving.

Martial sits on the bed, looking devastated, lost. And yet, bizarrely, Naivo does not believe him. He won't really know how to express this to the police, but something in Bellion's reaction does not seem natural. He will simply describe the scene to Captain Purvi, describe this handsome, self-assured, forty-year-old father collapsing like a child when he found the room empty. This playboy in his trunks sitting like a statue on the edge of the bed. Perhaps that was what struck him as sur-real in the moment it happened. The contrast . . .

The contrast . . . and the red stains . . .

Sweat pours down Naivo's forehead.

Red stains on the bedsheet.

Naivo stares. A dozen other red stains are spread across the beige carpet, around the bed, near the window, on the cur-tains. He falls silent. All he can see now is a room splattered with blood.

Indecision.

The moment seems to stretch, though in reality it lasts no more than a few seconds. Martial stands up, silent, and stalks around the room, throwing the clothes from the bed as if searching for an explanation, a note, some kind of clue. Naivo senses Eve-Marie staring over his shoulder. She has walked towards them, cloth in hand so she has an excuse. The cloth is the same turquoise color as the scarf she wears in her hair.

Martial stands up straight and finally speaks, in a toneless voice, as he picks up the vase and puts it back on the wooden shelf.

"I don't understand. Liane should be here . . ."

Naivo's gaze alights on the clothes he has thrown in a pile at the foot of the bed. T-shirts, cropped trousers, shirts.

All of them men's clothes!

Immediately, a door opens inside Naivo's brain, and a breeze blows through, sweeping away his morbid theories.

The girl has run away . . .

He could testify as an expert witness: Liane Bellion wears a different dress practically every hour of the day. You'd have thought her Corsair flight was accompanied by a cargo ship full of her clothes that were unloaded at the port. And yet, in this ravaged apartment, there is not a single trace of any lace knickers, frilled skirts or *pareos*, any skintight tops or low-cut camisoles . . .

Naivo is breathing more easily. He has forgotten about the blood.

"I don't believe it," Martial hisses, examining once more the two square meters of the bathroom.

"Monsieur Bellion," says Naivo, "can I do anything?"

Martial turns on his heel and speaks quickly, as if he had prepared his response in advance, learned it by heart.

"Call the police! My wife should be in this room. She came up here an hour ago. She didn't come back down." He slams the bathroom door and says: "So yes, you can do something. Get me the police."

Ever the professional, Naivo suppresses a worried frown. Calling the police to the hotel . . . The boss is not going to be happy about that. Between the *chik*[5] and the thousand-euro-plus cost of a flight from Paris, tourism is already suffering here. So the idea of having the police walking round the swimming pool, of every guest being interrogated, of blue flashing lights . . . No, the boss is not going to like that at all. But what choice does he have?

"Of course, monsieur," Naivo hears himself say. "I'll go down now and call them."

---

[5] The chikungunya virus.

His eyes meet Eve-Marie's, and a wordless flicker of understanding passes between them. Then he takes one last look at Martial. The man is prowling the room like a caged animal. The air conditioning is making all his muscles shiver, like a surfer lost on the Baltic Sea.

"You should put some clothes on, monsieur."

He cannot tell if the guest has even heard him.

"This . . . this is not normal," Martial Bellion whispers again. "Liane should have been here."

4
RETURN TO THE ATHENA

5:07 P.M.

Captain Aja Purvi curses as she slams on the brakes of her Peugeot 206. Just before the Cap de la Marianne tunnel, one of the two lanes of the coast road is closed off with an interminable row of orange cones.

Roadworks!

The tunnel entrance resembles a vast black mouth, slowly sucking in a necklace of multicolored metal sheeting. The 206 crawls forward for another ten meters or so, then stops behind a 4x4, level with a red pickup truck.

Irritated, Aja checks the clock on the dashboard.

How long will it take to drive the eight kilometers that separate her from the Hotel Athena? Thirty minutes? An hour? More?

Suppressing her fury, Aja stares out at the waves of the Indian Ocean crashing against the rocky outcrop that is supposed to look like Marianne in profile. Hmm . . . Aja has never been able to see the resemblance between this block of basalt and the symbol of the French Republic. They'd have been better off just blasting the thing with dynamite than spending billions on the Route des Tamarins, a few hundred meters higher up, a blot on the landscape that will not solve any of the island's traffic problems. All it will do is foster the illusion that an endless number of cars can continue to be registered here, thirty thousand new ones every year, ad infinitum. What they really ought to do is just face the truth: Réunion Island is a mountain that has grown out of the sea. Almost its entire population is crammed around the edges, and they all travel by car along the narrow, flat-ish strip of land between the ocean and the lower slopes of the volcanoes, going round and round in circles, no more free than protons in a cyclotron. A particle decelerator—the islanders are testing the concept.

Aja switches off the engine with a sigh of resignation. The man in the next car stares down at her from his pickup. A Cafre in a white T-shirt, his arm dangling from the truck's open window. This adds to Aja's annoyance. If she'd taken the gendarmerie's Jumper, or if she had a blue flashing light to put on the roof of her 206, she'd get past this crowd of vehicles in a few minutes; they would part for her like the Red Sea, including that Cafre, who is twisting his neck so he can get a good view of her cleavage . . . Unconsciously, Aja pulls the seams of her blouse together. Sometimes guys like that make her want to wear the veil, just to piss them off.

After all, when it's eighty-five degrees, a baseball cap is obviously a better option than a *chador* . . .

Or a policewomen's cap . . .

But the Athena's manager, Armand Zuttor, had been very insistent on that point.

"Keep it discreet, eh, Aja? Whatever you do, don't go scaring off the tourists!"

That Gros Blanc[6] hotel manager knew her when she was a child and came to the Athena with her parents, and he still talks to her with the same familiarity he did then. But Aja is no fool: she knows there is a fine line between affection and humiliation.

"This is a private affair, Aja, you understand, not an official investigation. Martial Bellion does not wish to press charges against anyone. Just come and see him, reassure him about his wife. I'm asking if you'll do this for me as a favor."

---

[6] Literally, "Fat White Man," a name given to island inhabitants from mainland France who have retained the wealth they gained during colonial days.

A favor? Incognito? Anything else? But how can she refuse? Tourism represents eighty percent of employment in Saint-Gilles.

Two hundred people work in hotels here, more than thirty of them in the Athena alone.

According to Armand Zuttor, there is no cause for alarm. This is a simple domestic case: a Parisian couple on holiday, the wife going off with her suitcase, leaving the husband alone by the pool like an idiot, with a six-year-old kid on his hands.

"Funny, isn't it, Aja? If this had happened to a Creole, everyone would just have laughed. Even if it was a Zoreille.[7] But a tourist . . . and then the husband won't face facts, won't admit that his little bird has simply flown away. He was the one who insisted we call the cops, that you get your arses over here straight away . . . You understand?"

Aja understands. And so the captain of the Saint-Paul gendarmerie had got in her car as fast as a fireman at the first hint of smoke appearing at the top of the Fournaise volcano.

Now here she is, stuck in traffic. At a standstill; no one is entering or leaving the tunnel at all. Aja sighs and restlessly opens the driver-side window. The air is oppressive, not a breath of wind. Tyre-meltingly hot. The sound of a *séga*[8] song flits over the motionless row of cars, emanating from the pickup's radio. The Cafre drums along to the rhythm with his ring-covered fingers, no doubt waiting for the Radio Freedom presenter to list all the kilometers of traffic jams on the island, while reminding his already depressed listeners that there are no alternative routes.

Aja throws her head back against the headrest. She wishes she could just leave the car here and walk to the hotel. The

[7] Someone from mainland France who lives permanently on Réunion.
[8] A kind of music and dance from the island.

Cafre seems unfazed by the traffic jam. In fact, he almost appears to be enjoying it. After all, he has music, sunshine, the sea . . . and a girl to ogle at.

As if he had nothing better to do with his day . . .

5:43 P.M.

Martial Bellion stands opposite Aja Purvi. He is very pale, the captain notes. She's the one who's been sweltering in the sun for the past hour, her arse stuck to the leatherette seat of her 206, and yet it is the tourist who is sweating buckets, despite the air-conditioned cool of the hotel lobby. As soon as she came in, he stood up from his plastic, imitation wicker chair.

"Captain Purvi?"

His mouth was open, as if he were gasping for air; it made him look like the exotic fish in the aquarium behind him.

"I . . . I apologize for disturbing you, Captain. I'm sure that, for a police officer such as yourself, a disappearance like this must seem very ordinary, unremarkable . . . but . . . how can I put this? I'm sorry, Captain, I'm not making myself very clear . . . What I mean to say is that, despite how it seems, there . . . there is . . ."

Aja tries to look sympathetic while Martial wipes his dripping forehead with his open shirt. He has only been speaking for a few seconds, and Bellion has already apologized twice. She finds it strange, this feeling of guilt, particularly at odds with his handsome face, the muscular pectorals visible beneath his Blanc du Nil shirt. What does he have to feel so guilty about?

Bellion sucks in air as if he's about to go for some kind of world record, then says in a gush of words:

"Captain, let me start again. I'm not stupid, I know everyone must think that my wife has just left me. Obviously . . .

There's no lack of temptation here, on this island. But listen, Captain, I'm sure that's not what's happened . . . She wouldn't have left like that. Not without her daughter . . . Not without—'

Aja suddenly interrupts Martial's stammering.

"O.K., Monsieur Bellion. There's no need to justify yourself. We're going to do everything we possibly can. You're lucky: Armand Zuttor takes very good care of his customers. The police force is all part of the service, ensuring the safety of the guests. Don't worry, I will investigate your wife's disappearance, as discreetly as possible . . ."

"Do you want to . . ."

Martial's linen shirt is sticking to his skin. Transparent with sweat. Aja smiles and turns to look at the yellow tang bossing the other fish around in the aquarium. There is something in this tourist's behaviour that continues to intrigue her.

"Listen, Monsieur Bellion, it's too late today, but you should come to the police station in Saint-Gilles tomorrow to make an official report of your wife's disappearance. You'll be required to show your ID, and to fill out a few forms. In the meantime, I'll see what I can do. Do you have a photograph of your wife?"

"Of course."

He hands her the picture. Aja observes the impeccable oval of Liane Bellion's face, the cascade of blonde hair, the fine white teeth. A pureblood! She is well aware that such a girl would stimulate desire in a racial melting pot like Réunion. Aja purses her lips sympathetically.

"Thank you, Monsieur Bellion. Armand Zuttor has already given me the essential details. Stay in the lobby or in the hotel garden, have a beer or a glass of rum—it'll do you good—but don't go up to your room yet, and don't touch anything. I'll come back to you in a few minutes."

5:46 P.M.

Gabin watches Aja walk around the edge of the swimming pool and approach the bar. The captain slaps the photograph on the counter.

"A beautiful girl like that in the hotel, I assume you must have noticed her, Gabin?"

The barman takes his time before replying. Usually, the eyes of the customers who stand on the other side of the bar sweep past him to the impressive collection of flavored rums that fill sweet jars over three shelves, like brightly colored potions in an apothecary's window. Aja, on the other hand, stares straight into his eyes. She couldn't care less about the rum. Like most Zarabes,[9] she doesn't drink alcohol. Not for lack of trying on Gabin's part. Many times, when Aja was a teenager, waiting for her mother and father by the edge of the pool, he would offer her a drink, just to taste. That was before the tragedy, of course.

As Aja is looking into his eyes, Gabin does the same to her. The head of the Saint-Gilles police force is quite a rare flower on the island. A Zarabe with Creole blood. Gabin has a fairly specific opinion on Zarabes, who rarely interbreed, generally preferring not to share their genes or their bank accounts with any other race. Discreet and efficient. Twenty-five thousand people, thirteen mosques, and no niqabs, veils or other outward signs . . . and they own every fabric, car and hardware business on the island.

Aja's Zarabe blood comes from her father, the Creole from her mother. Would he categorize her as pretty? Gabin wonders. Not an easy decision. Sometimes interbreeding produces masterpieces of universal beauty, but more often the results are like an interesting experiment. Aja is a case in point: a somewhat improbable combination of long black hair, blue almond-

---

[9] A Muslim inhabitant, of Indian origin.

shaped eyes, and thick black eyebrows that almost meet above her nose. There's potential for prettiness there, Gabin concludes, but in order to realize it, the captain would have to smile occasionally. He'd also have to see what she looks like in a bikini, which doesn't seem likely to happen. Aja is from the Hauts de Saint-Paul, the hilly interior of the island, from one of those squalid apartment buildings on the Plateau Caillou. He's known her since she was in secondary school. Even then, Aja acted like a *margouillat*[10] in a class of *endormis*[11]. Blessed with a rare level of intelligence, she was one of those studious types who never went out in the sun or swam in the lagoon, but spent all of her time working, working, working. Like many others from the island, Aja went to university in France. She studied Law at Panthéon-Assas, then went to police academy at Châteaulin, in Brittany. Top of her class. But unlike most of the super-intelligent kids from the island, she came back. Maybe she regrets that slightly now? It's not easy for someone of mixed race to climb the ladder of power here, and Aja got stuck with the local police squad at Saint-Gilles-les-Bains. But Gabin has seen her at work: she's tenacious, ambitious, gutsy, capable of making it all the way to the top. And her thirst for vengeance gives her added motivation. The Zoreilles of Saint-Denis will have trouble keeping her muzzled for long . . .

Aja waves the photograph in front of his face impatiently.

"So?"

"So, what? I don't remember hearing any sirens, Aja. I take it this isn't an official investigation?"

"Well, you know us cops. We won't get out of bed for a Creole who's been beaten up by her husband. But a tourist who runs off . . ."

Gabin gives a wide, toothy smile.

[10] Lizard.
[11] Chameleons.

"You're learning the art of diplomacy, Aja, that's good . . ."

Aja does not reply—she appears to be thinking about this—but then she asks him again.

"So, what do you know about the *tantine*?"[12]

"Hardly anything, my sweet. You know me: I just stand here behind my bar like a palm tree. I saw the girl walk past the deckchairs, take off her bikini top, wrap herself up in a towel, and then—*poof!*—she vanished into thin air. You should ask Naivo, on reception. He's new, you can't miss him; he's Madagascan, looks like a lemur in a shirt and tie. He was the one who opened the door of the room for Bellion."

5:51 P.M.

Aja enters the lobby. No sign of Martial Bellion. He must have taken her advice and made himself scarce so that she can get on with the investigation. Suddenly she smiles: Gabin wasn't exaggerating, the guy at reception really does look like a lemur. Naivo is sitting behind his desk, round hazel eyes like marbles, a crown of stiff grey hair stretching from one ear to the other; he is wearing a black-and-white-striped tie, as if he's wrapped his own tail around his neck.

And this lemur is not insensitive to the charms of a blonde. As soon as she waves the photograph of Liane in front of his bulging eyes, he suddenly becomes loquacious.

"Yes, Captain Purvi, I saw Liane Bellion go up to her room this afternoon. Yes, her husband came to fetch me to help him open the door to number 38. How long afterwards? I'd say about an hour. That poor guy looked so worried, panic-stricken in fact, standing there in his trunks and flip-flops. So I opened the door for him, and the room was—how can I put

---

[12] Girlfriend.

this?—in a state of some disorder. There were signs of a struggle. Or a shared siesta between a man and a woman, if you know what I mean, Captain . . ."

One of those hazel marbles vanishes behind the salt-and-pepper forest of an eyebrow. The lemur version of a wink, Aja supposes.

"Except," Naivo continues. "Except that all the women's clothing had disappeared. You can trust me: I have an eye for that sort of thing. Liane Bellion had packed her suitcase."

Another bizarre wink.

"But that was not the most important thing, Captain. The most important thing was that there were traces of . . . how shall I put this?"

Aja's eyes narrow. She has a feeling she isn't going to like what he says next. The lemur looks up at her again.

"Stains that looked very much like bloodstains." Aja nods, impassive.

"Let's go upstairs, if that's O.K. with you. You can show me the room . . ."

They take the lift. Second floor. Aja glances out through the bay windows at the hotel guests drinking cocktails and talking around the pool beneath the crimson sky; the women's bare backs, the wreaths of smoke, the kids splashing in the fluorescent water, colored blue, red and green by the underwater lights.

A tropical evening. Perfectly calm. Like paradise. Armand Zuttor was right: flashing blue lights would have been out of place here.

Naivo searches through the keys in his hand and moves towards room 38. He looks like a zookeeper about to open the cage of a gorilla.

"Captain, may I talk to you?"

The voice seems to come out of nowhere. Aja turns around

and sees an old woman standing behind her, holding a broom. The Creole, who came up behind her so stealthily, speaks again:

"You are Captain Purvi? Little Aja? Laila and Rahim's daughter?"

Aja doesn't know what irritates her more. The reference to her childhood from a woman she doesn't recognize, or the lazy rhythm of the cleaning lady's speech. She gives a vague nod.

"I see your mother often, you know, my little Aja," the Creole woman continues. "At the covered market in Saint-Paul, practically every other day. We talk about the past the way old women do."

Aja forces a smile.

"Go on . . ."

The lemur has not moved. Nor has the Creole. Stalemate.

"Can we talk alone?" she says.

"O.K.," Aja agrees, turning towards Naivo.

The lemur's eyes open wide with indignation but he reluctantly moves away to the other end of the corridor. The Creole woman with the broom seems to be searching for words. Aja waits for a few seconds, then interjects:

"How long have you been here?"

"Thirty years and six months, my little Aja." Aja sighs.

"I mean this afternoon, madame. How long have you been up here, in this corridor?"

Eve-Marie smiles, slowly checks her watch, then replies.

"Four hours and thirty minutes."

"That's a long time, isn't it?"

"Well, let's just say it's not usually this busy on my floor . . ."

Aja looks at the tiles, the walls, the paintings, the windows, all of it as impeccably clean as a hospital corridor. The cleaning lady's first name is embroidered on her jacket.

"Eve-Marie, you seem like a precise, organized kind of person to me. Tell me exactly what happened in your corridor this afternoon."

The old woman takes forever to lean the broom against the wall.

"Well, Naivo and the husband came up here around four o'clock to open the door to number 38. The room was empty and . . ."

Eve-Marie slowly adjusts the scarf in her frizzy hair. To speed things up, Aja takes control of the conversation once more.

"All right, Eve-Marie, so Martial Bellion came up here at four. Liane Bellion came up an hour earlier, about three o'clock. It's what happened in between that interests me. If you didn't leave your corridor, you must have seen Madame Bellion come out of her room."

Eve-Marie has spotted some invisible mark on the closest window, and she rubs at it with the corner of a turquoise cloth. It seems like an eternity before she replies:

"I saw people come through this corridor between three and four . . . But not the blonde . . ."

The words are like a hammer blow to the back of her head. "What do you mean?" Aja almost shouts. "Liane Bellion didn't come back out of her room?"

Again Eve-Marie takes her time to answer, slowly folding the cloth in four. The suspense builds. This woman should write thrillers.

"The husband came up."

"One hour later. Yes, I know."

"No, not one hour later. Long before that. I would say about fifteen minutes after his wife came up."

Another hammer blow. To the chest, this time. "Are you certain?"

"Oh yes, my little Aja, you can trust me. No one comes through my corridor without me noticing them."

"I don't doubt it, Eve-Marie. Please go on."

Eve-Marie shoots a suspicious glance at Naivo. The lemur

is pacing around in front of the lifts. The Creole woman lowers her voice.

"He went into the room. At the time, I thought he just wanted to have a bit of fun with his wife. After all, it was the siesta and the kid was downstairs with their friends. The husband came out of the room a few minutes later, ten minutes at most. He approached me, and asked me to do him a favor."

Aja observes her reflection in the window. Her blue eyes blend into the fluorescent glimmer of the swimming pool, four meters below.

"A favor?"

Eve-Marie takes forever to turn around to face the cart that contains her bin, her cleaning products and her brushes.

"Yes, a favor. He asked if he could borrow my cart. Not this one, but the big one, the one I keep all the towels and sheets in. It was empty. He went into the room with it, and came out two minutes later, and took the lift . . . then he just disappeared. I found my cart downstairs, on level -1, near the car park. It may seem strange to you, my little Aja . . . But we don't refuse the customers anything here."

The captain rests her trembling hand on the window ledge.

"The laundry cart . . . Did he tell you why on earth he wanted it?"

"Well, you know, we don't ask the guests questions here. *La lang na pwin le zo.*"[13]

Aja chews her lip.

"Did anyone else go in? Or come out? Was there anyone else in the corridor this afternoon?"

"No one! You can believe me, Aja. The *katish* from 38 never left her room."

---

[13] A Réunion proverb: "the tongue has no bones," meaning that one should be careful what one says.

And why wouldn't she believe Eve-Marie? "Your laundry cart. How big is it?"

Eve-Marie seems to think about this.

"Well, there's a sign on it saying it can carry up to a hundred and eighty kilos of laundry. I can see what you're thinking, Aja. Between you and me, I'd be surprised if the little blonde in her bikini weighed more than half of that."

While Eve-Marie's gaze finds more invisible specks of dust, Aja stares down at the garden. There are no more than twenty people there, chatting, drinking, waiting for the sunset. Aja spots Martial Bellion under a lamp post. He is sitting in a tall chair, a little girl of six on his knees.

His wife never came out of the room . . .

Naivo mentioned signs of a struggle. And bloodstains.

So much for the nice, reassuring theory that Liane Bellion went off with a lover somewhere . . .

Noticing that their conversation is over, the lemur advances down the corridor, keys in hand. Aja will have to explain to him, and to the hotel manager, that the nature of the case has changed. Armand Zuttor is not going to like it. There is every chance that the clothes scattered across room 38 now form pieces of evidence from a crime scene. Aja glances down at her watch. Ideally, they should search for fingerprints tonight, analyse the bloodstains, test samples for DNA, and all the rest of the protocol.

Now she will just have to convince Christos to get off his arse . . .

5
THE MOSQUITOES' BALL

8:34 P.M.

Sopha has not touched her grilled chicken or her rice. She is sulking, her nose buried in a collection of stories about Ti-Jean.[14] Martial Bellion is forcing himself to eat his smoked *rougail*. He is attempting to put a brave face on it, whereas Liane's disappearance does not seem to have diminished Jacques and Margaux Jourdain's appetite one bit.

The three of them eat in silence. Next to the pool, a guy in a floral shirt is bellowing '80s hits into a microphone. A woman in a skintight dress, a garland of bright red flowers hanging round her wrinkled neck, is moving around behind him. From time to time, she half-heartedly claps her hands or echoes a chorus.

Of the twenty or so guests at the Grain de Sable, the Hotel Athena's restaurant, not one applauds. Nobody is talking either. This must be what the singing couple are paid for: not for providing some atmosphere, but for filling the silence between all these couples. Jacques Jourdain pours Martial another glass of wine. His hand is shaking slightly and he hesitates, then leans towards Martial to make himself heard above the shrieking of the duo by the pool.

"She'll come back, Martial. Don't worry, she's bound to come back."

Martial does not reply. Jacques' sympathetic expression is not very convincing. Is this Parisian lawyer really saddened by the calamity that has struck a man he didn't even know five days

---

[14] A hero in many folk tales from Réunion Island.

ago? Martial doubts it. Jacques and Margaux seem more like the kind of couple who are relieved to have found someone more miserable than themselves. Their true sentiments, he guesses, probably lie somewhere between pity and indifference.

Martial forces himself to see the ironic side. Yes, his wife's disappearance probably has affected Jacques in a small way. He's not stupid. Staring at Liane's body as she lay by the pool was one of the lawyer's secret pleasures on this holiday.

Martial thinks about getting up, taking Sopha with him, and leaving them there, but decides against it. Overcoming his disgust, he chews a mouthful of cold *rougail*. No, this time, he will not give in to impulse; he must remain patient, keep up appearances, play the role of the husband genuinely affected by the disappearance of his wife. Not an easy task, he knows. Everything depends on the details, on his ability to hide the truth from the police. Suspicion will tighten around him like a noose around his neck, and even if they find no clear evidence, the doubts will remain . . . If things go badly, he might need the Jourdains—Jacques in particular. He must be extremely in demand as a lawyer, judging from the hundreds of emails he receives every day.

The silence is growing unbearable.

As is the duo's screeching. And yet none of the couples in the restaurant have left their tables.

Martial briefly imagines how tomorrow will unfold. The trap closing in on him. The police, the interrogations, the tourists confined to their hotel. The Jourdains summoned to the police station. Well, at least he'll have helped ruin those hypocrites' holiday! That's better than nothing.

9:17 P.M.

"Let's go upstairs, Sopha."

Martial approaches Gabin's bar, wallet in hand. Gabin passes him a *rhum arrangé*, a flavored rum. Hard to tell which fruit has been used in this one—some sort of yellow medlar.

When Martial passes him the banknote, the barman touches his hand. He shivers.

"It's a *rhum bibasse*, monsieur. A special batch. She'll come back, your wife, don't you worry."

At least this guy seems sincere. Martial forces himself to give a sad smile.

"You have to see it from her point of view," Gabin goes on. "She has taste, your wife. Who in their right mind would want to listen to this music? There's a good group on tomorrow night—she'll be back for that."

10:12 P.M.

The couple continue to wail out their songs. In the halo of yellow lights above the swimming pool, the mosquitoes are the only ones dancing.

Martial moves away from the window of room 17. It's on the first floor. He turns towards the child's bed that Naivo has, with great difficulty, squeezed between the double bed and the wall. Sopha has finally fallen asleep, after an hour of begging for her mother. Martial did his best to explain things, albeit clumsily.

"She'll come back, Sopha. She just went out for a walk. She'll be back soon."

He was wasting his breath.

The questions came thick and fast.

Why has Maman not called us?

Why didn't she give me a hug before she left?

Why didn't she take me with her?

Where is Maman? WHERE IS SHE?

Why aren't we sleeping in the same room as yesterday?

"Because a policeman has gone there to take fingerprints." But Martial couldn't tell his daughter that.

He read her the adventures of Ti-Jean, Grand-mère Kalle and Grand Diable several times over until, finally, she fell asleep. Lucky her. Down below, the duo is still caterwauling.

Martial takes off his T-shirt and trousers, and stands there, naked, in the shadows.

Anxious.

Nothing is going as planned.

Above him, in a few hours' time—tomorrow morning at the latest—a policeman will come and remove the seal on room 38. Naivo must have told them about the clothes scattered all over the room, the objects knocked down . . . and the bloodstains. Of course he did.

Martial walks over to the shower cubicle.

This evening, until dinner, he was in control of the situation. But in the last few minutes, something has gone adrift.

The water pours down on him. Almost cold.

His thoughts twist, slide over the smooth walls of his brain, disappear down a gaping chasm. Why on earth did he concoct this insane plan? Is he about to get caught in the trap he built himself?

He dries himself, wishing he could rub the towel so hard against his skin that it made him bleed, turning the white embroidered hotel logo a deep shade of scarlet.

Terrible images come back to him. Did he have any choice?

Martial walks back through the room. He stands, naked, at the window, barely concealed by the darkness. But no one is looking towards the window. There are only a few tourists left outside, couples embracing as they dance on the teak boards. The Jourdains aren't there. This isn't their scene.

The singers have moved on to the kind of interminable ballad that signals they will soon be packing up their equipment.

Martial takes a step back and watches Sopha's chest rise and fall as she sleeps on the cot that is almost too small for her.

His bed is too big. "Kingsize," as Naivo called it. The tactless moron!

Martial lifts up the cotton sheet, stiffened into a shroud by the air conditioning. The contact disturbs him. Suddenly he can't bear Liane's absence. Martial stuffs a corner of the sheet into his mouth and bites down to stop himself from screaming; he realizes that he is mimicking the very gesture that Liane made every night when she silently bit down on the cotton cloth to stifle the groans of her orgasm.

My God, what has he done?

What wouldn't he give to feel Liane's naked body against his now? To go back in time, just one day. Or a week, if he could.

Never to have set foot on this island.

At the window, the lights of the pool are going out, like dying stars.

Tonight, he will not sleep.

6
ORTHODOX EASTER

Saturday, March 30, 2013, 9:11 A.M.

Imelda explodes from under the sheets, like a volcano erupting.

"*Christos!* There's a message on your mobile from last night. 7:43 P.M. Don't you ever check your phone?"

"Not when I'm in your bed, no."

Christos Konstantinov stretches out, his head resting against Imelda's huge black breasts. She pushes him away unceremoniously, leans over the crate that serves as her bedside table, and reaches out to grab the mobile phone.

"It's your boss, Christos."

He has a stunning view of Imelda's majestic backside. Nothing else matters.

"Aja? So she's bothering the only Orthodox Christian on the island on Easter weekend? I'll sue her for harassment."

Christos groans and climbs across the bed to curl up against the Cafrine's[15] black skin. Imelda is a magical mattress that becomes an inch or two thicker every year. He once found, in a drawer, an old photograph album with pictures of Imelda when she was twenty; she was posing naked for a photographer who must have feasted his eyes as he took pictures from every angle of her tall, slender, goddess-like body, so perfect it could make a sleeping man erect. And yet, not for anything in the world would Christos swap that young body for the luscious form of his mistress now, twenty years later. How could any man love a woman

---

[15] Female Cafre.

with a wasp's waist when he has tasted the delights of a queen? Imelda is all chocolate and cream; he could gorge himself on her delicious body forever, her ever-changing curves, a cloud of sensuality that seems to mould itself to his desire.

If she knew . . .

Imelda pouts, phone in hand.

"Can I look?"

Christos sighs. It's against the rules as this is his work telephone. But who cares, if it makes Imelda happy? There is a pile of thrillers on the crate next to the bed. Imelda is a sort of Cafre Miss Marple, which is part of what he loves about her.

"If you like."

Imelda clicks on the message while Christos's hand slides up her thigh, explores the hills of her belly, then redescends from the mountain towards the damp pastures. Christos's fingers disappear into Imelda's bush. No waxing or shaving for her, thank God. The origin of the world, Christos thinks, in Réunion mythology . . . The primary forest, dark, protected, sacred, a part of our ancient humanity. Christos feels like a poet this morning. He's really not in the mood to clock in at the station.

He glances over at the pram next to the wall. Little Dolaine is asleep. With a bit of luck, she will stay that way.

"Hotel Athena," Imelda announces, her eyes riveted to the screen of the mobile phone. "You have to go there to check for fingerprints, bloodstains, DNA samples, and all the rest."

Under the insistent pressure of Christos's fingers, she spreads her legs a little wider.

"O.K.," Christos says. "I know the score. I'll go there this evening. Gabin Payet, the barman, makes the best flavored rums on the island. It would be criminal to turn up just for breakfast . . ."

"You'll end up getting yourself fired . . ."

Christos's index finger defiles the sacred forest.

"You'll feed me. What's one more in the family?"

"What would I do with a lazy arse like you? It's hard enough making the allowance stretch to cover my five kids . . ."

Christos puts his right knee between Imelda's legs. Then his left.

"You're calling Christos Konstantinov lazy?" the policeman gasps. "You shouldn't have provoked the stallion of the Mascarenes . . ."

He leans on his wrists. She helps him, placing her hot hands on his white rump and guiding him in.

The bed tips over, bounces back, is suddenly transformed into a trampoline.

Three monsters are jumping on the sheets: Dorian, Joly, Amic. One bushy-haired, one frizzy-haired, one shaven-headed. Twelve, seven and four years old. With the little one in the pram, the only child missing is Nazir. As far as Christos knows, Imelda's progeny are the offspring of three different fathers. He arrived eleven months after the departure of the last one. The family is a joyful jumble that is hard to categorise: Creoles, Malbars, Zoreilles. All crammed into a three-room apartment—or four rooms if you count the garden (the oldest child sleeps in a hammock).

The three kids jump on him. Christos protests feebly.

So much for authority . . .

"Aren't you working today, Jesus?"

"Christos, not Jesus! And yes, I am working! Clear off, you lot! Don't you have school to go to?"

No answer, just cascades of laughter, like the Salazie falls.

Imelda gets up and puts on a *pareo*. So much for that, thinks Christos. He gets up too, with a sigh.

"What else did the boss say?"

Imelda does not even have to check the phone; it's as if she memorized the information with just one glance.

"A tourist who has lost his wife. Oops! Off she's gone with her suitcase!"

"The idiot!"

Christos puts on a pair of ochre canvas trousers. A dubious shirt.

"You know what I'd do, to avoid losing my wife like that?"

Imelda doesn't reply. She yanks vigorously at the sheets, sending her brood flying.

"Same as I'd do to avoid losing my keys, in fact."

Still no reply. Imelda bends down to pick up the pillows scattered across the floor.

"I'd keep a spare!"

Christos leaves the room laughing, just before being hit in the face by three pillows.

10:03 A.M.

Hotel Athena. Christos heads towards the bar, instinctively, like a cat guided towards its food bowl. He wasn't kidding when he told Imelda that Gabin's rum is the best in Saint-Gilles. It may even be the best on the island. Usually when Christos comes here, it is late at night, to get away from the noisy, excitable young people emerging from the neighboring clubs, the Red White and the Loft. Gabin is a sort of local star, a cocktail artist, a virtuoso of improvisation. For ten years, all the bars on the island have been fighting over him, negotiating his transfer as if he were a high-scoring center forward in Réunion's premier division.

Gabin smiles as he watches Christos approach. With his long grey hair pulled back in a ponytail, his sun-bleached blue shirt and his ancient espadrilles, you would never guess this man had been a second lieutenant in the police force for over thirty years.

"Well, look who it is!" says Gabin. "The prophet himself. It's not too early. We were saving some croissants for you."

Christos gives him a thumbs-up, then slowly turns it down towards the ground. The barman does not push the matter. He has a degree in ethylotherapy; he observes his customers, listens to them, analyses them, then delivers a personalized service. He serves Christos a Mai Tai. Then a second, as he tells the policeman all the details of the case: the handsome couple, the kisses in the pool, the annoying six-year-old daughter, the mother who goes upstairs to her room for just a minute, and then—*poof*—vanishes into thin air.

Christos listens sympathetically, one eye on the ice cubes melting at the bottom of his glass, diluting the rum, the other drifting towards the pool, which is deserted.

"I tell you, Gabin, the Zoreilles should watch out. This island is one hell of a trap. Listen, I've got a good story for you: you know how I ended up here?"

Gabin shakes his head, smiling. His official title is psycho-ethylotherapist.

"I lived in La Courneuve," Christos goes on. "I was twenty-five years old. I applied for a transfer to the force in Saint-Denis. That was only about ten miles from my home. Even with traffic jams, it was just thirty minutes in the car. There was just one detail on the ad that I didn't notice. A tiny little detail, just a figure . . ."

Christos drains his glass, before concluding:

"The department number. It was 974, not 93. Saint-Denis here, not Saint-Denis near Paris! It had to be fate. So, I came over here with my whole life packed in a container. Thirty years later, I'm still here."

Gabin wipes the bar, indifferent.

"You don't think my story's funny?"

The barman replies without even looking up.

"That's the fifth time I've heard it! You always tell the same old jokes, Christos."

Christos shrugs. He swirls the ice cubes around in his glass, trying to convince himself that Gabin doesn't always mean what he says. Finally he gives up.

"You're a pro, Gabin, but you should work on your sense of humor. It's important for your customers. Anyway, I'll say goodbye. I'm going upstairs to take care of the honeymoon suite. Losing your wife, eh? That's pretty careless . . ."

He walks away, hesitates, then turns around.

"Hey, Gabin, you know what I do to make sure I don't lose mine?"

The barman rolls his eyes.

"Let me think. You keep a spare?"

Bastard!

10:09 A.M.

Christos places the briefcase on the bed and removes the BlueStar® Forensic vials, the test tubes, the Lumilight lamp and the miniature digital camera from their respective compartments. Apart from Aja, he is the only person in the Saint-Gilles-les-Bains force who knows how to use them. Competency comes with certain privileges, like being able to sleep in. He thinks again about the Madagascan on reception who opened the door to room 38 for him. Naivo Randrianasoloarimino.

Anyway, to work. What a crazy job . . .

Around each dark stain, on the carpet, on the sheets, in the shower, on the edge of the toilet bowl, he will spray a few drops of BlueStar® Forensic. But first it must be meticulously prepared. The preparation is only effective in detecting traces of blood when mixed with an activator composed of distilled water and a hydroxide salt. That idiot Gabin isn't the only one who knows how to make cocktails, Christos thinks. After that, if the room is reasonably dark,

each bloodstain should be transformed into a pretty, fluorescent blue lozenge.

Christos gets to work: the fluorescence lasts only about
thirty seconds, which is not a lot of time in which to detect the
stains with the aid of the Lumilight's black light as well as take
pictures of the scene. And if he doesn't get it done in time, he
will have to start all over again, ad infinitum.

Christos sighs as he aims the black light at the floor. The
blue stains vanish almost instantaneously, as if they've been
swallowed by the carpet, but one thing is already certain:
blood was spilled in this room, and not only on the floor but
on the bed and walls too. Try as he might to make arguments
to the contrary, Christos has to accept the reality.

Room 38 of the Athena is the scene of a crime. Shit.

Christos throws the Lumilight on to the bed. Most police
officers would be excited by such a discovery, like an entomol-
ogist accidentally stepping on a new type of anthill, or an astronaut discovering a new planet. But for Christos, it just pisses
him off. He has to mix the solution again, and spray it, meter
by meter, so that he gets photographs of the entire room. Any
time you watch an American crime series, there are always
about twenty policemen bustling around the corpse. In Saint-
Gilles-les-Bains on Réunion Island, he is stuck on his own, like
a big fat . . .

And decorating the place with blue light is only the first step.

Whose blood is this? Madame Bellion's? Monsieur
Bellion's? A mixture of the two? Christos knows that he will
have to stuff plastic bags with fragments of sheets and pil-
lowcases that he has painstakingly cut out. He will have to
crawl around on the floor, trying to tear off scraps of carpet.
He will go into the bathroom with tweezers and pick up any
stray nose hairs, arse hairs or pubic hairs he might find. He
will shove his hands into the toilet bowl, armed with a test
tube.

He thinks about Imelda's eldest son, that moron Nazir, high on *zamal*,[16] who spends his days watching episodes of *CSI* that his pal has downloaded for him. He should have brought Nazir in for a few weeks of work experience. Maybe that would have got rid of his taste for the grass that is turning him into a *bourik*.[17]

Or maybe he should have asked him to pass the *zamal* around. Right at this moment, Christos would have nothing against the idea of rolling himself a joint. It might pep him up.

He looks out through the window. The first female guests are claiming their deckchairs around the pool. Old and flabby. Christos knows from experience that the pretty, young ones do not sunbathe in the hotels around the lagoon. They put Pataugas on their feet and trudge between Mafate and the Piton des Neiges. Christos is too old to follow them. Not that he cares. He has always preferred women ten to fifteen years younger than him. And he is nearly sixty now.

Christos turns around and examines the wooden shelves. He thinks that he should also make an inventory of the room. According to the Madagascan on reception, all of Liane Bellion's clothes have disappeared: he should verify that. He tries to reassure himself. When it comes down to it, the most likely scenario is still that madame has run away. The discovery of bloodstains is not in itself evidence that a crime has been committed. For proof of a murder, you need a corpse. Or, at the very least, a weapon . . .

Christos has a sudden hunch. He gets up on the bed and carefully removes everything from the shelves. Sports bag, shoes, waterproof clothes, sunglasses, tennis racket, torch.

His hand comes to a halt over a barbecue kit: a high-tech model, made by an upmarket brand such as Nature et

---

[16] Cannabis from Réunion.
[17] Idiot.

Découvertes or Maisons du Monde, the type of gift your friends might buy you when they know you are about to go to a country where people still eat with their fingers. Christos rips open the Velcro that holds the black plastic case together. Inside there are compartments for everything: an XXL fork, a spatula, a scraper, a pair of tongs, a brush for the marinade . . . and, of course, a compartment for the knife. A solid kind of knife, good for slicing ribs of beef. With a nicely sharpened blade and a wooden handle.

Or that's what Christos imagines, anyway. Because there is no longer any knife in the case.

7
FIVE AGAINST ONE

3:13 P.M.

Aja is sitting behind the desk, facing Martial Bellion. Christos prefers to remain on his feet, a little further back. The Saint-Gilles-les-Bains police station, on Boulevard Roland-Garros, is composed of several concrete cubes of varying size, painted off-white and all connected to another cube—this one made of steel—that functions as the reception building. An ordinary, run-down station, like thousands of others in France, except that in this case the hideous cubes are located only about fifty meters from the beach. Standing in the main room, if the doors of the nearest boxes are open, you have a direct view of the beach and the port. Christos never tires of this. The yachts leaving the port, the surfers, the IMAX sunset when he leaves the office after 6 P.M. Which doesn't happen very often, admittedly. Aja, on the other hand, shrivelled up in her chair, could be teleported to Dunkirk without even noticing.

Martial Bellion is not interested in the tropical landscape. He has other things on his mind.

He was summoned to the police station for an interview at 3 P.M. He arrived twenty minutes early. He still looks like a beaten dog. Or a lost dog, searching for his mistress. A cuckolded dog, perhaps . . .

"Do you have any news about my wife, Captain? Have you found out anything? I'm going crazy. And as for Sopha, our daughter . . ."

Christos senses that Aja is about to explode.

And the bloodstains on the wall, my sweet? And the missing knife?

The captain is not the kind of police officer to treat her suspects with kid gloves. She won't put up with Martial Bellion's little game much longer.

"I do have some news for you, Monsieur Bellion."

Aja stands up. Christos admires the impeccable creases in her blue uniform, the buttoned-up blouse, the starched stripes. Christos stopped wearing his official clothes a long time ago, although Aja continues to try to make him wear a more suitable outfit when he's on duty. At least he could iron his shirt, and tuck it into his trousers, even if he can't manage to wear a tie, cap and epaulettes . . . Captain Purvi can be a stubborn pain in the arse, as Martial Bellion is probably about to discover.

Aja abruptly turns around.

"Monsieur Bellion, I've been patient. I've listened carefully while you've given me your whole 'traumatized husband' act. But now it's time for the next part of the drama, don't you think? Let's put our cards on the table. Eve-Marie Nativel, the cleaning lady at the Hotel Athena, told us all about your various trips to the second floor, about you borrowing her laundry cart and taking it down in the lift to the ground floor on the north-east side, where the car park is located . . ."

Bellion looks surprised. Not bad, thinks Christos. This guy could be a professional actor.

But Aja does not give up that easily: "Her testimony seems very different to yours, no?"

Bellion takes a breath, then says: "That woman is mistaken. Or she's lying."

Christos leans back against the windowsill, ready to enjoy the match, though he wouldn't bet a single euro on Bellion. First return into the net. Why would Eve-Marie lie? How could she possibly be mistaken? It's ridiculous.

Aja serves again.

"Eve-Marie Nativel is lying . . . Of course, Monsieur Bellion. Let us continue, then. In addition to Eve-Marie Nativel, Monsieur Tanguy Dijoux, the Hotel Athena's gardener, saw you in the car park at 3:25 P.M., pushing the infamous laundry cart. Not the kind of scene anyone is likely to misremember, is it, a Zoreille helping out a Creole cleaning lady? After that, three kids playing football behind the hotel saw you heading towards your rental car, a grey Clio, which you had left in the car park."

Aja moves forward and stares into the tourist's eyes.

"Now, Monsieur Bellion, do you still claim not to have left the pool before four o'clock?"

Another deep breath, longer this time, then Bellion spits out his response: "They're mistaken. Or they're lying . . ."

Aja rolls her eyes. Christos smiles. Martial is either very stubborn or very stupid. He's in a hole and he won't stop digging.

"I . . . I don't remember exactly, Captain. I was playing with my daughter in the pool. I'm teaching her to swim. I also slept for a while on a deckchair too . . . I . . . I didn't notice what time it was, but . . ."

Christos almost feels sorry for Martial, so pathetic is his defence. Swimming against the tide. He could throw him a lifebelt, but he feels sure his boss wouldn't appreciate that. Aja paces the room. Deliberately, Christos imagines; she is letting Bellion stew in his own juices, like a Caribbean-style chicken, until the bird's flesh comes away from the bones. Bellion stares fixedly at the red, white and blue posters on the walls that declare the glory of the overseas forces: to the right, the maritime police with their jet skis, speed-boats and diving suits; to the left, the air force—helicopters, rope ladders and abseiling. The thrill of life on the "intense island." Join the Police Force now!

Suddenly, Aja explodes. A button goes flying from her blue blouse.

"Monsieur Bellion, we're not going to spend all day doing this. Every member of the hotel's staff is testifying against you! And their testimonies all concur. Your version is full of holes. Eve-Marie Nativel is absolutely certain; she guards her corridor better than Cerberus guards the gates of Hell. Your wife went into her room at 3:04 P.M. and never came out again. The only person who entered, and came out, then entered again one hour later, is you. So, for the last time, Bellion, do you still deny going up to your room a quarter of an hour after your wife did?"

Martial hesitates. On the wall, a helicopter flies over the Trou de Fer. He seems to have decided to jump into that chasm, feet tied together.

Barely a whisper: "No . . ."

Christos winks at his captain. Good, Martial, now we're getting somewhere. Aja strikes while the iron is hot.

"Thank you, Monsieur Bellion. So, do you deny having borrowed Eve-Marie Nativel's laundry cart?"

Five seconds that seem eternal. Bellion stares at the policewoman in her wetsuit, sitting on a Zodiac inflatable boat.

"No."

Another wink. Just one word, almost a confession. Go on, Martial, don't stop there.

Aja's voice lowers by an octave, becomes almost soft.

"Why did you borrow that cart, Monsieur Bellion?"

Martial is staring into space now, his eyes roaming the posters, the walls, disappearing into the Bélouve Forest, the advertisement for the Roches Noires beach . . .

"I have to ask you this, Monsieur Bellion. Was your wife still in the room when you left? Was she still . . . alive?"

Christos nods his head. No reaction from Martial; he's no longer with them. He's no longer sinking, no longer trying to swim against the tide. He is floating at the mercy of the waves, waiting for the tide to turn. He could be in for a long wait, given the amount of evidence that is piling up against him.

At last, his eyes move.

"The room was empty, Captain Purvi, when I went up. We . . . things had not been going well between us since we arrived on the island. I simply thought she wanted to put some distance between us."

"That is not what you told me yesterday, Monsieur Bellion. When you summoned me to the Athena, you swore that your wife had not run away, that she would never have left without her daughter."

"That was yesterday . . . I told you that because I wanted you to investigate her disappearance."

Aja purses her lips, unconvinced.

"And the laundry cart?"

"A stupid reaction when I discovered that the room was empty. I threw all of Liane's clothes into it. She'd left most of them in the room. The suitcase she took with her was almost empty."

Christos smiles at his boss. Clearly, Bellion has not given up yet.

"We'll check that," Aja replies coldly. "No one, absolutely no one, saw your wife come out of her room."

Bellion has turned pale again.

"That's all I know, Captain. Maybe they weren't at their post and they don't want to admit it? I called you last night because I wanted you to find my wife. Why would I have done that if it wasn't the only thing that mattered to me?"

Aja just shrugs. A heavy silence falls. The captain goes back to the questions on her form, noting down each of Bellion's desperate replies. He doesn't understand the disappearance of the knife from the barbecue kit. Maybe his wife took it? Or one of the hotel's employees? He threw away his wife's clothes, stuffed in bin liners, at the Ermitage rubbish tip, on Avenue de Bourbon, a few hundred meters from the Hotel Athena. There were no bloodstains in room 38 before

Liane went up, alone. He is certain of that. Maybe she injured herself before she left?

The captain has understood that she is not going to get anything more out of Martial Bellion. Christos intervenes then.

"Monsieur Bellion, we are going to ask you to go into the next room, the infirmary. There, our colleague Morez will take a few drops of your blood in order to compare it with the blood found in your room. To be honest, I've spent all morning working on those bloodstains, and I am extremely curious to discover who they belong to."

3:55 P.M.

Christos watches Saint-Gilles through the window. About thirty kids are crossing the beach, dressed in flowery shorts and Day-Glo baseball caps, walking in a row behind their teacher. Do they have any idea how lucky they are? A school lesson taught by the sea, in a sandpit six miles long. Aja pays them no attention, her gaze fixed on the police recruitment posters.

"What do you think, Christos?"

The second lieutenant turns around.

"I think it's a total con. We should warn any kids on the island who are thinking of joining that helicopters and jet skis are pretty damn rare in local forces. And they are hardly ever piloted by Creoles . . ."

"Oh, give me a break, Christos! I was talking about the Bellion case. What do you think about that?"

Christos switches off the fan and opens the window. A warm wind blows into the interrogation room, carrying with it the children's shouts.

"After you, Aja."

Aja sits on the desk.

"All right, so we have proof that Martial Bellion is lying to us the whole way down the line. We have five testimonies against his. It's hard to imagine that all of the hotel's employees could be in league against the same man. Why the hell would they do that? Five against one."

"Six against none," Christos corrects her. "In the end, Bellion admitted he'd gone up there."

"Exactly, Christos. His wife might have escaped the notice of one hotel employee, but not all of them. And she obviously didn't leave the apartment on Sitarane's[18] back . . . If it's his wife's blood that's covering the hotel room, then that's it, we arrest him."

"And hold him in custody, Aja? Put the handsome Martial in the slammer?"

"We don't have a corpse, Christos. No murder weapon, no motive, no witness. Nothing. And let's not forget that he eats breakfast, lunch and dinner with a lawyer at the Athena. The prosecutor will laugh us out of court . . . Let's keep an eye on Bellion for a few hours while we wait for the test results. This is an island, after all. He can't easily escape."

Christos takes his time to reflect.

"It is strange, though, isn't it? He called the police station yesterday even though he knew all the witnesses would testify against him. He didn't even try to hide his damn laundry cart. He may as well have written a sign on it telling people he was using it to transport his wife's body. If he's guilty, if his wife hasn't just absconded, then his defence strategy is suicidal."

"Maybe he had no other choice, Christos."

The second lieutenant takes a seat.

"Explain that to me, boss."

"Imagine the scene. The girl goes upstairs. Her husband

---

[18] A Réunion witch who is the object of a Satanic cult.

joins her discreetly in the room. They argue. It turns nasty. He kills her, let's say by accident. What options does he have then? Leave her body in the room? If anyone finds the corpse, he's screwed. No, there's no other solution. In the end, he gets rid of the body. And the murder weapon too."

"In front of five witnesses? Leaving blood all over the room? Then he goes back to the crime scene shortly afterwards? That's suicide."

Aja shoots an irritated glance at her deputy's open shirt.

"No, it isn't, Christos—quite the contrary. Because there's no body. There's no weapon. No motive. And no confession. Even if all the evidence suggests Martial Bellion is guilty, he still has a good chance of being acquitted if it ever goes to trial. There are legal precedents. The Viguier case, remember that? Everyone felt absolutely certain that Jacques Viguier was guilty of murdering his wife, even though there was no body, no murder weapon, no confession. They pointed to the disappearance of Suzanne Viguier, her adultery as a motive, the signs of a struggle, the sheets washed by the husband. He even took the mattress to a recycling center. But he wasn't guilty. He was acquitted in 2010."

Christos's expression shows his scepticism.

"Hmm. Well, if you're right—if we don't find Liane Bellion in bed with some local *boug*[19]—then fame awaits us, Aja. Media briefings, appearances on the evening news. You can forget about arresting clubbers for disturbing the peace, or picking up drunks from the beach, or warning kids not to race each other on their scooters. This is the chance you've been waiting for, my girl. Your springboard to a great future!"

"Enough of your prophecies, Christos."

He sticks his head out of the window, savors the breeze on his face.

---

[19] Man.

"How long does it take to get the results of a DNA test, Aja?"

"I'll make them fast-track it. You know me. We should have a response this afternoon, tomorrow morning at the latest. And by that time, we might have found Liane Bellion's underwear at the Ermitage tip."

"O.K. Then I bet you a hundred euros that we will win the case. I bet you that the blood in the room is his wife's."

"Two hundred," says a voice behind them.

Morez, a first-class officer, enters the room. He's young, a nice guy. Generally, when he's on duty at night with Christos, he handles his Dodo beer better than his poker game.

"In fact, I'd go all in," Morez says. "When Bellion took off his T-shirt so that I could take his blood, guess what? He was wounded. A cut under the armpit, superficial but very clean. The kind of cut you get from a very sharp knife."

"How old was the wound?" Christos asks.

"No more than a day, I'd say."

"Christ," says Aja. "We really are getting there."

8
The Ghost of the Lagoon

Sunday, March 31, 2013, 9:31 A.M.

P apa, when will we go back?"
Papa is sitting on the beach. He answers without looking at me.

"Soon, Sopha. Soon."

I hope so.

I don't like the lagoon very much. There's hardly any water. It's like a small swimming pool but full of horrid stuff. Dirty stuff. Stuff that's sharp and cuts you. I have to put on my plastic sandals to go into the water, and the sandals make my feet go red.

Papa and Maman say it's better than the pool. They say if I look carefully, if I'm patient, I'll see lots of different colored fish. So yes, I've seen the fish, I'm not stupid. Little ones. Black and white. But they swim right next to the coral. Maman says the coral is beautiful, but it's really just some rock in the water, rock that hurts my feet and that the fish use as a hiding place. Whenever I use my armbands to float, I feel as if the coral's going to scrape the skin off my knees.

The lagoon is just a swimming pool that's dangerous, where all you can do is walk.

And even just walking, you have to be careful. Because there's seaweed at the bottom of the water too. When you get near it, you might think it's just a fish rubbing against your ankles, but it's not. It's like a sticky sort of lettuce that licks at you so it can stick its suckers on you. There are even some huge hairy slugs at the bottom of the lagoon. Disgusting! Maman says they're harmless, they're just sea cucumbers, and we call them that because Chinese people eat them. Imagine eating slugs! I'd be surprised if that was true, especially here, when all the shops have been bought by the Chinese, even the restaurants. Maman sometimes says the weirdest things. Like when Papa and Maman say I'm never happy, but they never come swimming.

"Papa, can we go back now?"

"Soon. Don't go too far, Sopha."

Papa is lying on the beach under the tree that has big roots like snakes. He never listens to what I say. I bet he wouldn't even notice if I took off my armbands. He always tells me to pay attention, but he never pays any attention to me.

Look, I'm making a face at him, just to see, just to check he's not looking at me. He always does that, Papa—he looks up at me, asks me if I'm all right, if I'm not too hot or too cold, don't go far away—and then, straight afterwards, he goes off with all his sad thoughts, looking to the side, as if there was someone else in the water. Not me, but an invisible child. Once, he even got my name wrong.

He called me Alex.

Like he was talking to a ghost that only he could see.

He's weird sometimes, Papa.

Especially since Maman left.

Anyway, one thing's for sure: I prefer the swimming pool. The water is warmer. Bluer too. It's not as big, that's true. I look out to sea, as far as I can. If I was brave enough, I'd keep going on, out to where the sea is deeper and the coral doesn't scrape your legs. Just to see if Papa noticed. Further out, the water is all broken up like it's hitting a window. The noise is a bit scary. It's the coral reef, Maman told me. The reef is a wall under the water that protects us. She said there are sharks on the other side.

"Papa, can we go back to the pool?"

I'm used to this by now. I have to say it at least three times, louder and louder, before he hears me.

9:33 A.M.

Martial does not hear. He stares out at the lagoon. Empty.

He has to do something, react; most importantly, he must not contradict himself. He has to respond coherently to the police's questions. He must work out a strategy and stick to it. And stay on his guard. He has no choice now. Things are speeding up. How much time does he have? A few hours, if that? He must remain focused.

And yet his thoughts escape him. His vision blurs. The lagoon is the same, except there are fewer houses around it. No pedalos to rent, no ice creams for sale. Just the casuarina trees watching over the beach. The sun is setting too. A few beach toys abandoned here and there. A red bucket.

A yellow spade.

A little figure in the water. A boy of six.

Alone.

"Papaaaa! I'm bored! Can we go back to the pool now?"

Martial resurfaces.

"Yes, Sopha. The pool? But we've just got h . . ."

He decides to let it go.

"All right, sweetheart, let's go back to the hotel."

The girl comes out of the water, takes off her armbands and plastic sandals.

"When is Maman coming back?"

"Soon, Sopha. Soon."

9
FEAST

D uring the thirty years that he has sipped a Ti' Punch on the terrace each day, Christos has seen Saint-Gilles metamorphose. True, he never saw for himself the old fishing village and the railway where trains arrived from Saint-Denis bringing husbands to their wives and children, obsessively white beneath their parasols. But he did live through the changes of the 1990s, when the island still believed it might one day be like its big sister, Mauritius. He followed the construction of the modern marina at the center of the island's tourist capital. It wasn't a bad idea . . . The Saint-Gilles gully had not been connected to the sea for a long time, except during storms; it died just as it reached the beach, like an exhausted runner collapsing a few meters from the finishing line. The developers opened the town to the ocean, methodically subdividing the marina into separate sections for boats, fishing and diving, and brightening up the whole place with a wild array of colors: the fresh paint of the fishing boats; the yellow plastic of restaurant chairs; the rich wood of the jetties of clubs such as the Corail Plongée; the pastel shades of the boats for toddlers in Captain Marmaille's miniature port; the pink roof of Notre-Dame-de-la-Paix; the grey of the foot-bridges over the stagnant gully; the white of houses eating up the arid hillside; and all of this set amidst palm trees that the developers shrewdly decided not to cut down.

There was some black among the colors, too.

With house prices going up, the Creoles were forced to take refuge in Les Hauts, in the Carosse district, but they still descend on the port en masse to fish for *pes'cavales* from the docks or from their rowing boats.

A success, then! Except that the developers had undoubtedly dreamed of a pedestrianized area buzzing with people, not almost empty bar terraces.

Well, at least Christos can't be accused of not making an effort on that score.

He, Jean-Jacques and René are the only customers at the Bar de la Marine. They have a perfect view of the yachts and of the twenty Creole fishermen's arses parked on their rainbow-colored ice boxes.

Not that Jean-Jacques cares: his eyes are riveted to the *Journal de l'île de la Réunion*.

"So tell us, Messiah, you still haven't found the *nénère?*"[20]

Christos takes a sip of his drink. The Marine's rum is not as good as Gabin's at the Athena, but the view is incomparable.

"It's top secret, O.K., guys?"

"Top secret, my arse," replies René. "For once, something is actually happening on this side of the gully."

Christos pushes back his chair to escape the parasol's shade.

"In that case, you'd better get me drunk . . ."

While Jean-Jacques pours his Dodo beer into his glass, he eyes the bottle of Charrette rum on the table, the bowl and the ice cubes, the pistachios, the samosas. Why not? With customers being so rare here, the bars have to take good care of them.

"All of this island's misfortunes can be summed up by that bottle," the Creole declares. "Rum, dulled wits, violence, idleness . . ."

Christos loves it when Jean-Jacques says something profound.

---

[20] Girlfriend.

Jean-Jacques has one job and one passion: pétanque player and philosopher. Or maybe it's the other way round.

In the heat of the sun, Christos closes his eyes and opens his ears.

11:48 A.M.

At the far end of the port in Saint-Gilles, among the rocks that make up the sea wall, the waves are methodically tearing off shreds from the corpse's flesh and then, in the backwash, washing its wounds. A colony of red crabs is also taking part in this cleansing operation. The smallest ones slip inside every orifice and empty the body from within before the carrion insects can get to work. The largest ones nibble the most tender areas of the body's surface. The mouth, the eyes, the penis, the testicles. New crabs come along, but the old ones don't complain. There is enough for everyone to have their fill at this feast.

11:49 A.M.

René turns his "974" cap around on his bald head as if it were fastened to his skull with a screw. He stares at the ox cart on the label of the rum bottle.

"Well, I don't want to die in ignorance, Jean-Jacques. So you'd better enlighten me on the connection between this island's misfortunes and that bottle."

Christos keeps his eyes closed, but doesn't miss a single syllable of the conversation. It is the time of day when Jean-Jacques becomes a poet.

"The connection is the exploitation of mankind, my poor René. Alcohol and the enslavement of the laboring masses.

Slaves, freedmen, poor whites, all lovers of the cane-sugar mistress, millions of liters of molasses rum, while the prestigious *rhum agricole* sails off towards the mainland. Unlimited alcohol for the damned of the earth—vodka for the Poles in the mines, tafia for the Creoles in the fields, the alcohol of the poor, burning their revolutionary neurones . . ."

Stephano, the barman, who is listening to all this from behind his counter, feels duty-bound to intervene.

"Hey, Jean-Jacques, the man selling tafia says 'screw you.'"

"Me too," agrees René, lifting his glass.

René is a fisherman. Or was, rather. A deep-sea fisherman, for twenty years, in Saint-Pierre, until the price of the fish he sold wasn't enough to cover the cost of diesel for his trawler. René then moved to Saint-Gilles, planning to make a living from tourism. His idea was to take tourists out to see swordfish, dolphins, sharks, humpback whales, sailing far out, as far as Kerguelen if he had to. Satisfaction, or your money back: that was the concept. You only paid if you saw some sea monsters. But no one saw anything, or at least that's what the tourists said when they came back from his trips. René was often too drunk to dispute the matter. In the end, he'd even added mermaids to his programme.

"Tafia or Charrette, who cares?" says René, draining his rum in a single gulp. "I drink to the health of the island's cultural heritage . . ."

Jean-Jacques sips his beer slowly. "Cultural heritage, my arse."

11:54 A.M.

The red crabs are now attacking the corpse in a more orderly fashion. Like a column of ants, they are becoming organized. The bluish putrefied flesh, which has turned the texture of papier-mâché, is being shredded by the strongest ones. The weakest make do with transporting it. The tastiest internal parts are evacuated first—bowels, viscera, brain—like furniture being carried out by efficient movers, leaving only a light, hollow carcass.

Suddenly the crabs all freeze.

The corpse has moved.

The most fearful have already run away and hidden under the massive rocks of the sea wall. Others, tiny, pour from the mouth, as if the dead person has spewed them out.

The body becomes stable again. The crabs warily watch the object that has collided with the corpse.

Round. Smooth. Cold.

11:56 A.M.

Jean-Jacques waves the *Journal de l'île de La Réunion* about as if it were a Bible, almost tipping over his plastic chair.

"Close your eyes and enjoy your drinks, my lads. Alcoholism, illiteracy, violence . . . It's all there, in black and white. Réunion is top of the league for all these things."

Christos opens his eyes, downs the contents of his glass, then finally intervenes in the conversation.

"Slavery's been abolished for a while now, René. If the people on this island drink, you can't keep blaming the Gros Blancs . . ."

Jean-Jacques twists around, then takes a *pil plat*[21] from his pocket.

"And what about this? Why do you think mistress cane sugar invented it? Twenty centiliters of white rum in the shops for the same price as five at a bar . . ."

---

[21] A flat flask of rum.

"Now you're speaking my language!" Stephano yells from behind his counter. "Solitary *bwar*[22] is the scourge of our nation . . . *Kantines*[23] going out of business, it's a crime against humanity!"

René nervously pours himself another glass of rum.

"I'm with you on that too, Jean-Jacques. The island's cultural heritage is Charrette, forty-nine per cent, and in a bottle, not this cough syrup in a hip flask with the alcohol limited to forty per cent by the government."

Christos leans forward on his plastic chair. He loves their hypocrisy. He watches the sails of the boats moored nearby billowing gently in the calm breeze. The sun beats down. Paradise, three hundred and sixty-five days a year. Until he came here, he had no idea that such a place could exist on this earth. As long as you can survive a tropical storm once every three years. Two days spent huddled under the duvet. It's not so bad.

Jean-Jacques has not given up. He sticks the flat bottle of rum under René's nose.

"Taste it, you moron . . . It's forty-nine per cent. All you need is a Bag-in-Box, three liters of Charrette in a soft plastic container with a built-in tap, and you can fill your own *pil plat.*' The latest of mistress cane sugar's inventions in order to keep the masses in a permanent daze."

He gets to his feet and starts imitating a drunken puppeteer.

"Listen to me, my friends. Global capitalism has the people of this island dangling like puppets by two threads, one in each pocket. The *pil plat'* and the mobile phone."

René stupidly pats the pockets of his jeans.

"And I don't care!" proclaims Jean-Jacques. "I don't give a flying fuck! As long as all the island's welfare cases suck at their

[22] Drinking.
[23] Bars.

hip flasks before taking aim on the pétanque court, I will remain the best player in Réunion."

As a finale to his sentence, Jean-Jacques lifts his Dodo up to the sky. René bursts out laughing, then picks up his glass of rum and lifts it towards Jean-Jacques' beer to make a toast.

He tries it in a Provençal accent. "*Peuchère*,[24] you old nutcase, we can still get along."

Jean-Jacques stares at him sorrowfully.

"Don't talk to me like a pétanque player from Marseilles. That really . . ."

"Think about it, you dick. I'm talking about reconciling rum and beer."

Jean-Jacques stares at his Dodo sceptically.

René gives a triumphant laugh.

"*Canne-bière*,[25] *peuchère*! *Canebière*!"[26]

Christos laughs so hard he almost falls off his chair.

Jean-Jacques sighs, close to losing his patience.

"Fucking hell, René," says Stephano, bringing over another bowl of samosas. "That last joke was a bit lame."

12:01 P.M.

"There's a dead body, Kevin. Oh God, there's a body!"

"Stop messing around, Ronaldo! Just get my ball and come back here. You said you'd try to beat my record of thirty-two keepy-uppies. Stop wasting time."

"I'm not messing around, Kevin. There's a dead body, I'm telling you. There, on the rocks, half-eaten by the crabs."

---

[24] Never mind.
[25] Rum-beer.
[26] The historic high street in Marseilles.

12:05 P.M.

Jean-Jacques is reading the *Journal de l'île de La Réunion* again, weary of his companions' jokes. René has tipped back his head towards the clouds covering the peak of Maïdo.

Christos savors the moment. He never tires of this ambience, it's like a permanent carnival. The comparison to the festive melting pot on the Canebière is not entirely misleading; there are no crowds here, but there is the scorching heat, and it lasts all year round. Christos had had enough of the cold in France. Bringing in the garden furniture. Bringing in firewood. Bloody hibernating. Those cretins on the mainland sometimes ask him if he doesn't miss the seasons, if he doesn't get tired of seeing blue skies every morning, of the leaves that never fall from the trees, of the sun that sets every day at the same time. They claim they can only really appreciate the spring after three months of rain; that going on holiday would not be the same if they weren't leaving behind grey skies . . .

Idiots.

As if you have to get older to appreciate the passing of time, or go on a diet for a week just to enjoy a good meal. Depriving yourself in order to earn pleasure. That old Judeo-Christian morality. Or Muslim. Or Buddhist.

Christos wonders if maybe he's some kind of anomaly. Generally, a Zoreille does not stay more than five years on the island, putting aside his fifty-three per cent of supplementary earnings as a government employee, investing his savings in local property to avoid paying tax on it, then, boom, back he goes to France to buy the suburban house of his dreams. Doing it for the kids, they all say. For the good schools.

Well, it's true, he doesn't have any kids.

A Creole officer from the Saint-Benoît force once told him that Christos reminded him of the character Lucien Cordier, played by Philippe Noiret in the film *Coup de Torchon*. At the time, Christos felt insulted by this. Then he thought about it. Appearances can be deceptive . . . The character is a police officer in a small West African town. Bored shitless, he regards life in the tropics with cynicism, and goes on to kill off all the idiots that surround him. He, Christos, is the complete opposite. Here, he is happy as a lark, as a clam, happy as a ripe fruit on a branch high enough not to be eaten. The officer in Saint-Benoît must have made that comment out of jealousy, because over there, on the windy coast, they get up to six meters of rain each year. It's the world record. But here, in Zoreilleland, not a drop.

Christos can live peacefully until he retires in this little corner of paradise. It belongs to everyone—and, consequently, a little bit to him too—because the island was uninhabited until the seventeenth century. No one can claim the land is theirs because they were here before the others; they are just a bunch of men and women all in the same boat, anchored in the middle of the Indian Ocean.

There's a definite hierarchy, of course. As on an overcrowded ocean liner. Jealousy too. Mutiny sometimes. But no racism.

All in the same boat, like a labora . . .

It is at this precise moment that he sees, through his sunglasses, the two kids running towards him. They're waving their hands like lunatics. What's up with them?

Christos lifts up his Ray-Bans.

Bloody hell!

The first kid, the smallest one, wearing a Barcelona shirt with Unicef emblazoned on it, looks like he's seen a ghost. The second, behind him, yells at the top of his voice:

"It's Rodin! It's Rodin!"

Jean-Jacques leaps out of his chair.

12:08 P.M.

Christos runs to the end of the sea wall, panting. The kids are five meters ahead of him. Jean-Jacques, behind him, can hardly breathe. René is walking, or rather, staggering after them.

"There it is! There!"

The sea wall seems to go on forever.

It's Rodin.

Only with thirty years of experience in the Saint-Gilles force is he able to decipher this message. Christos had once read a maxim in an old book of colonial images: "The Creole is naturally contemplative." Rodin is the personification of that maxim. As long as anyone can remember, Rodin has spent his days staring at the horizon from his black rock, at the end of the sea wall of the port in Saint-Gilles, his back to the island, the port, the bars, the nightclubs, the car park. And that's all he does. If all Creoles are philosophers, Rodin is Diogenes.

Rodin is there. He must have fallen onto the rocks, five meters below.

If you lean over, you can see his body.

Christos gets his breath back. The second lieutenant is thinking that he will have to go down there, to check. Just in case the Creole is merely injured . . .

It doesn't seem likely.

The kids stare at him unblinkingly, as if he's Horatio Caine. They won't be disappointed.

Christos starts climbing down the slippery rocks of the riprap intended to break the waves and protect the concrete sea wall. He makes slow progress. The stones are covered with seaweed and his polished shoes keep sliding. You're not dressed for this, Horatio. If only he'd known.

"So, Christos?" asks René anxiously from above.

So what? What does he expect? That Christos will bring Rodin back to life with his bare hands?

Christos yells at the red crabs to scare them off. The less alert ones are crushed underfoot, their shells crackling like dead leaves.

The corpse is lying face down. Feet turned towards the ocean.

Definitely dead. No sign of any wound.

Christos swallows, as the realization hits him. He must turn the body over to understand fully. Rodin has had excellent sea legs since time immemorial; he could stick to the concrete like a mussel. He didn't fall. He was pushed.

He hears Jean-Jacques weeping, up on the sea wall. Rodin was the perfect example, the very quintessence of Creole wisdom.

Christos decides not to think about it too much and grabs the corpse by the belt around its jeans. The body is surprisingly light and easy to turn. Its crab-eaten face is offered up to the sunlight.

Shit!

Christos just manages to stop himself falling. His hand digs into the soft coral that seems to cement the blocks of stone together.

This is all we need!

There is a knife sticking out of Rodin's chest.

Christos makes the connection instantly. Even the most obtuse police officer would be able to see it. It's a good, solid knife. Only the ivory handle is sticking out of the corpse, carved from the horn of an animal that does not exist on this island. Christos takes a closer look. The brand is engraved on it, just in case the cop who found Rodin was not the sharpest blade in the box.

Maisons du Monde.

The type of bourgeois-bohemian brand sold all over the planet, but which you cannot buy on Réunion Island.

Christos tries to think as quickly as possible.

Why kill Rodin?

He looks up towards the sea wall. Jean-Jacques is sobbing onto René's chest. The bigger of the two kids is holding the smaller one's hand, and the smaller one is holding the ball.

Why kill Rodin?

Not to rob him, that's for sure. Rodin had no possessions, not even a roof over his head. Christos turns around, observes the channel of the port. A theory begins to form in his mind, crazy but plausible.

What if Rodin had turned around, for once in his life? A noise behind him, a scream, someone calling for help. Just the briefest glance.

One single second, against an entire lifetime spent contemplating the sea.

What if Rodin was the victim of the most incredible bad fortune, one of those cruel ironies in life that sometimes make us smile?

Turning his head, for one time only . . . but at the worst possible moment.

4:01 P.M.

Martial hesitates. He should do it straight away: go up to the room, pile clothes into a suitcase. The police will be here soon, that is now certain. He should yell at Sopha to get out of the pool, so they can make their escape. Get a head start. At least.

But Sopha is having fun. For the first time since they arrived at the hotel, she has made some friends. She jumps into the pool with her Dora armbands. The other kids are ranged around her, like a court around a queen. Sopha laughs. A very small, long-haired blond boy, his skin tanned the color of caramel, whispers something into her ear. Sopha splashes him and bursts out laughing.

Martial feels a pang.

Don't go all soft. He needs to move! Get Sopha out of the pool.

Escape.

Don't ruin everything. Not now.

4:03 P.M.

On Rue du Général-de-Gaulle, the police van powers along the embankment, crushing the leaves from the tree heliotropes and the purple flowers of the beach morning glory. Morez presses down on the accelerator. The cars coming the other way swerve to one side. This time, Aja has given up on diplomacy;

she has ordered that Martial should be interrogated immediately, joyfully sacrificing the peace of the Athena resort. In addition to the police van, which is driving at top speed towards the hotel, the captain has summoned officers from the Saint-Paul and Saint-Leu stations. Four other vehicles, with more than twenty officers, are now converging on the area. The objective is to cut off Saint-Gilles completely; to block all roads out of the town, in case the arrest does not go smoothly.

Who can predict how Bellion might react?

Ignoring the jolting of the van, Aja, sitting in the passenger seat, rereads, one last time, the analysis supplied by the forensics lab in Saint-Denis. The documents confirm that the blood Christos collected from the sheets, the carpet and the bed belongs to Liane Bellion. The samples were compared to information sent by the Keufer laboratory in Deuilla-Barre, where Liane Bellion had had her blood taken previously. But it was the results of the test on the knife found in Rodin's chest—received fifteen minutes ago—that triggered the decision to arrest Bellion. In addition to the Creole's blood, the knife blade was also stained with that of another person: Liane Bellion.

One weapon. Two victims.

One culprit.

To narrow down the investigation further, there were very clear fingerprints on the knife's handle.

Martial Bellion.

In Avenue de Bourbon, Morez slams on the brakes, raising a cloud of dust. The Hotel Athena is located straight ahead, between the Aqua Parc and the nightclub district. Aja regrets not having locked up Bellion the previous day, when he was giving her his spiel at the station. Two officers spent all morning rummaging through the rubbish at the Ermitage and they did not find a single trace of Liane Bellion's clothes. So it must have been her body that Martial was transporting in the laundry cart. Aja feels sure that he is a man who was overtaken by events: in all probability, he stabbed his wife without premeditation, during an argument, out of jealousy perhaps, in a fit of rage, maybe even because of the kid . . . And then he panicked . . . And killed someone else: an inconvenient witness.

In cold blood, this time.

God only knows what he might be capable of.

4:05 P.M.

It's hard, running in flip-flops.

Papa is holding my hand too tight. He's going to rip off my arm, pulling at it like that. I never wanted to leave the pool in the first place.

"Papa, slow down, you're hurting me!"

"Hurry up, Sopha."

Papa leads me behind the hotel towards the place where our holiday car is parked.

"Papa, you're going too fast."

I've almost lost a flip-flop. I sort of did it on purpose, but Papa doesn't care, he just keeps dragging me along by the arm. There's gravel between my toes now. I stop and scream. Papa doesn't like that.

"Sopha! Come on! I'm begging you."

It's strange, Papa isn't shouting. He's speaking almost in a whisper, as if he's frightened, as if there's an army of ogres running after us. His big hand crushes mine. He forces me to follow him, hopping on one foot. I complain as much as I can, but Papa isn't listening.

The car is there ahead of us. Papa opens it with the remote control, but he doesn't slow down. The concrete hurts my feet. I shout, louder than before and have a tantrum—I'm good at that—until Papa lets go of my hand.

He suddenly stops. At last.

But it's not because of my shouting.

He stares at the car as if there's something wrong with it, as if someone's stolen one of the tyres, or the steering wheel. His voice trembles.

"Quick, Sopha, get in."

I don't move. I'm intelligent—Maman always says that. I already know how to read nearly every word there is.

Like the ones written in the dust on the side window of the car:

Anse dé Cascade

Tomoro

4 P.M.

Be ther

Bring the gurl

I don't really get it. I would like to read the letters one more time, to try to understand. Or at least to remember what it says.

But I don't have time. Almost straight away, Papa rubs them out with his hand, leaving big, dirty streaks behind.

"Get in, Sopha. Quickly."

I have never heard Papa speak to me like that before. He seems so serious and I'm a bit scared, but I do what he says. I climb into the back, onto my car seat.

Why did Papa wipe away those words, as if I wasn't supposed to read them?

Who was supposed to read them? Who wrote them?

Papa?

Maman?

Just before the engine starts, I hear yelling behind us.

4:08 P.M.

Aja is the first one to enter the lobby of the Hotel Athena, followed by Morez. Christos watches the action from a distance.

Naivo springs up from behind his counter like a jack-in-a-box. Less than three seconds later, Armand Zuttor also appears. The manager is wide-eyed, the hair on one side of his head sticking up like a hedgehog, the hair on the other side plastered to his face, as though he's just woken from a siesta. Aja does not even glance at him. She barks orders:

"Morez, upstairs, room 17. Christos, come with me to the garden."

The lift doors open. Eve-Marie gasps: "Don't walk on the . . ."

The three bastards in uniform and combat boots pay no attention as they tramp across the tiles, muddying the corridor all the way to the door of room 17. They lean against the immaculately clean wall opposite the door, then smash open the latch with a kick.

The door explodes inward.

The wet boots vandalize the carpet.

"No one in here!" yells Morez into his walkie-talkie. "He's gone, Captain!"

"Shit!" Aja curses.

She looks around the hotel garden. In front of her, the frozen tourists look like inflatable dolls abandoned by the side of the pool. Without her even giving the order, the officers disperse, searching the hotel and its grounds for any kind of hiding place. All of them except Christos.

Leaning against the trunk of a palm tree, the second lieutenant just stares at the bar and gives Gabin a questioning look. The barman shrugs. He's sulking, probably wondering if he should find a new place to work, with all this going on.

Christos frowns, signifying his insistence. Gabin is not as skilled at mime as he is at mixing cocktails, but he does his best. He waves his arms. With a little mental effort, one might see in this an imitation of a *Papangue*,[27] or a *tec-tec*,[28] or maybe even a butterfly. Something with wings, anyway.

Christos gets the gist. Bellion has taken off.

4:10 P.M.

Martial drives fast. He goes up Avenue de Bourbon, then takes Rue du Général-de-Gaulle. Saint-Gilles rushes past in a long, thin ribbon, between the lagoon and the forest. To leave the resort, he must get on the A-road, while avoiding the port, which would take him straight past the police station; he therefore has no choice but to drive along the backstreets of the housing developments, half of which are dead ends. It's like being caught in a labyrinth.

Another kilometer. Martial brakes suddenly and stifles a curse. The only bridge over the gully that will take him to the A-road is blocked. A tight row of cars stretches ahead for two hundred meters.

Martial swears.

Just the usual traffic jam or a police blockade? It hardly matters. There is no way he is going to get himself trapped in a line of cars. He has to find another way across.

U-turn. The Clio's tyres screech.

He goes back down Avenue de Bourbon the other way, then abruptly turns right, three hundred meters before the Hotel Athena. The track that runs alongside Ermitage beach for two kilometers is just about passable, as long as he doesn't run into the red beach train that carries people to and from the lagoon at a snail's pace.

To the south, the track joins La Saline-les-Bains. Martial forces

---

[27] A local bird of prey, and the island's only predator.
[28] The Réunion Island equivalent of a sparrow.

himself to believe that he still has a slight head start on the police. In a cloud of ochre dust, the Clio passes the Aqua Parc, the identical buildings of the Village de Corail, the bars and clubs of Mail de Rodrigues. Bicycles swerve out of his way. Women queuing outside the ice cream van cough as the vehicle speeds by. Bare-chested men, towels hanging from their shoulders, yell insults at him. Martial is aware that his escape is not exactly discreet. He won't get far at this rate.

And yet, he has no choice.

Dust flies into the Clio through the open window. In the back seat, Sopha cries.

"It's hurting my eyes, Papa."

Martial closes the window. Logically, he ought to continue heading south alongside the beach, go through La Saline, and then join the Route de Saint-Pierre after the Trou d'Eau beach. Saint-Gilles is a maze of streets with only three exits: the A-road that runs along the coast, heading north and south, and the D100 B-road that climbs towards the island's interior.

Back on tarmac, he is able to drive faster again. The crowds on the beach flash past like multicolored dots between the twisted trunks of the casuarina trees.

I'll be able to get through to the south, Martial forces himself to hope.

"Papa, don't drive so fast!"

In the rear-view mirror, he sees Sopha clinging on to her seat belt. Terrified. As if her father was some stranger, driving her towards Hell.

Suddenly, a kid emerges from a villa. Six years old. Barefoot. A bodyboard under his arm. He freezes like a rabbit, panic-stricken.

Martial slams on the brakes. Sopha screams. The kid bolts, disappearing into the courtyard behind the *guétali*.[29]

---

[29] A kiosk-like building typical of the architecture of Réunion villas.

Sweat is pouring down Martial's back. For a moment, he thought it was Alex.

He is going crazy. This mad dash is awakening all his demons.

He's hesitant to start driving again. His head feels like it's about to explode. He covers it with his clammy hands. Then he makes his decision. The Clio moves forward a meter, under the shadow of the gate, sending the pink gravel of the colonial villa's driveway spattering out from under its wheels, then suddenly reverses.

"Papa, what are you doing?"

Martial does not reply. He is aware, now, that he is entering the lion's den. Summoned by Captain Purvi, the police of Saint-Leu and Saint-Paul are bound to be heading towards Saint-Gilles. Their first reflex will be to park their vans by the side of the road and block access south and north along the coast.

So he has only one hope left. Going into Les Hauts. Driving towards the mountain.

And then . . .

4:14 P.M.

"A rental car!" Morez shouts.

The policeman is running from the car park behind the Hotel Athena. He takes a second to catch his breath, then adds:

"A grey Clio! You can't miss it. There's an ITC Tropicar sun visor in the front window and the rental company's sticker on the back window."

"O.K.!" Aja yells back into her walkie-talkie. "All the roads are blocked, he won't get far. Go and join your colleagues at one of the roadblocks on the coastal road exiting Saint-Gilles."

The captain prowls the hotel's lawn, barking out orders. The Saint-Gilles officers, with the exception of Christos, follow her around like a squadron of bodyguards. At the pool-side, some of the tourists are getting dressed. Others remain glued to the spot, only their necks twisting round as they follow the movements of the police, unwilling to miss a single moment of the show. The children have all taken refuge in their parents' laps, except for a little boy with long, blond hair who seems to be defying adult authority.

Aja meets the little surfer kid's eyes for a second. Suddenly she freezes, the walkie-talkie suspended close to her mouth.

"No! Change of plan. The priority is to close off the road to Les Hauts. Issindou, Minot, are you still at the end of Avenue de la Mer? Go wait at the roundabout of the D100. We've got the coast road covered. Bellion's bound to take the road to Maïdo, either to head towards the calderas or to reach the Route des Tamarins. Be ready, for God's sake. I'd bet my life that he's heading inland!"

She catches her breath, then forces herself to speak in a calmer voice.

"Be careful, lads. I know this is a double-murder case, but don't forget there's a child in the back seat of that car."

4:15 P.M.

"Papa, I feel sick!"

I'm not lying this time. I really want Papa to stop the car. He's driving like a mad person. He'll end up running someone over. Or missing a turn-off. I'm tired. I'm scared too. I want to go back to the hotel. I want to go back to the pool.

I want to see Maman.

I do understand. I know I talked about ogres, but I'm not stupid. Papa drove away just when the police arrived, when he heard the sirens. I'm sure this has something to do with Maman. In the pool, the other children were saying she's dead, so I splashed them. I didn't want to cry in front of them so I started to laugh. But they kept saying it, staring at me and pointing their fingers across their throats.

"Your dad killed her!"

I didn't cry, I didn't let them see my tears. I just pulled a face and said, "That's a load of rubbish! How would you know, anyway?"

"My mum told me!"

The tallest one, the one with the long hair, seemed very sure of himself. Well, maybe he wasn't that tall. But maybe he was right anyway.

As if Papa can read my thoughts, he turns around to face me.

"Look, Sopha, look at the mountain over there. That's where we're going, up into the clouds."

"To see Maman?" I ask.

4:16 P.M.

Martial does not reply. He continues to wind through the backstreets of the Ermitage—Allée des Songes, Allée des Cocotiers, Allée des Dattiers. All lead down to Avenue de la Mer. After that, he has to get through the roundabout that leads to the N1 and the D100.

And then he'll be free . . .

He accelerates again; they need to get through before the road is blocked off.

"Papa, is it true? Has Maman gone up to the clouds?" "No, Sopha, of course not."

"So, Papa, why are you—"

"Not now, Sopha!"

Martial raises his voice, and then feels bad immediately afterwards. He can't concentrate. He is haunted by a doubt, a feeling that grows stronger as he moves away from the sea.

He's not going to make it.

The police are communicating by phone and walkie-talkie, in real time. They are bound to have a description of the Clio and they must already have cars blocking the main roads out of Saint-Gilles. Including the one that leads inland.

The Clio yields to a Toyota. Martial lowers his window again. He can hear police sirens, quite clearly now, a few blocks away at most.

"Papa, can we go back to the hotel?"

He realizes that he has no chance of winning this game of hide-and-seek. His rental car could hardly be any more conspicuous. The police will have no trouble closing the net around him.

"No, Sopha, no. Not the hotel. I . . . I've got a surprise for you."

He is talking gibberish, anything to make Sopha quieten down so that he can think of a solution.

Should he park here and continue on foot? But that would be ridiculous—the police would almost certainly spot the car. And with Sopha, he wouldn't get a hundred meters.

"I don't want a surprise, Papa. I want to go back to the hotel."

Behind him, Sopha kicks her feet against Martial's seat.

"I want to see Maman! Do you hear me? Maman!"

Another siren howls over the housing development. Brief and piercing, like a ship's horn. Martial must find a way out, and reassure Sopha, and gain himself some time. He can't let himself be taken, or everything will be lost.

He cannot fail.

And to succeed, he must not hesitate to sacrifice anything that is holding him back.

"I'm going to take you to see something amazing, Sopha. Paradise. Did you ever imagine that you would see paradise?"

11
The Magician

T he car park of the Saint-Gilles police station usually looks like a patch of wasteland baking in the sun, and occasionally like a rather irregular pétanque court on which Christos, in partnership with Jean-Jacques, has remained unbeaten for over a decade.

Now, it has been transformed into the headquarters of the hunt for Martial Bellion. Twenty or so police officers are moving around five Jumper vans, all with their doors open.

Aja walks from one group to the next like a stressed theatrical director before a dress rehearsal. For a while now, she has been insulting her telephone.

"He hasn't had time to get through!" the captain yells. "Yes, I'm sure! All the exits are blocked. Trust us, we'll have him in a matter of minutes. For Christ's sake, I know this place like the back of my hand. We will corner him!"

Aja is furious. The police have been searching every street in Saint-Gilles and the surrounding area for more than an hour now, and they still haven't found any trace of the grey Clio, much less of Martial Bellion and his daughter. It's as if the car has simply flown away. Aja has had to call the ComGend[30] in Saint-Denis. A terrified underling took less than a minute to put her through to Colonel Laroche. A courteous, patient type who never shows the least sign of panic. On the contrary, he has adopted a condescending tone, as if he's trying to reassure her.

---

[30] The police command center for the island.

"Stay calm, Captain. We are certain that you and your men have done everything you possibly could. The GIPN[31] and our force will take over now . . . We'll be in touch . . ."

Everything you possibly could?

This jerk with his Zoreille accent has only been on the island for a few months and he's talking to her as if she were a child. Aja struggles to calm herself. And yet she has to win her team a few more hours. The ComGend consists of dozens of overtrained men eager to stretch their legs at the slightest excuse; motorized units, nautical units, aerial units, mountaineering units . . . The men of her force are not in the same league, but she hopes that Laroche is not particularly keen to unleash his troops on the island's biggest tourist resort. Launching a full-scale manhunt is more likely to scare away holidaymakers than a swarm of tiger mosquitoes.

Aja negotiates for several minutes.

"All right, Captain Purvi," Laroche finally says. "I'll give you two hours to catch your runaway tourist. After all, a murderer on the run with his daughter—we can't really consider that a kidnapping."

The colonel pauses, before concluding:

"Especially when the mother is no longer around to file charges."

Silence.

"I'm joking, Captain Purvi."

What an asshole!

Aja resists the desire to hang up on him. On the contrary, she reassures him that she will keep him in the loop and call every fifteen minutes. She thanks him again, then finally ends the call.

She is well aware that if she doesn't find Martial Bellion soon, the concession she has wrung from him will prove a

---

[31] The National Police Intervention Group.

hollow victory. The investigation will be handed over to Laroche's ComGend and she will only be involved again when the case goes to court.

Christos, a little further away, watches the scene from the shade of two casuarina trees between which is strung a moth-eaten hammock. Surreal. A few meters from the car park that has metamorphosed into the nerve center of this manhunt stretches out the Saint-Gilles beach. Tourists walk by, observing the action, discomfited by the radios that buzz like insects. The more clued-up ones perhaps imagine that the volcano has reawoken, or that a huge operation against drunk-driving is being planned for the Easter weekend. And that is, in fact, the explanation Aja has asked the officers to give to anyone who asks why there are roadblocks on the way out of town.

This place is about to explode, thinks Christos. A storm is going to descend on our little resort . . . You'd better make the most of it, all you lazy bums, make the most of the clownfish, and the sunset cocktails with parasols and slices of orange in them, before the state of siege is declared. You'll hear about it soon enough . . . There's a killer on the loose. He murdered his wife, maybe even his own daughter by now. Perhaps he's even buried them in the sand where your children are digging . . .

Aja, indifferent to her surroundings, turns her back on the beach and enters the principle room of the station. All the doors and windows are open. A projector linked to a laptop is displaying a 1/10,000 map of Saint-Gilles across the main wall. Four meters by two. An officer enters the real-time location of the roadblocks and areas searched on the computer; different colors represent how many times the patrols have been through each one.

Aja watches the map for a while as it changes color. Yellow. Orange. Red. It will take several hours to paint the whole thing.

Suddenly, she grabs a bunch of felt-tip pens and approaches the opposite wall, which is also an immaculate white. She stands on tiptoes and writes, as high up as possible, in huge capital letters:

In black: WHERE IS THE CAR?
In red: WHERE IS LIANE BELLION'S BODY?
In blue: WHERE IS HER DAUGHTER?
In green: WHERE IS BELLION?

She is putting the lid back on the last pen when Christos quietly walks up behind her.

"Maybe it wasn't such a good idea to bring in the cavalry to pick Bellion up from the hotel?"

The captain turns around, visibly annoyed.

"What do you suggest? That we should have gone in there wearing our trunks and bikinis and surrounded the pool?"

Christos does not take offence. He understands. Little Aja is ambitious and has a certain sense of self-worth, and yet she has screwed up the first criminal operation worthy of the name that she has ever conducted.

"Don't feel bad, Aja. You used all the forces you had at your disposal."

He puts a hand on the captain's shoulder, looks over at the policemen in the car park, bustling around like panic-stricken ants, then continues:

"Don't forget, the last time the Saint-Paul, Saint-Gilles and Saint-Leu forces worked together, it was to hunt down nudists from Souris-Chaude. Enforcing the law passed in September 2005. And yet, half of them managed to walk naked all the way to Trois-Bassins!"

Aja barely scrapes up a smile.

"Bellion didn't get through, Christos. We blocked all the roads that lead out of town. I even sent Gavrama and Laronse to check on all the boats leaving the port."

The captain looks over at the immense map stained with orange circles.

"He's still in there, somewhere close by. I can feel it." Christos examines the map too, then grimaces.

"Well, Bellion must be a magician then. If he can hide a rental car and a six-year-old girl in a village with three and a half thousand inhabitants, when there are dozens of police patrolling the streets . . ."

Aja isn't listening. She turns on her heel, leaves the room, goes out into the car park again, then raises her voice.

All the officers turn to face her.

"The ComGend is going to send reinforcements from Saint-Denis, lads. Because *they* think we're not capable of finding Bellion ourselves. So let's get moving! We all know that Martial Bellion cannot have left town. I don't just want you to check the boot of every car leaving Saint-Gilles, but every garage of every house, all the private estates, the villas, the closed buildings. Rich or poor, Creole or Zoreille, I couldn't care less. Every house! We're going to do this all night if we have to. He's driving a rental car, for fuck's sake, with an enormous 'ITC Tropicar' sign on it! We're going to catch him, lads. And we're going to do it on our own."

A sceptical silence greets the captain's tirade.

"Impressive," Christos whispers into her ear. "Like John Wayne, in fact. Now we just have to see if your cavalry is ready to charge."

Aja turns towards her second lieutenant, and continues in the same tone of voice.

"As for you, Messiah, give the prophecies a rest, would you? You're going to continue the investigation at the Hotel Athena. Grill the Jourdains, the hotel staff, the kids in the car park, everyone. I want a second-by-second reconstruction of what the Bellion family was doing prior to the crime."

12
SOPHA IN PARADISE

5:01 P.M.

Every time Sopha reaches out a finger, the leaves of the sensitive plant close up. It's amazing! You'd think the plant was a little animal. A few seconds later, the leaf unfolds again, shy and wary.

Sopha is captivated by the plant. A simple caress, a simple breath of air, a simple drop of liquid is enough to make the flower curl up on itself like a snail. To start with, Sopha was afraid, but now she's caught up in the game. And this is only the beginning. There are lots of other extraordinary plants to discover in the Garden of Eden.

Paradise. Martial hadn't lied about that.

He watches his daughter, reassured. For a few moments, Sopha forgets. He feels sure that outside the park, it must be chaos. The entire local police force will be searching for him, furious at having let him slip through their fingers. A thousand questions running through their heads.

It's only logical.

Who would have thought that the most sought-after criminal on Réunion, instead of fleeing or hiding in a house, would calmly visit the Garden of Eden with his daughter, the most prestigious botanical park on the island? What police officer would ever think to search for him here?

The police are looking for a grey Clio.

Where is the best place to hide a rental car?

Less than an hour ago, surrounded by the screaming of sirens and trapped between the police roadblocks, Martial had only a few seconds to make his decision. It had suddenly seemed obvious to him: the most brilliant way of hiding is always not to hide.

"Yuck!" shouts Sopha, laughing.

She has stopped in front of the evil-smelling java olive tree, and is reading the name on the wooden sign: *Poo-poo Tree*. She sniffs the flowers on the branches, holds her nose, then laughs again and continues on her way, skipping.

Martial follows her silently.

Not to hide.

Easier said than done. Martial had to drive back up Avenue de Bourbon, only a few hundred meters from the Hotel Athena, right under the noses of the police. At any moment, he might have found himself face to face with a police van. He had braked suddenly outside the fence surrounding the tarmac courtyard of a purple concrete building.

ITC Tropicar Rental Agency.

Five rental cars were parked in the yard, including two grey Clios. Clearly, business wasn't great. Moreover, the agency was closed for the Easter weekend, so customers—all of whom had been given the code for the gate—had to leave their keys in a letter box or call the manager (his number was painted in black on the purple wall). Martial had parked his Clio at the far end of the car park, under the casuarina trees, so it couldn't be seen directly from the road.

Five or six cars? One too many. But who could possibly know that, apart from the rental agency manager? And he wouldn't be likely to notice it until Tuesday morning at the earliest, when they opened up for business again. As for the cops, there was little chance of them checking. A fugitive hunted by the police rarely takes the time to return his rental car, particularly if the agency's car park is only three hundred meters from his hotel.

So that should give him two days . . .

*

Sopha enters the cactus garden. She leans down, amused, towards a big, round, hairy thing. Another plant that looks like an animal! Like a sort of desert hedgehog rolled up into a ball.

"Mother-in-law's cushion," Sopha reads out loud, following the letters with her finger.

She laughs again and runs towards the wooden bridge in the middle of the bamboo garden.

Martial walks behind her, lost in his thoughts. The ITC Tropicar agency had another advantage: its car park lies adjacent to a small wood, which meant they were able to walk around the edge of Saint-Gilles unseen for over half a mile, until they reached the entrance to the Garden of Eden. The botanical park is almost deserted this weekend: most Creole families are picnicking in the hills inland. The only people here are a few tourists, mostly older ones, holding their *Guide Bleu* guidebooks. Clearly, none of them is aware—yet—of the manhunt going on outside.

For now, the Garden of Eden is an inviolable paradise, the ideal refuge where they can bide their time.

For now . . .

Sopha looks up at the traveller's palm, entranced by the hundreds of leaves exploding in the sky like the rays of a green sun. Ever since she entered the garden, she has spent a long time trying to read the explanations written on the little signs in front of the flowers. Scholarly terms in Latin, complicated botanical names, many expressions she cannot understand.

Ravenala.

Sopha strikes a pose, frowning and running a hand through her long hair. Mimicking her mother, Martial thinks, whenever she goes to a museum or an exhibition. He is surprised that he has been able to breathe more easily for several minutes now; that he is able to enjoy the moment despite knowing he is the subject of a massive police search. Taking the time to watch his daughter. Sopha may be a pain in the neck, but she's an adorable pain in the neck. Gifted. Passionate. Strong-willed.

Liane has spoiled her, of course. What right did he have to oppose her? What right will he have from now on? Liane gave up her studies in sociolinguistics in order to raise Sopha. Liane was supposed to write up her PhD thesis during her pregnancy. That was the plan: nine months to write four hundred pages on the passage from the spoken to the written word via the most exotic and secret translations of *Le Petit Prince*. And it was possible, in theory, even if she had to work as a librarian three half-days a week at the Saint-Exupéry Foundation for the young people of Issy-les-Moulineaux.

Liane never even wrote the introduction. She gave up her work in the fourth month of her pregnancy, even though the Foundation was ready to grant her tenure upon completion of her thesis.

Pregnancy can transform a woman. How could Martial have forgotten that? Liane suddenly put all personal ambition aside so she could spend her time looking after a little girl weighing 3.512 kilos. "All personal ambition"—Liane would have screamed if he'd used those words in front of her. He didn't understand a thing! Never had Liane felt so in harmony with herself as she did following Sopha's birth . . .

He hadn't understood anything about Liane any longer.

Or about them, for that matter.

The pregnancy and then the birth had swallowed up the Liane who used to coil herself around him, the Liane who used to delight in their wildest erotic games. Not that they had no longer had a sex life after Sopha was born; but suddenly their lovemaking was a lower priority, planned in advance, one of many activities on the daily list of things to do. Necessary, of course, but no longer transcendent. And the same was true of him, in fact. Martial was still there, an important person in Liane's life, but not the most important person.

It wasn't easy to accept.

Sopha is still running along the parade of trees. Sometimes she lingers, sometimes she looks up at the sky, sometimes she stares, wide-eyed like an owl, at the carnival procession of elaborate foliage and plants. Baobabs. Breadfruit trees. African oil palms. Screwpines.

Suddenly she lowers her head and charges under the red bridge covered with bougainvillea. For a moment, Martial loses sight of her.

"That's life!" Liane pouted, as she rocked Sopha in her arms. "It's life, Martial! Just normal, everyday life. That's what connects us, till death do us part. All couples go through this, the ones who last anyway."

No, Liane! Martial had wanted to scream, on so many occasions.

No, Liane, not all couples!

Liane had never directly reproached him, but the silence between them was so oppressive, the unspoken inference so obvious. Was Martial capable of looking after Sopha? Of loving her, even? Was it possible to trust him? Liane never talked to him about before. She never pronounced Alex's name. Liane was a discreet, tactful girl, but Martial could read the doubt in her eyes and, each time, he lost himself in the spiral of questions that must surely plague her. Sopha, is your father a monster?

"Watch out!"

Instinctively, Martial reaches forward and grabs Sopha's wrist.

His daughter glares at him, more irritated than angry.

"The fishtail palm," Martial explains, pointing to bunches of green fruit hanging by the edge of the path. "It's poisonous if you eat it, and like the strongest itching powder in the world if you touch it."

Sceptical but wary, Sopha stares at the strange plant, then starts walking again without a word to her father.

Sopha, is your father a monster?
He has no response.

He mustn't let himself lose concentration any more. The garden closes at 6 P.M. In a few minutes, they'll be outside again. He does not have a plan. The whole town must be crawling with police, all of them searching for him and his daughter. His face has surely been shown repeatedly on the island's television channel. Sopha's too.

A father alone with his daughter.

Someone is bound to recognize them, and report them to the authorities. A tourist, a passer-by.

Sopha has stopped at the side of the path. A tiny panther chameleon is lazing on a stem amid a thicket of porcelain roses. The color of its skin changes from red to green as the flower sways from side to side.

With a little imagination . . .

This is not something Sopha lacks.

"Can you stay right there, sweetheart? I'm just going to the entrance."

Sopha does not reply, fascinated by the baby chameleon's eyes, each one turned in a different direction like two Beyblade tops. Martial shoots a final glance at Sopha, then walks under the pergola covered in creepers. He is aware they no longer have a car, that they have no clothes apart from the ones they are wearing, nowhere to sleep, and nothing to eat.

He knows no one on this island, least of all in this resort. Alone against the world. He is empty-handed, defenceless.

To enter or exit the garden, you have to pass through a gigantic barrel, an oak cask built in 1847 that originally contained 57,000 liters of rum, according to the sign next to it. Martial walks through and spots the girl on the reception desk, sitting behind racks of postcards. She is typing on her iPhone. Painted fingernails, African braids, nose piercing. Statistically, this girl is more likely to be looking at Facebook than reading a news story with a photograph of the fugitive.

Martial puts on his sunglasses. He has no choice: he has to try his luck. There isn't much to see in the reception area: pamphlets on a display stand detailing the main events on the island; the monthly magazine promoting the charms of the Saint-Gilles resort; various leaflets.

Nothing of any use, on the face of it.

On the face of it.

An idea germinates in Martial's mind.

All it requires is a bit of luck. And a lot of nerve.

13
GRILLED LAWYER ON TOAST

H ello, Aja?"

Captain Purvi shuts herself away in the main room of the police station. As she passes in front of the beam from the projector, the town of Saint-Gilles is suddenly eclipsed by a black shadow as if Aja were an encroaching storm cloud.

"Yes?"

"Gildas, captain of the Saint-Benoît force. Do you remember? We're the ones with the galoshes and the oilskins . . ."

Aja remembers him. Gildas Yacou has been the Saint-Benoît force's captain for twenty-five years, and in that time he has requested and been denied innumerable transfers, so that he cultivates his bitterness the way others cultivate cannabis. In Saint-Benoît, it rains a hundred days a year, almost half the inhabitants are unemployed, and the town has the highest statistics for violent crime on the island.

"What do you want, Gildas? We're a bit on edge here. If you're offering help . . ."

Gildas coughs.

"I have some information on the Bellion case, Aja."

Aja's legs weaken. Martial Bellion has slipped through the net. He is already on the other side of the island. He is going to disappear in Mafate or Salazie.

"You . . . you haven't *seen* Martial Bellion?"

"No. I wish I had, mind. It would have been nice to get five minutes of fame after decades of good and loyal service that no one gives a rat's arse about. No, listen to this. My student officer, Flora, who's on reception this week, well, she saw Liane Bellion."

Aja collapses into the first chair she manages to grab.

"Alive?"

Gildas coughs into the phone again. Aja has a sudden vision of him wearing a woolly hat and scarf, as if it were winter.

"Very much so. But that was five days ago . . ."

Aja wishes she was standing next to Gildas so she could strangle him with her bare hands.

"Stop messing around, Gildas. I'm working here."

The captain of the Saint-Benoît force ignores her remark.

"Liane Bellion came to the station on Tuesday the twenty-sixth."

Aja calculates: that was three days before she disappeared.

"What did she want?" she asks feverishly.

"Hard to say. As far as I know, what she said was pretty surreal. But if you want details, you'll have to ask Flora. She's the one who took the statement."

"O.K., Gildas. Can you come over here with Flora? We'll be waiting for you."

Gildas's cough mutates into raucous laughter.

"You don't change, Aja. A real little Napoleon! We have work to do here too, you know. If you want to meet Flora, get in your car and drive over. You're lucky—there's no storm forecast for the next hour or so."

"There's a killer on the loose here, Gildas."

"Yeah, I think I heard something about that. But I've got murders to solve. We get about one a week. Not to mention all the rapes and assaults."

"Give me a break, Gildas. The ComGend will come down on you like a tonne of bricks if you don't co-operate."

Gildas explodes, his humor gone.

"Don't threaten me with that crap, Aja! What do I care

about the Zoreilles in Saint-Denis? Let's just say that my priorities are not the same as yours, O.K., and then we can stay friends. I suggest we meet halfway. I'll drive to Tampon. Can you meet me at the Entre-Deux, opposite the Bras de Pontho cemetery?"

On the wall, Aja observes areas of the giant map slowly turning yellow, as patrols pass through each zone.

"I've got too much other shit on my plate, Gildas. They need me here."

"You have to learn to delegate, Aja."

5:21 P.M.

Christos asks the Jourdains to sit down while he installs himself in the luxurious leather armchair belonging to the manager of the Hotel Athena.

What a pleasure it was to throw Armand Zuttor out of his own office.

Sorry, big guy, you need to clear out! Needs must . . .

Christos enjoyed seeing the Gros Blanc's appalled expression as he ejected him in order to use his office for interviewing his customers. And the second lieutenant's rear end is happy too as it burrows into the comfortable chair, perfectly positioned so that the cool air from the ceiling fan tickles the back of his neck. He understands Zuttor, when it comes down to it. One quickly becomes accustomed to such pathetic emblems of power.

The couple opposite him do not seem very confident. The lawyer and his wife. Jacques and Margaux Jourdain.

Christos has placed the Maisons du Monde knife on the desk.

"Madame and Monsieur Jourdain, let me ask you again: is this Martial Bellion's knife?"

"Well, um . . ."

Not very articulate, this lawyer.

But Christos is not fooled. Jacques Jourdain recognized the weapon immediately, of course; he is simply reluctant to say so. A question of honor, perhaps; class solidarity, an unspoken pact. After all, he ate dinner with Martial Bellion only the night before.

A lock of Christos's hair is blown out of place by the fan. He rearranges it.

"Madame and Monsieur Jourdain, let me be frank. While the three of us take it easy here in the boss's office, all the police on the island are out on a hunt. A pack of hounds in pursuit of its prey, and between the one and the other, there is the life of a six-year-old girl. So try to think quickly."

Christos spins the knife.

"This weapon was found in the stomach of some poor guy, with Bellion's fingerprints on the handle. I'm not asking you to denounce anyone, just to confirm the facts."

Jacques Jourdain assumes a dignified, responsible expression. "It's difficult to say . . ."

Go ahead, treat me like I'm stupid.

Christos sighs, exasperated. He looks up and examines the room. The walls are covered with black and white engravings, obviously intended to make an impression on the hotel staff when they came into the manager's office; lithographs detailing the island's history, but a history that ended in 1946, when Réunion became a French *département*. Creoles lined up like convicts in sugar cane fields; ladies in crinoline dresses standing in front of colonial villas with carved lambrequins; bare-chested Creoles with white teeth and ebony skin; portraits of forgotten Gros Blancs, looking proud and arrogant under their sad moustaches.

The good old days . . .

Christos decides to take off the gloves.

"I understand you. Solidarity, eh? When things get tough, you have to stick together."

The lawyer reacts as if he's just sat on a sea urchin, jumping straight into the air.

"Why do you say that?"

To get a reaction out of you, dickhead.

"Because there's a killer at large on the island. Because he's already committed one murder, because he may kill again, because we need facts. You can't hide behind your professional discretion, Monsieur Jourdain. You're not Bellion's lawyer. You don't owe him a thing. This is not some foreign police force asking you to denounce one of your countrymen. Réunion Island is part of France."

Christos wonders if he has over-egged things a bit.

"It is his," Margaux Jourdain mutters.

"Are you certain?"

"Yes. We went up to Cilaos, three days ago. A traditional Creole picnic. We used one of those barbecues you find by the side of the road. We all used that knife."

Margaux takes a closer look at it, examining each imperfection on the blade and the handle, then nods: "It's his."

Jacques looks angrily at his wife. Just for show. He's actually quite pleased that his wife got landed with this. Christos puts the knife in a transparent plastic bag.

"Thank you. Now we're getting somewhere. So, what about the other afternoon? You were splashing around with the Bellions in the pool, I believe?"

A professional hypocrite, Jacques now takes the lead.

"That's right. Martial asked us to watch Sopha while he went up to his room to see Liane."

Christos pushes the clock across the desk, a clock that must date back to a time before the abolition of slavery. Around the dial, four little naked Creoles are carrying a basket overflowing with exotic fruit.

"I'm sorry, but you're going to have to be more precise. Liane Bellion went up to her room at 3:01 P.M. Naivo Randrianasoloarimino opened room 38 for Martial Bellion at 4:06 P.M., but the room was empty. The question could not be simpler: did Martial Bellion leave the hotel garden at any time between 3 and 4 P.M.?"

Jacques Jourdain replies a little too quickly.

"It's hard to say. You know how it is. Siesta time, reading, lazing around. We don't spy on each other. And we hardly ever look at our watches."

Well, well, well . . .

"Monsieur and Madame Jourdain, I don't want to give you the whole spiel again—the killer on the loose, little Sopha, the importance of your testimony."

Undaunted, Jacques attempts to open an emergency exit in the conversation.

"Lieutenant, I imagine Martial Bellion himself must have confirmed this particular point. I've also heard that you've had statements from the hotel's employees, and three children who were playing in the street. Isn't that enough for you?"

Christos glances up at the colonial lithographs, then looks back down at Jacques Jourdain.

"For me, sure. For others . . . To be honest with you, Martial Bellion's version changed quite substantially over time."

Again, it is Margaux who cracks.

"Martial left the garden fifteen minutes after Liane went up. Discreetly. Everyone was sleeping in their deckchairs. I was alone in the pool, doing lengths. He probably thought no one saw him go. He came back half an hour later, and stayed with us for about twenty minutes before going up again, openly this time. He asked us to look after Sopha."

"Are you sure?"

"Certain. At first, I thought he was meeting his wife for a . . . debauched siesta, let's say . . . and I thought to myself how lucky she was."

Take that, lawyer! A solid blow from the right.

"Then, as time went on, I thought, gosh, she really *is* lucky."

A good left hook.

Christos grins. Scratch the surface, and the shy-seeming Margaux Jourdain is not lacking in sex appeal. Jacques Jourdain keeps on smiling his courtroom smile.

"But you see, my darling, in reality she wasn't very lucky, was she?"

The lawyer ducks and dives, then unleashes an uppercut.

His wife's eyes cloud over suddenly. Almost sincere, she asks: "Lieutenant, do you really think Martial killed his wife and that . . . um . . . native?"

Be careful, my lovely, you're skating on thin ice there. Never, ever use that word on the island. Your lawyer husband can explain it better than I can. Maybe you're getting what you deserve in bed, after all.

"It's possible, Madame Jourdain. I just hope he doesn't kill anyone else."

14
FOR RENT

S itting on the chair, Martial hides his face behind the Saint-Gilles newsletter, a small four-page leaflet printed on glossy paper, just in case the girl behind reception should lift her eyes up from her iPhone. It doesn't seem likely though: she is tapping away at her phone as if she were some kind of piano prodigy performing Mozart at the Royal Albert Hall.

Martial's attention is caught by the headline on the front page of the newsletter:

The end of ITR. Property market holds its breath in Saint-Gilles-les-Bains.

From these simple words, the outline of a strategy begins to take shape in Martial's mind, but he needs to know more. Like everyone else on the island, he has heard about the ITR pension benefit, but he can't take any risks; he must gather as much information as possible.

He lowers the newsletter for a second to check that Sopha is still in the Garden of Eden. She has left the chameleon on its stem and is now concentrating on the butterflies. Her eyes attempt to follow the orange and black wings of a monarch as it flies between two orchids.

Reassured, Martial goes back to reading the article. Since 1952, any French government employee taking retirement on Réunion Island—on the sole condition that they do not leave the island for more than forty days per year—has received a thirty-five per cent increase on their pension. More than thirty thousand people have benefited from this measure, including a few hundred who never, or almost never, actually live on the island. The Jégo reform of 2008 proposed to end this privilege, but only after twenty years. No way were they going to suddenly cut off the supply of golden eggs: retired people injected hundreds of millions of euros into the island's economy, especially in the property market in Saint-Gilles.

Martial glances over at Sopha. She is fine, and has gone back to tormenting the chameleon once more, placing one of her arms behind it to see if it will turn pink.

He focuses on the article. In truth, he doesn't care about the details, or the future of pensioners on the island. Only one aspect matters to him: the fact that there are lots of empty apartments in Saint-Gilles, theoretically occupied more than three hundred days per year by French people who, in reality, rarely set foot there. Martial suspects that a number of them are trying to have their cake and eat it. Not only do they receive an increased pension by claiming residence in an apartment they never (or hardly ever) live in, but they can also rent out that apartment. Who could resist the temptation? An abode in the tropics with a view over the lagoon.

Martial drops the newsletter. The receptionist's fingers continue to skate over the screen at Olympic speed. Even if the police do come to interrogate her, he doubts she will be able to offer much in the way of a description.

Back under the pergola and into the Garden of Eden. Sopha stares at him imploringly.

"Papa, can I go back and see the sensitive plants again?"

"Yes, Sopha. But be quick. We need to leave soon."

Just for a second, he wonders if he shouldn't leave Sopha here and escape on his own. Does he have any idea what will happen over the coming hours? Can he even imagine how he will react? Liane would never have let him go out on his own with Sopha. Ever since their daughter was born, she was always against the idea, for one simple reason.

Fear.

But Liane is no longer here.

Drops of sweat roll down Martial's forehead. He mustn't panic. His hesitation is ridiculous. He has no choice: Sopha *must* stay with him. His daughter is his hostage. An accommodating hostage, docile and willing.

Currency, when the moment arrives.

Martial takes his mobile phone from his pocket, a BlackBerry Curve 9300. He bought it under the counter from a Chinese guy, three days ago in Saint-Denis, on Rue de l'Abattoir. He didn't even have to provide his name, so there's no chance the police will be able to use it to locate him. The internet connection is good. He clicks on www.papvacances.fr.

The site is an open door to over fifty thousand private rental ads.

A drop-down menu offers to scour the entire world.

Region or city?

His thumb moves quickly over the keyboard.

SAINT-GILLES-LES-BAINS

After barely four seconds, Martial is looking at a list of forty-seven ads. He quickly scans them. Most are for apartments. He sighs. Too risky. He returns to the drop-down menu.

Type of accommodation?

Martial adds a criterion.

HOUSE OR VILLA

Three seconds later, the list has been reduced to eighteen.

Feverishly, Martial clicks on the *See details* icon. Using Google Earth, he is able to check the location of each house, then concentrate on the owners' addresses. This takes him less than a minute. With the twelfth ad, he finds what he is looking for. The building is situated less than three hundred meters from the Garden of Eden, on Rue des Maldives. The four photographs in the gallery give a more precise idea of the property: a discreet little garden protected by a concrete wall, and a *varangue*[32] with a large bay window.

Perfect.

Contact: Chantal95@yahoo.fr

There's even an address in France.

Chantal Letellier

13 Rue de Clairvaux

Montmorency

Martial checks the house's availability again. It seems to be available for five weeks a year—the next five weeks. It almost seems too good to be true. Martial can't risk taking any chances, so he clicks on Google Images and types in the woman's name and city, checking his spelling as he goes.

Chantal Letellier Montmorency

In the second that follows, fifteen thumbnail photographs of a smiling, blue-haired woman in her sixties appear on his screen.

Martial clicks on the first one.

www.copainsdavant.liternaute.com

Martial finds Chantal Letellier's biography. It is brief. A nurse for thirty-eight years in the Bichat hospital. He clicks on the second picture and finds himself on a Facebook wall. Blue-eyed Chantal has covered her profile with photographs of her grandchildren. No husband, apparently.

Martial can hardly contain his excitement. It's ideal! Chantal Letellier rents her Réunion villa for five weeks per year. If the nurse is honest, this constitutes the legal period during which she can return to France to see her grandchildren. If she's defrauding the government, she never sets foot in the tropics and rents her house for five weeks a year that are, on the website, always the following five weeks.

---

[32] A type of veranda typical of Creole architecture.

In either case, the house is empty, close by, and isolated.

Perfect.

He memorises the address—3 Rue des Maldives—then finally looks up.

Sopha? Where is Sopha?

There is no sign of her anywhere.

Sopha?

Martial panics. It is too risky to ask a visitor, never mind shout out his daughter's name. He puts his phone in his pocket and starts to run.

One path, two paths. He knocks over plants. He should never have left her unsupervised. Liane was right. He is careless. There's a pond at the far end of the Garden of Eden. A natural pool filled with eels, guppies and other fish of all colors. What if she's . . .

Sopha is there.

Staring curiously at the Zen garden.

The impressive silence of the place contrasts with the deafening birdsong heard elsewhere in Eden. Ochre soil. Raked grey gravel. White stone paths snaking between small hills of black sand. Martial puts his hand gently on Sopha's shoulder.

The girl looks up at him imploringly.

"Papa, can we stay a bit longer?"

"No, Sopha, we have to go."

She smiles at him. Just for a moment, she seems to have forgotten the frightening reality. The police sirens. The car chase.

Her *maman*.

Just for a moment.

15
The Meeting

Aja parks just outside the Bras de Pontho cemetery. The gravestones are ranged along a gentle slope, spread out, as though each one should be able to enjoy the benefit, for eternity, of the panoramic view of the Bras de la Plaine, the gully of lemon trees and the natural chapel of its basalt columns.

The temperature is mild; the imposing shadow of the Piton des Neiges offers the illusion that dusk falls less suddenly here than elsewhere.

Aja looks at her watch and curses. In less than an hour, the ComGend will take over the case. Every minute counts, and here she is, wasting her time in the middle of nowhere, waiting for that prick of a cop who is now late and has probably dragged her out here for no good reason at all.

6:25 P.M.

Finally Gildas Yacou turns up. He gets out of a yellow Jeep. Shirt open. Flowery tie. Like a Bollywood version of *Hawaii Five-0*.

The fat policeman has his arm round the waist of a trembling young Creole who is not especially pretty, except for her long eyelashes that flutter like the wings of a butterfly. Fortunately, they are her most striking asset. Flora stares at the ground.

"Flora, this is Aja. I knew her when she was a kid, just like you.

She saw her first action with me. She's a fighter."

Gildas shoots Aja a smile that he would like to be complicit, then continues.

"She is also a pain in the arse, it has to be said—more irritable than a Zoreille who's just landed here—but she has integrity."

Aja's foot kicks at the dust. "Have you finished?"

"Certainly."

"Well, let's get started, then. I'd be in Saint-Gilles now, if it weren't for all this nonsense."

"Take it easy, Aja. It's not the girl's fault . . ."

"I'm not pissed off with the girl, I'm pissed off with you." Gildas's eyes sparkle like those of a fisherman facing down a massive storm.

"Calm yourself, Aja. The girl's only been with us for two months. She's from Hell-Bourg, in Les Hauts. She's had a hard time getting to where she is now. You should understand that. So you can question her, but don't take it out on her."

The captain's arm moves paternally up to Flora's shoulders. She is trembling slightly. Aja can't tell if it's because her boss keeps touching her, because he has told her about Aja's fierce reputation, or because of what she is about to say.

"So, you saw Liane Bellion?" Aja asks Flora.

The student officer hesitates, squirms.

"Yes . . . on Tuesday. Five days ago."

Gildas presses his big fat belly against Flora's stomach and whispers in her ear:

"Go on, love, she won't bite."

Aja concentrates. These two are hiding something. The girl has made some kind of blunder, and that pig Gildas is trying to cover for her.

Flora talks in a whisper.

"She . . . she came to the Saint-Benoît station."

"Sorry?"

The pit bull in Aja awakens. Calm down. Let the kid talk.

Flora works up some momentum and the words begin to emerge, gradually speeding up.

"I was on reception. On my own. She came in the morning, just as we opened, about nine o'clock. She asked me something weird. It was all a bit vague, but I finally worked out that she wanted us to protect her."

Aja keeps a tight hold on the leash attached to her pit bull. She wants to scream.

"She went to ask for police protection. And you think that's weird?"

Gildas's fingers grip the girl's waist. He strokes her back through her blouse, as if telling her what to say through some kind of braille. Flora gets flustered.

"No, Captain Purvi. No, that's not what I mean. Liane Bellion didn't phrase it like that. She asked me if the police could ensure the protection of individuals . . . individuals in general . . ."

"But she was talking about herself?"

"Yes, that seemed obvious."

Aja attempts to control the adrenalin that is fizzing through her veins.

"You're not stupid. I assume you tried to get her to explain what she meant?"

"Of course, Captain Purvi. I tried to make her talk. I asked her, following the rules, 'Protection for whom? Against what?' That was when Liane Bellion got stuck. She replied something like 'protection for individuals who cannot reveal what is threatening them.'"

"What?"

Flora starts to look more confident. She has taken a few steps forward, and Gildas's arms can no longer fondle her.

"Exactly, Captain . . . '*What?*' That's what I said to Liane Bellion. After that, her explanations were all mixed up and she started talking in the first person. She was talking in circles. 'I'm scared, madame,' she told me. 'And it's because I'm scared that I can't tell you anything.' Then she asked me what the police would do if she told us more."

"And you replied?"

"I said that we would check out the facts. What else could I say? That's when she got angry. 'That would only make things worse!' she yelled. 'Don't you understand? You have to trust me. If you can't take my word, if you launch an investigation, then there will be more than just one threat.'"

Aja opens her mouth to speak. Gildas tries to reach out and grab hold of one of Flora's arms, the hem of her blouse, a patch of bare skin. Flora lifts her hand authoritatively, refusing any interruption.

"I insisted, Captain Purvi. Believe me, I insisted. 'You have to tell me more,' I said to Liane Bellion. 'How can we help you if you won't give me any details?' She cracked. Liane Bellion was a very beautiful woman, and she seemed very sure of herself, but in that moment she just lost it. 'Don't you understand?' she shouted at me. 'Are you even listening? I can't tell you anything! I just need you to protect me!'"

Flora suddenly falls silent. The two black butterflies that frame her eyes turn towards the Piton des Neiges. Aja tries to speak in the gentlest voice possible.

"After that, Flora, how did you deal with the matter?"

"I continued asking her for details, or at least a hint of what was going on, something tangible we could work with, and gradually she calmed down. She didn't tell us anything more about whatever danger she thought she was in, but she wanted us to supply her with a bodyguard, or get some undercover officer to follow her around. After a few minutes of negotiation, she suddenly cut short the interview, as if she regretted ever having come in. As she left, she said something along the lines of: 'Never mind, it doesn't matter. I was probably panicking about nothing.'"

That's it?

Aja inwardly curses this stupid girl. She has difficulty concealing her anger.

"You let her go, Flora? Did you believe her?"

"No . . . No, Captain . . . Not really, but . . . What else could I do? She didn't want to file charges, she didn't want to talk, she apologized for having bothered me with such a small thing . . ."

The student officer promptly bursts into tears. Gildas takes full advantage of the situation. He moves close to her again and glares at Aja. At least he is tactful enough not to say anything.

Flora is sobbing.

"Captain Purvi . . . Do you . . . do you think it's my fault? Do you think she didn't dare say she felt threatened by her husband because she was too frightened of what he might do to her?"

Aja's response is cold and cutting.

"Not what he would do to *her*. She was frightened of what he might do to her daughter."

"If I'd . . . if only I'd . . ."

"No, sweetness, no, of course you couldn't . . ." Gildas comforts her.

Aja does not have the heart to say anything else. What's the point? Could the tragedy have been averted if Flora hadn't thought Liane Bellion was lying or exaggerating? The answer is unimportant. Flora's testimony simply adds another item to the long list of evidence against Martial Bellion.

Well, that's something, at least.

Aja looks out over the cemetery. Most of the graves do not have headstones or marble plaques. The dead have to make do with a rectangular cage placed in the grass. Sometimes the bars of the cages are decorated; more often they are rusted. The captain turns back to the two police officers.

"In your opinion, why did Liane Bellion go all the way to Saint-Benoît to visit the police?"

Gildas responds this time. The front of his shirt is wet with a mixture of sweat and Flora's tears.

"Anonymity, Aja. Battered women rarely file charges at their local station."

Exactly, Gildas.

Gildas is a dirty old man with wandering hands—she experienced them when she was Flora's age—but he is not a bad police officer.

Flora continues snivelling. Her well of shame is not yet full.

"I . . . I couldn't have known, Captain . . ."

Aja says nothing. Behind her mask of integrity, she too is essentially a hypocrite. She feels just as responsible as Flora does. She let Martial Bellion slip through her fingers. She is floundering, and so is her investigation. This student's mistake is nothing compared to her own incompetence.

She looks at her watch, then at her phone. Nothing new. She has failed. Any minute now, the ComGend and that bastard Laroche will take over the investigation.

And yet it is evident: Liane Bellion was afraid for her safety, afraid for the safety of her daughter.

Aja cannot tear her eyes away from the little flower-covered cages scattered across the cemetery, slender rectangles in wrought tin. Aja can no longer see a single grave, just dozens of children's cots; an open-air room where infants sleep, buried alive.

16
The Old Lady's House

Through the net curtain at the window, Martial discreetly observes the other houses on Rue des Maldives. The halogen lamp, turned to its lowest setting, projects a light that is so subtle it cannot be seen from outside.

Getting into Chantal Letellier's house proved even simpler than expected. The house was described in great detail on the site www.papvacances.fr. Judging from the map and the photographs, the bathroom window was both the most concealed and the easiest to break. The most difficult thing, in fact, had been explaining the broken window to Sopha.

An old lady is letting us borrow her house, sweetheart, but she forgot to leave us the keys.

His daughter didn't reply. She'd just waited for him to open the bay windows on the veranda, then entered and looked around at the walls, staring with curiosity at the photographs of this unknown, blue-haired grandmother with her blond, tanned grandchildren: a boy of about ten, and a younger brother who was more or less Sopha's age. Happy pictures of kids posing in the middle of Croc Parc, the crocodile farm in the Etang-Salé; in front of the silver threads of the Voile de la Mariée waterfall; in a field of sugar cane three times their height.

Martial continues to survey the deserted housing development for the slightest sign of life. A patch of shade under the casuarina trees, a ripple on the surface of a swimming pool, the

sound of footsteps on the pavement. In this almost uninhabited area of retirees, the few permanent residents probably
spend their days on the lookout for any unusual activity. The
type of people who would call the police over a twitching curtain, a light left on.

An open garage door . . .

Martial preferred to take that particular risk: he had left the
iron gate to the garage ajar, just wide enough so that, from the
street, it would be obvious that the garage was empty. He saw
some policemen two hours ago, at the other end of the development. They looked as if they were opening garages, more or less
randomly, almost certainly on the hunt for a grey Clio. If the
police pass by Chantal Letellier's house and see only a locked-up
house, silent and dark, the garage empty, they won't stop.

Or probably not, anyway.

Martial takes a step back and grabs the remote control for
the small television. He switches it on and lowers the volume,
then collapses onto the couch.

Sopha is sleeping in the room next door, which must belong
to one of Chantal Letellier's grandsons—a nice bedroom,
around eight square meters, decorated with Creole puppets,
shellfish and starfish, kites and miniature sailboats.

Sopha has been obedient. Too obedient. Almost silent. In
truth, Martial has no point of comparison; this is the first time
he's ever been alone with her. What ideas might be running
through the mind of this child, who's been protected, ever
since birth, as if she were a doll made of glass? What inner
resources does she possess that might help her to withstand
this avalanche of events? Of course, she had kissed him good
night, she had smiled at him, she had replied, "Yes, Papa" to
his clumsy "Good night, sweetheart."

But, deep down, what does she really think of him?

8:45 P.M.

On Réunion 1, the island's own television channel, the news has been on a loop for almost the last hour. For the third time, Martial sees the photograph of Liane on the screen, and then the following image announces the launch of Operation Papangue (named after the Réunion harrier, the native bird of prey that is in fast decline). The number for the ComGend rolls continuously along the bottom of the screen, while his own photograph appears above, followed by one of Sopha. The voice-over lists the charges against him—double murder—and cites damning evidence. Dangerous and perhaps armed . . . a plea for witnesses . . .

The portraits of Martial and Sopha disappear and are replaced by the face of the outraged journalist, who stresses the urgency of the search, the need for vigilance, prudence.

Martial settles himself on the couch and puts his feet up on the coffee table. He feels strangely calm, at one remove from the panic he has created, even though he is aware of the terrible consequences. Like a careless child who's lit a match in a hay field or thrown a stone off a bridge onto a motorway; observing the damage he has caused without any way of altering the chain of events.

8:51 P.M.

Papa's killed Maman!

I thought it might be true when the other kids at the pool told me, but now I'm sure. They've said so on the news, several times. Papa's turned the volume down, but I heard what they said all the same.

They're showing our photos.

Papa killed Maman.

I feel like I've been standing here behind the living room door for hours now. I did try to go to sleep, for a long time, but I couldn't.

It's impossible.

So I got out of bed and crept over here, behind the open door. When we first came in, Papa told me not to speak too loud, or knock anything over, or turn on the lights.

Now Papa is on the couch, but from where I'm standing I can only see the ends of his shoes on the little table. Except when he gets up and goes to the window and looks out through the curtain.

Just like that, the sound of a car in the street is louder than the words on the television. There's a sort of flash of headlights going across the room, and then nothing. The car is gone.

But Papa keeps on looking.

I am not going to talk loud, just loud enough so that Papa can hear me above the people on the television.

"Papa, did it hurt Maman, when you killed her?"

8:52 P.M.

Martial turns around instantly, as if he's been electrocuted. The only thing he can think of in response to Sopha's question is to put his finger to his lips. Lights go on in the nearest house. Neighbors coming home, probably. Martial still has the remote control in his hand; he mutes the television.

"Be quiet, Sopha."

He twists his neck round to look at her. The whole world spins.

His legs can no longer carry him.

Sopha is lying on the living room floor. A small pool of blood beneath her forehead.

17
PRIDE AND LAZINESS

9:02 P.M.

Aja has settled on the veranda behind the station. The inner courtyard is cloaked in darkness, except for the table, which is lit by a dim lamp hanging from a wire wrapped around a beam. The night is incredibly warm. Aja loves ending her days like this, outside with her laptop, surfing the internet. Just the feeble glimmer of the bulb and the blue glow from her computer screen. Listening to the birds sing nervously, as though this were the first time they had ever encountered dusk. Her father taught her how to recognize the songs of *tuit-tuits*,[33] *tec-tecs, oiseaux-la-vierge*,[34] but especially of her favorites, the *salanganes*,[35] which only come out at night and which use echolocation to find their way around.

The words swarm across the screen. Aja types quickly, without even correcting her mistakes. Colonel Laroche is expecting her report before midnight. He made it clear that he personally would send it on to the various departments of the ComGend.

Headquarters' decision reached her at precisely 8 P.M.: Operation Papangue is officially launched. The ComGend is taking over the co-ordination of the hunt for Martial Bellion; the media plan is to broadcast a missing persons appeal across all television channels and radio stations. Liaison with forces in mainland France as well as those on the island, mobilization of the National Police Intervention Group, the GIPN.

[33] Réunion cuckoo-shrikes.
[34] Mascarene paradise flycatchers.
[35] Mascarene swiftlets.

The full monty.

Aja didn't even have to negotiate. Laroche has left her in charge of the investigation within the perimeter of the Saint-Gilles commune—as well as the roadblocks and the house searches—until morning. Until further notice, he will oversee everything else.

Behind her, inside the station, Aja hears the crackle of radios. Muffled orders. Some laughter, and a lot of swearing from her exhausted colleagues. At the last checkpoint, on the very edge of Saint-Gilles, the traffic jams caused by the searching of every vehicle are now several miles long. The unfortunate cops in charge of the searches have had to put up with a constant stream of insults. Fifteen other officers are systematically searching houses with garages, more or less at random. For the moment, they have no leads at all.

Not even the tiniest clue.

Aja closes her eyes and makes out, in the distance, towards the cliffs, the sound of *paille-en-queues*[36] protecting their nests. She must have missed something.

Too young, too female, too Creole. A triple handicap. They'll make sure she understands that tomorrow morning.

And so, she revises the report. The process is enlightening.

Tuesday, March 26. Proven fact: Liane Bellion goes to Saint-Benoît to ask for police protection. She says she feels threatened.

Friday, March 29, 3 P.M. Fact: Liane Bellion leaves the garden of the Hotel Athena and goes up to her room. All the hotel guests and staff have confirmed this. Eve-Marie Nativel is positive: Liane Bellion did not come out of her room.

3:15 P.M. Fact: Martial Bellion goes to join his wife in their room. Confirmed by the testimonies both of the Jourdains and hotel employees.

---

[36] Tropicbirds.

3:25 P.M. Almost a proven fact: Martial Bellion leaves the hotel room, pushing a laundry cart that may or may not have contained a body. He goes down to the car park behind the hotel. The testimonies of Eve-Marie Nativel, the hotel gardener, Tanguy Dijoux, and the children playing in the car park all concur. This is also confirmed by Martial Bellion's confession.

3:45 P.M. Fact: Martial Bellion returns to the hotel swimming pool.

4 P.M. Fact: Martial Bellion goes back up to his hotel room. Again, all the testimonies of the hotel staff agree on this. In the room, signs of a struggle are observed, as well as bloodstains belonging to Liane Bellion.

Between three and four, Amaury Hoarau, aka Rodin, was murdered at the port in Saint-Gilles, around half a mile from the hotel. The murder weapon, a knife, belongs to Martial Bellion. The analyses leave no room for doubt: the knife's blade is covered with traces of Liane Bellion's blood. The only fingerprints found on the handle are those of Martial Bellion.

Sunday, March 31, 4 P.M.: just before his arrest, Martial Bellion escapes from the Hotel Athena in a grey Clio, a rental car, taking his daughter Josapha with him.

He has not yet been found.

Doubts concerning Martial Bellion's guilt: none.

Problems: no apparent motive. No corpse for Liane Bellion.

Most likely hypothesis: an argument between Martial Bellion and his wife turns nasty. He accidentally kills her. He panics, then becomes caught in a violent spiral of events.

Subsidiary question: what might he be capable of if he really freaks out?

Aja lifts her eyes from the screen. She keeps stumbling over that last phrase, "freaks out." She would like to find more appropriate wording for the ComGend, but she can't think of anything better.

The initial investigation in mainland France has not produced anything substantial—the Bellions seem to be a normal couple with an unremarkable past. Martial Bellion works in a gymnasium in Deuil-la-Barre. He has been married to Liane for eight years. She quickly gave up her PhD in sociolinguistics in order to raise their daughter, Josapha.

Above Aja, near the wire attached to the bulb, a gecko is creeping carefully along the beam, like a tightrope walker, in an attempt to move closer to the light. An Icarus without feathers.

Aja forces herself to smile.

No one becomes a murderer just like that. There has to be something in Martial Bellion's past. The police station in Deuil-la-Barre is supposed to send over all the information they've discovered about the Bellions some time this evening. Apparently, they are still busy at work, even though it is nearly 7 P.M. in France and, for the moment, the ComGend does not seem to believe in the psychological aspect of this case. Or perhaps it just doesn't care. The simple explanation, a domestic row that went drastically wrong, is probably enough for them. And the priority is to catch this guy before he kills again. After that, they can start looking at any extenuating circumstances.

Except it's not that. Aja has met Martial Bellion on two occasions now, and something just doesn't make sense. A guy who killed his wife by accident then gave in to panic would already have been caught. Why call the cops, why turn up at the police station voluntarily, why confess, and then run away? This whole scenario seems like it's been planned in advance with a particular objective in mind.

But what?

It would be hard to mention her gut feeling in a report. She would immediately be accused of trying to avoid responsibility, of inventing a Machiavellian enemy so that she didn't have to admit she has been duped by an amateur.

She doesn't care.

The words on her screen are all underlined in red and green. She sighs. Surely there are more pressing needs than correcting her spelling mistakes just to satisfy the Zoreille administrators . . . And yet, even if she is bored out of her brains by all this bureaucracy, she will go through the report again meticulously.

It's a question of pride.

9:05 P.M.

"Good night, Gabin!"

The barman turns around but does not hold out his hand, which is black with charcoal. He has been cleaning the Athena's huge barbecue for the past fifteen minutes. It is Armand Zuttor who chooses the menus for the Grain de Sable, the hotel restaurant. On nights when the food must be grilled, in addition to making cocktails, Gabin has become a chimney sweep. Well, orders are orders.

He looks at Eve-Marie Nativel. The cleaning lady stands in front of him, gripping her canvas bag. Clearly, she is about to go home.

"I won't shake your hand, Eve-Marie. See you tomorrow."

The old Creole woman smiles under her blue headscarf but she doesn't move an inch. Slowly, she turns her head and checks that there are no tourists within hearing distance. Most of them have already left the pool to escape from the mosquitoes.

"No," she replies. "Tomorrow I'm working for a Gros Blanc. A bastard, even worse than Zuttor, but he pays me four times as much . . ."

"Well, Happy Easter then."

The barman looks down at his sooty arms, resigned. He's going to be spending quite a while yet cleaning out the fireplace.

Him, an artist, the king of Ti' Punch, obliged to sully his skin and his throat with clouds of ash.

Eve-Marie still hasn't moved. She seems to be turning a word around in her mouth the way some people chew on a cane stalk.

"What did you say to the cops?"

Gabin almost sits down in the charcoal.

"To the cops?"

"Yeah, little Aja and the prophet. What did you tell them exactly?" Gabin forces himself to reply without thinking.

"I just told them what happened. What I saw from behind my bar. What else was I supposed to say?"

The old Creole woman closes her eyes. Out of tiredness or exasperation? It's hard to tell. When she opens them again, her two blue irises are glaring at the barman.

"You could have mentioned the past, for example. Martial Bellion's past."

Gabin takes his time pulling a Marlboro from his pocket.

"I didn't say anything about that, Eve-Marie. The police didn't ask. I'm a disciplined type; I only reply to the questions I'm asked."

"Bullshit, Gabin! You know it's only a question of time. The police are bound to check everything."

The barman leans over the barbecue and blows on the embers in order to light his cigarette.

"We'll see. I'll come up with something. I'm used to it."

"I'm not."

Eve-Marie hangs her head as if the wooden cross she wears around her neck weighs a tonne. Then, in a weak voice, she adds:

"I have even more to lose than you have."

The barman takes a long drag on his Marlboro. The smoke from the cigarette curls up into the sky around the Croix du Sud.

"You still blame Bellion?"

Eve-Marie Nativel blinks, then stares at the barbecue, like a seer who can read the future in its fatty residue.

"I'm counting on you, Gabin. The cops are going to stir up the ashes. Blow on the embers. I . . . I don't want Aloé's name mixed up in all this. I've spent years protecting her. You see what I mean, Gabin? *Pis pa ka rété assi chyen mô.*"[37]

Gabin flicks his cigarette into the hearth.

"I understand. But Aja is stubborn. And she knows this place better than anyone."

Eve-Marie slowly turns towards the exit.

"I'm counting on you, Gabin. Pass the message on to Tanguy, Naivo and the others."

The barman watches the old lady walk away. He tries to think of something to say to prove to her that he is on her side, not the cops'.

"Don't worry, Eve-Marie. After all, the most likely thing is that Bellion will be shot by the police and buried straight away, without them having to dig up anyone else instead."

9:09 P.M.

Christos enters the station's veranda, a can of Dodo beer in one hand. Aja barely looks up from her laptop.

"Good work on the Jourdains' witness statement, Chris."

Christos drains his beer, indifferent to the compliment.

"Anything new, Aja?"

"No, nothing."

She clicks an icon on her computer. The map of Saint-Gilles, showing each house that has been searched, appears on her screen.

---

[37] Réunion proverb: fleas do not stay on dead dogs. Misfortune separates friends.

"But we're making progress, Christos. We'll catch him. There are only a couple of officers working in the Carosse district, both rookies. Maybe you could give them a hand?"

Christos throws the empty can into the bin and stretches his back.

"I'm off, Aja. I'm going home."

Aja's arms fall onto her thighs. She doesn't even try to conceal her surprise.

"You're doing *what*, Chris? We have until tomorrow morning to find this guy. After that, the—'

"No, Aja . . . I'm sorry. We have to work in shifts. That's how it goes."

"Fucking hell, Christos. There's a killer on the loose."

"And not just one. Drug dealers too. Paedophiles. All sorts of lunatics. Widows to protect. I know what my job is. And so do my colleagues."

Aja sits up. Her thick eyebrows form a single dark line.

"You don't have a choice, Christos. You've been seconded to this assignment, like everyone else. Operation Papangue, remember?"

"What are you going to do to me, Aja? Give me an official reprimand? I'll be here again tomorrow morning. Early. But I need to sleep. You should do the same, by the way."

Disconcerted, Aja listens to the strange symphony of birdsong mixed with the static from police radios. She gives a tired smile, then says:

"You're completely irresponsible."

Christos just smiles cynically, then takes two steps into the garden.

"You have nothing to prove, Aja. To anyone. Even if you catch Bellion, you won't get the credit for it."

Her response is immediate: "I'm going to catch this guy before he kills anyone else. Full stop. I couldn't care less about the rest."

Christos applauds silently in the darkness.

"Respect, Aja. You're a saint. Don't forget to call your partner and your kids."

Aja looks up and the light from the bare bulb burns her eyes. She thinks in a flash about Tom, about their daughters, Jade and Lola. Lola is barely three months younger than Josapha Bellion. Tom sent Aja a text just after the announcement about Operation Papangue was made on Réunion 1. She has not had time to reply yet. In any case, he's already understood that she won't be coming home tonight. He'd explained that to the girls before telling them a story and putting them to bed. Tom is her perfect man.

She blinks and stares at Christos's shadow. She experiences small green flashes of light on her retina for a few seconds longer.

"You're making me waste time, Christos. You're right, it's probably best if you just piss off."

18
AIRE DE JOSAPHA

You can hardly see the flesh-colored plaster on Sopha's forehead. By tomorrow, there won't be any trace of the bump or the scratch. Martial is sitting next to Sopha, on the bed. He has pushed aside the embroidered cushions and the cuddly toys. He has kissed Sopha's wound better. He has undressed her. Put her to bed. Martial is acting like a father again. It feels almost unreal, as if he is doing these things to a lifeless doll as part of some training programme.

A doll that's in shock.

He switched off the television. Sopha did not say anything more, her last words still ringing in his head.

Did it hurt Maman, when you killed her?

Now Martial grips the book about Ti-Jean in his hand, feeling like an idiot. Is reading her a story the right way to communicate with his daughter? Almost since her birth, Liane has read stories to Sopha every night.

A never-ending ritual. An ordeal.

Martial had always hated their bedtime intimacy, as he was excluded from it. He felt like a spy if he listened in, and an outsider if he walked away. He gets to his feet and puts the Ti-Jean book back on the shellfish-covered shelf. He sits down on the bed again carefully.

"I'm going to tell you a story, Sopha. Better than that one. I'm going to tell you a secret."

No response. Sopha curls up under the pastel duvet.

Martial insists, his voice calm and reassuring.

"Do you know why you have that strange name, Josapha?"

Still no response, but Sopha's breathing has accelerated slightly.

"I'm sure Maman never told you about this."

A head emerges from under the duvet, the curiosity overwhelming; Martial smiles.

"You see, Sopha, Papa and Maman wanted a baby. Their desire for a baby was very strong. To make a baby, a Papa and a Maman have to hug, they have to hug each other very tightly, as tightly as they want the baby. Do you understand?"

Sopha's eyes are wide open. Inside the frames hung on the walls of the bedroom, the little boy of her age is stroking the immense shell of a turtle, a *"Ferme Corail"* cap on his blond head; in another photograph, his grandmother is setting him on a sledge in the Parc du Maïdo. Dream holidays. Happy, peaceful.

Martial's voice trembles slightly.

"That day, Maman and Papa had decided to go on holiday. Not far away, and not for long. Just to the nearest seaside town from where we lived. Deauville, in Normandy. We went back there last year, do you remember? The beach with all the different-colored parasols, where you thought the water was too cold?"

Sopha pulls a face at the memory. Her lips open but no sound emerges.

"But the day I'm talking about was long before you were born. That day, Papa had booked a hotel room with Maman. We could see the sea out of the window. It was a surprise for Maman's birthday. We went in the Picasso. Your car seat was not in the back yet. To go to Normandy, you have to take the motorway: it's not far, but the roads are often very busy. Papa and Maman left late in the evening—it was almost night—in order to avoid the crowds. Maman was eager to get to the hotel. We were both eager to hug each other, to hug each other very tightly, so that the baby would come quickly . . ."

Sopha climbs out from under the duvet. Her arm is touching her father's shoulder now.

"On the motorway, after the tolls, there is a rest area, the only one before the sea. Papa and Maman were so eager for the baby that they couldn't wait to get to the hotel. So they stopped there, in a car park by the side of the motorway . . . You know what the name of that place is, Sopha?"

Her lips move slowly, as if they are numb.

"N-no . . ." Sopha whispers at last.

"It's called the Aire de Josapha, sweetheart. I don't know why it has such a pretty name. There's nothing else there: no village, no houses, just a tarmacked car park and a few trees. But that's where Maman and Papa made you come down from heaven, darling. When we got back in the car, your Maman held my hand very tight and said in a soft voice: 'Don't you think Josapha is a nice name?'"

Sopha's little hand slides into her father's. It is clammy. Hot. Martial leans forward, his voice barely audible now.

"You are the only girl in the world with that name, Sopha. It is something to treasure. And only Papa and Maman—and you, now—know the secret of that name. Do you realize that every day, millions of cars and trucks go past that sign—'Aire de Josapha'—and none of the drivers has any idea that it's also the name of the prettiest little girl in the world?"

A tear rolls down Sopha's cheek.

She still doesn't dare speak, but she stares at her father and he understands. Sopha is lost.

So why did you kill Maman? her wet eyes ask him. *Why, if you loved her so much?*

Martial sees another picture of happiness on the wall. Grandma visiting the Maison de la Vanille with her grandson. Sopha's hand is limp in his and her bare arm trembles slightly.

It is covered with goose bumps. Martial exhales, looks away, and then speaks.

"You have to trust me, Sopha. You have to believe me."

He coughs, clearing his throat.

"I . . . I didn't kill Maman. I didn't kill anyone, sweetheart. No one at all!"

Sopha's hand feels like a sliver of soap melting between his fingers. Martial stares at the wall, the photographs, incapable of any other form of intimacy, of holding his daughter in his arms, hugging her tight to his chest, or stroking her hair.

He doesn't even look at Sopha. Three short phrases dance obsessively before his eyes.

Anse dé Cascade

Be ther tomoro

Bring the gurl

He speaks. He is aware that comforting Sopha is only the first step. After that, he must convince her. He needs her.

"You're going to have to be very brave, Sopha. Do you remember the message on the car window yesterday, in the hotel car park? That message told me to meet someone at the other end of the island, under the great volcano, in a place called Anse des Cascades."

Martial presses five tiny wet fingers against his palm; a sponge to soak up the tears.

"We have to get there, Sopha. Tomorrow. It will be difficult. Very difficult. There are police everywhere, searching for us, but we have to get there . . ."

Sopha sniffs. Between three hiccups she manages to ask her question:

"To find Maman? Alive?"

A very long pause, almost an eternity.

"I would love that, Sopha, I would really love that."

9:34 P.M.

Martial opens the bathroom window, the one that overlooks the small interior courtyard that is invisible from the street. He only pushes it an inch or two, just enough to allow the smoke to escape up into the starry night sky.

Martial holds the improvised cigarette between his fingers. He hasn't smoked *zamal* for years. He bought the grass from the Chinese guy on Rue de l'Abattoir, the same one who got him the BlackBerry.

Buying zamal . . .

It made him laugh. He had felt like a retired baker going out to buy his daily bread. He almost ended up giving the Chinese guy some advice about his business.

He takes another drag. The stars pass behind a cloud for a second, then shine out again, even brighter than before, their numbers multiplied in a kaleidoscope through the broken window.

In the courtyard, a few nightbirds are singing. Martial has forgotten what they are called. Nowadays the only birds he can name are the little grey sparrows of the Parisian suburbs.

He has forgotten almost everything.

When he went to Rue de l'Abattoir, three days ago, he drove past the old bus station. A dozen whores were standing under the street lights, in front of the vast graffitied wall. Without thinking, Martial slowed down.

He looked for Aloé, among the line of mixed-race prostitutes. She wasn't there. His eyes slid over girls who were barely legal, Creoles with platinum blonde hair, fat girls squeezed into mini-dresses, but none of them looked like her. Either that, or he didn't recognize her. He hasn't heard from her for more than five years. He knows she has changed her name. Maybe her hair color too. She might even have kids.

Another drag.

What would Aloé's life have been like if she'd never crossed his path? If she hadn't become so attached to Alex?

Three days ago, he had talked about this to Liane. They had argued, as they always do whenever he mentions this part of his life. Or at least the part that Martial has revealed to her.

A row . . .

All of it seems so pointless to him now.

That was before the point of no return.

Martial crushes the butt of his joint against the window.

He has become so used to lying. To Aloé, in another life. To Liane, this week. To the police, three days ago. And now, to his daughter.

Hiding. Lying. Escaping. Killing.

Does he have any other choice?

19
THE CAVE OF THE FIRST FRENCHMEN

9:26 P.M.

C hristos's old Renault 5 moves slowly through Les Hauts de Saint-Louis. He slows down even more at the tight bend on Rue des Combavas. A dozen Cafres, beer in hand, are standing halfway across the road, waiting for one of the white plastic tables to become free outside the mobile snack bar. Above the tables, a rainbow-colored sheet of canvas is strung between two palm trees.

Rainbow nation, my arse, thinks Christos.

Another three bends to go.

The few high-rise buildings give way to houses, tiny corrugated-iron constructions surrounded by gardens that are more like rubbish tips: rusty bikes; flowers rotting in pots; rubble and scrap metal.

Slum villages, the casuarina trees masking the worst of it.

Christos cuts across the next bend. He only really understood Réunion Island the day he got a bird's-eye view of it; not from a helicopter, no need—he simply used Google Maps. He discovered the flat satellite image of the island, covered by thousands of little white squares: houses, all identical, surrounded by the same tropical landscape, bathed in the same golden sunshine, with only one distinguishing detail: sometimes there was a little blue oval next to the white square, sometimes not. From above, the equation is simple: the closer you get to the beach and the closer you get to the lagoon— where you can swim without fear of rocks, sharks or currents—the more houses there are with a blue oval next to them. There is no exception to this rule: the density of swimming pools on the island is strictly in inverse proportion to the theoretical need for one.

At the station, Christos had shown this map to Aja, who had merely shrugged. But he found the pattern incredibly significant. "One island, one world,' Réunion's tourist slogan proclaimed. And, fundamentally, that is not untrue. A representative sample of the inequalities between the people of five continents is gathered here, over twenty-five square miles.

A human laboratory.

This island is a terrace at the edge of the world, where you can sit and observe humankind. In the shade, while wearing flip-flops, and drinking a glass of punch.

Christos parks on Rue Michou-Fontaine, a gently sloping alley lined with rusted cars. Imelda's house is the fourth in the street. There are three youngsters smoking outside it, sitting on the three worm-eaten planks that serve as steps.

Nazir is the eldest of Imelda's sons. Fifteen. Long legs, like a heron in shorts. He blows out a mouthful of smoke and looks up at Christos.

"Hey, you're here, Chief Inspector Derrick!" he says, referring to the popular German TV show. "Aren't you supposed to be out catching public enemy number one?"

Fifteen feet away, a radio placed on a plastic container bellows out noise. The hunt for Martial Bellion is clearly this evening's entertainment.

Nazir sucks at his cigarette and goes on:

"And here I was, thinking you were James Bond . . ."

Christos puts his foot on a step.

"I'm going to bed, kid. Even Derrick sleeps, eats, and shits. So does James Bond, for that matter."

Nazir's two friends giggle. Not Nazir. He's too cool for that.

"I don't get what my mother sees in you. A Zoreille, a cop. And a dick."

Christos climbs two steps, then looks down at the teenager.

"But also a romantic. Learn that lesson, kid. Sleep, eat and shit, but do it romantically. That's the secret. Now give me a drag of that."

Nazir pinches the joint between two fingers and hides it behind his back.

"Don't touch it, man. It's illegal, ain't that so?"

"All the more reason. Don't forget you're talking to a sworn officer of the law."

The boy's eyes sparkle with defiance.

"Oh yeah?"

"Yeah! In fact, you can forget the joint. Just give me the bag of *zamal* you've got stuffed in your pocket. I'm confiscating it!"

Unfazed, Nazir takes a ball of compacted leaves from the pocket of his shorts. He waves it in front of the policeman.

"You talking about this, man? I'll let you have it for 150 euros. It's worth twice that much, but since you're almost family . . ."

Christos holds out his hand.

"Deal. I'll give the cash to your mother."

"Bullshit."

The plastic packet is returned to the boy's pocket. Nazir has kept just a single leaf between his thumb and his index finger.

"Here you go, Derrick. On the house! Freshly picked from our garden this morning."

When Christos enters the house, cigarette in hand, Imelda has her back to him and is leaning over the sink. The three children, Dorian, Joly and Amic, are sitting on the edge of the table.

"Christos, for God's sake!" shouts Imelda, without even turning round. "Your cigarette!"

The policeman sighs.

"Not in front of the children! Or Nazir for that matter—I

heard everything you said, you know. He's only fifteen. You shouldn't be encouraging him. You're a role model."

Christos coughs.

"A role model? Is that it? How about his adoptive father while you're at it? Don't use that psychological blackmail with me, Imelda. Please."

The dishes bang against the chipped ceramic and the cutlery falls into the sink with a clatter.

"Well, anyway, would you stub out your ciggy. And tomorrow, please confiscate his pack of *zamal* and pull all the plants up in the garden. If you don't want to act like his dad, at least act like a police officer."

Christos crushes his cigarette butt on the floor. He grabs the bottle of Charrette rum, then collapses onto the wooden stool.

"Fucking hell, what an evening."

Imelda turns around and, in one smooth movement, picks up all the glasses and plates from the table.

"I listened to the news. Things are heating up in Saint-Gilles. I didn't expect you back so early."

The white rum burns the second lieutenant's palate.

"One less cop playing hide-and-seek isn't going to change things much."

Imelda shrugs. She strikes a match and lights the gas under the aluminium stewpot.

"I bet you haven't eaten, have you?"

Christos shakes his head. He adores this Cafre goddess. He adores her curry. He adores resting his arse in this crappy little house.

He has barely finished his glass before little Joly jumps onto his knees. Her long, frizzy hair smells of coconut shampoo.

"Can you tell me a story about a bad guy?"

Christos moves the bottle out of the child's reach.

"A real bad guy?"

"Yeah."

"A story about a bad guy who kills Creoles with a big knife. Who kills his wife so he can have their daughter all to himself?"

Joly bursts out laughing.

"Yessss!"

Imelda tidies away the dishes, placing them inside the Formica sideboard. Through the distorting glass of the rum bottle, Christos can see nothing but her queenly arse. God, he wants her, right here, right now.

Joly tugs at his sleeve.

"Hey, are you looking at Maman's bum or are you telling me a story?"

Little minx!

Christos jokingly tries to push the girl off his lap. She collapses with laughter. Dorian and Amic get back in the ring and start wrestling each other again.

"Careful, it's hot," Imelda warns Christos, placing the bowl of curry in front him. "O.K., bedtime, you lot!"

The kids' protests are cut short by a threateningly raised dishtowel.

Imelda turns towards Christos.

"Later, when we're alone, I have to talk to you. Seriously."

"Just tell me now."

Imelda continues with the same tone of voice, perhaps with an added hint of excitement.

"I need to talk to you about your case, you idiot, the killer at large! There's something in the story they keep telling on the TV that bothers me. Something odd that no one seems to have thought about . . ."

9:53 P.M.

Twenty minutes' rest. That is what Aja has given herself.

Watch in hand.

She has decided to get out of Saint-Gilles. As she often does, when she needs to take stock, she has driven her 206 to Saint-Paul and gone for a walk as night falls, around the deserted sailors' cemetery, around the empty marketplace, to the Grotte des Premiers Français, the cave where the first French settlers supposedly lived, which is buried under the casuarina trees.

Aja has just called home. Everything is fine. Tom is looking after Jade and Lola. Aja hates phoning like that, summing up a whole day in three sentences, hanging up almost straight away in case someone else is trying to get through, then rearranging in her mind the words spoken by her sympathetic husband and her two excited little girls.

Take care of yourself, darling! We saw you on the TV, Maman . . . don't worry, darling, I'll take care of it. When are you coming home, Maman? The girls wanted to wait for your phone call before they went to sleep. Papa read us *Ti-Jean*, Maman, and then he found the chameleon, it was hiding under the stones behind the house . . . Blow a kiss to Maman, girls, she has to go now.

Tom is perfect.

Tom has been a schoolteacher for the last six years in Les Hauts de Saint-Gilles. He looks after five- and six-year-olds at a primary school. He is calm. Reasonable. Sweet. Often, she wonders why such a perfect man puts up with a girl as annoying as she is.

You're not annoying, he always replies. You have integrity.

Integrity . . .

Aja sometimes has the feeling that she is married to a punching ball, very stable at its base, and the harder she hits it, the faster it bounces back. Intact. A beautiful, black velvet punching ball. A wonderful father. A tender lover.

Aja does not like sleeping without Tom.

Except when a killer is loose on the island, with a girl of Lola's age.

She checks the time on her watch. Seven minutes left. She has no reason to stress out: Morez is under orders to call her immediately if new evidence is found. But for the moment, there is radio silence.

Aja walks towards the Grotte des Premiers Français. In the distance, she can see the port at Pointe des Galets. According to legend, this is where the island's first inhabitants landed. The Bourbon Island, as it was known at the time, was uninhabited—no natives for the colonies to massacre. The island was simply a jewel in the middle of the ocean, belonging to no one. Or to everyone.

Aja walks past the sailors' cemetery. Her car is parked at the other end. She learned quite recently that her great-great-grandfather was buried here, in a little tomb surrounded by the graves of pirates. Abhi Purvi, her ancestor, arrived on the island in 1861, during the period of indentured servitude: the local, politically correct term used to describe slavery after it had been outlawed by the French Republic. After the Africans and the Tamils, thousands of Zarabes were brought over to work in the sugar cane fields. This was just before beet sugar production took over in France, causing almost immediate ruin for the island's economy. In an ironic twist, in this fledgling globalized economy, thousands of slaves suddenly found themselves unemployed. Aja's great-great-grandfather attempted, like other Zarabes, to make his fortune in the fabric trade. Ethnic solidarity. He got into the niche market of creating straw plaits to make hats. This enabled him to survive. Which was better than most Creoles managed; many were dying of hunger.

Jalad, Abhi Purvi's son, picked up the paternal standard. Straw hats would be sold as long as the tropical sun beat down on people's heads. He married in 1906 at the Noor-al-Islam mosque in Saint-Denis, the oldest in any French territory. He bought a plot of land in Saint-Gilles, without knowing that just opposite this rocky patch of earth by the side of a filthy little gully, the Zoreilles would build the Saint-Denis train station. His first thought was to move, because of the noise, the crowds and the smoke. Then he got used to it. In the end, he rented his house to inhabitants of Saint-Denis who wanted to spend their weekends at the lagoon. Five years later, in 1912, he abandoned the straw hat business and built a seven-room guest house.

Faris, Aja's grandfather, was born in 1915 in a large, colonial-style house in Les Hauts de Saint-Gilles. The Purvi family's business was at its peak. Not only the railway, but also the ocean liners that came into the Pointe des Galets port, continued to bring a select flow of tourists, business executives and middle-class families in search of an exotic experience. In 1937, Faris laid the first stone of a Réunion Island hotel worthy of the name, and the hotel opened two years later. His first guests stayed longer than expected: they were rich Europeans fleeing the Nazis, most of them Jews—the only religion that had been missing on the island.

Aja's father, Rahim, came into being the same year as the Hotel du Lagon, in 1939. An only child, he found a sister of his own age, Sarah Abramoff, in the daughter of a Jewish businessman who had taken refuge in the hotel during the war and had decided not to leave the tropics for the nascent state of Israel. Between the corridors of the hotel and the lagoon, they grew up together, inseparable. For Faris, Aja's grandfather, the marriage between Rahim and Sarah was already arranged. His business sense, allied to the bank account of the father-in-law, would allow him to create a successful union between Jews and Muslims the like of which only Réunion Island could produce. The promise of a tourist empire in the Mascarene Islands. When they turned eighteen, Rahim and Sarah were sent to the United States to study international business. Same college, same class. Rahim was shy and obedient, but less fascinated by the family business than by his supposed artistic gifts, which were expressed in collages of colored ceramic. Sarah, for her part, quickly gave up the *zouk* of her childhood for the pop music of the Beach Boys. She never returned. She got her hooks into a blond Californian and moved to San Diego. So that was the end of the dream. Her father, Natane Abramoff, left Réunion in 1967 and went to live in Tel Aviv. Rahim came back alone from the United States, without a dollar or a diploma to his name. And to top it all, no sooner had this unworthy son returned than he fell in love with the most beautiful girl at the hotel: Laila, a very young, illiterate Creole who cleaned the toilets there. His father was disillusioned and angry, but his threats made no difference. Rahim, who had never dreamed that a girl as pretty as this would even give him a second look, stood up to his father for the first time. To get away from the family's ire and the sarcastic comments of the Zarabes, he set sail with Laila for Madagascar. To make his fortune in the world of art and ceramics, he hoped. Again, though, he failed. Instead he scraped a living by transporting rocks for the construction of the dam in Lake Alaotra. He did not return to Réunion until six years later, upon his father's death. Laila was pregnant with Aja then. Once more he was penniless. Jobless.

Rahim was welcomed back like a leper. Since his departure, the Hotel du Lagon, which was on the verge of bankruptcy, had been bought by a large, multinational company, one of whose shareholders was—ironically—Natane Abramoff. The manager of the hotel, now renamed the Athena, was a highly educated Belgian who couldn't care less about the family's heritage. He hired Aja's mother because she was pretty, and incidentally because she knew the job and the place. He also gave Rahim piecemeal work, as and when Laila begged him, in his specialty: mosaics. Bathrooms, swimming pool, toilets. Aja remembers waiting patiently for her parents in the hotel corridors and seeing the other employees brazenly humiliating the son of their former boss. Well, it was only fair. Faris Purvi had not been the kind of man to be sentimental with his staff, and it was rare to see a Zarabe fail in business. She understood later that everyone considered Rahim to be an inbred degenerate who had only paired up with the most beautiful girl on the island in order to resuscitate his dynasty. Until she was ten, Aja's parents had lived in Plateau Caillou, an area containing a few dilapidated buildings which was cut off from Saint-Paul and Saint-Gilles by a cliff face two hundred and fifty feet high; then they had moved to a house in Fleurimont, a little further away.

Rahim died at the age of fifty-two. Aja was seventeen at the time. He left behind him a poor family and a house in which every surface was entirely covered in tiles. It became a local curiosity. Her mother still lives there.

Aja goes to visit less than once a month. Tonight, her mother will have spent all evening watching the television news, proud that her daughter's force is at the front line, and surprised, no doubt, by the disturbing coincidence: that the Hotel Athena should have been the scene of the crime.

Aja walks through the car park. Here, in a few hours' time, the most beautiful market on the island will be set up, as it is every morning. Even now, she can detect in the air, or at least in her imagination, a whiff of spices: cardamom, nutmeg, turmeric . . .

The phone rings just as she is getting into her car.

Morez.

"Aja?"

"Yes, Morez?"

"I have some news!"

"You've caught Bellion?"

"No . . . No. Don't get excited. But we do have some more information about his past. And guess what? Bellion has another death on his conscience. And my God, when it comes to being weighed down by guilt, I don't think you could imagine anything heavier."

10:13 P.M.

Christos's body moves smoothly up and down under the sheets. Imelda's body is hot, the folds of her skin are like a feather mattress, like a bath full of cream; he is swimming in a warm sea, rocked by waves; he is bathing in an ocean of amniotic fluid. Inside her, he becomes at once a lover and a foetus. He could stay like this for hours. Paradise.

"Can I put on the TV?"

Christos does not have time to reply: Imelda, without moving her body, which is trapped beneath him, stretches out her arm and grabs the remote control.

"You should be interested in this too, you know," the Cafrine says. "Every channel on the island is showing images of the Saint-Gilles police tonight, instead of *CSI: Miami*."

Well, quite . . .

"Do you realize you're fucking Horatio Caine?" She turns up the volume.

"Shouldn't you be out there?"

"No. We're working in shifts. I'll go back tomorrow morning, early. Full of energy. Aja likes to make sure her men get plenty of rest."

Horatio Caine gives a long, powerful pelvic thrust.

"You don't seem to be getting much rest at the moment." Christos supports himself on his elbows and enjoys her voluptuous body. The television offers unfair competition, but he refuses to give up.

"There's a little girl in danger, Christos."

"Yes, and there are also drug dealers, paedophiles, kids

dying of hunger in Les Hauts, slave drivers, and, if I have any time left over, drunk drivers and pimps hanging around outside schools. It never ends. So when am I ever supposed to get any sleep?"

Imelda moans a bit. She lets go of the remote control, and her eyes roll up towards the ceiling. Christos increases his pace. He knows by heart the sounds his partner makes; still a few seconds before the explosion. He loves it when Imelda's body begins to erupt.

"He's . . . dangerous," Imelda gasps between two sighs. "Dangerous for his little girl. He's already killed another kid. There's . . ."

Christos's head suddenly rears up from under the sheets.

"What? What other kid?"

Imelda takes a deep breath. The pressure falls again.

"The kid in Boucan Canot. Quite a few years ago now. Don't you remember?"

No, Christos does not remember. Only people born and bred on the island are able to keep a mental archive of every news story printed in the papers.

"Please go on, my love."

"This is just what I remember—it was at least eight years ago. An evening, I think. The father was watching his kid on the beach at Boucan Canot, or he was supposed to be watching him. They found the six-year-old boy the next morning, drowned in the ocean. No one ever found out what had really happened."

Christos feels his erection melt like an ice lolly left out in the sun.

"Jesus Christ. Are you sure that the father was Martial Bellion?"

"Absolutely. Same name, same face."

The policeman looks incredulous. Imelda continues: "Didn't anyone on the force make that connection?"

"We all thought Bellion was a tourist."

His excuse sounds almost unreal. They fall silent for a moment, the only sound coming from the television, which has moved on to some adverts. Christos's hand grips a breast, and his lips tease the pink nipple.

Imelda protests weakly:

"For God's sake, Christos, aren't you going to call your colleagues?"

Christos feels the blood surge once again into his cock. This woman is a witch: all he has to do is touch her skin and he gets as hard as a rock. She must be hiding headless black chickens under her bed, melting candles in coconut shells, burning cubes of camphor before he arrives; the whole gamut of the island's white magic.

"I'll tell them tomorrow. First thing. I swear."

He slips inside her.

"You're mad," she whispers. "You're a disgrace to the force."

"On the contrary, I have principles. A worker has the right to a break every now and then. What would it change, anyway, if I told them tonight rather than tomorrow morning? The guy has vanished."

He puts his head against her shoulder, and ventures deep into the labyrinth of secrets that are held inside Imelda's body.

10:32 P.M.

Imelda strokes Christos's hair. He fell asleep just after he climaxed, as he always does. Continuing to massage his scalp with her fingertips, she reaches out with her left hand and grabs a book from the bedside table. Dirty, yellowed pages. *Nemesis* by Agatha Christie. She turns the pages without really concentrating. She is thinking about the case on the island.

What they are saying about it on the television, what Christos has told her about it, the disappearance of that woman, Rodin's death, that man running away, what the hotel staff are saying. It all fits.

The worn pages of the book are hard to separate. There is something fishy about those witness statements, though. Even back when that kid drowned in the ocean, certain details of the case bothered her. She must try to remember. Perhaps find the newspapers from the time. Old Marie-Colette, on Rue Jean-XXIII, has been keeping copies of every paper on the island for more than thirty years.

What was he called again, that child who drowned?

She turns the pages of *Nemesis*. Nazir found the book for her at a car boot sale in Saint-Joseph. Christos likes to call her his Cafrine Miss Marple. He doesn't know how well the name fits: she reads more than a hundred novels a year. Everyone in the neighborhood brings her books, old copies mostly, as often as not with the final chapter missing. This case reminds her of a novel she read about ten years ago, *Kahului Bay*: the same story as Bellion's, even if it took place in Hawaii. All the evidence seemed to be against this guy.

Except that there was another character, a witness who only turned up later in the story, altering the whole chain of events. As always, Imelda had guessed the solution long before the end, despite the author's attempts to lead his readers down blind alleys.

Christos is snoring like a kitten.

Imelda has to get her brain working. Let's start with the simplest thing first. Put her elephantine memory to use.

What was his name, that six-year-old kid?

20
LITTLE BROTHER

Monday, April 1, 2013, 7:21 A.M.

In the mirror, I can see the blade shining in Papa's hand.
It's sharp. And pointy.
He puts it to the back of my neck. I can feel it, cold and cutting.

I bite my lips until they bleed.

I am trembling, but I'm too scared to say a word. Papa stands behind me. He must be able to tell I'm afraid, must feel me shivering, the goose bumps covering my skin.

Papa brings the blade close again. The point touches my neck this time. It's ice-cold. The blade moves up towards my left ear.

I force myself not to move an inch. I must wait, be perfectly still. I mustn't scream. I mustn't panic.

Papa could hurt me. By accident.

He's not very good at this.

More chunks of hair fall into the sink.

Tears come in the corners of my eyes. I promised Papa I wouldn't cry, but it's hard.

Papa's explained it all to me, though: to find Maman, we have to get up very early and leave as quickly as possible. We have a sort of meeting, at the other side of the island. He also told me that I have to be the bravest girl in the whole wide world.

I am, I will be, I promise, so we can find Maman. But still, I'm sad about my hair. I dreamed of it growing so long it would go right down past my waist, so it would be as beautiful as Maman's. I wouldn't have minded if it had taken years for that, if I'd had to spend hours each morning combing out the knots.

Papa cut it all off with five snips of his scissors. The pig!

What a weird idea, making me look like a boy! He said he got the idea when he was looking at the photographs. A little boy, almost the same age as me, sleeps here sometimes, when he comes to stay with his grandma. It must be nice to have a grandma on Réunion. Better than staying in that hotel. She looks kind, too—and a bit funny, with her blue hair. In the photos, she always wears necklaces made of shellfish or crocodile teeth.

"You could dress up as a boy," Papa told me. "It would be like a disguise."

He made himself laugh. When Papa tries to be funny, he usually isn't.

The scissors move behind my ears, cutting the hair even shorter.

Actually, I know why Papa wants to disguise me as a boy. It's not so no one will recognize me. Well, not just that.

I decide to take Papa by surprise. I turn around:

"Papa, is it true that I had a little brother? Before. And I've never met him because he's dead? Do I look like him?"

Papa almost drops the scissors. He catches them at the last moment, but the blade has nicked the skin at the top of my neck. I didn't really feel anything though, because I was concentrating too hard on Papa's answer.

Except Papa didn't say anything.

7:24 A.M.

Martial waits several minutes before speaking again. As if he hopes that, by leaving this silence, Sopha will forget her question.

"You make a very pretty boy, sweetheart."

She sticks her tongue out at his reflection in the mirror.

A few last snips of the scissors. He tries to make the fringe as straight as he can, attempting to concentrate on his amateur hairdressing when his mind is filled with one thing only.

Sending his daughter outside, alone, is a suicidal idea. And yet, there is no other solution.

"So you understand, darling? I've made the list. All you have to do is show it to the man."

"Can't I read it to him? I know how to read, Papa!"

He leans towards the back of his daughter's neck like an obsequious stylist.

"You should speak as little as possible, sweetheart. We don't want anyone to know that you're a girl. So, just show him the list and make sure he gives you everything on it. A 1/25,000 map."

"That's complicated."

"A compass."

"I know the rest. Some fruit and some sandwiches."

"And if anyone asks, you say that your name is . . ."

"Paul!"

"Good."

He forces himself to laugh again, but he is the only one laughing. "And you remember how to get there? Go towards the sea, straight down the main pedestrian avenue. All the shops are there. Don't talk to the people in the shops. Or to anyone else. Understood?"

"I know. I'm not a baby any more."

Martial removes the towel, which is covered in hair, from his daughter's shoulders. Sopha examines herself in the mirror, stunned at the way she looks with the horrible bowl cut. Ruined.

"When Maman makes a shopping list, she always adds two lines at the bottom. A surprise for her beloved daughter and a surprise for her beloved husband."

It's true. Liane had a kind of everyday grace that made a game of each chore. He hesitates, then replies:

"The best surprise, darling, would be for you to come back very, very quickly."

He walks over to the door, opens it and scans the empty street.

"Wait, Sopha, one last thing."

He leans over his daughter and puts a pair of sunglasses on her. He found them on the entrance hall table.

"Listen, Sopha, when you come back, you might not recognize me. I'm going to disguise myself too: cut my hair, shave my beard. You understand?"

"Yes . . ."

It is hard to read the girl's expression.

Is she frightened? Surprised? Excited by this new game?

Martial runs his fingers through his daughter's short hair. Scores of tiny cuttings stick to his fingers.

"All right, Sopha, now off you go."

7:51 A.M.

T ea, dearest?"
Aja's nostrils stir first, sniffing the hot steam. Then her eyes open. A breakfast tray. Three croissants in a basket. Christos has a fourth one in his mouth, and his beard is covered in crumbs.

"Did you sleep, Aja? You look like an insomniac *gramoune*."[38]

"Thank you, Chris. I love getting a compliment whenever I wake up. Yes, I must have got about an hour or so of sleep, in ten-minute instalments."

"I listened to Radio Cop on the way over here. Nothing new, then?"

"Nothing. It's as if Bellion has vanished into thin air. I've had Laroche on the phone—he's directing Operation Papangue. Six choppers have been searching all over the island since sunrise. No sign of a grey Clio, no sign of Bellion or his daughter. Laroche has only been on the island for six months. He's supposed to call me back when he's gone through things with the prefect. He . . . he seems competent."

"Say it like you mean it, Aja."

"What?"

"When you call him 'competent,' say it like you mean it."

Aja sighs. She stretches and clasps her hands around the hot mug. Christos sits on the windowsill.

"I do have some news, though, Aja. And it's bad."

---

[38] Old person

Aja's eyes shine; she's still halfway between dreaming and waking.

"Seriously? You work even when you're in bed?"

"That's truer than you can imagine. I got the information from a friend. A woman with a brain like a computer and a memory like a three terabyte hard drive, ideal for processing local news stories. Anyway, basically, my lady friend told me that Martial Bellion was mixed up in a shady case a few years ago: a kid who drowned off Boucan Canot."

Aja's gaze has lost its sparkle.

"What's wrong? You don't believe me?" Christos asks, disappointed.

"Oh, I believe you . . . It's just that we've had seven phone calls since last night, telling us the same thing. The people here have an amazing memory for anything unpleasant that happens on the island . . . a better memory than us, anyway. Not one single police officer made the connection between this tourist on the run and the case of the drowned kid. As you can imagine, we've done some digging overnight and I've had emails from France. I need to go back and read them in more detail, but, to cut a long story short, Martial Bellion lost his first child, by his first wife, the one before Liane. Alex was the boy's name. Six years old. He drowned in the ocean. Bellion was watching him, but clearly not well enough. Right now, I can't see a link between that and the double murder in Saint-Gilles. What I do understand, however, is that our tourist—supposedly lost in a foreign environment—actually knows this island like the back of his hand."

"Look on the bright side, Aja," Christos says sarcastically. "He may have completely fucked us over, but there are extenuating circumstances."

"Bellion lived on the island for nine years," the captain goes on, as if Christos had not said a word. "Between 1994 and 2003. He worked at the sailing club in Bourbon. According to

what the ComGend told me, Bellion still has a few acquain-
tances living on the island. A diving friend in Langevin, a sugar
cane plantation owner on the river Mât, an ex-girlfriend in
Ravine à Malheur. They all say they lost touch with him after
he returned to France, and that they haven't seen him since he
came back to the island. They're all being tailed and bugged,
of course. But there's not a single trace of Bellion."

Christos gulps down a second croissant.

"He's a clever one. Sorry about the dud lead . . ."

"Forget it. Sorry I gave you shit last night."

"I was asking for it. And you were exhausted. Now you're
even more exhausted. You should go back to sleep for an hour
or two."

Aja blows on her tea.

"No way. It's all about to kick off, I can sense it. Bellion
must have found a hiding place for the night, but he's going to
come out into the open, he has to. Like a rat sneaking out to
find food. He didn't run away for no reason, Christos; he has
something in mind. A specific aim."

"If I offered you some help that was, let's say, a bit border-
line, what would you say, Aja?"

"I'm not really in a position to turn anything down right
now."

"Well, it's my lady friend. She's a Cafrine, and her enormous brain was working on the case all night. She thinks
there's something fishy about this whole affair too. Some sort
of underlying logic we can't yet see."

"All good leaders must know how to delegate, Christos. Is
she a witch doctor, your girlfriend? Coffee grinds or goat
entrails?"

"She's more like Harlan Coben. Guesses the answer about
three chapters before the end."

Aja swallows some tea, burning her throat. She grimaces,
then makes a decision.

"Sure, why not? Tell her to come and see me. What harm can it do?"

Christos smiles.

"Cool, boss. You won't be disappointed. Imelda is a national monument."

He takes a bag of grass from his pocket, and rolls a cigarette.

"Christos, please tell me you're not about to smoke *zamal* in here? It's a police station, for God's sake! And today of all days, when we have the entire ComGend about to descend on us . . ."

"Chill out, Aja. We're on a veranda. By the sea. The wind will blow the smell away. Anyway, it's all in a good cause. I confiscated this packet from a kid before I left home."

Aja sighs, resigned.

"You really do wear me out, Christos. I don't want to have another row with you this morning."

Christos takes a drag.

"So what else is new, darling?"

"There's news coming in every minute. Operation Papangue, remember? There are dozens of men on the case, here and in France."

"Just give me the highlights then. The juicy details."

"Oh, I think this will be juicy enough for you. One of the latest things I've heard is that the computer guys at the ComGend have been digging around for information about the Jourdains. They have confirmed that the Jourdains didn't know the Bellions before meeting them here a few days ago, *but* . . ."

The second lieutenant sucks hard at his joint. He has a feeling he's going to enjoy this.

"But?"

"But then they decided to check the Jourdains' internet accounts. His, in particular. And guess what that sly old fox had hidden away on Picasa?"

"Dirty photos, right?"

"Bingo, Chris. Jacques Jourdain collects photographs of pretty young tourists, sunbathing topless on the beach. He must have taken some of them close up with his mobile phone, and others using a Konica Minolta with a telephoto lens, like a paparazzo."

"Whoa, I'm impressed! Never would have guessed that lawyer had it in him. So, can we lock him up?"

"Unlikely. Except that among his gallery of girls, there are a good ten or so snaps of Liane Bellion. She obviously didn't like to get tan lines."

Christos grins joyfully, the joint clamped between two teeth.

"I'm on it! Can I see the pictures?"

Aja bursts out laughing.

"The ComGend has several agents just as obsessed as you are and they have already volunteered for this particular task. You shouldn't have gone home last night!"

Christos drops his cigarette.

"I hate those ComGend bastards just as much as you do! So, you think Jacques Jourdain had a crush on Liane Bellion?"

"Who knows?"

The captain unhurriedly finishes her cup of tea, then looks up at Christos again.

"I've got something else for you. Seeing as you're an early riser, do you want to make yourself useful?"

"That's why I got up, dearest! I even forsook my morning screw so I wouldn't be late."

Aja sighs and puts down her mug.

"There's another lead that needs checking out. I got a call last night after one of those newsflashes on TV. A girl, Charline Tai-Leung, who works behind a flight desk at Saint-Denis airport. According to what she told us, Martial Bellion came to see her five days ago, forty-eight hours before the double murder, wanting to change his plane ticket. If this is true, then the whole thing starts to look premeditated. The girl is off work today. She lives in Roquefeuil, in Les Hauts de Saint-Gilles. She's at home, waiting for an officer to take her statement."

Aja holds out a card with an address scrawled on it.

"You know me so well, my lovely. I have a real thing for air stewardesses!"

Faced with his superior's weary expression, he adds:

"Come on, Aja, it'll be all right. The noose is tightening. We're going to catch him, soon. We're bound to."

22
BRITISH BULLDOG

8:04 A.M.

I walk down the main pedestrian avenue that leads towards the sea. On both sides there are cube-shaped houses painted in pastel colors, like brand new dolls' houses with roofs and walls that can be taken off. I spot the street name on a sign beneath the green cross of the pharmacy: "Mail de Rodrigues."

Ever since Papa closed the door behind me, I have obeyed all his instructions. I've been a very good girl. I haven't run. I've walked on the pavement. I've gone down the steps. I've crossed the road. Now I'm on the big street with no cars, but I still haven't run.

And I remember what I need to do next. Go into each shop and show the shopkeeper the list.

Wait. Pay.

Easy, even if I can't see very well, wearing these enormous sunglasses, especially when I'm in the shade.

Papa was very strict, though. He said I mustn't take them off!

Down there, at the end of the street, near the beach, there is a policeman wearing a uniform. He's on his own. Standing completely still, only his eyes moving, like a lazy cat watching sparrows.

He's looking at me now. I must have done something that surprised him. At least I didn't cry out or anything. I've been holding it all in as much as I can. Even though, in my head, everything has turned upside down.

That's me, in the newspaper!

Big pictures, on the front page, with Papa and Maman. There are piles of newspapers outside almost every shop. But I have to keep walking normally, just like Papa told me. I have to be clever. In the picture in the newspaper, I'm wearing my yellow dress and I have long hair, and you can see my eyes too. Nobody will recognize me like this. Certainly not that big pussycat, anyway.

I go straight into the grocer's. "What can I do for you, my dear?"

I play dumb and hand the list over to the lady behind the till. Bread, ham, biscuits and bananas. The lady takes ages to put it all in the bags. When she's finished, and taken forever to give me back my change, I just say in a very quiet voice, almost a whisper:

"Thank you, madame."

Papa told me not to change my voice, just to speak as quietly as possible, as if I was very shy.

I come out of the shop. The big police cat is still there. He's not moving, but he looks like he's come closer, like he's playing a game of statues.

I keep walking as if I haven't noticed anything.

Four shops. Two clothes shops, one flower shop, one crêperie.

I walk on. Forcing myself to go slowly.

A bookshop.

I go in.

"What are you looking for, little boy?"

I look up. Straight away, I get scared. The man is Chinese.

I'm afraid of Chinese people. They're the scariest people in the world, after ogres and the pirates of the Caribbean. Even in Paris, in restaurants, I'm afraid of them. Maman likes eating Chinese food when we go shopping, but I don't. In school, Timéo, told me that they eat weird things, like stray dogs and spiders and fish without eyes. Here, they eat sticky cucumber. I slowly unfold Papa's sheet of paper, and tell myself I'm being an idiot. I know Timéo talks rubbish. Anyway, this Chinese man sells books.

And newspapers.

There's my picture again, right in front of my nose, in a pile of papers as high as my chin. Inside my head, I try to read the big black letters.

KILLER ON THE LOOSE.

"Do you want a paper, son? Can you read already?"

I lower my head, frowning and looking down at my sandals. I only have one thing to buy, but I have to read it out to ask for it, and the shop is too dark, even darker than a troll's cave. What else can I do? I take off my sunglasses and read out the words.

"A 1/25,000 map. The 4406 RT."

The Chinese man hesitates for a second, then hands me a blue map folded in a rectangle.

"Are you going on a picnic with your parents in the mountains, little man?"

I don't reply. I hand him the money and look down at the floor again. My sandals are ugly. It's probably a good thing he's Chinese, after all. He must think I'm scared of him. He must be used to it.

I've got everything now so I leave.

The policeman has moved again. He's cheating, he's walked up the street and he's ahead of me now. I'll have to walk past him to get back to the blue-haired lady's house, where Papa is waiting for me.

It doesn't matter. Doesn't matter. Doesn't matter. He couldn't possibly recognize me!

Another twenty meters.

All right, that's enough of statues. We're going to change the game. I'm the best at British Bulldog. The trick, to get from one end to the other without being caught, is to make people forget you're there. Not to run like mad like those boys who think they're so great. They always get caught before me.

I walk past the policeman, going the same speed, not even turning my head. Maybe he's watching me, maybe his eyes are on me, maybe he's staring at my back. But I don't care, I don't care, he can't possibly have recognized me, that stupid bull-dog.

Another thirty meters.

All I have to do is cross the road. Now I can turn around.

The policeman is far away, he's walking towards the beach, at the other end of the street.

I'm the best!

Once I'm over the road, there's just twenty steps to climb and after that I can run, really fast. I can't wait. I just have to let the cars go past first.

There's only one car. Big and black with very high wheels for driving on mountain tracks. It slows down. It stops to let me cross.

I step onto the crossing. Without thinking, I turn my head towards the car.

The man behind the steering wheel is so strange! His skin is so dark, it's almost orange, and he's wearing an Indian shirt. On his head there's a green cap with a big red tiger embroidered on it. A Malbar, that's what Papa calls people like that. There was one in the hotel who cut people's hair. This one's wearing sunglasses too.

The orange man turns towards me as I cross the street. I climb the steps, avoiding the palm tree in the middle. I have a very bad feeling, I'm shivering all over, crazy ants are crawling over my legs. I can't see the man's eyes, but I'm almost sure—he's seen through my disguise.

He knows I'm a girl! He wasn't fooled like that stupid policeman or the Chinese ogre in the bookshop.

Now that I think about it, I'm more afraid of Malbars than I am of Chinese people.

My legs are trembling as if I've had to cross a whole haunted forest instead of this street with three palm trees.

I'm being an idiot. I'm almost back. Papa is waiting for me, there, after the turning. I can almost see our house. I'm running now, along the pavement, not turning around. The big black car has probably moved off by now anyway.

Papa!

The house door opens, and I recognize Papa even though he looks strange with his hair cut so short. His lips look weirdly small without his beard and moustache. I rush into the hallway. Papa closes the door behind me. He hugs me.

I love it when my Papa hugs me. He doesn't do it much. Actually I like it, I think, being on my own with Papa. We do more strange things than we do when Maman is there. Play new games.

Games where I'm the best! I give the bags to Papa. I won the treasure hunt and I didn't get caught! And, best of all, this afternoon, we're going to see Maman.

Papa goes through everything in the first bag. He looks happy, he's very proud of me. He roughs up my hair.

Thinking about my hair makes me want to cry. I wonder if it was really worth cutting it. I could have just worn a cap, a big green one with a tiger on it, like the Malbar wore.

Papa has checked all the bags, including the last one, the one with the map in it.

"You're a champion, darling!"

"Are we going to find Maman now?"

He takes me in his arms.

"Listen carefully, Sopha. I'm going to lock the house. I'm going to put the TV on for you. Leave the volume turned down low, and whatever you do, don't open the door to anyone. Don't move from the couch. Now that you're back, I'm going to take a shower. I'll be done in five minutes, and after that, we're out of here."

8:21 A.M.

I've been watching *Titeuf* for ten minutes, no more than that, when I hear a car outside, just in front of the house. I don't get up.

I turn the sound down even lower on the television. That shuts Titeuf up!

There are noises coming from the garage. Papa left it open.

As if a car has gone in there.

I wish I could go to the window to check. I really think that the car hasn't parked in the street. It's here, very close, I can hear the engine.

There is a door between the garage and the house. And it could be open.

Someone could come in.

Without knowing why, I think about that Malbar with the orange face in his big-wheeled black car. I should call Papa, but he told me not to make any noise. And I'd have to shout loud for him to hear me over the noise of the shower. I can't go into the bathroom, because I'm not allowed to leave the couch.

Unless . . .

I get up. I walk quietly to the bathroom door. The thick carpet muffles my footsteps.

Nothing. I can't hear any noise at all now.

Not Titeuf, not Nadia, on the television both of them are silent. No noise in the garage either.

I can't even hear the sound of the shower.

23
CAP CHAMPAGNE

8:32 A.M.

For God's sake, Colonel, don't you understand? Lifting the roadblocks would be the stupidest thing we could do."

Aja grips the phone in one hand. Laroche called her just after his interview with the prefect. Ten minutes at the most; the same prefect who must have been speaking to a minister. Two minutes at most. Clearly, someone is not happy . . . and that has caused a bureaucratic snowball that has gathered speed, descending the administrative echelons until finally it has landed on her with an enormous splat.

"Since last night, your damn roadblocks have taken up the time of thirty men, Captain Purvi," Laroche tells her. "And what have we got? Nothing but the biggest mess Réunion has seen since the coastal road collapsed in February 2006."

"Colonel, you have to trust me on this! Bellion will come out of his hole. Last night, he'll have hidden somewhere, so that his daughter could get some sleep—he didn't have any choice—but he's bound to try something now. We just have to be patient."

Aja looks at the map of Saint-Gilles projected onto the wall of the station. A good third of the houses in the commune have been searched.

"Unless Bellion is already on the other side of the island."

Laroche says this calmly. Coldly. Indifferently.

Aja explodes.

"That's impossible! Bellion is caught in our noose. All we need to do now is pull it tight. I know this area, Colonel . . ."

"I don't doubt that, Captain Purvi. Better than I do, anyway, if that's what you're implying. But that doesn't stop me knowing my job and having competent colleagues. It's Easter Monday, the traditional day for a picnic in Les Hauts. Every village on the island will be empty. Your roadblocks are going to completely foul up the island's traditions."

"Exactly, Colonel, and Bellion knows it. He's going to try to take advantage of that fact to slip through the net."

Laroche falls silent, as if he's thinking. Logically, Aja ought to tell him about the desk attendant who saw Martial Bellion at the Roland-Garros airport. Keeping this type of information to herself is unprofessional, and she knows it. Except she's not really keeping it to herself, just delaying the moment when she passes it on. She'll inform Laroche just as soon as Christos has made his report. If it's important.

At the other end of the line, Laroche sighs.

"O.K., Captain Purvi. We'll maintain the roadblocks around Saint-Gilles for another few hours. People will be complaining about this all the way to Place Beauvau, but for the moment we don't have any other leads."

Aja leans back against the white wall of the station. She's won.

"Thank you, Colonel. The men here are exhausted. They've been searching for him all night, but they won't give up, not if I ask them to keep—'

"Don't go overboard, Captain Purvi."

"What do you mean?"

Laroche does not become annoyed. Aja is sure he has files on all of the island's officers. Captain Aja Purvi's character traits must be mentioned therein. Underlined in red, probably.

"How shall I explain this to you, Captain? To put it simply, let me return to your metaphor of the tightening noose, you remember that? It's an interesting metaphor, but an erroneous one. Incomplete, to be exact. Operation Papangue is an extremely complicated plan, even on an island such as Réunion.

We are not using a noose, but a net, composed of multiple cords all linked together. That is the most important thing, Captain, the way in which the cords are knotted together. This is not a simple structure, but consists of several interconnecting circles, ranging from the first, the simplest, around a perimeter of a few hundred meters from the place where Bellion disappeared, to others that are more complex, involving many different agents, modes of transportation, surveillance networks, specialised brigades . . ."

Get to the point!

"Let me assure you, Captain Purvi, we absolutely trust you . . ."

A silence. Calculated this time.

". . . to pull together the cords of that first circle."

Aja imagines Laroche's hypocritical smile. She doubts he can imagine the finger she is giving him.

8:36 A.M.

Aja is sitting in the hammock between two casuarina trees, with her laptop on her knees. She has always found it ridiculous, this hammock suspended in the station's car park—another of Christos's ideas—but she didn't want to get on the wrong side of her colleagues over such a trivial matter. And today, after a night during which she has barely slept at all, she finds it pleasant to be rocked gently while she checks her emails.

The slanting sunlight, the sea breeze blowing through the houses, the shade of the palm trees . . . all of this offers the perfect conditions for a quick break from the manhunt, which in turn allows Aja to concentrate on trying to understand Martial Bellion's psychology. Even if she is not especially convinced by all the woolly theories about serial killers that were reeled off at the police academy by supposed profilers: their modus operandi, signature, their narcissistic tendencies, catathymic crises, and all that crap. She has always believed that that type of officer was just masking their incompetence by using a load of hot air; a bit like teachers who were incapable of educating children training other teachers.

The ComGend has been busy. It has sent a secure email containing four attachments to every force involved in holding one of the cords of Laroche's precious net. The email was written in a hurry by the police station in Deuil-la-Barre. It includes a brief biography of Martial Bellion.

Born in Palaiseau in 1973. Childhood in Orsay, then in Ulis.

After two years spent studying to be a PE teacher at Paris-11, he left the university without any diploma except for two certificates stating that he was a qualified to be a lifeguard and a kayak instructor. He then went to Réunion Island. He was twenty-one years old. He got a job supervising sporting activities at the sailing club in Bourbon de Saint-Gilles. He stayed there for nine years. In September 1996, he married Graziella Doré, the manageress of the Cap Champagne bar-restaurant on the beach at Boucan Canot. Graziella was three months' pregnant. Little Alex was born on March 11, 1997. His parents divorced eighteen months later and Martial had custody of the child every second weekend.

On Sunday, May 4, 2003—Martial's weekend—Alex's body was found by tourists in the ocean. He had drowned. The story made the front page for several days. The judge hesitated for a long time between "involuntary manslaughter" and "accidental death." After much debate, he finally went for accidental death, allowing Martial to avoid an appearance in a criminal court—which also explained the absence of any trace of the affair in the police files.

Martial Bellion left Réunion Island in the months that followed. He returned to France and met Liane Armati in 2005. Josapha was born in January 2007. They were married the following year. Since 2009, Martial has worked in a gymnasium in the Parisian commune of Deuil-la-Barre. Liane Bellion gave up her studies to raise their daughter.

That's all there is.

Aja yawns. The sun, filtering through the leaves of the trees, warms the back of her neck. The hammock sways gently. She feels as if she is floating on an inflatable mattress in the middle of the sea.

A sea with Wi-Fi.

She yawns again and clicks on the second file.

It is a brief report on Alex Bellion's death, written by the judge, Martin-Gaillard.

On the evening of the tragedy, Martial Bellion was looking after Alex. The incident happened between 10 P.M., when Martial Bellion picked up his son from his ex-wife's house at Boucan Canot, and 6 A.M. the following morning, when six-year-old Alex's body was found on the beach. The judge's investigation appears damning towards Bellion and establishes without any doubt the father's failure to take adequate care of his child. All the customers at the Bambou Bar, some one hundred meters from the Boucan Canot beach, testified that Martial Bellion was there, drinking rum, at the time when his son must have drowned. To make matters worse, Martial Bellion never reported his son as missing. It was the police who came to give him the dreadful news the following morning, at his apartment in Saint-Paul. Martial Bellion had 1.2 grammes of alcohol in his blood and 150 nanogrammes of *zamal* in his urine.

My God.

Aja closes her eyes. Naturally, she is thinking about Jade and Lola.

How could a parent survive such a tragedy?

What do they have left? How could anyone rebuild their lives afterwards?

Did Martial Bellion become a monster through negligence? Almost by chance? She imagines the chain of events, so stupid, so sordid: "Don't move from here, Alex, Papa's just going for a quick smoke and a drink over there, at the other end of the beach. I'll be back soon. It's not a place for children."

Can he really have lost everything just for a few glasses of rum? First one life, and then others.

Liane Bellion. Rodin. Sopha Bellion.

Aja clicks on the third file. A PDF of an article from the Réunion daily newspaper appears, dated July 1, 2003, two months after the accident. The short piece announces the closure of the Cap Champagne bar-restaurant, managed by Graziella Doré. The journalist goes for the sentimental angle, mentioning the tragedy of Alex's death. But, while he can fully understand Graziella Doré's inability to go on living beside the waves that brought her son's lifeless body back to her, the consequences of the restaurant's closure have been severe: seven Creoles made unemployed overnight. Barmen, waiters, chefs . . . cleaning ladies . . .

Aja notes the strange coincidence. Her own parents were employed for years at the Hotel Athena. It was a precarious kind of work, just like the jobs held by the seven Creoles mentioned in the article. Frowning, Aja extends this line of thought to its logical conclusion: there were probably, among those Creoles who lost their jobs due to the death of Alex Bellion, some who sought employment at the Athena. And yet none of the hotel staff interviewed following Liane Bellion's disappearance mentioned the previous case.

Gabin Payet.

Eve-Marie Nativel.

Naivo Randrianasoloarimino.

Tanguy Dijoux.

Why not?

Aja makes a mental note that she must verify the identity of the seven Cap Champagne employees. So far, her entire investigation has rested on the assumption that Martial Bellion is the only possible culprit. Five testimonies against one, including that of Eve-Marie Nativel, who swore that Liane Bellion never left room 38. She remembers word for word the conclusion she voiced to Christos: "It's hard to imagine that all of the hotel's employees could be in league against the same man. Why the hell would they do that?"

Five against one. She's delirious.

She must get some sleep.

Her body keeps telling her this, is insistent. Apart from her fingers, which are dancing over the keyboard, all her other limbs and organs seem to be functioning in slow motion, as if they're already on standby. Her thoughts drift towards the beach at Boucan Canot. She can't help thinking about the curious fate of that iconic location. Its whole attraction was that it was dangerous, because of the swell of the sea and the slope of the beach. There is no lagoon at Boucan Canot, only waves that were perfect for surfers of all abilities. Until, in September 2011, the most famous bodyboarder on the island was eaten by a shark only fifteen meters from the beach. It proved a traumatic event for the tourists, and a catastrophe for the hotels, restaurants and shops—far worse than an accidental drowning, ten years before, that had already been forgotten.

Aja yawns again. She is fighting against sleep when she opens the fourth file.

She discovers a long interview with Alex Bellion's teacher, Agnès Sourisseau; clearly another document that was added to the case folder by the judge, Martin-Gaillard.

Judge's question: *What kind of father was Martial Bellion?*

Aja reads the teacher's response.

Martial Bellion was mostly an absent, scatty, rather uninvolved parent. Graziella Bellion, on the other hand, was very down-to-earth. She assumed sole responsibility for Alex's education. On the whole, a fairly classic male-female divide, according to the teacher. Martial Bellion was simply not quite ready to be a father. Not ready to sacrifice his passions for a child.

His passions?

Sport, friends, alcohol, *zamal* . . . women.

Women?

Martial Bellion was a handsome man. Athletic. He liked to party. All he had to do was click his fingers and girls would fall at his feet. Although, a couple of months before Alex's death, he did seem to have calmed down a bit. He was more or less in a steady relationship with a young Creole girl.

Are you saying that this tragedy didn't surprise you?

No, I didn't say that. Martial Bellion was not a very responsible father, but it's a long stretch from that to even imagining such a terrible accident . . .

Exactly. So what could have happened?

Who knows? The beach at Boucan Canot is dangerous, unlike any of the beaches by the lagoon, because of its steep slope. You're quickly out of your depth there. But Alex didn't know that. He was a little boy who loved swimming, just like the big boys. It's terrible to say this, but he idolised his father. Whenever he drew pictures in class, they were always of his father, surfing or windsurfing, surrounded by fish. For his part, as I told you, Martial Bellion preferred his friends, pretty girls, nights out . . . He wasn't a bad man, just more of a big brother than a dad. And yet . . . everything I'm saying is based on hindsight. If you'd asked me this before the tragedy, I'd have said that little Alex was a well-balanced kid who, despite his parents' divorce, would enjoy a wonderful upbringing on this island, benefiting from his mother's authority and level-headedness and his father's spontaneity.

How did the other children in the school react, after Alex's death?

Aja does not read the reply. Not straight away, anyway.

She has fallen asleep, rocked by the trade winds and the hammock's gentle swaying.

24
The Garage Door

I'm scared.

There are no sounds any more, nothing in the house or the garage. All I can hear are my little fists banging against the bathroom door.

Louder and louder.

Finally, Papa comes out of the shower. He's changed his clothes. He takes me in his arms.

"I'm here, sweetheart. I'm here."

It's weird. He doesn't ask me why I was banging so hard on the door. Suddenly, I don't dare tell him about the car I heard in the garage. Just there, behind that door. I think about something else, something even stranger. Papa's hair isn't wet. He must have dried it. Either that or he didn't put his head under the water. That's my favorite bit of taking a shower, putting my head under the water.

"Shall we go, darling? We don't want to hang around any longer."

Papa crams clothes into a large bag: trainers, trousers, sweaters. Apparently it's cold where we're going. I find this hard to believe. Ever since I've been here, on Réunion, the weather has been hotter than it's ever been in France. And the boy who lives in this house, the one whose shorts and shirt I'm wearing, is a bit bigger than me, and I would have liked to take my time choosing other clothes, and trying them on.

"That'll do," says Papa.

He's also told me I mustn't be difficult, that the blue-haired old lady has already been very kind, lending us all her things as well as her house.

Papa empties the cupboard over the sink. He grabs packets of cookies and shoves them into the bag.

I pull another face.

"Not those ones, Papa, they don't look nice."

Papa says nothing. He takes out the biscuits and puts them on the table. He's annoyed. He looks at me strangely again, the same way he did earlier, when he came out of the shower. Maybe it's because of my big brother, who's dead. I think he probably looked a bit like me and that's why Papa's asked me to disguise myself as a boy.

I wish I had a photograph of my big brother. Papa grabs the bag. I look up at him.

"Are we going far, Papa?"

Papa's voice sounds annoyed too.

"Yes, I told you . . . we're going to the other end of the island, to find Maman."

He moves towards the garage door. I hesitate for a second, and then it comes out.

"Papa . . . I heard a car noise earlier, while you were taking your shower. As if it stopped just there . . . in . . . in the garage."

Papa gives me a frightened look, as if I've just told him that I phoned the police and told them where we are.

"Did you . . . did you see anything?"

"No, Papa. Nothing. The garage door didn't open. No one came in."

Papa strides through the house and I jog behind him. Papa opens the garage door and turns back to me.

"Stay there, sweetheart. I'm going to check." He closes the door behind him.

I'm expecting to have to wait for hours, but Papa comes

back almost straight away. He smiles at me, but I can tell he doesn't mean it.

"So?"

"It's nothing, Sopha. You must have been mistaken. There's . . . there's no one there."

Papa is lying. And he's not very good at it. I know this, but I play along anyway.

"Well, that's good, Papa. I was a bit scared."

"Stay here, Sopha. I'm just going to take a look around the garden to make sure the coast is clear. As soon as I call you, come on out."

"Be careful that the police don't see you."

"That's nice of you, sweetheart."

He hugs me, then goes off outside.

What is there, in the garage?

What is Papa hiding from me now?

I have to know.

I open the door.

In the garage is a yellow car. Small, round and shiny. I don't know what make it is.

I walk towards it.

There's someone behind the wheel. I move closer. I recognize her now. *It's the old lady with blue hair.*

She sits there, stiff, on the driver's seat. Her blue glasses have fallen from her nose. I move forward again, silently. It's as if she's fallen asleep.

I put my hand on the yellow door and stand on tiptoes. Straight away, I'm sorry I did this.

For a second, I can't believe what I'm seeing.

Then I start screaming!

The blue-haired old lady has a knife sticking out of her throat!

There's blood all over her collar, on her chin, on her chest, like she can't eat properly and has spilt something all down herself. The blue dress she's wearing is all wet, almost purple, the same color as her hair where it's soaked in blood.

I'm about to scream again, to scream loud enough to wake up the whole neighborhood, but a hand closes over my mouth.

A big, hairy hand belonging to a man, although all I can see of him is his shadow.

25
Honey for the Detective

C hristos parks the Mazda pickup under the archway of the brand new building in Terrasses de Roquefeuil. The recently constructed development in Saint-Gilles lies very close to the lagoon and is a perfect example of sustainable urban planning; a clever mix of houses with swimming pools for the rich, surrounded by walls and gates, and apartments for people of more modest means built over several storeys, with all these people supposed to send their kids to the same schools, to shop in the same stores, to walk in the same parks.

Hmm, thinks Christos, not really convinced by the apparent diversity. His personal belief is that there is only one place on the island where all the races truly mix: the beach! Everyone naked, everyone equal. Curiously, the more out in the open the color of one's skin, the more people tend to forget about it.

The second lieutenant climbs three steps, enters the building's lobby, and checks the names engraved on the small copper plaques.

Charline Tai-Leung. Stairway B. Second floor. Number 11.

Fewer than one per cent of the island's inhabitants have agreed to give up their houses or villas in order to live in apartment buildings, so they're being dolled up to make them more attractive. High-rise buildings are the only solution to the problem of housing the ten thousand or so extra people who come here each year, or are born here; it is the only way of stopping the anarchic urbanisation that is devouring the island's natural spaces as surely as a fire devours forest.

A silent lift. A pink doormat. A red door. A golden doorbell. Classy!

After ringing the bell, Christos indulges in his fantasy about an Asian air hostess, roused from her bed . . .

At last, the door opens, revealing a small bombshell of a woman, five foot three at most, who stares at the policeman with round, sleepy eyes. Her plump face is flanked by straight, black hair, a bit like Dora the Explorer's. Christos forces himself not to look down too far. The T-shirt she is wearing covers so little of her thighs that he has the impression that, with every breath the girl takes, there is a chance of it revealing her pubic hair.

He shows her his card. She rubs her eyes and racks her foggy brain.

"Oh yes, that's right, the guy from the airport. Come in."

This sexy Dora first offers him a place to sit on the couch, and then a coffee.

Christos is happy. He appreciates the beautiful panoramic view of the Indian Ocean or, if he turns his head a little, of Charline's tanned, voluptuous buttocks as she bends over to reach the breakfast tray. Coffee, biscuits and honey.

"I didn't know you policemen were such early risers!"

Christos adopts a serious expression.

"This is an urgent matter, miss. There's a murderer at large. I'm sure you understand. Every second counts."

She understands. She sits down next to him and crosses her legs. The T-shirt lifts up to the very top of her thighs. Dora playing Sharon Stone. Christos purses his lips to stop his tongue lolling into his hot coffee. The girl smiles, seeming unembarrassed, and perhaps a little amused by his reaction.

"Maybe you could give me a couple of seconds, though? I'll put something on."

What a shame.

She disappears into the bedroom. Christos's erection has barely had time to soften before she returns. She has put on a pink poplin summer dress that covers a good half-inch more of her thighs than the T-shirt did.

This, apparently, is Dora's version of modesty.

In compensation, the round neck of the T-shirt has been replaced by the dress's acrobatic décolletage: two slender straps that fight against her breasts' desire to see the light of day.

Christos turns his face towards the sea. A surfboard takes up all the space on the balcony.

So she's sporty, too.

The police officer coughs.

"So, you met Martial Bellion at Roland-Garros airport? Five days ago."

Charline giggles.

"Yes. Public enemy number one. Quite a handsome man. If he wasn't a murderer, I might have thought about it."

She jumps back on the couch, three feet away from Christos, and adopts a Lolita pose. Knees drawn up to her chest.

God, this minx is turning him on! Is she really one of those girls who fantasise about the heroic forces of law and order? He's not sure, but settles for crossing his hands over his crotch to mask his revived hard-on.

"What did Martial Bellion want?"

"Nothing extraordinary. He just wanted to change the date of his return ticket."

"Did he say why?"

"The first article in our charter is about respecting our customers' right to privacy."

Christos scowls.

"And did he manage to change his ticket?"

"No, it was impossible. He wanted to go back to Paris as soon as possible, but all the flights were full. He'd have had to wait at least a week to get a seat on a direct flight, which was almost the day of his return anyway, April 7."

"How did he react?"

"He panicked, to start with. He wouldn't take no for an answer. We tried everything we could. It was complicated, he didn't have a passport. The only possibility involved a stopover, either in Sydney or Delhi, and was three times as expensive."

"And?"

"Eventually he said no. But he did hesitate."

"Ah."

Christos forces himself to concentrate on the shadowy zones in the investigation rather than those situated between Charline Tai-Leung's dress and her skin. So Martial Bellion was secretly trying to get away. At almost any price, apparently. For a prosecutor, that could imply that the murder of his wife was not simply an accident, but premeditated. On the other hand, why go back to France? Because it's easier to hide in a large country than on an island? Hmm, maybe . . .

"So Martial Bellion didn't say anything else to you?"

"No. He seemed like a nice guy, really. Annoyed, but nice."

The girl smiles as she leans over acrobatically to grab a biscuit. The dress pulls up over her bum, while her little breasts dance under the second lieutenant's nose. Remaining impassive, not even making a pass, would be the worst kind of rudeness. Christos reaches out his hand to the breakfast tray, brushing against her breast.

"Was there something else you wanted, Detective?"

The girl has not moved an inch. Skin against skin. Christos stammers.

"Some . . . some honey . . ."

God, what a stupid reply!

While he hesitates between making a more obviously flirtatious allusion and simply placing his palm on that dangling breast, Christos's lewd thoughts are drowned out by the sound of a toilet flushing. Then the sound of tap water running. The creak of a door.

A guy in red Turkish trousers enters the living room. Barechested and muscular, with tousled long blond hair like the Little Prince. The kind of guy who could fuck all night. And surf all day.

"Honey, Detective?" asks Dora the minx.

"Thank you."

The taste of sugar takes away some of his bitterness.

The surfer is not exactly a chatterbox. He flops down on a chair and drinks a litre of water.

"Miss Tai-Leung," stammers Christos, "did Martial Bellion seem like he was trying to escape?"

"What exactly do you mean by 'escape,' Detective?"

"Well, did he seem desperate to leave the island? Did you have the impression that he was afraid of something?"

The surfer stands up and scratches his balls through the fabric of his trousers. Charline glances up at him lovingly, then turns her doll-like eyes back towards Christos.

"Yes, Detective, that's it exactly. He looked like he was afraid."

26
The Woman in the Car

The hairy hand on my mouth is choking me.

I can't breathe.

I am suffocating. Suffocating with fear. I want to bite the hand, tear into it with my teeth like a wild animal, rip off each finger and spit it out, one by one.

Behind me, the monster breathes hot air against the back of my neck.

"Shh, Sopha. You mustn't scream. Whatever you do, don't scream."

Papa?

The hand releases its pressure. I turn around, confused.

Papa?

Papa is standing in front of me. He crouches down so that his face is level with mine. His eyes look into mine.

"Calm down, sweetheart. I came running as soon as I heard you screaming. Please don't start again. I've closed the garage door, but the neighbors could still hear us. They could call the police. They could . . ."

I don't want to listen to Papa any more. I put my hands over my ears and scream.

"She's dead, Papa! The old lady with blue hair is dead!"

Papa strokes my hair, his hand cold and hairy like a spider.

"Shh, Sopha. You mustn't think about that. We have to leave. Quickly."

A huge and deadly spider.

"The old lady has a knife sticking out of her neck, Papa. You killed her."

My eyes look into his.

"It's you, Papa. You're the one who killed her!"

Papa moves closer.

The spider rests on my shoulder, its legs creeping up my neck.

"Of course I didn't, Sopha! How could you believe that? You must never say anything like that to anyone, Sopha. Do you hear me? Never. You have to trust me, always, always, no matter what people tell you, no matter what you see. Now, come on, we have to leave. We have to get the bag and go."

I'm shivering. I don't care. I won't move.

"I *know* you killed her, Papa. We're the only ones in the house."

"Don't talk nonsense, Sopha. I was with you the whole time."

The spider moves down towards my heart, while another one comes to rest on my hair again. I'm trembling. I'm crying. I know I'm right.

"You didn't take a shower! You killed the lady to get her car. To get her house too. And her things. And these boy's clothes I'm wearing."

I realize I'm yelling louder and louder. Suddenly the spider flies towards my face. At first, I don't understand.

The slap makes my cheek sting.

I take a step back, shocked into silence.

"That's enough, Sopha! We don't have any time to lose! Turn around!"

"No!"

The spider is lifted into the air again, threateningly.

This time, I give in.

Papa opens the passenger door of the yellow car. Very quietly, almost without making any noise at all.

Even if I don't look, I know what Papa is doing.

He is taking the old lady out of the car. He doesn't care about the blood on the seat. He doesn't care that the grandma is dead. He doesn't care that she can never again play with the boy whose shorts and shirt and trainers I'm wearing.

He doesn't care about anything.

All he wants is a car, so the police won't catch him. Because he killed Maman, I'm sure of it now.

Because he killed her and he doesn't want to go to prison.

9:11 A.M.

"You can turn around now, Sopha."

There is blood all over Papa's blue shirt.

I see the old lady's feet poking out from behind two old tyres and a lawnmower.

"Get in the car, Sopha. I'm sorry I slapped you, but I didn't have any choice. Even if you're only a little girl, you have to understand. We must keep going, no matter what. You'll see, Sopha, there are some extraordinary places here, wonderful places like you've never seen before."

Wonderful places?

I'm sitting on the back seat of the car. A dead woman's car. Papa is crazy.

"I don't care about places. It's Maman I want to see!"

Papa has calmed down again.

"Then you will have to come with me, Sopha. And trust me. If you want to see Maman again, we have to get to the other side of the island by this afternoon."

"Promise?"

I don't know why I'm asking him that. It's not like I'll believe his answer anyway.

"Yes, sweetheart. I promise."

9:17 A.M.

Martial keeps moving his head from side to side, glancing in the rear-view mirror of the Nissan Micra to check on Sopha, then looking straight ahead again, watching out for anything suspicious. For now, the streets of Ermitage-les-Bains are more or less deserted.

Martial drives for one kilometer, his fingers tense on the steering wheel.

In front of them, the road to Saint-Pierre is blocked. A line of cars several hundred meters long stretches out from the police roadblock, just before the roundabout at Chemin Bruniquel. Martial moves out to the right a little bit so he can see what's going on. The police are stopping every vehicle, checking the driver's papers, looking at each passenger, then opening the boot. There is no way they will let him through, even with Sopha disguised as a boy, even though he has altered his own appearance by shaving his beard and eyebrows, by putting on thick glasses and a cap with the visor pulled down low.

A father and a six-year-old child.

Without any papers.

They are bound to be suspicious.

It's over. They're caught in a trap.

A 4x4 honks its horn behind him. He parks farther off the road, crushing the roots of some beach cabbage.

Martial glances at Sopha, who is lying on the back seat, and goes over and over the unsolvable equation in his head.

The police are searching for a father and a six-year-old child.

There is only one way of solving this equation. A terrible solution for Sopha, more monstrous than everything he has already made her suffer, more traumatic than that face-to-face meeting with the old woman's corpse in the garage.

And yet, once again, he has no choice.

Sopha rolls her eyes at him, surprised, as he manoeuvres the car as discreetly as possible.

"Papa, why are we turning round?"

27
GOLDILOCKS

9:19 A.M.

"A ja! Aja!"

The captain finally wakes up. The faces of Christos and Morez are swaying in the sky, like bobble-headed angels. It takes Aja a few seconds to understand that she is the one who's moving, lying in the hammock, the laptop having slid down her chest so that it looks as if she's wearing an enormous silver medallion. Christos holds out a hand, and she grasps it. Carefully, she rolls out of the hammock.

"Any news?" the captain asks anxiously, checking her watch to see how long she's been asleep.

Two hours and eighteen minutes. This seems both perfectly reasonable and far too long.

Morez is the first to reply.

"Yes and no. We're not sure, in fact. That's why we preferred to wake you. There's been a report of a missing woman: Chantal Letellier, sixty-eight years old, lives on Rue des Maldives, in L'Ermitage. According to the friend she was staying with, she was just supposed to go back to her own house this morning, around 8 A.M., before meeting him at La Saline, with some other retired people. They belong to the same club, they play Go there. You know, the Chinese game? The club is called Go du Dodo. Seriously! Anyway, she still hasn't arrived. They've been calling her house for the last thirty minutes, but no one's answering the phone."

Aja stretches, visibly disappointed. She touches her fingers to her face. She imagines her skin must be covered with little diamond-shaped lines from the cords of the hammock.

"Hmm, well . . . She's probably stuck in a traffic jam. Or she's fallen asleep. Is there any connection with Bellion?"

"Well, it's shaky," says Morez.

His eyes are bloodshot from lack of sleep. He keeps blinking, as though his eyelids are being blown open and shut by the wind, like two bougainvillea petals.

"There is a connection, but it's tenuous. Chantal Letellier lives very close to the Garden of Eden. Now, late last night, the receptionist there called us to report that a man and a girl who looked very much like Bellion and his daughter had visited the garden."

Aja's brain shifts into gear. She has slept for two hours, now she has to make up for lost time. Laroche's extended deadline must be close to expiring. She has to find proof that Bellion has not been able to get through the roadblocks around Saint-Gilles before the ComGend opens the floodgates.

"Morez, did you take the call from the receptionist at the Garden of Eden?"

"Well, yes, but the girl didn't sound too sure of herself. A father spotted with his daughter, two vague figures, that's all she could tell us. The receptionist was a bit dopey, to be honest. We've had fifty similarly hazy reports since last night."

Aja slaps her own cheeks to wake herself up. The harlequin wrinkles on her face begin to fade. Morez and Christos wait for her reaction. Suddenly Aja explodes.

"But fifty vague reports in the same location? That's a fucking sign! Come on. Rue des Maldives, right? Let's go!"

9:27 A.M.

Aja paces the empty living room. She savors the order, the slightly starchy, old-fashioned arrangement of the furnishings, the fleeting calm, well aware that in a few minutes the house will become a crime scene, and that every square inch of it, every piece of furniture, every knick-knack will be taken away and examined by an army of forensic scientists. She touches the wallpaper with her finger and takes a close look at Chantal Letellier's photograph. The old woman has blue hair! She's a character, no doubt about it. Her grandchildren must adore her.

Morez rushes in. His bulging eyeballs are now turning yellow and he is blinking as fast as a dragonfly's wings.

"We've searched everywhere, Aja. There is blood all over the garage. On the ground. On the lawnmower, the tyres, on the sheets of tarpaulin. But there's no sign of a body."

"Jesus, what does that mean?"

Aja chews her lips.

Christos spent fifteen minutes on the phone with Chantal Letellier's boyfriend, so they now have the beginnings of an explanation. Chantal Letellier lived on the island all year round, but spent most of her time at the house of this man, another retiree, a former doctor whom she met at the Go club in Saint-Paul. As her house was rarely lived in these days, Chantal Letellier decided to put it up for rent through a private website, excluding the times when her children and grandchildren came over to visit her. Bellion must have consulted a rental website, read the ad, thought that Chantal Letellier lived in France and her house was therefore empty.

And it was. Almost.

Before going to the Go club, as she did every morning, Chantal Letellier had dropped by her house around 8 A.M. This was unusual, but a neighbor had called the boyfriend's house to say she'd forgotten to close her garage door. This had come as a surprise to her; she wasn't losing her marbles yet, and she really thought she had closed that damned door. But with the story of a killer on the loose, she'd wanted to be sure.

Aja takes a picture off its hook on the wall. In this one,

which is slightly blurred, Chantal Letellier is posing in front of the Voile de la Mariée waterfall.

Fate is sadistic. Chantal Letellier made the wrong choice. That open garage door was the clue that should have allowed them to catch Bellion. All it would have taken was a phone call to the police.

The captain sets the photograph down on the living room table. She is going to ask Morez to fax it to all the stations on the island. Just in case. As they haven't yet found Chantal Letellier's body, there is perhaps a slim chance that Bellion hasn't killed her. That he has only taken her hostage.

Although with blood all over the garage, it's a very slim chance.

At the moment, Aja has no DNA analysis and no finger-prints—the forensics team will take care of that—but all the evidence points the same way. They even found the butt of a joint in the bathroom. She has no doubt.

Martial Bellion and his daughter slept in this house last night.

She contacted Colonel Laroche a few minutes ago. The entire staff of the ComGend is being helicoptered to Saint-Gilles.

Their tails between their legs.

Aja was right all along. The fish had been caught in the net she had laid. She had almost hung up on Laroche after telling him this, so that he'd understand how much energy and time they had lost by his insistence that the manhunt should cover the whole island.

9:29 A.M.

Christos comes back into the room with a cynical, indiffer-ent smile on his face: exactly the attitude that Aja hates in her second-in-command. She asks him, anxiously:

"Still no sign of Chantal Letellier's body?"

"No, but I found something else."

He holds up a plastic bag, then, without any explanation, empties the contents onto the living room table, right in front of Aja. For a few seconds, there is a cloud of hair in the air, then slowly it falls onto the table and the floor around it, making the living room tiles look like the floor of a hairdresser's.

Long blonde hairs. Fine. Almost artificial.

As if some madman had shaved the heads of a hundred Barbie dolls.

Or maybe just one. A little Goldilocks.

Aja's gaze turns once again to the framed photographs on the walls. This time, she doesn't look at the grandmother, but at the six-year-old boy next to her, in his baseball cap and checked shirt, watching the crocodiles.

She understands.

"For God's sake!" she suddenly screams. "They mustn't get through!"

28
The Fireman's Dream

Here you are, Officer. These are my mother's papers."
Martial opens the wallet and hands over the identity
card, the car registration document, the insurance
papers. The policeman gives a routine smile. He must have
checked hundreds of vehicles this morning. He looks inside
the yellow Nissan. The old lady is sleeping in the passenger
seat, a tartan rug tucked over her knees and a scarf around her
neck, as if she were cold in this eighty-five-degree heat; on the
back seat, the kid is sulking, surrounded by a hammock and
the Creole picnic boxes.

Even the Zoreilles are at it now.

The cop, conscientious despite his weariness, carefully examines the vehicle's papers.

"What about your papers?" he asks Martial.

Martial lowers his head apologetically.

"Sorry, I don't have them on me. We're just taking
Grandma to get some fresh air in Les Hauts. Look at her. I bet
if we could have found a hat, she'd have put that on too."

The policeman laughs. He's a Creole. He can sympathise.

He hands the papers back to Martial.

"It's the same for me. I get every other weekend off, but I'm
not as lucky as you. I've still got all four grandparents to bring
with me."

He takes one last look at the back of the car. The expression
on the kid's face is priceless. He even looks as though he's been
crying. The cop gives Martial an understanding wink.

"The kids hate it, don't they? They'd rather just go swimming in the lagoon. Mine are the same. All right then, have a good day."

Martial calmly steps on the accelerator.

He's through!

To start with, he drives slowly along the Saint-Pierre road, until the Trou d'Eau. At least the roadblock has the advantage of reducing the amount of traffic: there's no one on this road, and he'll be able to put his foot down and get away quickly.

He hugs the coastline leading to Saint-Leu, crossing the estuaries of the Trois-Bassins, the Grande Ravine and the Ravine Fontaine, glancing briefly at the vast bridges on the Route des Tamarins, half a mile inland. The traffic is still sparse. Too sparse. He'll be too easy to spot.

Suddenly Martial brakes. Between dwarf palms and giant cacti, the roundabout at the entrance of Saint-Leu has taken him by surprise. In spite of the seat belt holding it in place, Chantal Letellier's corpse slides down the passenger seat and the bloodless head falls against his arm.

Martial shivers. His fingers tighten around the steering wheel; he is sickened by the touch of the cold skin, which detonates unbearable memories inside his mind. Whenever he drove anywhere with Liane, even for just a small distance, she would always fall asleep after a few kilometers, and her soft blonde hair would spread over his shoulder.

In the same affectionate position as this corpse.

This corpse that has now started to bleed again.

His shirt is soaking again.

In the back seat, Sopha is crying.

With the exception of the few minutes at the roadblock, when the cop was watching, she hasn't stopped crying since they set off. Martial has no choice but to continue, though, to keep moving forward, even if he knows that the body of this murdered old lady, disguised as a tired granny sitting in her mother's place, will haunt his daughter her entire life.

For years . . . or for a few hours.

Who knows?

He is not in control of anything any more.

9:37 A.M.

Martial leaves L'Etang-Salé. In a few kilometers, after Saint-Louis, he will have to choose between continuing along the coastal road or turning in towards the heart of the island, towards Tampon. His decision depends on questions to which, for now, he doesn't have the answers. How long will it take the cops to notice the disappearance of Chantal Letellier? To identify her car? For the officer who let him through to make the connection? For them to issue a missing persons report? Minutes? Hours?

He is hesitant. To reach the Anse des Cascades, the coastal road is the shortest route. Saint-Pierre. Saint-Joseph. Saint-Philippe. An almost continuous succession of houses, round-abouts, pedestrian walkways, traffic lights and speed controls. This is the road on which he would be most vulnerable, a sort of funnel between the mountains and the sea. It would be easy for the police to trap him as soon as they knew which road he had taken out of Saint-Gilles.

He sees the sign to Tampon on the RN1. Straight ahead. Instinctively, he accelerates. He will follow the Route de l'Entre-Deux for a while, until he reaches the Plaine des Cafres. Then there are three different ways to get to the Route du Volcan, which winds its way towards the Piton de la Fournaise.

It's a dead end. And that's what he's betting on.

Hundreds of tourists go up there every day, photograph the

Piton, then come back down by the same road. If there's one road the cops won't think to look for him on, this is it.

9:42 A.M.

The Nissan Micra steers through the first curves of the Route du Volcan. The gently rolling fields of thick, green grass are enclosed by wooden posts. White and beige cows raise their necks above the wire fences to get a better look at passing tourists. The houses with their pointed roofs look like colorful chalets.

It is one of the most unusual landscapes on the island. Hard to believe that, a few hundred meters below, they have just left behind coconut trees, cacti and scorching heat.

Martial glances in the rear-view mirror. Sopha is still lying down on the back seat.

"Have you seen how different the landscape looks here, sweetheart? You'd think we were in Switzerland."

Silence.

Sopha sniffs.

Again, Martial pushes away Chantal Letellier's corpse, which collapses on top of him every time the road curves to the left. The dislocated dummy has been emptied of all its blood; now it is just a sort of pale, almost transparent ghost, its flesh gradually turning blue, the same color as the dyed hair on its head.

But this ghost is beginning to rot.

At every bend, the corpse passes in front of Sopha. She doesn't say anything, but Martial can see her biting her lips, sees the disgust in her eyes.

She's traumatized.

My God!

He should stop right now and throw the corpse out onto

the side of the road. That is the only solution, if he doesn't want his daughter to go completely crazy. Or at least park the car, and move the body to the boot.

But that would mean leaving a huge clue for the cops, or losing precious time.

It would mean taking a massive risk.

The risk of ruining everything.

No, it's impossible. He has to keep going, to the end of this madness.

9:45 A.M.

Sopha is shivering now.

Chantal has calmed down over the last few minutes. Martial gave her a more abrupt shoulder barge, and now she is leaning against the passenger door, her mouth stuck against the window, as if she too is admiring the passing landscape. Dribble mixed with blood leaves smears on the glass.

Another bend.

Martial remembers the way. There is at least another hour to go, and dozens of curves in the road. Sopha won't make it, at this rate. He has to do something. Anything. His throat feels like it's blocked by some enormous obstacle. He coughs several times, then finally speaks.

"Sopha, sweetheart, you asked me a question earlier. You asked me if you looked like your big brother. Remember? Alex. Your big brother who . . . who died before you were born."

A look in the rear-view mirror. No perceptible reaction on the girl's face.

"I have time to answer your question now, if you want. Yes, sweetheart, you do look like him. You look a lot like Maman, of course. But you also look very similar to Alex."

Sopha lifts her head. Hollow-eyed. Miles away.

"I'm going to tell you a secret, Sopha. This is the second time I've driven along this road. The first time was just over ten years ago. And Alex was sitting exactly where you are now. In the back seat. He was almost your age, just two months younger. The two of us were alone in the car. I wanted to show him the volcano."

Sopha is listening. Martial can tell. He has to keep speaking to keep her mind focused, so that she doesn't lose it completely.

"The big volcano on the island, the Piton de la Fournaise, had started erupting again. All the newspapers and television shows kept explaining that you shouldn't go near it. And yet, all the people on the island did exactly that. They drove there to see it—the most beautiful fireworks display you could ever imagine."

The yellow Nissan is now passing one of the little picnic huts every two hundred meters. The last one, just below the summit of Nez de Boeuf, vanishes in a cloud of barbecue smoke.

"I wanted to surprise Alex. I didn't say anything to him about it in advance, or to his mother. You don't know her, but she was very strict and serious. She wouldn't have wanted me to take him there. She'd have told me I was reckless, dragging a six-year-old child to see a volcano erupting, when all the sane people on the island were telling us to stay away. Maybe you won't agree with this, Sopha, but there are some things even mothers can't understand."

No reaction. Sopha doesn't even blink.

Martial goes on, even if Sopha has walled herself up in her privacy, listening to her music through the earbuds of an imaginary MP3 player. What he says now is as much for himself as for his daughter.

"I was already reading Alex the adventures of Ti-Jean back

then. The same books I've been reading to you. As you know, Grand-Mère Kalle and her friend Grand Diable live somewhere under the lava of the volcano. That's why Alex was a bit scared on this road. You're not scared, are you, sweetheart?"

Inwardly, Martial curses his own stupidity. Did he really need to mention that story about the devil, on top of everything else? He starts talking again straight away, he must not let the silence triumph.

"I'm going to tell you something else, Sopha. Ever since he was little, Alex had a favorite toy that he took everywhere with him—a little fire engine that he'd found on the beach. You know what I mean, Sopha? Just a little metal car, small enough to fit in the palm of your hand. Nothing special. A bit rusty. He played with it everywhere. On his bed. In the sandpit. On the grass. On the gravel. On the table of a high chair. In his car seat. You get the picture, don't you? Alex was only six, but his little fire engine had already driven miles and miles. When we arrived at the Pas de Bellecombe, up there, the car park at the base of the erupting volcano, it was impossible to go any further. The road was blocked. And do you know what fascinated Alex the most?"

In the rear-view mirror, Sopha's face remains impassive, but her hand has moved, as if, on hearing the description of the toy, she too wants to reach out for something—a friend, a cuddly toy, a comfort blanket. Any kind of object on to which she could project her demons.

"You're not going to believe this, Sopha! Alex wasn't interested in the incredible jets of flame spurting out of the Piton volcano, or the sparks exploding against the coal-black sky. No. He was interested in all the fire engines! There was a row of them blocking the way and dozens of firemen all running around like Martians in their fireproof suits. We quickly got out of the car. There was no danger: we were several miles from the crater, even if the heat was infernal. And we weren't the only ones there. There were hundreds of people around us, holding up cameras, binoculars, video cameras . . . It was almost impossible to get close to the barrier to get a better view. But then this big, fat lady let Alex past. She was a Creole and she had a huge cross hanging around her neck. 'It's the devil coughing, my sweet,' she said to Alex. 'You must remember that. It's the devil, and he's angry with people!' Alex couldn't have cared less. He was watching the lava flowing down the mountainside like an endless, fiery snake. Believe me, Sopha, I had never seen his eyes shine like that before. But the old Creole lady kept on with her stories about God. 'Little one, do you know what you must do to stop the devil getting angry? Hasn't your Papa told you? You must pray, my sweet, pray to all the saints of the island. The devil is afraid of them.'"

Martial falls silent and glances up at the summit of the Piton de la Fournaise. Above the Dolomieu crater, the sky is an immense blue, with the exception of an almost imperceptible heat haze. A vague idea begins to form in his mind, the rough outline of a way out at the end of this impasse—narrow, but perhaps wide enough for two people to slip through. Why not? He must think about that, later. Right now, he has to concentrate on his story. He mustn't abandon Sopha.

"Alex didn't care about saints any more than you do, and you've never even set foot in a church. But he was polite, and the old lady kept talking, as if God were speaking through her mouth. 'I won't lie to you, little one. Listen to me carefully: between the volcano and the sea, there is a small village, Sainte-Rose, with a little church named Notre-Dame. When the volcano erupted in 1977, the lava covered everything: the sugar cane fields, the houses, the roads. All the inhabitants of the village took refuge in the church and they prayed to the saints, fearing the lava would burn them alive. You know what happened, little one?' Alex shook his head. No, he didn't know, and he didn't care. He was watching the firemen walking up towards the crater in their amazing outfits that made them look like spacemen. But the old lady went on: 'Well, little one, the saints were stronger than the devil and the devil got scared. The lava came to a halt just in front of the church and nobody died! Ever since then, the church has been called Notre-Dame-des-Laves. You can still see the dry lava climbing up to the bottom step of the chapel and stopping there, as if it didn't dare go inside. If you don't believe me, you can ask your father to take you there.' Alex turned around then and asked the lady: 'Did the saints have a red fire engine, to stop the lava?' You can imagine the scene, Sopha. The fat Creole lady was surprised. She laughed, a bit embarrassed: 'No, little one, of course the saints didn't have a fire engine.' Did they have shiny helmets, then? Alex demanded. 'No.' Were they dressed like spacemen, then? Did they have a big gun that spat out water? 'No, little one, your imagination is getting the better of you. Saints dressed as spacemen, carrying a gun?' In the distance, men in uniform were rushing around urgently, as if every second mattered, when really there was nothing to be done but watch the lava running down the mountainside. Alex shrugged and turned his back on the Creole lady. 'It must suck to be a saint, then!' He stared up at the volcano, holding his little red fire engine tight in his hand. 'When I grow up, I want to be a fireman.'"

Another glance in the rear-view mirror.

Still no reaction from Sopha. No laughter. No smile.

Nothing from Chantal Letellier either. She seems to have found the most comfortable position and has fallen asleep. A bump in the road has even made her shut her mouth.

Martial forges on.

"And he would have been, Sopha, believe me. At six years old, your brother was already a very brave boy. More than just brave, in fact; he was intrepid. He would have become the greatest fireman in the world."

Outside, the picnic huts rush past the window, all of them occupied by Creole families and already piled high with tin lunchboxes, folding chairs, towels hung up to protect the youngest and oldest from the sun during the siesta hour. Around the volcano, the landscape opens up; they pass the Mare de Scories, the Piton Textor, the Pente Zézé, all appearing in a damp blur through the windscreen.

The marks Chantal Letellier has left on the window aren't the only reason for this blurriness. Martial can no longer hold back the tears that prick the corners of his eyes.

The road straightens out for a short while, and he takes advantage of this to twist round towards Sopha. She, too, is crying. He keeps one hand on the wheel and reaches with the other hand towards the back seat of the car. He feels Sopha's little fingers touch his. Five fragile insects that he captures with infinite care.

"It's a shame he died so young, your big brother. He would have saved lives, lots of lives. You would have been so proud of him, sweetheart."

The five insects vibrate gently in his warm hand, as if they were sprouting wings. Martial wishes this moment could go on forever.

Above them, a helicopter passes in the sky.

29
IMELDA IN THE FRIDGE

9:50 A.M.

Quentin Patché, standing in the car park of the Saint-Gilles police station, stares at his feet like a naughty schoolboy caught smoking in the toilets. He is six foot tall, has a third dan in aikido, and does not have a single blunder on his conscience in twenty-one years as a policeman. The girl facing him is ten years younger, twenty centimeters shorter and weighs thirty kilos less.

You would never guess it, though.

"A guy on his own, for God's sake!" Aja screams. "With a six-year-old child on the back seat. And no papers! And you let him through?"

Quentin Patché begins to stammer his excuses, but Aja interrupts. She knows what he's going to say: the grandmother's corpse on the passenger seat, Sopha disguised as a boy, a driver who didn't really look like the photograph of Bellion. The announcement radioed to all patrols came through only a few minutes too late. Most cops, in his situation, would have been fooled. This cretin Patché is no worse than the rest. Aja knows all that, but it doesn't stop her yelling at him.

"We had him, Lieutenant. All you had to do was open your eyes."

Patché is a well-trained cop. At the station, as in the aikido club, he has learned to take the blows thrown at him without flinching. Aja machine-guns insults at him for a while longer.

She needs to get it out of her system.

She also needs to make an impression on Colonel Laroche.

He is standing next to her, under the shade of the casuarina tree. He arrived ten minutes ago in a brand new Ecureuil AS350 B that whipped up a sandstorm as it landed on the beach, which had been evacuated by the police a few minutes before.

Christos has been silently watching this scene since the beginning. Finally, he decides to step in. He leans towards the captain's ear and whispers:

"That'll do, Aja. I think you've given him enough of an ass whooping. Quentin's been at work for more than thirteen hours straight. Give him a break, eh?"

Aja nods.

She turns around to Laroche while Quentin Patché walks away. The colonel is taller than Aja had imagined when she was talking to him on the phone. More charming, too. A handsome forty-something, clean and smooth, with just enough humor in his gaze to hint at the skilful diplomat hidden behind the façade of a cold bureaucrat. He looks like the manager of an NGO, a microfinance banker, a socialist councillor.

Intelligent. Energetic. Trustworthy.

Annoying.

Laroche waits until Patché has returned to the station before he speaks.

"Let's not waste any more time on this, Captain Purvi. Officer Patché's error has only cost us a few minutes. We have already sent out the details: a yellow Nissan Micra with a registration number that Bellion cannot possibly have had time to change. He won't get far. All the ComGend's helicopters have been mobilized: eleven EC145s are in the air above the island as we speak. You've done a good job, Purvi, and I mean that sincerely. First in trapping him, and then forcing him out of his hiding place. He can't have more than a thirty-minute head start on us. He has no chance of escaping."

While he speaks, Laroche draws little circles with the sole of his shoe in the gravel scattered over the tarmac car park.

Despite his apparent self-assurance, Aja detects in this movement a suggestion of nervousness. Before he climbed into his helicopter, the colonel had donned combat trousers, a bulletproof vest and combat boots. The whole "Ken joins the Marines" outfit. At the time, the colonel must have thought it exotic to leave behind his usual suit and tie for a baptism of air in the Ecureuil and his visit to the natives. But, deep down, he surely wasn't expecting Operation Papangue to be like some welcome-to-the-island gift?

Aja frowns so hard her eyebrows meet in the middle, demonstrating that a few insincere compliments are not enough to win her over.

"And in the meantime, Colonel? What do we do while we're waiting for the choppers to return: get the speakers out and turn 'Ride of the Valkyries' up to full volume?"

Laroche gives the captain a good view of his perfect teeth. A smile that anyone would swear was frank and complicit.

"You keep quiet and you pray to Saint Expeditus,[39] Captain Purvi. Isn't that how things are done round here?"

9:57 A.M.

"Aja, can I speak to you? In private."

Christos pulls Aja by the sleeve, away from the other men.

"Is it important?"

"Yes."

Christos watches Laroche, who is a few meters away, as he tries to find the best place to get a signal on his iPhone.

"It has to be private," Christos insists. "Not in front of Laroche. You'll understand, he won't. Shall we go to the fridge?"

---

[39] Roman martyr venerated in Réunion.

The fridge is a small, windowless room, containing thirty years of the force's archives, two chairs and a table, all made of metal. The officers of Saint-Gilles gave it that nickname because it is the coolest room in the building, but above all because the absence of windows makes it the perfect place to cool down any suspects held in custody who are refusing to talk.

They go inside and Christos closes the door. Turns on the light. It's a modern fridge: the light stays on inside even when the door is closed.

There is a woman waiting for them there in the cold. A Cafrine. Tall. Strong. Tasteful Creole make-up: crimson lipstick and indigo eyeshadow.

Christos handles the introductions.

"Aja, this is Imelda. My friend. I told you about her this morning. You told me she could drop by, remember? You should listen to her. She's given this case a lot of thought. And she's got more distance from it than we have, if you see what I mean. She—'

"I remember," Aja interrupts, then speaks directly to Imelda. "So you're the only woman in the world who can get the libertarian prophet Christos Konstantinov to work overtime. And, if I remember correctly, you also have a gift for criminal detective work, Harlan Coben style? Forgive me, madame—or forgive Christos, more to the point. He should have consulted me beforehand. I would have told him that there was now no need for you to come here. Certainly not straight away. Martial Bellion is currently being pursued by a dozen police helicopters. He should be caught any second now."

But Christos does not give up.

"You should really listen to what she has to say."

"You're pissing me off, Christos."

Aja walks around the room, mechanically straightening the archive folders. She throws a sympathetic glance at the Cafrine.

"I'm sorry, Imelda, I have nothing against you. But—'

"That's all right," Imelda smiles. "Don't worry about it, madame. I understand. I'm too old to get upset."

She stands up and turns to Christos.

"Your boss is right. I should go back home. I told you I had no business coming here. My kids are waiting for me, I've got three tonnes of laundry to wash, I have to go to Saint-Paul to buy vegetables for the curry, and—'

Christos, who is staring up at the blistered ceiling, suddenly bangs his fist on the table, raising a cloud of dust.

"For fuck's sake, Aja, would it really cost you anything just to listen to her for five minutes? Imelda is a witness. She's a goddamn witness! She was observing and archiving in her memory every news item on this island long before hard disks and search engines were invented."

Aja sighs, checks her watch.

"O.K., five minutes. And not a second longer."

Christos pulls out a chair and wipes it with the back of his hand.

"Go ahead, Imelda."

Imelda steps forward. Under the sole bulb, her large shadow almost covers Aja.

"Ever since this case began, madame, I have found Martial Bellion's attitude illogical."

As Imelda moves around, Aja's face passes from shade to light, as if she were the one being interrogated.

"Be more specific, Imelda."

"Well, to me it almost feels—how can I put this?—as if we are dealing with two different men. At least according to what the press is saying. And what Christos has told me."

Aja frowns, but she doesn't interrupt.

"To begin with, madame, it all appeared to be the result of a simple domestic row. A fight. An accident. Martial Bellion panics, calls the police, makes his confession."

"O.K.," says Aja impatiently. "O.K."

"Then suddenly he does a complete U-turn. Bellion runs away. He escapes from the police. He is transformed into an organized, elusive criminal, as if he were following a carefully premeditated plan, or at least, had a specific goal in mind."

"O.K., Imelda. I'm sorry to be so forthright, but we have already considered all that."

Christos leans back against the yellowed archives. His eyes move from one woman to the other.

"I'm sure you have," Imelda says quickly. "I'm sure you have, madame. So I'm going to cut to the chase. It all comes down to a single question: what happened between Friday, March 29, at 4 P.M. and Sunday, March 31, exactly forty-eight hours later?"

After looking surprised for a second, Aja replies in a cutting voice:

"Nothing! Nothing at all. It was afterwards that everything got out of hand, when we tried to catch Bellion."

Imelda does not take offence. Instead she pursues her argument, becoming more eloquent.

"Let me explain my reasoning, madame. On Friday, from 4 P.M. onwards, after the disappearance of his wife, Martial Bellion co-operated with the police—he asked you to search for his wife, even sought her protection. Two days later, a complete metamorphosis."

Aja glances irritably at her watch.

"In the meantime, Imelda—as you know, because Christos does not seem to be able to tell the difference between professional secrecy and pillow talk—we collected quite a lot of evidence. Blood samples. DNA. The killing of Amaury Hoarau. The murder weapon. Suddenly Bellion found himself cornered."

"But he already was, madame. Bellion isn't stupid. He already knew about the blood, the DNA, and the fingerprints that were bound to be found on the handle of the knife. I stand by what I said, Captain Purvi: Bellion changed his strategy completely, and we don't know the reason for this sudden U-turn. To be perfectly frank, this story reminds me of another story involving my son—my oldest, Nazir—three years ago, when the Jean-Lafosse School called me because he had stolen a friend's MP3."

Aja looks at her watch again, but Christos signals her to be patient.

"To start with, Nazir was perfectly calm and obedient towards the school's prefects. He even admitted the theft. Until one of his friends spilled the beans: Nazir hadn't just stolen an MP3. He was responsible for a whole network of crime at the school: MP3s, MP4s, mobile phones, video-game consoles, *zamal* . . . As soon as he found out that one of his accomplices had snitched on him, my boy ran away to the Plaine des Makes. He was only twelve. It took the police three days to find him."

Aja stands up, at last showing some interest. She tries to make the connection between this story and the murky areas of the investigation. Liane Bellion's visit to the police station in Saint-Benoît, Bellion's attempt to change the date of his return flight. Bellion's past, too: the pretty girls, the booze, the *zamal*.

"What are you getting at, Imelda? That Martial Bellion is hiding something else from us? Worse than what he's already accused of? You think he's escaped so that we won't find out whatever that is?"

Christos, smiling proudly because Aja has clearly been convinced by this reasoning, whistles between his teeth.

"Worse than three murders . . . Interesting, eh? Makes it worth digging a little deeper into Bellion's past."

Imelda lifts her arms theatrically. She does not have time to say anything else, though, because the fridge door suddenly bursts open.

Laroche appears, his hair almost out of place. The bullet-proof vest is buttoned up to his chin.

"We've spotted them, Purvi!"

"What?"

"After the Plaine des Cafres, on the road to the Piton de la Fournaise."

"That's a dead end! We've got them. I'm on my way."

A metal chair falls backwards in a cloud of dust. Laroche waits for the echo to die down.

He is visibly irritated.

"All the choppers are in use, Captain Purvi. There's no room for you. The men who are going to carry out the assault are professionals: the air and alpine sections of the mountain police. Your force should continue the investigation in Saint-Gilles. That is crucial, as there are still quite a few missing elements in this case. The murder of Chantal Letellier, and—"

Aja explodes.

"Are you kidding me?"

Behind Laroche, two guys in uniform with shoulders wider than the door are hopping around as if they need to pee.

"Captain Purvi, twelve helicopters are about to converge on Bellion's Nissan. Thirty men. Most of them elite snipers. Every single one is merely a cog in the wheels of Operation Papangue, perfectly trained and without ego. Without ego—do you understand that, Purvi? I have to go now."

The clicking of footsteps fades away, leaving the fridge door open on a vast and empty silence. Christos purses his lips. Imelda withdraws towards the shelves, her back pressing against the archive boxes. Both wear the same sorrowful expression.

The metal table is suddenly sent flying. It crashes against the metal shelving, making a terrible racket.

"Bastards!"

Aja rushes out of the fridge and enters the main room of the police station. Morez leaps out of his superior's way as elegantly as a football player who doesn't want to commit a foul in the penalty area. Aja does not notice the cable that is running across the room, or at least she doesn't bother avoiding it. She rushes forward and, the very next moment, the video projector connected to this cable smashes on the tiles. Hundreds of yellow and orange houses in Saint-Gilles vanish into darkness.

Eight hundred and sixty euros. A quarter of the station's annual operating budget.

"What a bunch of fucking bastards!" Aja shrieks.

She runs out into the car park.

Sand and gravel are being whipped up into a storm.

Laroche's Ecureuil AS350 B passes less than thirty meters above her head, the casuarina trees nodding theirs frantically for fifteen seconds.

"Son of a bitch!"

Aja watches the Ecureuil move away, holding up her middle finger.

10:14 A.M.

Laroche's helicopter is now merely a speck on the horizon. Aja prowls around the car park, her shoes kicking out at stones like the hooves of a stallion locked in a stable. Not a single officer dares speak. Christos leans against a tree and lights a cigarette while he waits for the right moment to break this silence.

Letting the storm clouds pass.

For several long minutes, the captain continues to stare at the empty sky, as desperate as a baby bird abandoned in its nest. Suddenly, Aja puts her mobile phone to her mouth and yells into it:

"Jipé? Yeah, it's Aja. This is an emergency! Do you have any choppers left?"

The silence lasts only a few seconds.

"You do? Fantastic, I love you! It's for a special mission. Don't move, I'll call you back in two minutes."

Aja hangs up.

Christos stares at her, incredulous.

"Who's this Jipé? Your ex?"

"Almost. The guy who's taken me higher than anyone else in my life."

"Your lover?"

"No. My flying instructor."

30

THE FIVE-STAR GRAVE

10:17 A.M.

A bouquet of flowers in every color, said Papa. The biggest we can make! For the old, blue-haired lady who died. Like in a cemetery. Dead people like flowers.

Papa told me to stay under the trees while I pick them, and not to go too far away, but not to come too close to the hole either. It's actually more than just a hole, it's a sort of huge well that seems to go down into the center of the earth. It's VERY dangerous! The wooden barrier in front of it is damaged, and there is orange plastic tape around it and big yellow triangles.

I turn around so I don't get lost in the bushes. Papa is standing near the yellow car, about thirty meters away.

I get it.

Papa came off the road as soon as he saw the helicopter. He turned off straight away, but he continued along a dirt track, being very careful to stay under the trees. The helicopter couldn't follow us—it would have had to land—but we were already a long way away. Afterwards, Papa parked next to the hole. Just in front of the sign attached to the barrier. I read the words: *Commerson Crater*.

We got out of the car. Well, Papa and I did, not the old lady, obviously. I wanted to go up to the edge, but Papa wouldn't let me.

"It's almost a thousand feet deep," he explained. "You could put the Eiffel Tower down there and only the very top would poke out."

I found this hard to believe, but without leaning over it, all

I could see was the edge of the well and black rocks full of holes like dried-up sponges.

Then Papa sent me to pick some of these flowers.

I've got enough now—I can only just manage to hold all the stems in both hands—so I head back to the yellow car, still being careful to stay under the trees. Papa has taken off his shirt. It's true that, even up here in the mountains, it's really hot, even hotter than it is by the lagoon, because there's no wind. Papa has taken everything out of the car. The bag, the water, the map.

It's strange.

It looks as if the car has moved.

I walk towards him, holding the flowers.

"Don't come any closer, Sopha!"

"What are you doing, Papa?"

He's all sweaty and his hands are on the car.

"What are you doing, Papa?"

He crouches down so his face is level with mine. I like it when he does that.

"You've seen graves in cemeteries, right, Sopha? People dig holes so that dead people can sleep without being bothered by all the noise, the rain, the sunlight . . . So they can sleep forever, you understand?"

I nod. I understand. But being dead is not sleeping. Being dead is never waking up.

"On this island, there's no need to dig holes in the earth, because there are already lots of really big ones, craters made by the volcano. Five-star graves. Like five-star hotels, you see?"

I nod again.

"Stand back, Sopha."

Papa moves the yellow triangles out of the way, then starts pushing the car. He doesn't push it towards the wooden barrier, but a bit lower down, through some bushes and straight towards the hole. He pushes it as hard as he can. The car rolls along slowly.

The old lady is inside. I can see her blue hair sticking out.

With one hand, Papa tears off a strip of orange plastic tape. One last push. The car tilts over.

It's funny. At first there's no noise, as if the hole really has no end, like when Alice fell down the rabbit hole.

But then suddenly, there's a loud bang. As loud as thunder when it's very close, just a little while after the lightning. So loud I almost imagine the rocks are shaking around the edge, and that they are going to come loose and fall into the hole, blocking it up forever.

I take two steps back. I'm not as brave as Alice.

10:22 A.M.

Martial pushes Sopha further back into the cover of the *avoune*[40] and looks up at the sky. He can see three helicopters now, all quite far away; two are flying over the Piton de la Fournaise, while the other is headed towards the Piton des Neiges. He imagines policemen leaning out over the void, binoculars clamped to their eyes, searching for any clue that might help them spot their prey, among the *avoune* or in the Forêt des Tamarins. One car, two fugitives, hiding somewhere between the edge of the volcano and the Rivière des Remparts: the search perimeter has narrowed considerably.

And that was his plan.

Attract the helicopters by driving the Nissan, very conspicuously, along the Route du Volcan. Wave a red flag to get them excited. Then, as in Saint-Gilles, suddenly make the car vanish, covering their tracks and continuing on foot. Swinging over to the other side of the volcano, towards Piton Sainte-Rose, the ocean, and Anse des Cascades.

---

[40] A sort of local heather consisting of low bushes.

*

Martial smiles at Sopha, then crams the rest of their things into the bag, while trying to memorise every detail of the OS map, the differences in height, the wooded areas, the gullies, forcing himself to create a 3D image in his mind.

As soon as they have left the scrubland around the Commerson Crater, they will be confronted by two major problems.

Firstly, they must cross the Plaine des Sables, over a mile of black ash, under the full sun with no shade at all—it has a record low albedo, as it absorbs almost all the solar radiation without reflecting any of it. A barbecue the size of five hundred football pitches, large enough to grill sausages for the entire island's inhabitants for a century. They must cross the Plaine des Sables completely exposed, as easy to spot as ants on a white tablecloth.

And if, by some miracle, they get past this, they must descend the slopes of the volcano towards the ocean.

Nearly ten miles. A five and a half thousand feet descent.

Sopha will never be able to follow him . . .

10:25 A.M.

"Come here now, sweetheart. That is a beautiful bouquet."

I hesitate. I press the bunch of flowers against my heart. I feel like the hole is still trembling.

"Come on, sweetheart. You don't feel dizzy, do you?"

"No."

"Give me your hand. You're going to throw the flowers into the crater so that the old, blue-haired lady will have them in heaven."

I want to tell Papa that if he hadn't killed the grandma we wouldn't have to bother with all this nonsense—heaven, flowers, pushing the car into a hole—but I don't want him to get angry again.

So I walk towards him. My feet are very close to the edge.

Papa's hand is damp.

The hole looks like a huge mouth. A hungry mouth that doesn't just want to swallow my flowers but me too, like the big teeth of a horse when you offer it some grass through a fence.

It wants the fingers too. The hand. The arm.

I stand on the rocks, right on the edge. I want my flowers to fall all the way to the bottom.

"Hold me tight, Papa!"

Maman would never have let me do this.

I lean over. I'm almost leaning over the hole now. Papa holds my left hand while my right hand whirls around, then suddenly I let go of the bouquet.

The flowers rain down.

They fall in silence. I look down. I want to watch them fall as far as possible, until they reach the center of the earth.

All I can hear is the wind blowing through the leaves, and insects buzzing high in the sky. Or maybe that's the helicopters?

"You won't let go of me, will you, Papa?"

31
Greetings from Mauritius

10:32 A.M.

Everyone has flown the nest.

Christos finds that he is the only one on duty at the Saint-Gilles police station, like a cat that has been left to its own devices while the owners have gone off on their summer holiday. He has the big house and the garden all to himself.

Alone. Well, not exactly.

Imelda is still here. The Cafrine is in his office, reading *ZENDARM' LA RÉUNION*, the monthly magazine published by the ComGend, a few pages written by young hopefuls for the glory of the Republic, the overseas forces, and their officers. Christos has barely ever glanced at it. There are so many better magazines on the island, usually with topless girls on the covers. Who could possibly want to read a yellow and green magazine in which the very best you could hope for was a short article praising some young, female recruit?

Christos is feeling especially dirty-minded this morning. That desk girl really got him going. He looks over at the hammock and tries to imagine how he might, by some gravity-defying miracle, get Imelda up there and then get on top of her. It would be fun . . .

He didn't insist on going up with Aja in the helicopter belonging to the famous Jipé. It would have given him the chance to get an amazing, panoramic view of the island's tourist highlights: the Trou de Fer, Maïdo, Mafate, Salazie . . .

A unique experience: man alone with the wilderness. And all for free.

But someone had to stay behind to hold the fort. And besides, Christos had no desire to watch Laroche's elite snipers in action. Thirty guys kitted out for a safari, falling from the sky like exterminating angels.

And, facing them, some poor lunatic and a six-year-old girl. Not his thing.

Christos delves into the fridge—the real one, in the little kitchen—and gets himself a Dodo, then goes to find Imelda in the office that he shares with Aja. The Cafrine has given up on *ZENDARM' LA RÉUNION*, and is now reading books on criminology. She looks enraptured.

"Is this O.K.?" she asks.

"Make yourself at home. It's an open house today. Read whatever you want."

Imelda takes him at his word. Christos, beside her, grows bored. He has to face up to facts: the chances of him and his lady friend ending up playing hide-the-salami in the hammock are very low indeed. All the same, there are more plausible alternatives: handcuffs in the top, right-hand drawer, and the bars of the cell in the first room to the left . . . spicy enough to make up for the screw he skipped this morning.

"What are you thinking about, Christos?"

"Nothing."

Imelda puts down a dog-eared book, *Mémoires du RAID*,[41] and stares greedily at the folders piled up on Aja's desk. Christos empties his beer and replies wearily:

"Go ahead. Take a look. It's open bar."

---

[41] "Research. Assistance. Intervention. Deterrence." A special operations unit of the French national police.

10:45 A.M.

Imelda is sitting in Aja's leather chair. On the desk in front of her, two little girls laugh inside a rectangular frame. The captain's kids, no doubt. They look like her own children, except for one difference: they have a Papa to hug them tight.

Imelda carefully reads through all the evidence collected by the force. Interviews with the Hotel Athena's staff and guests. Witness statements relating, directly or indirectly, to Martial Bellion. DNA analyses. Police photographs of the alleged crime scenes—room 38 of the hotel and Chantal Letellier's house—and other pictures supplied by civilians: of the Hotel Athena car park during the afternoon when Liane Bellion disappeared; the Saint-Gilles port around the time when Rodin was murdered; the Garden of Eden, where Bellion and his daughter probably hid out for a few hours.

Imelda tries to memorise it all. Contrary to what Christos believes, she has never thought of herself as having great deductive powers. She simply never forgets a thing. She compiles information, puts it in order, and is therefore able to find what she needs very quickly.

Christos, next to her, is beginning to nod off. The centerfold of *ZENDARM' LA RÉUNION*, where the few women in the marine force pose proudly, falls from his hands. He has come to terms with the reality of the situation. Imelda is a passionate, sensual woman who loves sex, but she is also fairly conventional. Away from their bed, screwing her is mission impossible.

As for his professional duties . . . The telephone in the police station has not rung for more than twenty minutes.

10:51 A.M.

It is at that very moment that he comes in, waking Christos from his nap.

At first glance, the policeman doesn't recognize him in his Ray-Bans, his white linen suit and with droplets of sweat hanging from the little tuft of salt-and-pepper hair under his chin.

"I would like to speak to Captain Aja Purvi."

The second lieutenant identifies his voice immediately, however. Armand Zuttor, the manager of the Athena.

"Sorry, she had to go out."

Christos makes a hand movement that no one but him could possibly recognize as a helicopter taking off.

"Shit," says Zuttor.

"What's up? Lost another guest?"

The hotel manager wipes the sweat from his beard.

"Two!"

"Bloody hell . . . That's all we need. Do I know them?"

"Slightly, yes. It's Jacques and Margaux Jourdain."

The policeman's fingers tense around the glossy paper of *ZENDARM' LA RÉUNION*. He glances at Imelda, bewildered. Zuttor doesn't even seem to have noticed the Cafrine's presence in the room.

"The Jourdains have disappeared?" Christos repeats stupidly.

Zuttor does not appear to be panicking. He sits down, carefully removes his Ray-Bans, takes out a beige silk handkerchief, and pats his forehead dry.

"No, not exactly, Lieutenant. They have simply left the Hotel Athena. They informed me of their decision to spend the rest of their holiday on Mauritius."

Christos rolls his eyes, the magazine in his hands as rigid as a truncheon.

"You can't really blame them," says the hotel manager in

the same blasé tone. "Operation Papangue was not exactly part of their holiday plans."

"The pricks," Christos mutters.

Armand Zuttor smiles. The policeman recalls Jacques Jourdain's favorite pastime: collecting suggestive pictures of girls, including several of Liane Bellion. Suddenly he stands up.

"I don't care if he's a lawyer. Jacques Jourdain and his wife can stick their holiday in Mauritius up their arses. They are key witnesses and as long as Bellion is at large, they're not leaving the island."

The hotel manager shakes his head, seeming either relieved or embarrassed.

"Tanguy Dijoux, the gardener, took them to the airport early this morning."

He falls silent and looks at his watch.

"They're on the plane right now. They have nothing to—'

"You stupid bastard!" Christos yells at him.

Armand Zuttor's complacent smile freezes in place and sweat breaks out over every wrinkle of his face.

"How much did they pay you to keep quiet about this until the plane had taken off?" Christos continues.

Zuttor's thin beige handkerchief is now saturated. The second lieutenant leans towards the hotel manager, towering over him by at least a foot.

"*The customer is always right*—I get it. But spare me your crap about the economic crisis. Don't worry, Zuttor, we'll have someone waiting for them on the runway in Sir Seewoo,[42] or whatever it's called. And that lawyer and his blonde missus had better co-operate if they don't want the Mauritian version of Operation Papangue on their backs."

---

[42] The Sir Seewoosagur Ramgoolam International Airport is the only international airport on Mauritius.

Zuttor looks at his watch again.

"You'd better hurry up, then, Lieutenant. They're due to land in ten minutes."

The police officer whistles through his teeth and applauds sarcastically.

"What can I say, Zuttor? Nicely timed! Mauritius is an independent republic that tends to be rather protective towards its rich foreign visitors."

Christos throws the ZENDARM' LA RÉUNION like a javelin, straight into the stainless-steel waste paper basket.

Clink.

He turns back towards the Athena's manager.

"Then again, Mauritius is not the Cayman Islands. We have agreements in place with all of the Mascarene Islands, to prevent illegal immigration. The judges and the cops will play ball. Your guests shouldn't harbour any illusions: by tomorrow morning, we'll have all the authorisation we need to take them their breakfast in bed. Do you know where they're staying on Mauritius?"

Zuttor grimaces. He twists his Ray-Bans between his fingers.

"The Sapphire Bay Hotel. I found them the hotel myself."

"Why that particular one?"

"The Sapphire Bay consists of fifty beach huts on stilts, sitting right next to a lagoon. My customers didn't have to think about it for very long."

"On Easter Monday . . . Wasn't it fully booked?"

"I know the manager there."

Christos wishes he had time to let this particular hotel manager cool down in the fridge for a few hours before grilling him afterwards, just for the pleasure of it, but he has bigger fish to fry.

"O.K. Give me the address and phone number of the Sapphire Bay, and then piss off."

Zuttor stands up and slowly puts on his sunglasses. For the first time, he notices Imelda's presence behind the desk. The hotel manager stares at the Cafrine.

"And she is . . . ?"

Christos doesn't like the look on his face. In the hotels by the lagoons, the managers probably pay more attention to the palm trees, the deckchairs and the parasols than to the Cafres, Malgaches and Comoriens who work so hard to keep the place clean, like invisible shadows. He decides to lay it on thick.

"Officer Cadet Imelda Cadjee. Don't be fooled by her silence. She's the brains of this place."

Zuttor gives her a suspicious look, then leaves.

11.09 A.M.

"Sapphire Bay Hotel? Do you speak French?"

The guy on the other end of the line answers with a British accent: "Yes, a little bit, monsieur. How can I help you?"

"I'd like to speak to the manager."

The voice hesitates, then simpers:

"Could you give me the reason for your—"

"I'm calling from the Saint-Gilles police station on Réunion Island. It's a matter of life and death. There's a killer on the loose here, Operation Papangue, you'll have seen it on the news?"

The Mauritian receptionist does not seem overly impressed.

"Of course, monsieur. Let me find out if the manager is available."

His composure irritates Christos. He listens as the guy from reception talks to someone else.

"Mike, is Miss Doré in the office?"

Click!

Christos yells into the receiver:

"Graziella Doré? She's the manager of the Sapphire Bay?"

"Yes, monsieur, but—'

"For fuck's sake. Put her on the line!"

This time, he hears footsteps, moving rapidly away. Christos looks out of the window. Zuttor has disappeared.

He doesn't have to wait more than a minute.

Lighter footsteps approach, moving more slowly than the ones that went away. Christos identifies the sound of high heels on tiles, maybe even marble. They come to a halt. There is silence for a second, and then suddenly a cold voice speaks.

"Yes?"

"Graziella Doré?"

"Speaking."

"Second lieutenant Christos Konstantinov. I'm in charge of the investigation into your ex-husband, Martial Bellion."

A sigh of irritation precedes Graziella Doré's reply.

"I have already spoken to the man from the consulate yesterday who questioned me here at the hotel. He assured me he was working in collaboration with the ComGend in Réunion."

Christos signals Imelda to pass him the Bellion folder. He turns the pages with one hand. Almost immediately, he finds three stapled pages. Statement by Graziella Doré, taken down by Officer Daniel Colençon, on Sunday March 31, at 9:17 P.M., in the Sapphire Bay Hotel, on Mauritius. *Daniel Colençon . . .* Christos knows him vaguely, a former officer at the central police station in Saint-Denis who fell into a depression after the riots in Chaudron, and then chose the safety of the consulate on Mauritius. The statement arrived by fax this morning, sent by the ComGend just before everyone rushed off to Chantal Letellier's house. Therefore no one had read it. There was no time. It was just slipped into the folder. And who cared, after all? Bellion was guilty. The only thing that mattered was tracking him down.

"Are you still there, Lieutenant?"

Christos looks up from the statement. He's bored shitless by all this paperwork. He needs to play for time.

"So what are the Jourdains doing at your place?"

She sounds surprised.

"You're very direct, I must say."

"We don't have much time."

"The Jourdains . . . you mean the lawyer from Paris and his wife? Armand Zuttor called me earlier. He's an old friend of mine, so I made a room available. Returning a favor. Shouldn't I have done that?"

"It's fine. It all just seems a very strange coincidence."

Christos reflects that Armand Zuttor must already have been running the Hotel Athena when Graziella Doré was managing the Cap Champagne bar-restaurant in Boucan Canot. People of the same class . . .

Christos puts his finger on the statement. The words dance under his gaze.

"Madame Doré, can you give me a brief summary of what you told Officer Colençon yesterday?"

"Don't the police communicate with each other?"

"We've been a little overwhelmed the last couple of days, sorry. What is your view?"

"I beg your pardon?"

"I imagine you've seen the hunt for your ex-husband on television? There are three people dead so far."

"You want my opinion?"

"Exactly."

"I said this to the man at the consulate yesterday. You are all making a mistake. Martial has nothing to do with these crimes. He wouldn't hurt a fly."

Martial Bellion?

Wouldn't hurt a fly?

Christos curses inwardly. He should have taken the time to read this woman's statement. Daniel Colençon is a bit of a sun-loving layabout, but, as far as Christos can remember, he was pretty good at interrogating witnesses.

"Your ex-husband was found guilty of the accidental death of your son."

For the first time, Graziella Doré's voice sounds less calm, and becomes louder and shriller, like feedback from a microphone.

"What did you read? Judge Martin-Gaillard's report? The newspaper reports? What do you actually *know* about what happened that night? Which statements are you basing your opinion on?"

Christos takes his time before replying. He has the strange impression that the entire investigation is about to be turned on its head, so he weighs his words carefully.

"Martial was not responsible for the death of your son, Alex. Is that what you're telling me?"

"I already told your colleague all this yesterday. Martial wasn't to blame at all, but he shouldered the guilt anyway. They had to have somebody to blame."

Christos tries to think as quickly as possible. What if they've got their thinking back to front, right from the beginning? What if Martial was *not* responsible for the death of his son, but was trying to avenge it, Monte-Cristo style? What if he came to Réunion for that very reason? Christos wishes he had time to ask Imelda's advice.

"Was there someone else on the beach at Boucan Canot that night?"

"It was a long time ago, Lieutenant. It took us years to get over it."

"You have to tell me more, Madame Doré."

"What would it change? What difference would knowing the truth about Alex's death make to your Operation Papangue?"

"Leave the connections between the past and the present to us, Madame Doré. You haven't answered me. Was there someone else on the beach at Boucan Canot?"

"I already explained all this to the man from the consulate yesterday."

Christos closes the Bellion folder. If there had been any interesting evidence in Graziella Doré's statement, the ComGend would have told them about it.

"You didn't tell him anything at all. Nothing about your employees at the Cap Champagne. Nothing about any possible witnesses to Alex's death. Nothing about your reasons for closing the restaurant two months after the tragedy, and leaving the island a few weeks after that."

"Are you studying psychology or something?"

Christos flashes a complicit grin at Imelda.

"Yeah, evening classes."

"Very good, Lieutenant. Don't give up. But listen, for the third time, all I can tell you is that you've got the wrong man. Martial never killed anyone. He wouldn't be capable of it."

"Madame Doré, I'll need more than that to get your ex-husband off the hook. At this very moment, eleven helicopters and more than thirty officers are hunting for him."

"I hope they're using a net. Your men are running after someone who's no more dangerous than a butterfly."

"They're using rifles, madame. And they won't take any risks. They'll shoot him if they get the chance."

For the first time, Graziella Doré seems to hesitate. Christos realizes that he has to offer her a way out. He remembers some of the hare-brained theories he discussed with Aja.

"Madame Doré, could you simply provide me with the names of your employees at the Cap Champagne? The ones who were working there when Alex drowned?"

"It's a long time ago . . . There were lots of them."

"We will find those names, Madame Doré, one way or another."

"Your brain works fast, Lieutenant. Very fast."

"Your turn, then. The ComGend is about to pin down your harmless butterfly and stick him to a board."

"Let me think. If you give me your phone number, I'll—"

"There were seven of them, Madame Doré. I want all seven names."

"That's right, Lieutenant. Seven Creoles. You're better informed than the guy I saw yesterday."

"It's our job. We search, we dig, we make progress. One other thing. Have you heard from the Jourdains?"

"No, nothing yet. There are two glasses of vanilla punch and a bouquet of anthuriums waiting for them on the glass table of their beach hut."

"Ah, paradise! As soon as the Jourdains arrive, please inform Officer Colençon, the man from the consulate. Or there's a good chance the roofs of your beach huts will be blown off by the helicopters of some big bad wolves from the ComGend . . ."

Graziella Doré's voice becomes cold and neutral again, the voice of the manager of a luxury hotel.

"I'll think about it, Lieutenant."

"So, my love, what do you think?"

Christos has just hung up and is waiting impatiently for Imelda's opinion. The Cafrine listened to the entire conversation on loudspeaker.

"It sounds great."

The second lieutenant looks baffled. "What?"

"The Sapphire Bay! Beach huts on stilts by the lagoon. A bouquet of anthuriums. It sounds really nice. You could take me there."

"To Mauritius?"

Christos sits on the desk. The Cafrine is sitting on a chair behind it.

"Isn't Mauritius just a place for young lovers?"

Imelda grabs an eraser from the desk and throws it at Christos. He ducks, laughing.

"Young lovers with no kids!"

While Imelda searches for another projectile, Christos looks down at her. The curves of her ebony skin are visible beneath the low neckline of her dress. He knows how best to win over his black Miss Marple.

"And the Bellion case, my love? Do you have any idea how to solve this strange mystery?"

Imelda forgets her irritation and thinks out loud:

"I don't know, I need to go over it again in my mind. The Jourdains, Armand Zuttor, the employees of the Cap Champagne from ten years ago, those of the Athena today, the relationship between Martial Bellion and his ex-wife, the relationship with his new wife. And with Alex, and Sopha . . ."

Christos is tormented by the desire to pop a button or two on Imelda's dress, just for the pleasure of seeing it. He reaches out. The Cafrine, lost in her thoughts, does not see his hand approaching.

"There's a connection between all these things," she goes on. "Violence doesn't occur by chance. There is always a soil in which it grows."

The second lieutenant leans over further and blows on the Cafrine's neck.

"And there's no lack of fertiliser on this island," he says. "The divide between rich and poor. Mass unemployment. Even racism, if you dig deep enough."

"But that's where you're wrong! That's not the driving force behind violence on the island."

Christos replies automatically, his nose almost pressed between his lover's breasts. He wants to add sex to the long list of motives.

"So what is it then, my love?"

"I don't know . . . I dissect the news every day. There is crime taking place all over the island—abandoned kids, battered women, neighbors killing each other with swords—but the origin of these crimes is somewhere else . . . somewhere hidden."

Imelda follows the thread of her reasoning, thinking about the different fathers of her children. The usual spiral, always the same. Inactivity. Poverty. Drunkenness. Malice. While the women of the island receive and spend their family allowance, the fathers and stepfathers gradually lose whatever dignity they once had.

She whispers, as if it were a secret:

"Hidden inside each man."

Christos does not hear this. He lifts his other hand and leans forward; his fingers are aiming for the top button of Imelda's dress, but then his bottom starts sliding off the desk. Unable to keep his balance, he stops himself falling by desperately grabbing at Imelda, his right hand on her shoulder, his left on her breast.

Imelda recoils.

"Get your hands off me, you filthy pig! I've been here too long already. I need to go home and make curry for my kids."

11:23 A.M.

Imelda's Polo is parked in the post office car park, just after Boulevard Roland-Garros, about fifty meters from the police station. She walks towards it, counting the change in her purse. Almost every day, an old Creole from Grand-Ford parks his van here and sells *chouchous*[43] at unbeatable prices. The tourists never buy them more than once. Generally, they hate *chouchous* as intensely as people from Réunion love them.

---

[43] Edible plants also known as chayotes.

Imelda crosses the street.

Three cars are parked in front of the post office. The farmer's van. A blue Picasso. And a 4x4—a black Chevrolet Captiva.

Imelda cannot take her eyes off this last vehicle—it's a type rarely seen on the island, especially this one, with its twin exhaust pipes and its chrome bull bars protecting the front bumper, the headlights and the bonnet.

Imelda closes her purse, her hand trembling. As incredible as it seems, her memory leaves no room for doubt.

She has seen this 4x4 before! Less than an hour ago, on a photograph in Captain Purvi's file relating to Bellion.

Instinctively, Imelda takes a step sideways to hide behind the flame tree that shades the corner of the street. The *chou-chou* vendor's toothless smile falters as he watches her in amazement. Repeated reading of thrillers has taught Imelda never to believe in coincidences. And yet she has to face facts.

The Chevrolet parked in front of her, a short walk from the Saint-Gilles police station, was also parked in the car park at the Hotel Athena three days ago, on the very afternoon when Liane Bellion disappeared and Rodin was murdered.

32
PLAINE DES SABLES

11:24 A.M.

W e have to keep going, sweetheart."
Martial squints at the horizon. As far as he can see, there is nothing but an ocean of dark ash, a lunar landscape dotted with small, fire-colored islands of lava and blocks of basalt that look like petrified monsters. He judged the distance on the map quite precisely. Even taking the most direct route across the Plaine des Sables, the walk is well over a mile. Over a mile of total exposure between the tree-covered areas of the Plaine des Remparts and the Savane Cimetière.

With each footstep, they leave marks in the ash behind them. The wind is not strong enough to blow away the traces of their footprints completely, but it is strong enough to blow the dust up into their nostrils, their eyes, every orifice. They walk with their mouths closed.

In front of them, Martial spies the road that winds across the plain. Tiny pieces of reddish scoria accumulate along the banks and cover the asphalt, making the road look like a huge slab of rusted iron.

They have to cross it. Then continue. Straight on.

"It's too hot, Papa."

Sopha won't move. She coughs. She is refusing to continue. Martial understands. His daughter is not being capricious. It is sheer madness to expect a small child to cross this desert.

"We have to keep going, Sopha. We have to . . ."

Keep going—where to?

Ahead of them, the black earth seems to have been devoured

by a forest fire, each tree torn down, charred, the hills and the valleys all flattened. As if an angry god wanted to be certain that nothing could live on this plain. That nothing could even pass through and profane its silence. Sopha screams:

"I can't breathe, Papa!"

"O.K. I'll carry you, sweetheart. I'll carry you on my back. We have to cross this place. Once we get to the trees, we'll be fine."

"But there aren't any trees!"

To his left, above them, Martial can make out the car park of the Pas de Bellecombe. The road ends there, on the edge of the volcano's caldera: just beyond it is a basin that extends for more than a thousand feet, the Enclos Fouqué, at the center of which is the Dolomieu Crater. In the half-hour that they have been moving across the plain, Martial has seen three helicopters landing at the car park. Another is moving across the sky in the distance, behind the Piton des Neiges.

Martial's forehead is covered in sweat beneath the 974 baseball cap that he is wearing to hide his face. Above the Pas de Bellecombe, dozens of bright stars reflect the light of the sun.

Car windows? Binoculars? Rifle sights?

Martial reaches out his arms towards Sopha.

"We have to keep going, Sopha, if you want to see Maman. You remember? We mustn't miss the meeting."

11:26 A.M.

Colonel Laroche lets the binoculars fall to his chest. He can see Martial Bellion and his daughter with his naked eye. He turns back towards Andrieux, the GIPN commander who is in control of the sixteen elite snipers awaiting his orders in the car park of the Pas de Bellecombe. The tourists have been moved further back, beyond the helicopters, near the grey building that provides snacks, a picnic room and toilets. And there are no more visitors arriving, because the road has been blocked at Bourg-Murat. Commander Andrieux turns his Sako TRG-42 towards the Plaine des Sables.

"Bellion doesn't appear to be armed. At this distance, I could shoot him without touching the girl. It would all be over before he knew anything about it."

Laroche gazes out towards the caldera of the Enclos Fouqué, and the tiny volcano of Formica Leo. He has worked all over the world, but this island is like nothing he has ever seen before. The dark dust, the canyons, the hills of volcanic debris: it reminds him of the landscape in a western or, worse, a post-apocalyptic thriller. One by one, Laroche looks at the sixteen elite soldiers gripping their precision rifles. The most difficult thing now will not be capturing Martial Bellion, but avoiding any blunders.

"Calm down, Andrieux. The girl isn't Bellion's hostage, she's his daughter. How would it affect her psychologically if she saw her own father being gunned down in front of her? We have scores of men, and Bellion is in the middle of an open, exposed area of over two square miles. All we have to do is surround them and we can take them alive."

11:26 A.M.

"We have to keep going if you want to see Maman," Papa told me.

We have to keep going if you want to see Maman!

It's not true. Papa is a liar!

And I can't keep going. I'm too hot, I'm too weak. I stop and scream:

"I don't believe you any more, Papa. You're lying! You lie *all* the time. Maman is dead. You killed her just like you killed the old lady with the blue hair. What are you going to do now? Kill me too because I can't walk any more?"

Papa reaches out with his arms as if he wants to carry me. But I'm not going to let him.

I sit down. I throw off my shoes, then put my bare feet on the black sand. I put my hands on it too.

It's burning hot! I feel like my skin is going to melt. But I don't care. The black grains of sand bite into my skin as if I was sitting on thousands of ants. I don't move. I wait for them to eat me alive. It shouldn't take more than a few seconds.

I want to die . . .

I want . . .

Without realizing it, I start to fly.

I find myself on Papa's back.

I kick him, but he ignores me. Papa bends down and picks up my shoes. He walks, taking long strides, almost like an astronaut leaping across the moon.

He says, panting loudly:

"You have to believe me, Sopha. I haven't killed anyone, I promise."

"Why are they all after you, then?"

Two other helicopters roar through the sky.

All around us, as if the stones are coming alive, black shadows are moving, forming a circle.

Papa is crazy, with all his talk about a meeting. They've caught us.

The policemen will never let us through now.

"You're hurting me, Papa, you're holding me too tight."
"We have to go faster, Sopha. Look how close they are."

I don't answer, I just kick my feet into his sides. I want to hurt him as much as I can.

11:33 A.M.

Martial's footsteps sink into the ash as if it were wet sand.

The sweat is pouring off him. Sopha is too heavy and she's moving about too much. He won't be able to carry her much further. If he's to have any chance at all, he has to convince her to trust him, to walk next to him.

To gain some time.

"You have to listen to me, Sopha. If the police arrest us, you will never see Maman again. Never."

Sopha's feet kick him in reply. "Liar! Liar!"

Martial sees the dark uniforms swarming on the horizon. He has no choice. He gently puts the little girl on the ground, crouches down and looks her in the eye. He knows there is no room for error now.

And yet, he's bluffing. He has nothing in his hand, no ace up his sleeve.

"Listen, Sopha. Listen carefully. Maman is not dead. If we get past this volcano, if we get to the other side, she'll be there waiting for you. Do you hear me, Sopha? She's waiting for you. Alive!"

Sopha freezes, her face incredulous. Three more helicopters buzz over them.

The plain is shrinking. The stones are moving towards them, closing in on them.

Martial insists:

"She's alive, Sopha. I promise."

And, in his head, he prays that this is true.

PART TWO

33
Inferno

The basalt cave overlooks the Indian Ocean. The swell breaks ceaselessly against the black rock, as if the ocean were determined to win back the few meters of land stolen by the volcano with each eruption. Sometimes, more powerful waves rise up the rock face and a few drops of foam reach the interior of the volcanic cavern. As soon as they touch the rock, they sizzle into a cloud of steam.

The eternal struggle between water and fire.

The sauna of the Danaids.

Liane is going to die here.

Liane's hands are tied behind her back and her feet are bound by metal wire. She woke up like this, in this cave overlooking the ocean. If she crawled, she might be able to reach the entrance of the cave and kneel, but all she would see is the sea, stretching out towards the horizon. It would be suicide to jump into the water: the waves would smash her against the rocks in an instant.

At least that would put an end to her ordeal.

And yet, she has to hold on.

For Sopha.

She has not stopped thinking, ever since she woke up here. It seems likely that she is somewhere between Sainte-Rose and Saint-Philippe, on the east of the island, in one of the cracks formed by lava from the volcano that ran down to the ocean after crossing the coastal road, one of those crevasses accessible only by sea. The last eruption was in December 2010. No geographer bothers making relief maps for such an ephemeral landscape.

Liane can scream and shout all she wants; no one will hear her. The continual roar of the waves drowns out all other sounds. Not that this has stopped her trying, for hours on end. But she no longer has the strength to continue. Her throat is on fire. The sulphur dioxide fumes eat into her larynx with every breath she takes.

What temperature is it in here? A hundred and twenty degrees? More? Her naked skin is permanently covered in sweat and she moves as little as possible. She forces herself to remain clear-headed. To ask herself the right questions.

Though there is only one question, really.

Where is Sopha?

Is Martial with her? Alone with her?

Sopha is in danger. Liane has been over the chain of events ten, twenty times in her head. Everything is clear now. Her own life doesn't matter, not any more. Her death is just a pretext, her body bait, a piece of flesh rotting deep inside a trap.

Sopha is the real target.

Liane doesn't care about dying, but she is enraged at the thought of dying here, powerless. She must hold on, while there is any hope at all.

Where is Sopha?

The only reason she is still alive, after all these hours, is because she needs to find out the answer. She had lain down on the hot rocks and, with her feet, had pushed the most crumbly stones towards the ocean, one by one, gradually digging a little furrow that she slowly enlarged into a tiny basin. Then she began, next to it, to dig ten other little depressions in the rock.

She waited.

When one of the bigger waves crashed into the rocks below, splattering the cave with sea spray that instantly turned to hot steam, a few drops remained trapped in the small crevasses, forming little pools of lukewarm water, no more than a few millimeters in depth. Liane had put her face there—mouth, nostrils, eyes—to capture the dampness on the surface before it evaporated. She did this once, ten times, so that her skin didn't crack like a clay pot that had been left too long in the kiln.

In vain. She quickly realized that this wouldn't be enough and, in any case, she knew she shouldn't drink the salt water. Also, even when it was trapped, the water disappeared too fast through the thousands of tiny fissures in the rock. It was like trying to put out an inferno with a syringe full of water. The few fleeting puddles she caught would only allow her to survive a few hours longer.

Liane sat up to think. She had to find another solution before she went completely crazy.

Where is Sopha?

Liane had torn at her clothes with her teeth, her hands tied behind her back: trying to remove her short skirt, her white cotton camisole, her bra. She spent endless minutes contorting her body, her silk knickers ripped to shreds by the rock. Finally, she was more or less naked, except for a few fragments of cloth that were stuck to her skin, melted into a single layer of magma, like small bits of paper sticking to a forgotten sweet.

Then, Liane had dragged herself to the mouth of the cave and dropped the torn rags into the bowls she had dug in the rock, feeling the sea air against her bare skin. The cloth gradually became wet, holding the moisture a few moments longer before the water escaped into the bowels of the rock. Liane immediately applied the damp fabric to her eyelids, between her breasts, against her belly, until the scraps of cloth dried up.

And then she started again, repeating the same mechanical gestures over and over.

During her contortions, she had managed to break off a piece of rock, a bit like a stalagmite. She quickly abandoned the idea of using it to sever her wire handcuffs, but she did try rubbing it against the rock in order to sharpen it. Liane calculated that the shard, which was less than four inches long, could be held in her palm without it being seen.

A weapon.

If she was ever untied, then maybe she would be able to use it. She had forced herself to believe that it might happen, to prevent herself from going mad.

Where is Sopha?

Now Liane realizes that she has made all the wrong choices; that all her efforts are merely speeding up her death. This pathetic weapon . . . what a ridiculous idea! Her wrists are bleeding profusely from all the movement. She shouldn't have removed her clothes either, as every time her naked skin scrapes against the rock it feels like torture.

Burning.

The fiery coals biting into her feet. The sweat running down her limbs, digging hot furrows into her skin. She feels consumed, irradiated from within.

Was it worse before she stripped off? She can't remember.

And yet she must hold on.

Come up with an answer.

She must find Sopha.

Alive.

34
UP AND AWAY

"There!"

Jipé points to two figures, one tall and one short, walking amid the sea of sand. In the next moment, the Eurocopter Colibri describes a brief arc then swoops down towards the volcano.

Aja's hand tenses around the handle above the door. It has been a long time since she was last in a helicopter. Seven years and six months, to be precise: the day she found out she was pregnant with Jade. Jipé has insisted, several times since then, that this stubborn woman should go up with him again. Aja had known him at primary school in Plateau Caillou; a boy more often to be found perched in the tamarind trees or on the roofs of nearby buildings than in the school playground. He had founded Up and Away at the age of twenty, when Aja was studying law in France. Within a few years, helped by a network of friends, Jean-Pierre Grandin was able to offer the more daring visitor the whole range of island flyovers: by glider, microlight, hang-glider, paraglider, paramotor—and of course, the unmissable helicopter rides.

The Colibri suddenly veers to the right. Straight towards the Dolomieu Crater. Aja has never felt so in the grip of vertigo. Inside each volcanic chimney, she can make out incandescent depths, as if they were flying over a dragon's lair, over Mordor, a forbidden territory from which a fatal burst of flame might leap out at any moment.

Jipé adjusts his sunglasses.

"No need to panic, Aja," he quips. "The volcano's still sleeping. But there is a lot of traffic around this morning . . ."

He points towards the three GIPN Ecureuils flying over the Plaine-des-Palmistes.

"I won't be able to get very close. They'd be only too happy to take away my licence."

Aja understands. Helicopter flights over the island are mainly offered by the two official companies who have a gentlemen's agreement to charge exorbitant fares. More than a thousand euros per hour; the all-inclusive price of an unforgettable experience. Jean-Pierre and his association massively undercut those prices, although Up and Away is not strictly a commercial enterprise; Jean-Pierre is simply happy to take friends on island visits in his personal helicopter, the way others might use their car . . . friends who are members and donors to his association, which costs on average about a hundred euros. Despite the pressure exerted upon it by the official companies, who claimed that the competition was unfair, the court in Saint-Denis had found nothing wrong in Jipé's activities. Up and Away is on good terms with the inhabitants of Les Hauts and their elected officials. During the most recent hurricanes, Dina and Gamède, Jean-Pierre Grandin was one of the few pilots to risk his life in order to take supplies to those living in the Cirque de Mafate, in the famous villages built miles from any tarmacked road, cut off from the rest of the world . . . at least if you disregard the incessant ballet of helicopters full of tourists staring down through their telephoto lenses.

"Shall I drop you at the Pas de Bellecombe car park, Aja? I get the feeling your friends are not going to wait for you before they launch their operation."

The Colibri turns to the left.

Aja grits her teeth. The transparent sides of the helicopter's cockpit enable an extraordinary, 360-degree view of their surroundings. Below them, five Ecureuil AS350s and four police vans are parked in the car park. A dozen armed men are moving around, while twenty others continue to spread out across the Plaine des Sables, slowly encircling the two fugitives. At the center of this circle, Aja sees Martial Bellion, leading Sopha by the hand.

"They've got no chance," she mutters.

Although Aja has not forgotten the three murders committed by Bellion, she cannot help being touched by the escape attempt being made by this man and his daughter: like two exhausted gazelles surrounded by predators that have been cunning enough to drive them onto an exposed plain and then block every exit. The fugitives are still several hundred meters short of the first line of trees, where they might be able to hide themselves, but a barrier of twenty officers, all armed with long-range rifles, is blocking their way. All it would take to end this desperate flight is a single order from Laroche.

It's just a question of seconds now, thinks Aja. Laroche isn't stupid. He wants them alive.

She turns to the pilot.

"Game over, Jipé. Sorry to have bothered you for this, but I'd prefer it if you took me home. I don't really feel like going down there just to congratulate that bastard of a colonel."

"As you wish, honey."

The helicopter begins to ascend again. Aja hangs on, cursing.

"All the same, it's strange that Bellion should get caught out here, on the side of the volcano, in the middle of the Plaine des Sables . . . There are thousands of other places he could have hidden, vast forests, yet he chose the most exposed place on the entire island."

Jipé smiles.

"Is this guy a tourist, or does he know Réunion?"

"Both, actually. But yes, according to his biography, he should know the area quite well."

"You don't say."

The pilot lifts up his sunglasses and smiles with his pale blue eyes. Suddenly he seems highly amused, looking down at the figures of the man and his daughter with admiration.

"What do you mean?"

"If you want my opinion, your Public Enemy Number One has planned a very clever trap, and all the cops on the island have fallen into it."

Aja scans the sides of the volcano. There are dozens of men in position, with Bellion and Sopha at the center. She doesn't understand.

Jipé takes the helicopter up a little higher.

"Not above us, honey. Just behind."

Aja turns her head. She sees the canyon of the Rivière des Remparts. Her gaze wanders down to the river's mouth, the Pointe de la Cayenne, and the housing developments of Saint-Joseph that nibble at every bit of land between the ocean and the ravines.

Suddenly she understands.

She freezes, incapable of staring at anything but the bottom of the deepest ravine on the island, a drop of almost 2,000 meters.

Oh my God . . . Martial Bellion had it all worked out. The precise location. The precise timing of his escape. He has brought all the helicopters to the place he has chosen. He has lured all the cops on the island pursuing him to a single point. And that bastard Laroche fell for it, charged without thinking, him and his army of Zoreilles. Martial has been playing double or quits, but he is the only one who knew the rules.

In the cockpit, Aja shouts:

"We have to land, Jipé! We have to get down there right now and warn them."

"Your wish is my command."

The helicopter heads straight for the volcano. Aja tries to calculate in her head: how much time is left?

A few minutes at most.

And then, the trap Bellion has laid will close on Laroche's men before they even have time to notice it.

35
THE BLACK CHEVROLET

I melda has not moved for more than ten minutes. She continues to stand behind the flame tree, lost in thought, observing the black 4x4.

On the opposite pavement, the *chouchou* vendor watches her suspiciously. Imelda pretends to look in her bag for her mobile phone, then to check one of the apps. No one would guess that her old telephone is incapable of doing anything other than make a simple call. Imelda thinks. The Chevrolet Captiva in front of her was definitely in the Athena's car park on Friday afternoon, the day Liane Bellion disappeared. From experience, the Cafrine does not believe in chance. There is always a good reason why things are where they are. And the same is true for people.

The casing of the phone is warm in her palm. Imelda hesitates. Logically, she ought to call Christos, explain everything to him, give him the registration number. The affair would be dealt with and she would be able to forget about it.

Christos would make fun of her, of course, but if she insisted, he would research the matter. Christos is not a bad man. In fact, he's the best man she's ever known. He is probably also the laziest, the most unfaithful, and the oldest too, the one who comes inside her the quickest and who falls asleep as quickly afterwards; the biggest drinker, the one most hooked on *zamal*, the whitest man she has ever known . . . And yet, there is no such thing as chance. She has observed Christos when he is not playing one of his macho roles—the disillusioned cop, the cynical lover—when, for just a second, he automatically picks up Joly's doll, when he secretly checks that Nazir's scooter is safe, or even when she is reading and she senses his gaze over her shoulder.

Not the gaze of a man made horny by sunshine and alcohol.

But a gaze full of unspoken tenderness.

Yes, when you look more closely, Christos is a man who deserves to be loved.

The Chevrolet Captiva blinks.

Its headlights flash three times. Imelda steps even further behind the tree's trunk, furtively scanning the car park. A man is pointing his key at the vehicle—a Malbar, a barrel-chested man squeezed into a *kurta*, with a khaki cap decorated with a red tiger on his head. He must weigh at least as much as her, but he is a good six inches shorter. Under his left arm, he carries a brown bag stuffed full of food bought at the Case à Pain.

In the next moment, the Malbar vanishes inside his car.

Imelda has to make her decision quickly.

Call Christos and look like an idiot.

Let it slide, and never be able to stop thinking about it.

Or get in her old Polo, which is parked ten meters away, and follow this 4x4. To see where it leads her . . .

There is no such thing as chance.

11:37 A.M.

Print.

Christos leans towards the computer and clicks on the icon.

The old printer wheezes and groans as it spits red letters onto an A4 sheet. Christos had to change the color of the PDF file that Graziella Doré emailed to him, because there's no black ink left in the cartridge and he's never figured out how to change it. The manager of the Sapphire Bay took less than half an hour to make her decision and send him the list of her employees at Cap Champagne. From ten years ago.

Seven names.

The file is dated. Stamped. Signed.

Christos knows he ought to take the time to verify this list, to cross-check it with official registers, to contact each witness and get their version of events.

Later.

His compass is Imelda's instinct. He has to find the connection between the past and the present, the employees of the Cap Champagne and those of the Athena.

Christos snatches the sheet from the printer and curses. The red has turned out pale pink. Apparently the toner is almost finished too.

In the police station, two speakers linked to a PC relay the communications between the various police forces and the ComGend. Christos can follow the hunt for Bellion almost second by second, his imminent arrest, the orders choreographing the helicopter ballet . . . All of them, including Aja and Laroche, have better things to do than to look into a ten-year-old accident and the Creole witnesses who may not have had anything to say.

Christos holds the page close to his eyes. Even in this ludicrously pale ink, he can still read the seven names.

Mohamed Dindane
Reneé-Paule Grégoire
Patricia Toquet
Aloé Nativel
Joël Joyeux
Marie-Joseph Insoudou
François Calixte

Or maybe that should be *Françoise Calixte* . . .

The second lieutenant reads the list again, hesitating over the fourth name, his forehead wrinkling in concentration. Then he folds the sheet and shoves it in his trouser pocket.

He has made his decision.

As he has nothing better to do, he will pay a visit to Armand Zuttor and his employees. Even on Easter Monday, there must be a few of them on duty. It's barely a kilometer from the police station and the rum there is excellent.

11:39 A.M.

The black 4x4 comes to a halt before the stop sign at the exit of L'Ermitage. Imelda has let three cars get between her Polo and the Chevrolet. She has followed it, though, her curiosity too great. And it turns out that tailing someone on the island is not very hard at all: there is only one coast road, and vehicles tend to drive along it for miles without overtaking. Thank goodness—her old red Polo is especially conspicuous with its orange left rear door, which she picked up from a scrapyard. Christos never even bothered repainting it.

The 4x4 goes through Les Avirons. On the road overlooking the gully, a few goats are sharing the sparse tufts of grass, nicely wrapped up with litter. Imelda curses. Is the Malbar going to continue all the way to the windward shore?

With one hand on the steering wheel, she dials her home phone number.

"Nazir? It's Maman."

"What the hell are you doing? We've all been waiting for you!"

"I'm going to be a bit late."

"But you're coming home for dinner, right?"

"Maybe not. Can you look after Dorian, Joly and the little ones?"

"What? No way!"

Inside her Polo, Imelda stifles a curse. The Chevrolet drives slowly through L'Etang-Salé. She imagines Nazir, joint between his lips, too lazy even to get off his arse. She raises her voice:

"Yes, you can, my boy! There's chicken curry in the fridge. Not enough, but you can add some vegetables. Just see what you can find in the garden."

The 4x4 enters Saint-Pierre then turns towards the housing development of Ligne Paradis. Nazir coughs into the phone.

"For God's sake, you can't just . . ."

"You can sort yourself out, for once. Ask Joly to give you a hand." Silence.

For once, Imelda repeats inside her head, they can do without her. She feels like a kid sneaking out to go clubbing, a young lover with a pounding heart. She needs to calm down.

"You'll manage, won't you, eh?"

"You sound excited, Maman. You've found a bloke, haven't you? A real one this time? A Cafre?"

As they approach Ligne Paradis, there is less traffic on the road. Imelda has to be careful if she's to avoid being spotted. She slows down.

"I have to hang up now, Nazir. You're not stupid—you'll manage."

She switches off the mobile phone and places it between her thighs.

The Chevrolet turns left, then right. A few seconds after it, she enters a labyrinth of seedy backstreets. The 4x4 finally goes down Chemin Sapan. A dead end. She parks the Polo at the side of the road. A skinny dog comes over and sniffs at her tyre and a curtain flicks opens in the house opposite; an old woman in a dressing gown stares out at her. Children kick a ball between two rubbish bins.

The *kartié*, or local housing estate, is exactly the same as her own, back in Saint-Louis. At least she feels at home. She gets out of the Polo and walks towards the entrance of the cul-de-sac.

The Chevrolet is parked in front of a little house with a corrugated-iron roof. The luxuriousness of the gleaming 4x4 clashes with the poverty of the house, but Imelda knows that some Creoles would rather live under the stars than deprive themselves of a brand new car.

The Malbar gets out. Vanishes inside the house.

Imelda waits. A minute passes. Her phone rings.

"Maman, it's Nazir."

The Cafrine rolls her eyes. "I'm busy!"

"Maman, can we just have rice instead of the stupid vegetables from the garden? Dorian, Amic and Joly all agree."

For God's sake.

"I'm busy, my boy."

"I understand, Maman. So that's a yes, then?"

Imelda sighs.

"All right. But now listen to me very carefully, Nazir. No more phone calls. If there's an emergency, send me a text. O.K.?"

"O.K.! I'm happy for you, Maman. Enjoy . . ."

Idiot!

He hangs up.

Another minute. Again, Imelda thinks about calling Christos. When she reads thrillers, she is always cursing the protagonists who refuse, for completely implausible reasons, to ask the police for help, then end up getting into deep trouble, if not actually being bumped off.

And now she is making the exact same stupid mistake.

The Malbar comes out of the house. Over his shoulder, he is carrying a bag almost as wide as his torso. He stuffs it into the boot of the Chevrolet. A few moments later, the 4x4 vibrates and the twin exhaust pipes cough out carbon dioxide.

Imelda is unsure whether she should get in her Polo and follow it or stay here and take a closer look at the house. In the end, she is more curious about the house. Besides, the 4x4 has already disappeared up the street.

Imelda waits for several minutes. What if it's a trap? The Malbar might have spotted her car, just like the rest of the *kartié* has—the old woman with her nose stuck to the window, the dog now sniffing her other tyres, or the kids who have, on three separate occasions, come very close to hitting the Polo's bodywork with their ball. And they are getting better.

Imelda gets out of the car.

She has decided just to take a look around the garden. Maybe have a peek through a window, see if she can spot anything. She'll call Christos if she finds anything unusual.

The gate squeaks when she opens it. Imelda pushes a dry eucalyptus branch out of her way, then walks on. The windows are so filthy that it's difficult to see anything inside the house.

Not that there's any need.

The front door is not closed. It's just been pushed to. Besides, the rusty lock does not look like it's been used in several years.

Imelda is aware of how stupid it would be to enter the house. She's read these scenes a thousand times: overly curious witnesses are always caught that way, by being naïve and guileless.

She looks back at the street.

What could happen to her in this *kartié*? In broad daylight? She grew up in a *kartié* just like this one; she has lived there all her life. She knows its codes, its rituals, its spies, the kids yelling in the street, the men you only see after sunset.

Imelda clutches the mobile phone in her hand and checks that she has a signal.

Then she pushes open the door of the house.

11:40 A.M.

The voice, amplified by the megaphone, echoes across the Plaine des Sables.

"Bellion! You are surrounded. Move away from your daughter and put your hands in the air."

Martial squints. Through the grey halo of dust, he can see twenty or so men, separated by gaps of about thirty meters, standing absolutely still like a row of totem poles on the treeless plain. Each one of them is pointing a rifle in his direction.

Sopha's little hand grips his index finger. She speaks in a whisper:

"Are they going to kill us, Papa?"

Martial squats down.

"No, sweetheart. Don't worry. Keep your hand in mine. Whatever you do, don't let go."

Martial stares defiantly at the cops. The closer he comes to the moment of confrontation, the more he experiences a strange feeling of power; a heady sense of invulnerability that makes him more determined than ever. He has the desire, for instance, to position himself between his daughter and those rifles, to protect her from the mercenaries.

But he shouldn't let himself be led astray by this strange euphoria: this paternal boldness is merely a reflex, the survival instinct, an illusion to mask the reality.

Never has he been so irresponsible. Any one of these cops could suddenly lose his cool and press the trigger.

He whispers into his daughter's ear:

"Can you run fast, sweetheart?"

Sopha hesitates, then smiles.

"Yes! I'm the best in the school. And even the boys don't catch me when we play British Bulldog."

"O.K., I believe you. Well, you're going to have to run faster than ever now. But only when I tell you."

The megaphone thunders again:

"Bellion. This is Colonel Laroche. I'm head of the police command on this island. Don't force us to open fire. Move away from your daughter and put your hands in the air. There are at least twenty rifles trained on you."

Martial has to gain himself some time. Just a few seconds more.

Behind the police line, the volcano is calm. There is nothing to hope for on that score: the Piton de la Fournaise is one of the most closely monitored craters on Earth. Each time it awakens, there is a wave of media coverage that leaves no room for surprise.

"Do exactly as I do, Sopha."

Martial lifts his left hand, slowly and very obviously, but leaves his right hand holding his daughter's left.

This is not enough for the megaphone.

"O.K., Bellion. If you refuse to co-operate, we will come and get you. If you move a single step, then you'll get a bullet through your head. With your daughter watching. Understood?"

Off in the distance, Martial sees a helicopter land in the Pas de Bellecombe car park. The occupants start running as soon as they emerge from the doors. He thinks he recognizes Captain Purvi, the policewoman from Saint-Gilles.

He sees her for just a moment.

And then he can't see anything any more.

The helicopters disappear first, along with the volcano.

Five seconds later, the police in front of him are swallowed up.

Another five seconds, and he can't see more than three meters ahead of him.

One second after that, he can't see his feet, or Sopha. All he can feel is her warm hand in his.

"Now, Sopha. Run straight ahead!"

They sprint through the fog.

Double or quits.

Martial has gone hiking on the volcano dozens of times, and each time he has been amazed by this incredible local phenomenon, a temperature inversion. The sudden passage, in the space of a few seconds, from a radiant sun in a clear azure sky, to a bank of fog carried by the sea breeze; first channelled by the canyon of the Rivière des Remparts, but then abruptly bursting out like a swarm of bees, cutting off visibility for kilometers around. Martial has seen so many tourists in T-shirts suddenly shivering in the damp mist, clutching their stupid cameras; he has led so many frustrated visitors through the pea-souper to the panoramic views of Makes, Maïdo, the Pas de Bellecombe . . .

All sound is muffled by the fog. Orders disordered. The noise of footsteps, covering his and Sopha's.

They won't shoot.

Martial knows he must run faster: the fog in the Plaine des Sables could lift at any moment. They will only be saved if they can reach the *avoune*, because the mist hovers around the brush for hours. They will remain invisible long enough to get a significant head start. Then they will lose themselves in Les Hauts de Sainte-Rose. The cops will have no way of guessing in which direction they've gone.

"Do *not* disperse!" Laroche screams into the megaphone. "Form a line! Bellion must not get through."

Martial imagines the cops blindly holding hands, as dangerous as children playing blind man's bluff.

*

Something scratches him, and he could cry for joy.

They have reached the avoune*!*

He hears Sopha panting next to him. They must not say a word, must keep going, keep going, deep into the scrubland.

Martial uses his free hand to push aside invisible branches that claw at their faces and bodies. They move forward as quickly as they can.

They are getting away. They can no longer hear the cops yelling to each other.

They've done it!

All they have to do now is get down to the ocean; reach Anse des Cascades.

They will be there in time for the meeting. They . . .

Suddenly, Martial trips. He lost his concentration, just for a second. A root, a hole in the ground. He puts his hand to one side to regain his balance.

Sopha's damp hand slides from his.

He bites his lip, then whispers:

"Sopha?"

It's impossible to shout. He can't even speak normally—that would be stupid. Sopha must be there, a few meters from him.

The sound of breathing in the pale night.

"Sopha?"

No response. Martial's hands grope about in the mist. White brambles tear at his skin.

He speaks again. As quietly as he can.

"Sweetheart, don't move. I'm coming to find you."

Martial's thoughts are moving at lightning speed. He knows this place. The Savane Cimetière ravine is strewn with uprooted trees, sharp-edged stones, cracks in the earth. Sopha could get lost in an instant, as quickly as a nomad in the desert, surprised by a sandstorm.

"Sopha, I'm here. I'm going to find you. I beg you, don't move."

He said this louder, throwing caution to the wind.

No response. Not even an echo in this cotton-wool air.

Martial forces himself not to scream. He is reliving his worst nightmare.

He is standing on the beach. Alone.

He is screaming at the empty sea.

Screaming his child's name.

"Alex . . ."

37
THE MALBAR'S HOUSE

11:41 A.M.

Encouraged by the heat from the sun at its zenith, Liane moves her pretty white breasts above Martial's stubbly chin. She straddles her husband, the muscles of her long legs so taut that her red G-string bikini looks like it might burst. Lucky Martial, lying beneath her, seems unsure where to put his hands. On that flat stomach? On that back, glistening with oil and sweat? On those round buttocks? Or should he use his mouth to suck those proffered nipples, or to kiss those lips surrounded by a cascade of blonde hair?

Martial has a hard-on: the enlarged A3 photograph leaves no doubt about that.

Little Sopha is playing in the sand, six feet away, in the shade of a palm tree. The Bellions are alone on a beach of black sand. It's L'Etang-Salé: Imelda recognized the spot immediately.

A picture of happiness.

Who could have taken this photograph?

Imelda takes a step back and repeats this simple question in her head.

Who could have taken this picture, this one and the dozens of other photographs of the Bellion family that are pinned to the walls of this filthy house?

Imelda has counted thirty-seven in all, printed in A3 and A4. The strange display makes it look as if a paparazzo has been following the Bellions around ever since they first set foot on the island. The photographs have clearly been taken with a powerful telephoto lens, without Martial and Liane being aware of it. On the terrace of a restaurant, in Saint-Gilles, in the marketplace; outside the Hindu temple of Colosse in Saint-André; in front of a rack of postcards on the main street of Hell-Bourg. But most often it is the stills of little Sopha that seem to have interested the anonymous photographer. Disturbing close-ups of her blue doll's eyes, her freckles, her little dimples. Like any other kid who is the consenting victim of the digital camera, thinks Imelda. Except that the person who took these pictures didn't bother asking Sopha first.

Why?

While she is considering this puzzle, Imelda continually peers through the window to check that nothing has changed on the street outside. Next, she takes a tour of the house. The lair of the Malbar in the black 4x4 looks as if it has been requisitioned at the last moment. The two main rooms—the living room and the bedroom—contain barely any furniture at all: two folding chairs and a Formica table, a mattress on the floor, supplies piled up on the shelf of a cupboard hidden behind a dirty curtain: tinned food, packets of pasta and rice. A gas camping stove has been placed by the side of the sink. The bins are overflowing with pizza boxes and empty cans. Against the wall, there is a row of ten jerrycans of petrol. For what? Imelda wonders. A helicopter? Or a 4x4 that was intending to lose itself for weeks in Les Hauts?

This was the hideout of a criminal on the run, surely. Unexceptional . . . except for those photographs.

All the evidence suggests that the paparazzo was the Malbar himself. She was right: it was not by chance that his Chevrolet Captiva was in the car park of the Hotel Athena the day Liane Bellion disappeared. Imelda feels her excitement growing: she loves such moments, when she begins to see a pattern in the information she's discovered. All she needs is a little bit of time and some concentration and she will be able to solve the puzzle.

Damn it!

A brief, sharp beep indicates that she has just received a message on her mobile phone.

She curses, then reads it.

All fine mum. Got Dori and Jol to cook. Take yr time????

Imelda smiles, almost disappointed that her kids are able to manage without her. She types a brief reply, but continues to think about the Bellions.

Is the Malbar acting on his own account? Or is he being paid to spy on the Bellions? A private detective, perhaps? Not that it really matters; the crucial question is *why*? Why spy on the Bellions? Blackmail? A question of revenge? Jealousy? The possibilities are infinite. And what about the identity of the person who paid for such a service—a family friend? Some lunatic they happened to meet? Or perhaps it was even Liane Bellion herself? There are a multitude of reasons why a woman might pay for someone to spy on her husband, particularly when he has a troubled past and a reputation.

Imelda looks at a picture of Liane Bellion sitting on the terrace of a bar, probably in the port at Saint-Gilles. A short *madras* skirt, bare back, her blonde hair tied in a bun, revealing the nape of her neck. Attractive . . .

Unless it's the other way round, Imelda thinks. Unless it's Martial Bellion who is questioning his wife's fidelity. But, in that case, why ask the photographer to concentrate on pictures of the family? And why ask a Malbar? A Malbar who lives in this miserable *kartié*?

Imelda thinks again about the file she read in the police station, about the way all of the witness statements given by the Hotel Athena's employees put the blame on Bellion. The Hotel Athena was founded by Malbars—the Purvis, a dynasty whose sole heir is now the captain in charge of this investigation.

Another coincidence?

Before going into the windowless bedroom, Imelda again looks out into the street. Everything seems normal. The dog is still trotting around, sniffing at things and adding its urine to the ambient filth. The kids playing football have just begun their thirteenth half-time at the end of the street.

Suddenly, Imelda jumps.

Another message on her mobile.

No worrys. Shd even be sum cury left for tonite. Hope yr imprest! Have a grayt time.

Imelda shivers as she reads the text. Nazir is a good boy really. All he needs is a father to give him a kick up the arse now and then.

Cautiously, she lifts the dirty sheets and then the mattress.

A feeling of triumph explodes inside her: there is a handbag hidden between the bed and the corner of the wall! It seems unlikely that it belongs to the Malbar.

Excitedly, Imelda opens it. Her fingers and her eyes compile a quick inventory. A crimson lipstick, a tube of lip gloss, a Lancel wallet . . . its contents have fallen out into the bag and Imelda rummages around, picking out objects at random: an identity card, a credit card, a Navigo transport pass.

All in the name of Liane Bellion.

The neurons connect inside Imelda's brain. Drawers open in which she can file hypotheses. Did Martial Bellion hide his wife's body here? Did he entrust that vile task to the Malbar? Or has everyone been barking up the wrong tree right from the very beginning? What if Liane Bellion was not murdered in the hotel, but made her elopement look like a murder and then took refuge here, in this house, while all the police on the island were searching for her body?

But why? Was she waiting for someone? Did she want to disappear again? Where would she have gone?

Imelda's fingers suddenly stop rifling through the bag. Out in the street, the dog is barking.

In the next moment, she hears the purr of a car as it slows down outside the house. She instantly recognizes the sound of a powerful engine equipped with a twin exhaust pipe.

A 4x4.

No need to look out of the window to see that it is black and is being driven by a Malbar wearing a baseball cap. She hastily puts the handbag back in its hiding place and rushes back into the main room. She quickly looks around, to check that she has not disturbed anything, then searches for a place to hide.

There is only one, and it's not ideal.

The cupboard.

She yanks the curtain open and assesses the tall, straight compartment where the broom is kept. Imelda is twice as wide as the space, but she pushes in anyway, without even thinking. Her bulging body squeezes between the walls, gets stuck. On the verge of tears, she grabs a hook and pulls with all her might. Her skin is scraped by splinters of wood, her dress is torn, but inch by inch, she manages to squash herself between the cold planks, like thick dough overflowing a tin that is too shallow.

Despairingly, she closes the curtain and, in terror, watches as it sways to and fro for several long seconds.

Imelda holds her breath.

The front door opens.

Through the curtain, she can just about make out the stocky shadow that ambles into the room. The sounds are more explicit. A bag thrown onto the table, the closing of the toilet door, the sound of the flush, of water running into the sink, a few last drops, and then silence once more.

Still Imelda doesn't breathe.

The footsteps prowl around the room, passing the curtain without slowing down, then move off towards the bedroom.

After nearly a minute without breathing, Imelda sucks in some air. Her armpits and her nether regions are damp with sweat. She listens carefully and thinks she can recognize the sound of fabric against skin, the soft thud of clothes hitting the floor, the sharp, brief noise of a zipper, perhaps the zipper of a suitcase.

As if the Malbar is changing his clothes.

The seconds pass slowly, endlessly.

Footsteps approach again. The sound of breathing. The curtain trembles, caresses Imelda's belly.

The sound of water in the sink again, the sound of glass against stainless steel, a bag sliding on a tabletop, and then footsteps fading.

A door bangs shut.

Nothing more.

Imelda waits, all her senses alert.

She waits for a long time. An eternity. The house is silent. She thinks she can almost hear the shouting of the kids, far off, in the street.

But still the Cafrine doesn't move. She has not heard the soft roar of an engine in the street. The Malbar is still there, somewhere close by; she must remain hidden behind the curtain. With infinite caution, she takes the mobile phone from her pocket. She has made her decision: she must get in touch with Christos. She is not taking a risk. Her phone does not make any sound when she sends a text.

Only when she rec—

The ringtone suddenly explodes in the room.

Imelda's eyes look down, terrified, as if hypnotised by the small screen.

All dun all cleand up. Proud of us mum? Do U no wher dish towls r? and the hous keys? and the zamal that Derrik hid?

The message brings a strange smile to Imelda's face.

She was wrong: her kids can't manage without her.

Her final thought.

Suddenly the curtain is wrenched open. The shadow stands before her, a kitchen knife in its hand. Imelda tries to escape. In vain.

She has forced her body into a coffin that is too small for her. She has buried herself alive.

First, she feels the pain in her heart, intense and brief. Her hands try to grasp the curtain, but close on nothing. They tense, paralysed for a few seconds, before falling eventually to her sides, like two weary leaves at the end of two dead branches.

38
UNDER THE CLOUD

11:43 A.M.

P apa?"
It's not a cry, just a whisper in the white night.

Martial's pulse speeds up. Sopha is there, a couple of meters away from him.

"Sopha?"

Their hands find each other instinctively. They do not pronounce another word. Martial pulls his daughter along with him, his stride now confident. The ground descends as they walk. Then it begins to slope more steeply, and the fog thickens.

In the muted atmosphere, everything grows increasingly faint—the policemen's voices, orders bellowed through the megaphone, shouting, random footsteps. The police are now just invisible ghosts scattered by the wind.

Martial and Sopha continue to move further away. Martial knows this place like the back of his hand. He has memorized each square centimeter of the map, he has a good sense of direction, and—if necessary—a compass in his pocket. First they must go along the Savane Cimetière ravine. The terrain, if you cut across to the east of the gully, isn't too dangerous. In general, he keeps to a marshy bit of land that has enough trees to make them invisible from above, even if the fog disperses. The ravine then joins the Rivière de l'Est. After that, they must turn fully towards the east, crossing through Les Hauts de Sainte-Rose and the Bois Blanc forest. A forest of tamarinds, palms and other species, interspersed by lava flows that turned hard and cold decades ago, but also covered in hiking trails that they must avoid. Next, they will approach, under cover until they are as close as possible, Anse des Cascades. Les Hauts de Sainte-Rose is an area planted with sugar cane, ten foot tall, that extends almost as far as the ocean.

According to his calculations, they are about fifteen kilometers from the coast, and it is downhill all the way, a descent of around one thousand seven hundred meters. Sopha will walk for as long as she can. They'll take breaks. He'll carry her.

They are so close to their goal now.

They'll get there.

Just to set his mind at ease, Martial takes the compass from his pocket, then heads north-east, towards a tiny crater whose shape can just be made out through the mist.

"Don't let go of my hand, Sopha. We'll be walking downhill like this for hours yet."

"And Maman will be waiting for us at the bottom?"

"I hope so, sweetheart. Don't talk too much. We should save our strength."

Martial knows that, in about an hour, they will be underneath the layer of cloud again. Then they must be even more vigilant.

12:48 P.M.

Papa looked at his watch and told me we were a bit ahead of time because I'd walked so fast, and not complained. He also told me that all we had to do now was go down into the big field with plants four times taller than me and, afterwards, we'd be there.

"At the meeting?" I asked Papa. "Will we be on time?"

"Yes, sweetheart, if you keep walking like this."

I didn't reply. I still have the message I saw on the car window inside my head.

Anse dé Cascade
Tomoro
4 P.M.
Be ther
Bring the gurl

It's going to be hard.

I haven't said much to Papa, but my feet are hurting, and so are my legs. Everywhere hurts. Maybe Papa guessed that already, because he said we could take a break by the river.

Papa says it's a gully, not a river. A river without water, or hardly any, just a few drops running along the bottom. There's fruit here too. Papa told me we could eat some. All we had to do was pick it from the branches of the trees. There were a few different kinds—grapefruit, clementines. He taught me some other names too—Kaffir limes and guavas.

At the beginning, on the way down, Papa talked to me a lot about all the trees and flowers and fruit. But ever since we stopped for a break, Papa's been far away. Not far away from me, that's not what I mean. He's sitting right next to me, on a rock. It's just that he's not thinking about me any more. That happens a lot. I think he's with my big brother. Alex. The one who's dead. The corners of Papa's eyes look wet.

That's how I guessed he must be talking in his head to Alex, and maybe also some other ghosts from before I was born.

1:03 P.M.

Martial has got up to pick some guavas from the branches that are poking through the mist here and there. He makes a pile at his feet. He'll let Sopha taste them later. He watches his daughter playing. She is trying to build a miniature dam across the gully.

He is amazed by his little girl.

She has already understood when she should transform herself from a charming little chatterbox into someone quiet and discreet, taking refuge in her imagination so that he can be alone in his.

Martial exhales. He pats his pocket with his fingertips and suppresses the desire to roll a joint. Not here. Not now. Not in front of Sopha.

He looks up at a timid patch of blue sky that appears like a small tear in the mist. The patch is in the shape of a heart, with a single white stripe across it.

Just the vapour trail of an aeroplane. His imagination does the rest.

Without knowing why, he starts thinking about Aloé.

Why now?

Why here?

Because of that white arrow? That pierced heart?

The question has tortured him for years. Yet another question without any hint of an answer.

Would Alex still be alive if he hadn't let Aloé take the plane?

39
An Ice Cube, a Girl

1:05 P.M.

C *link. Clink. Clink.*
Christos shakes his glass of punch, making the ice rat-
tle like some jingle from a radio show.
"So?"

The employees of the Athena are all sitting on grey plastic
imitation wicker chairs in a semicircle around the bar where
Christos is standing. The only ones missing are Eve-Marie
Nativel, the cleaning lady, and Tanguy Dijoux, the gardener,
who went to take the Jourdains to the airport. Actually, it's a
little strange that he's not back yet, thinks Christos. It wouldn't
take two hours to get back from Saint-Denis.

The wall that encircles the garden protects them from the
high sun with its shadow. Behind them, in the baking heat, a few
tourists laze about in deckchairs, far enough from the pool not
to be splashed by the children, who are taking turns diving in.

Armand Zuttor is sitting at a distance from everyone else—
both guests and employees—under the shade of a palm tree,
his chair leaning against the trunk.

"So?"

Christos reads the seven names again. Quietly. Slowly.
Pronouncing each syllable as if he were giving dictation to a
class of illiterates.

Mohamed Dindane
Reneé-Paule Grégoire
Patricia Toquet
Aloé Nativel

Joël Joyeux
Marie-Joseph Insoudou
François Calixte . . .
or Françoise . . .
Clink. Clink. Clink.
"Never heard of any of these good people?"

Zuttor looks at his watch wearily, as if he were keeping a record of how many minutes his employees have spent at this interrogation.

On a bank holiday, too.

Christos turns back to the bar and pours himself another glass of punch.

"What, none of them? Come on, Réunion is hardly Australia!"

Gradually, the protective shadow being projected by the wall is moving towards the swimming pool. Christos hasn't planned this, but he hopes that it might help loosen a few tongues. Those who don't reply will risk having to bake in the sun.

Gabin Payet, sitting on the chair directly in front of the second lieutenant, is the first one to feel the heat. Finally he speaks:

"It was a long time ago, Christos. Nearly ten years. Lots of hotels have sprung up since then. With hundreds of beds. Thousands of Creoles who have changed the sheets, served breakfasts, collected the towels. They work for a few weeks, a few months, and then they're off."

Naivo Randrianasoloarimino, who still has another couple of minutes in the shade, adds:

"And they all have the type of Réunion surname very common around here. You know, Hoarau, Payet, Dindane . . ."

Christos grabs the ball.

"But Nativel . . . Are there so many Nativels on the island?"

Gabin, soaked with sweat, his flowery shirt sticking to his brown skin, suddenly stands up. He goes behind the bar, uncaps a Perrier, drops an ice cube and a slice of lemon into a glass, and returns to his seat without a glance at the other employees.

"She's Eve-Marie's niece."

Christos breaks into a grin.

At last, the connection between the past and the present. Eve-Marie Nativel is the main witness against Bellion, the only one who can testify to whether or not Liane Bellion emerged alive from room 38 of the Athena.

"So, what do you want to know about her, Prophet?"

"Everything. Just spit it all out. I'll work out what's important and what's not."

"Won't take long. There's not much to say. I worked at the Bambou Bar at the time. Aloé was employed as a waitress at the Cap Champagne, at the other end of the Boucan Canot beach. She was cute. Really cute, in fact. A pretty little island girl, you know the type. The guests liked her. So did Martial Bellion."

The shadow of the wall has moved further away. Now, all the employees are sweating in the tropical heat. Only Armand Zuttor remains in the cool, beneath his palm tree. Not that this prevents him from looking extremely unhappy. Christos has no desire to speed up the interrogation and spare them all heatstroke.

He drains his punch and asks Gabin:

"So, you knew from the beginning that Martial Bellion wasn't just a tourist but a Zoreille who'd gone back to France? We could have saved ourselves a lot of time if you'd mentioned that earlier."

"No one asked me."

"We might have caught Bellion earlier," Christos continues. "And then maybe Chantal Letellier would still be alive."

"How was I supposed to foresee that? You're the one who's the prophet."

The second lieutenant does not rise to the bait. Aja will deal with Gabin later. He pieces together the scraps of information the barman has given him, and then says:

"O.K. So, Aloé Nativel . . . How much did Bellion like her?"

"She was his mistress," the barman replies, placing his Perrier on the armrest of his chair. "Aloé was just Martial's type."

"Before or after his separation from Graziella Doré?"

"Years after . . . They got divorced in 1999, and Aloé wasn't hired to work at the Cap Champagne until 2002. She was only eighteen. A sweet girl, and a smart cookie too. She was the eldest of five or six kids. And she was totally smitten by little Alex. His mother, the restaurant's boss, spent a lot of time working. The waitress spent more time with the kid. He used to play between the tables on the terrace."

"And Martial Bellion? When did he come onto the scene?"

"He used to come and fetch Alex twice a week from the Cap Champagne. Aloé was there. Little Alex told his dad about his new girlfriend. Bellion wasn't stupid—Aloé Nativel had two qualities that were especially attractive to him. She wore very short skirts that didn't cover up her pretty little arse, and she could take care of a kid who was a bit of a burden for a single father like him."

"She didn't have someone already?"

"Yeah, she did. Some guy who worked out of the port in Pointe des Galets, but he was at sea more often than he was on land. Aloé Nativel was like Super Nanny! A top-class babysitter that Bellion would invite over to his house whenever he could. He'd put her up for the night, feed her dinner, then fuck her brains out."

While Gabin drinks the last of his Perrier with a satisfied sigh, Christos tries to assess the possibilities suggested by Gabin's revelations. Zuttor looks as if he's falling asleep behind his Ray-Bans. Naivo is on his feet, handing out glasses of water to the Athena's employees. The second lieutenant does nothing to stop this, preferring to concentrate on his conversation with Gabin.

"Was Aloé Nativel present the night Alex drowned?" The barman shakes his head.

"No idea. I didn't go to bed with them. You should ask her aunt." Christos curses inwardly. Eve-Marie Nativel appears not to be working today. According to the other employees, she has another client on Mondays, cash in hand. No one knows the client's name. Eve-Marie does not have a mobile phone. To contact her, Christos will have to wait until she gets home, in Kartié Carosse, around 6 P.M. at the earliest.

For fuck's sake.

"So what happened to Aloé?"

"Nothing good. First she was made redundant, like everyone else, when the Cap Champagne closed. And, after Alex died, Martial Bellion had other things to worry about, and he certainly didn't need a babysitter any more. Aloé went back to her sailor."

"And?"

"According to the rumours, he dumped her too. The last I heard, which was at least five years ago, she was working as a whore in Saint-Denis, near the old bus station. I'm not sure I'd even recognise her now if I saw her."

Christos registers this information in silence. He doesn't know why, but Aloé's fate makes him think about Imelda's girls, Joly and Dolaine. About Nazir and his *zamal* too. On this island, if you fall either side of the ridge line, you almost always end up in trouble. Windward or leeward. You either stay in the shade or you spend your entire life getting burned.

The second lieutenant shakes the remains of the ice cubes in his glass one last time.

Clink. Clink. Clink.

The countdown has begun. He has to find Eve-Marie Nativel before 6 P.M. If her testimony isn't solid, then the whole case will collapse. Liane Bellion might have been alive when she left room 38 . . . And if she's not dead, then the charges against Bellion make no sense, despite the bloodstains and the fingerprints on the handle of the knife.

Christos decides to stop formulating theories. It's all becoming too complicated. If he has time, he will call Imelda to keep her up to date and ask what she thinks. He turns to Gabin for one final question:

"I don't suppose you remember his name, do you, Aloé Nativel's sailor boy?"

"I do, actually. I still see him from time to time. A short, stocky guy. He delivers crates of beer to the clubs in the area. He's called Mourougaïne Paniandy."

"Paniandy? He's a Malbar?"

40
The Parable of the Dodos

Laroche looks like an overwhelmed general, taken by surprise by an unforeseen development on the battlefield. He stands on the roof of a police van while the blanket of fog swirls about his face, making his hair go white and lending him the beard of a patriarch. The night-vision binoculars with their infrared beam, which are theoretically capable of helping them track a person in extreme conditions, hang uselessly around his neck.

About twenty officers are wandering around, barely able to recognise each other in the slowly fraying fog, like a riot squad in a square full of smoke after the protesters have thrown all their grenades then dispersed.

Aja approaches, accompanied by Jipé, who is clearly amused. Aja's cool demeanour clashes with the wild-eyed expressions of the other cops. Laroche stares down at her from his high perch. He is too upset to bother with his usual diplomacy.

"Purvi . . . fantastic, that's all we need! Aren't you supposed to be leading the investigation in Saint-Gilles instead of sticking your nose in our business?"

Ordinarily, Aja would have replied without any attempt to be conciliatory, but she does actually feel sorry for the colonel, perched up there like a cockerel crowing orders at the hens below. The news will undoubtedly already have reached France—probably as high up as the Ministry—that a man and his six-year-old daughter have somehow managed to slip through the net, despite there being an unprecedented concentration of forces on the island.

Poor Laroche. He'll probably end up being transferred to Kerguelen, or Crozet, or Tromelin. A police station all of his own, amid the terns and the penguins.

"You think this is funny, Purvi?"

The captain waves the white flag.

"No, Colonel, it makes me feel sorry. Most of all, sorry that I realized too late the cheap trick that Bellion was preparing."

Laroche crouches down and jumps nimbly from the van, testing the grip of his new boots. He acts tough, as if an excess of authority can somehow make up for a lack of efficiency.

"No need to be sorry, Captain. He has us all fooled."

Nervously, he lights a cigarette, then stares with surprise at Jipé's helicopter. The company name, Up and Away, is painted on the side, along with the association's logo—a wading bird in flight. He finishes his inspection with a glance at Jipé's open shirt.

"Captain, did you thumb a lift here? You islanders are obviously more resourceful than I realized . . . And I don't mean that bastard Bellion."

A man wearing a white police hat is moving towards them, clutching a map that flutters in the wind. Rough concentric circles have been traced on it in felt-tip pen. Laroche points at it and gives orders. Spread out in a radius around the volcano. Make a systematic search of the area. Maintain radio contact at all times.

It's a hopeless task, thinks Aja. One hundred square kilometers of forest to search . . .

"Are you interested in the island's inhabitants, Colonel?" she asks. "I have a personal theory that our people are infinitely resourceful. I call it the Dodo Syndrome."

"Aha?"

Laroche watches his men move away through the curtain of mist, their radios crackling like a chorus of cicadas. He takes a drag on his cigarette. If there's any news, he'll be the first to know.

"All right, Purvi, I'll listen. What harm can it do? Teach me about your island. What is this Dodo Syndrome?"

Jipé winks at Aja. The captain doesn't wait to be asked twice.

"People are often surprised, when they come to this island, to discover inhabitants who are not on holiday, who aren't wearing flip-flops or flowery shirts over their tanned torsos. In fact, there are even people here who rush around all day, wearing ties, carrying folders, stuck in traffic jams, as stressed-out as Parisian commuters. So my Dodo Syndrome theory is really just a way of explaining why this idea—that Creoles are lazy by nature, with a tendency to daydream and other such crap—is all just a stupid cliché. You know about the dodo, don't you, Colonel?"

Aja continues, without giving him time to reply:

"You will have seen images of it on the label of Bourbon beer bottles. It's the island's mascot. To be more precise, the experts here call it the *solitaire*. It's very similar to the dodo found in Mauritius. Anyway, the experts think that the dodo, or the *solitaire*, arrived on Réunion by flying here. And then it stayed. Why wouldn't it? This place was an Eden, an island with no predators. No mammals. No great apes, no big cats, no human beings. Not even any snakes or spiders. Our dodo originally resembled an ibis."

Aja points at the slender bird painted on Jipé's helicopter.

"According to studies, it was a kind of streamlined, supersonic bird that could fly across entire oceans. But a few hundred thousand years spent living in paradise changed it completely. Without any enemies to threaten you, why bother flying? The skeletons found on the island are surprising in every possible way. Over successive generations, the dodo's wings gradually atrophied, becoming nothing more than ridiculous, useless little appendages. And then why bother running? Over time, the slim ibises became more like fat geese.

Then why bother reproducing? Egg-laying became rare. Why bother sticking together? The communities fragmented into thousands of isolated families. The skeletons reveal exactly the same evolution in the dodos of Mauritius, the *solitaires* of Réunion Island, the Rodrigues pigeons . . ."

Laroche listens, amused, to Aja's fable, while remaining alert for the faintest crackle from his walkie-talkie.

"So what, Purvi? You can't blame the birds, can you? They discovered paradise in these remote islands. They chilled out for hundreds of thousands of years. As for your aesthetic judgements about their obesity . . . well, at least your fowl had the privilege of becoming a species that was completely unique."

Aja smiles. It's not that Laroche is stupid. It's simply that she doesn't want to play on the same team as him. She watches the last members of the commando unit move across the Pas de Bellecombe car park. Helicopter pilots. Elite snipers. Radio operators. All of them white. Every single one.

Aja looks Laroche straight in the eye.

"The dodos were fatally naïve. They forgot that there is no such thing as paradise. No one will ever know how many thousands of them were here when the first colonists arrived on the island in 1665. The dodos did not flee from the sailors. Quite the contrary. They had forgotten what fear was. And by the time they rediscovered it, it was too late. They no longer had wings to fly with, no longer had the strength to run away, no longer had the courage to unite and defend themselves. The dodos were all slaughtered in less than one generation. By the end of the seventeenth century, there was not a single one left on any of the Mascarene Islands."

Aja falls silent. Laroche spits his cigarette stub out onto the ground.

"And the moral of your story, Captain Purvi? I presume there must be one?"

"You're an educated man, Colonel. I don't need to dot the i's for you. All of the dominant majorities, every elite, has sought to transform us into dodos. They want a nice, quiet henhouse. Comfort, safety, laziness. Those islanders who calculate their welfare benefit in terms of how many liters of Charrette rum it will buy them wouldn't disagree."

Laroche pulls a face and Jipé laughs. The colonel hesitates, then claps his hands.

"O.K., Purvi, I get it. Dodos, inhabitants of remote islands, women in the police force . . . same fate, same battle. Thank you for the geography lesson. I'd like to continue our discussion some day. I've been around a few of the other French islands—the Antilles, Mayotte, New Caledonia—and I would say you don't realize how lucky you are here. Your island is a pacified Garden of Eden, it's almost unique in the world, without any racism or ethnic tension."

Aja maintains eye contact with the colonel. She doesn't confirm or deny his statement.

Laroche smiles, shrugs, and puts his hands on his belt. Like a cerebral cowboy, straight out of a Clint Eastwood film.

"Well, Captain, we can sermonise on this later, if you like. Just one thing: I don't suppose you've had any news about the murders of Rodin or Chantal Letellier?"

"I've delegated, Colonel," Aja replies. "If I had any new information at all, you would be the first to know."

Laroche nods, then turns around to talk to a technician while Aja walks towards Jipé. She checks that Laroche is not listening to her any more.

"There's one question that keeps bugging me, Jipé. Why the hell do you think Bellion climbed up here with his daughter?"

"That's obvious, isn't it? Because of the microclimate. Because the fog is at its densest here, this is where it rises out of the canyon the fastest."

"All right, but if Bellion had wanted to disappear into scrubland, he could have left his Nissan wherever he wanted and gone straight into a forest. Bébour, Bélouve, Plaine des Lianes . . . there's no shortage of them. And he wouldn't have had to take any risks, or give us any clue to his whereabouts."

"What are you thinking, Aja?"

"I've been turning this over in my mind. If he came up here, there's only one explanation. He wanted to get to the other side of the volcano. He'd have had no chance along the coast road— he'd almost certainly have been caught. So there was only one solution: cut across the peak and try to get there on foot."

Jipé thinks about this, going through his mental map of the island.

"So Bellion is headed somewhere between Saint-Benoît and Saint-Philippe? That's nearly sixty kilometers of coastline to search."

"Too much, I know. Especially as I feel sure he'll reappear somewhere, and then go and vanish again straight afterwards. It's what he's done so far."

Jipé looks up. Laroche is walking around the car park in his boots, mobile phone clamped to his ear.

"Are you going to mention this to the boss?"

"No fucking way!"

Halfway down the mountainside, the fog is beginning to disperse. At last, Aja can see a patch of ocean, to the east.

"Jipé, we have to be able to react if Bellion appears again . . . and we have to do it quickly. Could you lend me some equipment?"

"What kind of equipment?"

She hesitates, lowers her voice, and pulls the pilot further away from Laroche.

"Equipment for making a descent of two thousand meters in less than a minute. You know what I mean. A deltaplane, a paraglider, something like that."

Jipé purses his lips, then looks over at the last members of the commando unit on the Pas de Bellecombe.

"I don't want to make things difficult for you, Aja, but if I stick one of those X-men in a glider and let them go with the trade winds, they'll end up in the middle of the Dolomieu, burned to a cinder."

Aja winks and says in a whisper:

"I'm not talking about those clowns, Jipé. If you can get the stuff up here in one of your containers, I can pick out twelve of the most qualified and experienced officers from the island."

Suddenly the sky opens up and sunlight floods down on them. Jipé grabs his sunglasses with professional efficiency.

"You'll never give up, will you?"

She laughs.

"No way! It's the Dodo Syndrome! I don't want to end up all fat and flightless, ready to be plucked."

"Laroche isn't going to like it."

"Who cares?"

1:27 P.M.

"Aja? It's Christos! Are you still on the Pas de Bellecombe?"

"Yes. Have you been listening to the radio? Are you calling for a laugh?"

"No, just the opposite."

"What?"

"Just wait a bit before you take out Bellion. I think I've uncovered a fault in our theory, the kind of thing that could make a whole cathedral come tumbling down."

"Could you be a bit less abstract, Christos?"

"I have my doubts about the impartiality of Eve-Marie Nativel's testimony."

"Fuck! Can you give me the details?"

The second lieutenant fills her in on Armand Zuttor's visit to the police station, the Jourdains' escape to Mauritius, the telephone conversation with Graziella Doré, the list of seven employees, the interrogation at the Hotel Athena, Gabin's account . . .

"Fuck," Aja curses into the phone again. "How on earth will we make the ComGend swallow that? Laroche is not the kind of guy to change his mind over some vague family connection between Creole witnesses to an accident that happened ten years ago."

"Mmm. But there's more to it than that. It's strange. When the ComGend drew up the list of Martial Bellion's possible contacts on the island in order to put them under surveillance, why did they never mention Aloé Nativel, his ex-girlfriend? They must have known about her existence."

Aja takes some time to think about this, but can come up with no explanation.

"I'm stuck here, Christos. Bellion might appear out of the mist at any moment. But I want you to forsake your siesta and find me Eve-Marie Nativel before sundown."

"Easier said than done, Aja. According to the other employees, she spends all day Monday working for a Gros Blanc who pays her under the counter. And no Creole is ever going to snitch on their employer . . ."

Aja does not reply. All Christos can hear is the sound of the wind blowing.

"Aja? Are you still there?"

"I think I might have an idea."

"You know a Creole who'd flip the old Nativel woman?"

"Yep . . . Laila . . ."

"Who?"

"Laila Purvi. My mother!"

41
The Lady with the Umbrella

3:27 P.M.

Martial and Sopha push through the huge stalks of sugar cane, being careful to remain hidden from view by these plants that grow up to ten feet high. They are climbing the lower slopes of the Piton Moka.

"Move out of the way, Papa, I can't see anything."

The green and yellow fields slope down in bands towards the ocean, bordered by narrow grey lava flows. Probably the most monotonous-looking landscape on the island. Only the bell tower of Notre-Dame-des-Laves rises above the sugar cane, like a miniature replica of Chartres Cathedral emerging from the middle of the Beauce plain.

A natural labyrinth; Martial has studied the map of it in detail. The Piton Moka is an old eroded crater with a peak of less than five hundred meters. It pales in comparison to the gigantic Dolomieu, in the shadow of which it lies, but it does offer a panoramic view of the entire south-east coast of the island.

Sopha, standing on tiptoes, stares wide-eyed.

"Why is the blue lady down there holding an umbrella?"

Martial's gaze lingers on the spot pointed out by his daughter, almost directly beneath the dirty, pink bell tower of Notre-Dame-des-Laves. The statue of Mary wearing a crown, praying with her hands together, stands at the entrance to the village of Sainte-Rose and is unremarkable, with the exception of one incongruous detail: above the head of the Virgin is a large umbrella, painted the same azure-blue as her tunic, which is fastened with a gold clasp.

"She's the lady who protects us from the volcano erupting, sweetheart. She's famous here. You see all those flowers at her feet? Those are to thank her."

"Is it because of her that the police didn't catch us?"

"Maybe."

"Then I'll bring her some flowers too. I'll come with Maman."

Martial can feel his heart racing. He steers his daughter behind him so that she remains hidden by the vegetation. At this altitude, the fog has completely disappeared. He takes the 1/25,000 map from his pocket, just to check their location. There is less than a kilometer to go. They just have to descend through the Ravine des Bambous to reach the ocean.

"We've made it, sweetheart! Look down there, do you see the big black rocks stretching into the sea. That's Anse des Cascades."

"And that's where we'll find Ma—'

Martial's hand covers Sopha's mouth before she can finish her sentence. A horrible wet handkerchief tears at her lips and pushes into her mouth.

3:41 P.M.

"You're hurting me, Papa."

The thing with the hankie was because I wanted to talk about Maman. Every time I mention her, Papa finds some way of not answering me.

Finally, Papa pulls the cloth from my mouth and shows it to me.

I take a step back. Frightened.

The handkerchief is all red!

I put my finger to my face. I don't understand—it doesn't hurt.

Papa continues to smile, as if it's no big deal. It takes me a few seconds to understand. It's true, I'd almost forgotten: a little bit higher up, we found fruit in the trees. Guavas, they're called. I *loved* them and I stuffed my face, almost as much as I do when I go blackberry picking with Maman in the Fôret de Montmorency.

Papa explained to me that here, guava trees take the place of other trees so quickly that people tear them down whenever they find them.

That's just silly.

"Am I clean now, Papa?"

"Nearly. You looked like you were wearing lipstick. Do you want me to carry you, sweetheart?"

"I'm not tired."

And it's true. I'm not tired . . . I'm exhausted! But I don't want Papa to know that. I haven't walked all the way down the mountain from the moon just to fall asleep now. In a few more minutes, we'll see Maman again!

Down there, in Anse des Cascades.

Unless Papa has been lying to me from the beginning.

"You have been an incredibly brave girl," he tells me. "But before we reach the sea, we have to cross one more road, and they mustn't recognize us. The police are searching everywhere for us. And now they know you're disguised as a boy."

"What difference would it make if you carried me?"

"Papa has thought of everything."

Papa leans down and takes a dirty, ugly blanket from the bag. I recognize it: he took it from the garage belonging to the blue-haired lady, who is now in the bottomless hole with her car.

"I'm going to wrap it around you, sweetheart, and I'm going to carry you in my arms. It might look as if I'm carrying some wood, or cane stalks for burning, or screwpine leaves for weaving, the way people do here."

I have no idea what he's talking about. Papa holds out his arms to me.

"Come on, darling."

For a long time I hesitate, but then I do as he says. I hold out my arms to Papa.

As soon as my feet leave the ground, I feel tiredness falling on me like a blanket, covering my whole body, even warmer and darker than the real one wrapped around me.

3:43 P.M.

Martial sets off. Walking down the Ravine des Bambous takes him less than ten minutes. Sopha, shattered, yawns in his arms. As they get closer to the coast road, he covers her head with the blanket.

The last hurdle.

The road seems deserted. Martial was expecting this; it is the quietest part of the island, about ten kilometers of coastal land without a single inhabitant. Over the past decade, streams of lava have flowed down to the ocean in this area every other year, burning everything in their path. What kind of madman would build a house here?

Martial, hidden at the edge of the cane field, waits patiently, cautiously scanning his surroundings. He must remain vigilant, even if the cops have no clue as to the direction he and Sopha took after leaving the Plaine des Sables. Sopha is sleeping sweetly in his arms, and his arms are trembling, though not from his daughter's weight.

They are trembling with apprehension.

He thinks again about those words traced in haste on the window of the grey Clio.

Anse dé Cascade
Tomoro

4 P.M.

Be ther

Bring the gurl

So close to reaching his objective, it suddenly crosses his mind that he might have been better off letting the cops arrest him. Confessing everything. In trying to save Liane, hasn't he put Sopha in even greater danger? Martial strokes the blanket softly, gently singing a Creole song into her ear.

It's been ten years since he last sung it.

In the Hauts, lost in the mountains

No fog, no lil' birds, few lil' streams

Just call Marla, to get there, you must be brave.

Sopha is rocked to sleep in his arms. Her breathing grows steadier, calmer, more trusting.

Call Sopha, to get there, you must be brave

He checks his watch. He'll be on time.

3:57 P.M.

Martial waits for two cars and a rental van to pass, then crosses the road. No sign of any police.

L'Anse des Cascades suddenly appears in all its glory. An aquatic wonderland set among palms, tropical almond trees and screwpines that look as if they have been planted there by a meticulous gardener. The landscape is backed by an enormous ridge of volcanic rock from which thunders an endless waterfall. The water is whisked away by a stream that winds between a bridge and rocks, then joins the sea, disappearing into a beach of huge coal-black pebbles. In stark contrast to this romantic oasis, waves crash down onto the rocky coastline with such ferocity that it is hard to imagine how the dozen fishermen's boats lined up along the fragile pier could ever risk venturing out onto the ocean.

Martial advances cautiously. Picnickers have taken over the huts, tables and wooden benches beneath the shade of the forest. Their cars are parked on the neatly mowed lawn that serves as a car park.

Only one vehicle has broken the rules. It is parked in the most inaccessible spot, beyond the pier, behind the pebble riprap.

A black 4x4. A Chevrolet Captiva.

A man stands in front of the 4x4. Short, bulky, dark-skinned, wearing a khaki cap with a tiger's head embroidered on it.

Martial does not understand. His fingers tense around the beige blanket.

He walks another ten meters.

The Malbar stares at him, smiling, as if he has been waiting for him. Suddenly Martial freezes. His heart is pounding inside his paralysed body.

Now he recognizes the person in front of him.

42
Fé lève lo mort

3:29 P.M.

The old Creole lady does not go inside the police station. She puts her large canvas bag on a step and simply waits in the doorway for someone to notice her.

Christos sees her when he goes out for a cigarette in the car park: how long has she been standing there? A few minutes? An hour?

"Lieutenant Konstantinov?" she asks in a slow voice. "It was Laila Purvi, the mother of your captain, who convinced me to come here. I hope it's important. The bosses don't like it when you leave their veranda half-*déblèyée*."[44]

"Well, that depends on you, Eve-Marie. Entirely on you. Please, come in."

Christos puts his packet of cigarettes in his pocket but Eve-Marie Nativel has not moved. Did she even hear him?

"No," she mutters finally. "No. I haven't come to make a . . . what do you call it?"

"A statement?"

"Yes, a statement. I've just come to . . ."

The old Creole woman stares at the red, white and blue flag that hangs limply over the police station.

"To tell me a story?" the second lieutenant guesses. "The story of your niece, Aloé?"

"Because I promised Laila."

[44] Cleaned.

Christos looks up. The old woman's eyes are the same lagoon-blue as the Creole scarf that covers her hair. Fifty meters in front of them, between the houses, he catches a glimpse of the almost empty beach.

"Would you prefer to go for a walk?"

Eve-Marie smiles.

"That's a good idea, Lieutenant. Would you carry my bag?"

They walk side by side towards the beach, in the middle of the street. There are no cars to disturb them. They pass the orange sign for the hairdressing salon, Mandarine Coiffure.

"You're a secretive person, Eve-Marie."

The old Creole woman breathes heavily as she walks.

"I told the police everything I thought was relevant, Lieutenant. Not once did I lie."

"So you still maintain that you never saw Liane Bellion come out of room 38 of the Athena?"

A deep breath.

"Yes."

"And that Martial Bellion borrowed your laundry cart?"

A pause. In the middle of the road. Two scooters almost run them over, before disappearing towards the port.

"Yes, that too. Everything happened exactly as I told you."

"But you forgot to mention that you knew Martial Bellion. That he used to live with your niece, Aloé Nativel, ten years ago."

They start walking again. The beach is straight ahead of them, after the Paul et Virginie restaurant. Thirty meters. An eternity.

"Lieutenant, what possible link could there be between that old story and the disappearance of Liane Bellion?"

"You tell me, Eve-Marie. Tell me about your niece."

The old Creole stops again. A few tears well up in the corners of her wrinkled eyes. Christos takes her arm, like an attentive son-in-law. He supports her as they move forward, step by step, towards the sand.

"Aloé was a wonderful girl, Lieutenant. An adorable child who raised her four brothers and sisters without a single word of complaint. So pretty! And she smelled good too. Like vanilla. There was always vanilla growing in my garden in Carosse and she used to spend hours there, every evening after school. That's why I didn't tell you about her. *Fé lève lo mort*,[45] Lieutenant . . ."

Fé lève lo mort?

They walk down a short concrete stairway to the beach, Eve-Marie stopping on almost every one of its nine steps. When they reach the last one, she leans on the second lieutenant's shoulder and takes forever to remove her shoes. Holding her canvas sandals in one hand, she walks carefully over the sand.

"I already know this story, Eve-Marie." Christos chooses his words carefully. "I know she had a hard life, that her boyfriends left her . . . Martial Bellion, Mourougaïne Paniandy. That the Cap Champagne closed down. But I need to ask you a very precise question, Eve-Marie. Aloé was very close to little Alex Bellion. She took more care of him than his own parents did. Was she at Boucan Canot the night he drowned, on May 3, 2003? Could she, in any way, be considered responsible for that little boy's death?"

Eve-Marie stands still. For a long time, she watches a tropicbird gliding above them, then responds with a hint of anger:

"So that's what this is about? That's what you're so worked up about? You think I lied to protect my niece?"

Eve-Marie's cracked laughter echoes over the lagoon.

"My God . . . Poor Aloé . . ."

---

[45] It is dangerous to bring back the past.

The old Creole woman sits down and pours thousands of grains of sand through her wrinkled fingers. Christos hesitates for a moment, then sits down beside her.

"Aloé and Martial Bellion made a lovely couple. He was much better suited to her than that brute Mourougaïne, even if he was older than her, even if, with each passing week, he was taking more care of his son. His pretty, young Creole nanny was becoming less useful to him. Aloé could see the way things were going: he would leave her eventually, for another girl, not so young perhaps, but just as pretty."

"You haven't answered my question, Eve-Marie. Martial Bellion was accused of having caused an accidental death. He was the only one named by the judge, Martin-Gaillard. Where was Aloé on May 3, 2003, the day Alex drowned?"

"Far away."

Eve-Marie's eyes stare up at the sky.

"Further away than the tropicbirds fly."

Is this woman crazy?

The Creole woman anticipates the second lieutenant's doubts. She takes his hand, her fingers trembling almost as much as her voice.

"Aloé thought she was seizing the opportunity of a lifetime. She had gone to an audition on the beach, in the summer of 2002. She had to dance in a bikini on a podium under coconut trees, in front of a beautiful sunset. That kind of thing. They called her in the autumn that year and hired her for a video shoot that was going to take place in France. The song wasn't even a *séga* from Réunion, just some Antilles *zouk*, I think. Her flight and hotel were all paid for. The video was shown on television quite a few times back then, mostly on Channel 6. You could see my little Aloé, dancing behind a handsome black singer, surrounded by a dozen other mixed-race girls in bikinis, all of them just as pretty as her. Then she came back to the island and they never called her again."

"So, on May 3, 2003, Aloé was in France?"

"Yes. It shouldn't be too hard to check. There must be records of that kind of thing."

Another strange coincidence . . . Of course, they will check.

And yet Christos hears himself saying: "I don't think there's any need. Would it be possible to meet Aloé?"

The wrinkled hand turns to dead wood. Eve-Marie's eyes fill with tears once more.

"You haven't understood?"

Christos gently strokes the old woman's withered arm, as if he were trying to calm down a frightened *tec-tec*.

"Understood what?"

"Why I never told you about Aloé."

"When things went wrong for her, she sold her body. Is that what you didn't want to tell me?"

The fingers of Eve-Marie's left hand trace small circles in the sand.

"She called herself Vanilla. That was the only name her clients knew her by—I found that out later. She never came back to see me in Carosse. She was in great demand, apparently. Rich men. She made a lot of money."

The palm of her hand covers the circles like a sudden sandstorm. "But she spent more and more of it. And the more money she needed, the less she earned."

"*Zamal?*"

Eve-Marie smiles.

"Heroin, Lieutenant. Her body was found on November 17, 2009 in the pool by the Maniquet waterfall, just above Saint-Denis. An overdose, according to the experts. The newspapers here ran a few lines on the death of a *pitin*[46] nicknamed Vanilla. No one ever knew her real name, apart from the

---

[46] Whore.

police, her brothers and sisters, her parents, and me. Even Martial doesn't know."

"I'm sorry, Eve-Marie."

"Don't be, Lieutenant. It's not your fault. At least you can understand now why I didn't want to talk about my little Aloé. It's not easy to hide family secrets on this island."

Eve-Marie allows a few last grains of sand to cascade through her fingers.

"Shall we go back, Lieutenant?"

4:00 P.M.

Christos and Eve-Marie are standing in front of the station door. They walked here in near-silence from the beach. Not once did the idea that Eve-Marie might be lying to him cross the second lieutenant's mind.

"Thank you for the walk, Lieutenant."

"My pleasure, Eve."

Christos realizes he means it.

Eve-Marie picks up her bag, then shuffles across the car park. Before she is out of earshot, she turns back to the policeman one last time.

"I can tell that you're going to keep racking your brains, trying to find out who is responsible for Alex's death. But, Lieutenant, maybe there is no one to blame. Maybe it was just chance, maybe there was nothing anyone could have done to change it. That is where all the hatred in this world comes from, Lieutenant, all the wars: we always have to find someone to blame, for all the misfortune in the universe. Even when there is no one to blame, our mind invents someone or something. That must be hard to admit when you're a cop, the idea that we are so desperate to find someone to blame that we make them up."

Christos is immobile, unable to interrupt the Creole woman's tirade. Her blue eyes stare into his.

"*I fé pa la bou avan la pli*,[47] Lieutenant. Do you understand that? When we are unhappy, we survive by blaming the whole world, or sometimes just one person—one person we can attack in order to make ourselves feel better. Don't you think?"

"I don't know. You're saying that no one is responsible for little Alex's death, yet we have a murderer on the loose on this island . . ."

The policeman is engulfed in Eve-Marie's gaze.

"That is what I'm trying to explain to you, Lieutenant. *I fé pa la bou avan la pli*. When tragedy hits us, we refuse to admit that there is no one we can punish. So, to reduce our suffering, we invent an act of revenge."

We invent an act of revenge, Christos repeats in his head.

Is the old woman crazy or is she trying to tell him something else? A coded truth? The name of a murderer who is not Martial Bellion?

As a swarm of contradictory theories fly around his head, inside the station a telephone rings.

---

[47] Réunion Island proverb: One should not confuse the consequences of an act with its causes.

43
Joint Custody

Martial has stopped twenty meters away from the Malbar. Incapable of walking any further. He puts the blanket in which Sopha has fallen asleep on the ground. The Malbar, behind the black 4x4, watches him do this, his face shaded by the khaki cap. Behind him, the waves pummel the black rocks of L'Anse des Cascades in an explosion of foam.

Martial is unsure whether he should keep moving forward or just run away.

He doesn't move.

He stares intently at the Malbar and thinks again about the message.

Anse dé Cascade

Be ther

He realizes that he cannot fight his memories any longer; they overflow, rising to the surface, electrifying all of his senses. This time, he lets the past conquer him.

His thoughts are wild, panicked. Images from long ago rush at him, his lips recounting the past to himself, opening and closing though no sound emerges.

It all happened on May 3, 2003.

It was evening, a Saturday, and it was Graziella's turn to look after our son. Unusually, I was alone. My girlfriend at the time, Aloé, had just flown to France for a video shoot. The break was quite well-timed, and I think we both knew it. Time to go our separate ways . . .

*

4:02 P.M.

Graziella Doré tucks a strand of long hair behind her ear. She does it carefully, as if afraid she might tear it out, then turns towards the Indian Ocean.

For a second, she thinks about her phone conversation with that officer. Is he capable of working anything out? No, probably not. He didn't seem overly zealous. He'd go running off after shadows as soon as anyone waved some puppets in front of his eyes.

A lazy little lapdog.

She should concentrate, instead of endlessly rewatching the same old film. Act. React. But is it even possible to forget?

Each wave that crashes at her feet reminds her of Alex.

How can she fight it?

Flashes of memory submerge her. The lagoon. The Hotel Athena. Martial's escape. The dead. Some of whom died recently, others a long time ago.

The dead pull at her legs so that she can't forget them. This time, Graziella doesn't push them away.

It was so long ago . . .

To be exact, thinks Graziella, it was May 3, 2003. I was obsessed with only one thing back then.

That Martial would never leave me.

He could cheat on me with other, prettier women—with little Aloé Nativel, for example—he could spend his nights drinking with other men, he could come round only when he felt like it and take advantage of my money, the cooks in my restaurant, my bed, my body, but he couldn't—mustn't—ever leave me.

He couldn't fall in love with anyone else.

I had invested everything in him, like a gambler staking all his savings on a single roulette number at the casino. I had chosen him from among dozens of possible men. I felt certain that I would be able to change him—and I did. He was young, as malleable as clay, a rough diamond to be cut and polished, a lode of some rare mineral that I alone had detected and knew how to exploit. All of my sacrifices were bearable because our relationship was a long-term undertaking, the strength and balance of which could only be measured years later. What I was building took time and patience.

I had gambled on Martial despite all my other dreams, my other passions, the infinite possibilities that life offered me, like a student ready to jettison her youth, to work night and day with the sole aim of gaining an unattainable diploma.

I had chosen him to be the father of my child.

No. So Martial couldn't just leave me for any little slut who happened to pass by.

That is why, that night, I backed him into a corner.

4:03 P.M.

Graziella called me less than three hours after Aloé's plane took off. I had driven Aloé to Roland-Garros airport. Graziella had probably found out that my girlfriend was leaving for Paris, and that no one seemed to know when she was coming back.

"I need you to look after Alex tonight. Yes, I know it's my turn, but I need you to come. I have a date tonight. With a man. It's the first time, Martial. Please, help me out here. Come to Cap Champagne and pick up Alex by 10 P.M. at the latest."

She was bluffing. I felt sure she was bluffing. There was no other man, no date. Once again, she was using Alex as a pretext to make me come running whenever she whistled, to yell at me about my supposed obligations to her and our son. Trying her luck, because she knew I was free again.

4:04 P.M.

Martial was too proud to believe it, but I wasn't bluffing that night. For the first time, I was being honest. I really had decided to give myself to another man. Fabrice Martin was an environmental lawyer. He was rich and he defended the island's biodiversity by expelling farmers from protected areas in Les Hauts, even if they had lived there for five generations. He wasn't very good-looking, now that I think about it. Even if he ran for two hours every day in the sun and took off his shirt and tie at every opportunity so I could admire his sculpted torso, he still looked like a balding civil servant with a long and perfectly proportioned nose supporting a pair of thick-lensed glasses.

He had been inviting me to dinner for weeks. And so that evening I agreed—to make Martial jealous, naturally. That little Creole child had finally cleared off. I could have fired her from the Cap Champagne months ago, but she was good for business. And she did a good job of looking after Alex, too. Martial had never been able to look after his son on his own, but that was all over. This time, he would have to choose.

Alex was playing on the beach at Boucan Canot, as he often did in the evenings. I watched him from behind the bar of the Cap Champagne. The beach was already getting dark and was virtually deserted. I had decided to close the restaurant at 10 P.M. Even if it wasn't his turn to look after Alex, Martial would have no choice but to come and fetch him. He knew that I always nailed him whenever he was late. My employees were my witnesses. Letters to the judge. Martial was a kid who had to be punished. And my methods were working. He was making progress. By the time he came back to me, he would almost be the perfect father.

Yes, Martial would come to fetch Alex. And then I would make him aware of his responsibilities. He couldn't mess me around any longer. From now on, he would have to take the competition into account.

Fabrice was a young, rich, athletic lawyer, with a good head on his shoulders.

Martial might lose me forever.

And there was no way he could bear that.

4:05 P.M.

If I didn't turn up at the Cap Champagne by 10 P.M., that crazy bitch Graziella would write another tissue of lies to the judge. Seemingly the word of a father holds no more sway against that of a mother than a black slave's does against his master. So, around 9:30 P.M., I decided to go and fetch Alex.

I drove to Boucan Canot, and arrived just after 10. The sun had already set and all that was left was a red sky like a volcano awakening. I deliberately parked the car under the casuarina trees, at the end of the beach, some distance from the first street lamp.

I walked through the darkness, along the black rocks opposite the Hotel de Boucan. From there, I could observe the Cap Champagne bar without being seen.

That bitch Graziella was standing there, behind her counter, watching Alex as he played on the beach on his own, about ten meters in front of her, beneath the glow of the bar's neon lights.

As I expected, her supposed date was just a lie to lure me over as soon as Aloé was out of the way. I kept moving forward through the darkness, then I crouched down and watched Alex play for a few minutes. I loved seeing him like

DON'T LET GO · 309

that, escaping from the world of adults. Talking with an imaginary boat, a pirate, inventing fantastical shellfish. Graziella couldn't stand it when he wasn't doing anything useful.

Irreconcilable.

4:06 P.M.

Even though Martial had hidden his car under the casuarina trees, even though he was hiding in the shadows on the beach, I knew that he had come to fetch Alex. He probably thought I couldn't see him, but he was betrayed by the illuminated windows of the Hotel de Boucan behind him. I discreetly watched his dark figure, turning his gaze towards Alex every time the boy looked round at me.

I had guessed his plan, this time. Martial would rather pick up his son without seeing me, without even asking me how I was.

Classic.

The judge, Martin-Gaillard, had told me that some divorced parents were incapable of even going near each other, that they hated each other so much they would exchange their child by leaving them alone for a few minutes in a safe, neutral zone, like the lift of an apartment building, or in a park, or on the terrace of a café.

Martial and I had not yet reached that point, but it was clear all the same. He didn't want to see me any more. He wasn't a bad father. He wasn't even a cheating husband by then. But something in me disgusted him. My threats, my plots, only seemed to make things worse.

I had bet on the wrong number. I had lost.

Fabrice Martin could dispense with a long, gallant seduction during our dinner. I would give myself to him that night. Maybe I would grow to love him, after all. And maybe Martial would hate him . . . hate him so much that he would start loving me again.

Maybe everything was not lost after all.

4:07 P.M.

I stayed in the shadow of the rocks for a few minutes. I didn't want Alex to see me. It was already quite complicated for him, getting used to the to and fro of joint custody. He wouldn't have understood what I was doing there, in Boucan Canot, on a weekend when he was supposed to be with Graziella. And he'd have found it even harder to understand when I left again straight away.

I checked my watch. 10:10 P.M. Casting one last glance at Graziella to make sure she was still watching the beach from behind the bar, I began walking back towards my car.

4:08 P.M.

I looked at Martial's car, parked under the casuarina trees, to make sure it was still there.

Oh well, I thought.

One night of pleasure, just one . . . why shouldn't I be able to enjoy that too?

I didn't have the heart to say goodbye to Alex. He was sitting in silence on the sand, a few meters away from me. I had told him that his father was coming to fetch him.

He didn't say anything, just played with the sand, allowing it to slip through his fingers.

Alex was a sensitive child, but very reserved. So distant, he would probably have ended up being diagnosed as autistic.

I stepped back, my decision made. I now felt almost afraid to find myself face to face with Martial. His shadow might suddenly appear on the dark beach at any moment, asking me for explanations about the dress I was wearing, that bracelet on my wrist, the make-up on my face . . . I put on a jacket, shot a final look over at Martial's car, and then, switching off the lights of the Cap Champagne, I grabbed my mobile phone.

It was 10:10 P.M. Fabrice would have been waiting for me for quite some time now in the Flagrant Délice, the best restaurant on the west coast. All I said to him, in a curt, cold voice, was that I was on my way.

I was going to make him suffer, that one. And I was going to enjoy it.

4:09 P.M.

I started the car and called Graziella as I reversed out of Rue de Boucan Canot. The lights were off and all I got was the bar's answering machine. At the time, it seemed like a stroke of luck that Graziella didn't answer. It saved me having to explain myself.

"Graziella, it's Martial. I'm not coming to get Alex tonight. You have to stop inventing ridiculous excuses. You have to stop using Alex. We need to behave like responsible adults."

Then I went drinking until late with some friends at the other end of the Boucan beach, the Bambou Bar, a tiny little dive where all the different ethnic groups on the island somehow managed to cram themselves around three tables and ten chairs . . . One of the main reasons I knew that Graziella would never set foot there.

4:10 P.M.

It was 6 A.M. when I discovered Martial's message on my answering machine. I hadn't slept at home that night: Fabrice was a rather unimaginative lover, but he did have stamina. I listened to the message once, and didn't understand. Then I pressed a blue button that was flashing like the light bar on an ambulance, and Martial's voice repeated:

I'm not coming to get Alex tonight.

And then I screamed. I ran to the bay window overlooking the ocean. I ran on to the beach like a madwoman. There was already a crowd of people there: a swimming instructor, some passers-by.

And, lying behind this forest of legs, Alex's lifeless body.

4:11 P.M.

When the telephone rang, I didn't understand.

"Monsieur Martial Bellion?"

The alcohol was pounding in my head, and this cop kept trying to yell his meaningless words even louder. Leaving a six-year-old child alone on a beach with no lifeguards. At night. A kid who loved the sea. On a beach as dangerous as that one.

Then I realized, and everything exploded in my head. I didn't even try to offer an explanation to the policeman . . . I just ran, ran the five kilometers between Saint-Paul and Boucan Canot like a madman, screaming my rage at the ocean.

At first, I tried to make the cops understand that it had been Graziella's turn to look after Alex that night, to highlight the importance of those few minutes before and after ten o'clock, to tell them about the message I had left on the Cap Champagne's answering machine, which she denied ever having received. Graziella brought together a dozen witnesses who stated that they had heard her asking me to look after Alex, and confirmed that they had seen me parking my car around 10 P.M. near the Hotel de Boucan. Fabrice Martin, the lawyer, stated that Graziella was sitting at a table with him at the Flagrant Délice a few minutes after ten. Réunion Island is a small world, particularly among the Zoreilles who run the health system, the education system, the police force and the judiciary. Fabrice Martin was a second cousin of the judge, Martin-Gaillard, who was in charge of the investigation.

It was so much simpler to take all the blame myself that I had no desire to fight the charges by hiring a lawyer to negotiate my percentage of the responsibility for Alex's death. The judge bought my silence by passing a verdict of accidental death, so that I was free to go.

I left Réunion the following month and vanished into the greyness of France. That was ten years ago. At the time, the idea that I could start living again seemed unreal. Even more so, the possibility that I might ever look after another child. Essentially, Graziella had won. I was ready to shoulder the feeling of guilt on my own, to carry it, to drag it around with me. The fact that Graziella shared the same feelings did not lighten the burden for me in the slightest.

Divorced couples share responsibility for living children, not corpses.

4:12 P.M.

Martial was the only one to blame.

I have considered the matter a great deal since that night. Alone, not with a psychiatrist or any other confidante.

It was not my fault.

It was all Martial's fault. Coming like a thief in the night, hiding in the shadows, spying on our son and then leaving again without a word, getting drunk only a few meters away . . .

Martial had no excuse. Not for that evening, nor for the days leading up to it. Nothing would have happened if Martial hadn't abandoned Alex and me. My little boy would still be alive if Martial had simply agreed to keep loving us. Or to pretend, at least. If he hadn't sown death around him, like a malevolent angel.

After the verdict, Martial ran away—as he always did.

I stayed.

I tried to survive. I fired the *kafs*[48] and I closed the Cap Champagne. I moved to a different island, a different sea, but the waves still brought Alex's corpse back to me.

Every morning.

So yes, it was all Martial's fault. Worse than that, in fact.

I have thought about it a lot since then.

Martial wanted Alex dead.

Alex's death was a godsend for him. A chance to leave me forever. To put nine thousand two hundred kilometers between us. Martial must have wished for Alex's death so many times. Then finally he killed him that night, May 3, as surely as if he had put a knife through his heart.

Accidental death . . . That judge was an idiot, even more stupid than his cousin. The truth was there, right in front of their eyes. It was murder, pure and simple.

Premeditated.

Martial had decided to sacrifice Alex for a very particular reason.

He stole his life because he wanted to give it to someone else, a few years later.

A little blonde girl named Josapha.

It takes a few moments for Graziella to return to the present. She puts her hand on the black 4x4 and lets the tears roll down her ochre cheeks. What does it matter? There'll be plenty of time for them to dry later. Her make-up no longer matters.

---

[48] Racist slang term for Cafres.

In front of her, Martial moves forward with the girl in his arms.

Everything is going to plan.

She forces herself to smile, to speak in a natural voice, even if she almost has to shout to make herself heard over the din of the waves breaking against the rocks.

"Hello, Martial. You're on time, for once."

4:01 P.M.

H ello, is that the Saint-Gilles police station?"
Christos had uncapped a bottle of Dodo before lazily
picking up the receiver.

"Well, yeah, what's left of it."

"Christos? It's Moussa Dijoux. Of the Saint-Pierre municipal force. Do you remember me?"

Christos pictures a tall, jolly man with a propensity for calling the main police station any time there was even the slightest problem, slapping them heartily on the back and ending
each conversation with the words: "All right, well, I'll leave
you to do your job . . ."

Moussa Dijoux continues: "I expected to get an answering
machine. Aren't you all out on the bear hunt?"

"Well, no, as you can tell. I'm too old for all that."

Dijoux doesn't even pretend to laugh. It's a bad sign.

"I'm lucky I got you, then, Christos. Guess what? I've got a
corpse on my hands. Kartié Ligne Paradis. And you won't
believe it, but the person who reported it was an eleven-year-
old kid who called me on his mobile phone. A Cafrine, thrown
into the gully, probably by some guy who parked up there and
tossed her straight out of his car boot. Knife in the chest. Can
you imagine?"

Before responding, Christos takes a swig of Dodo. The last
he heard, Bellion was still on the run somewhere near the volcano. It would be difficult to pin this one on him. Wearily, he
replies:

"A prostitute?"

"No, I don't think so. She's not that young, more of a mother-of-the-family type, if you see what I mean. Nice curves, though. Can you get over here?"

Christos drains his bottle. He can sense he's going to have to play his cards close to his chest to avoid this chore. He hasn't even had time to call Aja or Imelda to tell them about his walk on the beach with Eve-Marie.

"I'm the only one holding the fort here. Given the context—Operation Papangue and all that—I'm sure you can understand that it wouldn't be easy for me to get away."

Dijoux raises his voice: "Come on, man! I'm just a municipal employee. You're not going to leave me here with a stiff on my hands . . ."

Christos sighs.

"For Christ's sake. It never rains . . . Got any details?"

"Not many. There's no ID. No handbag. We just found the keys to a Volkswagen in her pocket, and a badly parked red Polo three hundred meters away, with a dented orange door. Do you want the registration number?"

The bottle drops from Christos's hand and falls, almost in slow motion, onto the tiled floor of the police station. It explodes and sticky liquid covers his feet.

Christos does not move a muscle. All the veins connecting his heart to his other organs have been severed. As if his life had suddenly lost its moorings.

"Hello, Christos? Hello, are you still there? So, are you going to show up, or not?"

45
CREDIT CARD HAPPINESS

H ello, Martial," repeats Graziella. "It's been a long time." As Martial walks towards the black 4x4, Graziella takes off her cap and places it on the hood. Freed from the khaki canvas, her long, light chestnut hair cascades down. Her dark skin, from her eyes to the bottom of her face, is etched with white stripes. Thin canals dug into the clay by her tears.

Graziella has been crying. Her voice is harsh, cynical, as if to push aside all pity.

"I was sure you'd find a way to get here."

Martial stops a meter away from her. He is holding Sopha's sleeping form in his arms once more. He speaks quietly so as not to wake her:

"I came, Graziella. With Sopha. Alone. I kept my promise. Where is Liane?"

"Take it easy, Martial. We're here, the two of us, to come up with a fair solution. There's no need to hurry or get angry."

Martial takes a step forward. He stares at his ex-wife.

"Tell me she's alive, Graziella. Tell me right now, or . . ."

Graziella sits down on the embankment of black rock. She did not choose this location by chance. The riprap shelters them from the eyes of other visitors to L'Anse des Cascades, and the noise of the waves makes it impossible for their conversation to be heard more than five meters away.

"You understand now, Martial. Responsibilities. Family. That fear in your gut. Please, introduce me to your daughter."

"She's asleep. Don't worry, I'll take care of her. What do you want?"

Graziella looks around. Twenty meters away, a Zodiac is bobbing on the waves, moored to the trunk of a screwpine. She raises her voice again to drown out the sound of the swell.

"I want us to find a fair solution, I've already told you. All debts must be paid, Martial, even if it's years later. There is no alternative, if we want the ghosts to leave us in peace. If you didn't want to see them, why did you come back to this island with your wife and daughter?"

Martial almost yells, as if raising his voice might somehow break the clinical calm of his ex-wife.

"Because those ghosts only exist in your head, Graziella. They went with you when you left the island."

"No, Martial. They stayed here, at the Athena, at Boucan Canot, at the Cap Champagne. They were sleeping. You woke them up by coming back."

She stares, in turn, at the ocean and the waterfalls, then looks Martial straight in the eye.

"Did you really think you could escape your past?"

Martial staggers slightly. The weight in his arms is becoming almost unbearable, but he doesn't want to give in. He must buy himself some time, in order to protect Sopha. He thinks about the phone calls received the day after they arrived on the island.

"It's important that you came back to pay your debt, Martial. When you buy your happiness on credit, sooner or later you have to pay it back. One life for another. The life of your daughter for the life of my son. Then we'll be even."

Graziella continues in the same neutral tone of voice, like a judge listing the facts of a case.

"You thought about calling the police. Perhaps you even met with them discreetly. But what could you say? Ask them to provide you with a bodyguard? How could they possibly charge me on the basis of some anonymous threats? And what policeman would ever take your word for it without at least investigating the case first?"

The menacing voice on the telephone, heard one week before, continues to echo in Martial's head.

"Josapha has had the right to a fair trial. There were years of investigation. It's too late for an appeal, Martial. If the police come anywhere near me, or ask me even a single question, I will execute your daughter."

The same cold voice that announces triumphantly now:

"I was certain you wouldn't take the risk. Parents who've been threatened with the death of a kidnapped child might take a gamble by calling the police. They imagine that the abductors' objective is the ransom money, not to kill their child. But for you, Martial, there was no question of probabilities, only deadlines; how to delay the execution and continue to hope . . ."

Martial says nothing. He thinks about Liane's visit to the police station in Saint-Benoît. She almost told the cops everything that morning. He was waiting in the car. He'd made her promise not to mention their name. There was no proof against Graziella, and God only knew what she might do in retaliation if the police began to investigate.

"I know you," Graziella says now. "You must have wanted to run away, but all the flights were booked, weren't they? Or you'd have had to pay a fortune for a connecting flight, which was way beyond your means. We are responsible for the weight we put on the scales: if you hadn't married a penniless girl, maybe you'd be far away by now. But you couldn't escape your sentence any longer. Imprisoned here on the island. Without any protection. The executioner could strike at any moment. So this time, you did pay close attention to your child, didn't you, Martial? You didn't leave her alone on the beach by the lagoon. You worried about her. You did your duty as a father.

You behaved impeccably, like a prisoner hoping to negotiate an early release for good behaviour."

Don't say a word. Play for time.

Occasionally, Graziella glances over at the Zodiac.

"Such a good boy . . . But you were planning your escape. I have to congratulate you, Martial. You tried to slip into a mouse hole that I hadn't spotted. It took me a while to understand your strategy. Liane disappearing suddenly, and you setting it all up so that you would be suspected of having murdered her. Two minor wounds, a few drops of blood scattered around the room, nice and obvious. So you borrow the cleaning lady's cart, making sure you're seen by several employees. Liane leaves her room without being seen, alive of course, while everyone imagines that you are transporting her dead body. All the evidence, all the clues, point to you as the killer. The police have no choice but to hold you in custody and to place Sopha under judicial protection. Two days later, Liane reappears, a few hours before the departure of your flight. She was just having a fling with someone, she will explain. The police apologise to you, free you, and the three of you fly back to France. It was a complicated plan, but a good one. You and your wife are no fools, Martial."

"Actually, the plan was all mine," says Martial. "To start with, Liane wouldn't agree to it. She didn't want to leave Sopha alone with me."

Graziella lifts her eyes up towards invisible shadows, beyond the waterfall.

"But then, to your great misfortune, she did listen to you. You forgot one detail, Martial: the ghosts are always wary. I was watching you the whole time. Liane had the opportunity to admire several touching family portraits on the walls of my house in Saint-Pierre. When you left her in the hotel car park and she got out of the laundry cart, a Malbar in a khaki baseball cap was waiting for her. And he kindly suggested she get into his Chevrolet Captiva."

This time, Martial can't restrain himself:

"If you've done anything—"

"Take it easy," Graziella interrupts, holding up her hands. "Don't try to pin this one on me, Martial. You're the one who tried to help your wife escape. You failed. You knew the rules. Punishment. Solitary confinement. Poor Liane—it's not her fault, when you think about it. The only thing she can be blamed for is meeting you. Do you realize you've dug a grave for your entire family all by yourself?"

Martial moves back a meter or so, and leans against the trunk of a screwpine to reduce the strain on his arms. He has to protect Sopha from this madwoman for as long as he possibly can.

"And you killed that guy in the port in Saint-Gilles? Rodin?"

"That's your fault, Martial. Entirely your fault. If it wasn't for your stupid plan, that *kaf* would still be alive. He turned around at the wrong moment, just as I was putting Liane in the boot of my car. You provided me with the murder weapon, it was in Liane's bag: a knife with her blood on the blade and your fingerprints all over the handle. I was more hesitant to kill that old woman whose house you were staying in. I saw your little Sopha in the streets of Saint-Gilles, disguised as a boy. A boy, Martial! A boy of Alex's age! As if you, too, had realized that you had no choice but to exchange one life for another. The rest wasn't too complicated. I followed her. I hid about ten meters from the house. A few minutes later, the old lady turned up. Imagine what would have happened if I hadn't stopped her, if she'd found you in her house? You'd have been forced to put a knife in her neck yourself to keep her quiet . . . I'm right, aren't I? Would you rather have sacrificed your daughter?"

Graziella looks at her ex-husband and goes on:

"No, of course not. But, once again, you make out that nothing is your fault. Can I ask you something, Martial?"

Martial has managed to create a makeshift, uncomfortable seat for himself by leaning against the pyramid of roots attaching the trunk of the screwpine to the ground. He chooses not to answer. A few more seconds gained. Graziella continues:

"I wonder exactly when you realized your plan had failed. That first night, I suppose. Liane was supposed to call you, to tell you everything was all right, that she'd found a hiding place as you'd planned, so that you could then perform your pantomime for the police . . ."

Graziella pauses for effect.

"But she never did call you, did she?"

In spite of himself, Martial remembers his gathering terror after reporting the supposed disappearance of his wife to the Saint-Gilles police. No phone call from Liane that evening. Then the murder of Rodin. Then the message written on the window of his rental car. *Tomoro . . . be ther.* How could the cops possibly understand how a guy willing to let himself be accused should completely change his attitude only a few hours later?

It was impossible.

Martial clings on to three words.

"Where is Liane?"

Graziella gives a reassuring smile.

"She's still alive, Martial. At least for a little while. It's nice and warm where she is. She's tougher than I expected."

Suddenly the smile freezes.

"Enough talking, Martial. I don't care whether your wife survives or not. She was just bait to lure you here with your daughter. Wake her up now. Set her down on the ground. Let's get this over with."

Martial tries to think as fast as he can. It's already a miracle that Sopha has not heard Graziella's confession and threats. Is his ex-wife really capable of murdering a little girl as cold-bloodedly as she killed two inconvenient witnesses?

His eyes plead for mercy.

"Please don't mix Josapha up in this, Graziella. She has nothing to do with our adult problems. She's . . ."

For the first time, a scowl of anger deforms Graziella's face.

"Oh no, Martial. No. Our problems are certainly not just about adults. Have you calculated how old Alex would be today? No, I bet you haven't. He would be sixteen. A handsome young man. I'd be worrying about his grades. I'd have found the best *lycée* for him: European, he'd be studying applied arts, engineering science. Maybe I'd have gone back to France to give him the best chance of getting into a good university. Wake up your daughter, Martial. She must give me back the life she stole."

Martial thinks about risking it all, grabbing his ex-wife by the throat and throttling her until she tells him where she has imprisoned Liane.

Too late.

Graziella has anticipated Martial's every reaction. Without warning, she takes a small black revolver from under her *kurta*.

"A Hämmerli," she tells him. "Swiss. Very expensive. They assured me it was the quietest gun on the market. Believe me, nobody will hear the gunshot over the sound of the waves."

She aims the gun at him.

"Put her down, Martial. Put the kid on the ground or I'll shoot."

4:14 P.M.

The dry gully in Kartié Ligne Paradis is an open sewer into which the local residents throw their rubbish. Rusty cans, flat tyres, a television with no screen, mouldy newspapers, dozens of empty bottles, a ripped settee, foam rubber, cardboard, metal, glass, shit . . . a foul slop that is carried down from Les Hauts to the ocean by each successive storm. Dead animals sometimes, too; the corpses of cats, dogs, rats.

And the corpse of Imelda.

Thrown down there like just another piece of garbage.

Christos descends into the gully and stands in the vile mud at its base. He holds the already cold body to his heart. His heart is filled with murder, it's a bomb, it's molten lava; he wishes he were a god so he could make it rain for forty days, rain until the end of time, so he could blow a wind that would unleash a tidal wave over the island, sweeping up tonnes of water, earth and shit from the windward side and pouring it down on the opposite shore, engulfing all skin colors, all races, all the poor people in shacks and the rich in their villas.

Up on the path overlooking the gully, Moussa Dijoux doesn't dare say a word. His wide, complicit smile froze on his face as soon as he saw Christos get out of the station's Mazda pickup truck.

As he saw him run.

Saw him flash his police card and cleave through the crowd.

Heard him howl over the dead body like a dog.

Christos kneels down. His hands disappear in Imelda's long, frizzy hair. His hunting instinct awakens, like a monster opening its eyes after a long hibernation.

All the questions he asks himself smash against walls of glass.

Who could have killed Imelda?

Why?

Why did she come to this rotten kartié, *almost straight after she'd said goodbye to him and left the police station?*

What will happen to her children?

The policeman tries to rid his mind of the image of the five kids.

Nazir's proud gaze. Dorian's *tec-tec* legs pedalling furiously in his overlarge shorts. Amic's shy concentration behind his glasses with their twisted frames. Joly's cascading laughter as she rocks on his knees. Dolaine's big, round eyes, looking up at him from the pram.

Five kids. He'll have to tell them about their mother.

Who could kill a mother who loved love so much?

The crowd above the gully is increasing in number. Old people in their straw hats, snotty-nosed kids in torn T-shirts, Creoles who weep and others who sneer. They must all think that Imelda was a battered wife.

Nothing out of the ordinary, even if they're intrigued by the crying cop.

Dijoux holds out a friendly hand.

"Come on, Christos. Take my hand. You can't bring her back to life."

Christos doesn't move. He rummages in his pocket for his mobile phone. He has to call Nazir. He's the oldest. He'll have to look after Joly and the boys. Little Dolaine too. Christos's fingers come upon a soft plastic packet, and he identifies it as the bag of *zamal* he confiscated from Nazir that morning.

Imelda had insisted on it. At 6 A.M. she had stood guard at

the door of the house and wouldn't let Christos leave until he'd found it—which he did easily, under the mattress.

Nazir, fifteen years old. Smoking cannabis. Selling it too. And now an orphan.

Responsible for his four siblings?

He needs to be responsible for himself first. And not move on to coke, for example.

Christos thinks about little Joly in her princess dress, made for her by her mother. About Amic who Imelda promised she would take to see the sea as soon as he could ride his bike without stabilisers. He thinks about the meals the kids won't eat any more, and the vegetables that will rot in the garden; about the house that will fall into ruin.

Christos thinks, without believing it, that maybe the kids have an uncle, a cousin; an adult of some kind that they can rely on. Then there's the welfare state too.

His hand grabs the mobile phone. He moves it to his mouth. He doesn't know what he will say to Nazir. He doesn't know who will answer. He wonders if phoning is really a good idea. Will he even have the courage to return to Imelda's house one day?

He blinks when he sees the screen of his phone.

A missed call.

He clicks on it.

From Aja.

And not just one missed call, but five.

Plus a text.

Call me back FFS!

Unthinking, Christos calls her.

Aja's shrill voice explodes in his ear.

"Bloody hell, Christos, what are you up to? I called the police station about twenty times. Where the fuck are you? I need you. Urgently."

"Go on. I'm listening."

Aja is silent for a moment, as if surprised by her deputy's tame response.

"The manager of the ITC Tropicar rental agency called. He's just found Martial Bellion's Clio! Christos, are you all right? You sound kind of strange."

"Don't worry about me. I'm bearing up."

"Are you sure? You don't sound like yourself. Where are you? Did something else happen?"

Christos raises his voice:

"Later, Aja. First tell me about this rental car."

"You'll never guess where the manager found the Clio. That bastard Bellion parked it in the agency car park, in the middle of all the other rental cars! On Avenue de Bourbon, less than three hundred meters from the hotel. If it hadn't been for a customer returning a car just now, the guy wouldn't even have spotted it until tomorrow. What do you think about that? Christos . . . are you there?"

"Yeah."

"Are you on *zamal*, or what?"

"I'm on my way there, Aja, don't worry."

"O.K., hurry. I trust you to make that damn car talk. Oh, and one last thing, Chris—'

"What?"

"I know you, man. Something's up, I can tell. I don't know what it is, and I'm not going to bug you if you don't want to talk about it, but just promise me you'll be careful. I care about you, you know."

"Thanks, Aja. That means a lot."

He hangs up. The hunter sniffs the ground.

Imelda was killed after reading through the police files on the Bellion case. Stabbed—just like Rodin, like Chantal Letellier. Except that for Imelda's murder, Martial Bellion has a cast-iron alibi: he was on the Plaine des Sables at the time, surrounded by at least thirty cops. So perhaps Bellion did not kill Rodin either. Or Chantal Letellier.

Perhaps the real murderer is still at large on the island.

The guy who put a knife through Imelda's heart.

Christos barges his way through the circle of onlookers.

He turns the key in the ignition. The Mazda's tyres squeal.

The siren screams. He speeds through the curves with the stink of burning rubber.

The other cars travelling towards Saint-Louis move to the side of the road to let him past.

The landscape opens up and then closes at each bend. The colored towers are swept aside like skittles—the mosque's blue minaret, the church's white bell tower, the monsters grimacing from the roof of the Temple du Gol—like so many charlatans on whom Christos slams the door.

The pickup barely misses fruit stands and pedestrians as Christos takes shortcuts.

So what if he goes too fast around a bend? So what if his brakes don't work? He doesn't care.

47
ONE LIFE FOR ANOTHER

4:17 P.M.

Graziella's fingers tighten around the trigger of the Hämmerli.

"I said, for the last time: put her down!"

Martial remains where he is, leaning against the trunk of the screwpine. He has decided not to give in until he has proof that Liane is alive.

"Where is Liane?"

"I'll shoot that kid, Martial."

"Where is Liane?" Martial repeats quietly, without making any sudden movements, to show that he does not want to do anything that might wake his daughter.

Graziella hesitates. Slowly, her index finger curls around the trigger. Martial holds the small sleeping body tight in his arms and prays that Graziella will not be content with a bullet fired at point-blank range. She has probably imagined a more formal execution for Sopha.

Keep her talking.

"Sopha crossed the whole island on foot to see her mother. You could at least give her that."

Graziella smiles and relaxes the pressure on the trigger.

"You haven't changed, Martial. Still as good as ever at pleading your cause. Come on, then, as it matters so much to you. Move."

She points the barrel of the Hämmerli towards the sea, straight at the moored Zodiac.

"You go first."

Martial moves cautiously over the black, wave-soaked pebbles. He concentrates on keeping his balance without being able to use his arms, for a few meters at least. Graziella is no longer insisting that he wakes Sopha. She must have realized that, with his hands full, he cannot attempt anything desperate.

"You're almost there," Graziella announces behind him. "Have a look in the boat."

Martial takes one more step forward. The Zodiac, moored to a screwpine by a six-foot length of rope, moves constantly in the swell. For the first time, Martial notices the two twenty-liter jerrycans of petrol attached near the motor.

Then he sees Liane.

She is lying at the bottom of the dinghy. Gagged, hands and feet tied together with metal wire.

But alive.

Martial turns around, his eyes filled with fury. "What did you do to her?"

Graziella's eyes gleam.

"So you're beginning to realize that this isn't all a game? A *kaf*, an old Zoreille, you don't care that they're dead, not really. But your two little darlings . . ."

Martial trembles with rage. He bites his lip and turns back to the Zodiac. Liane stares at him hollow-eyed, as if she isn't sure she recognizes him.

She is completely naked. Her skin is blistered, as if some evil torturer had inflicted hundreds of burns on her, all superficial, but covering every inch of her body. A torturer who paid particular attention to certain parts of her anatomy: her feet, blackened by a red-hot brand; her wrists, peeled raw; her crotch, smooth and scarlet, as if irritated by an interminable procession of lovers.

Graziella now stands between Martial and his wife.

"You're right. It would be a shame if Liane couldn't enjoy the spectacle too. After all, the only reason she's survived is the hope of seeing her daughter again. She deserves to be allowed to kiss her corpse."

Graziella caresses the Hämmerli's trigger once more.

"For the last time, Martial, why don't you introduce me to Sopha."

"Go fuck yourself!"

Instinctively, Liane moves inside the Zodiac. Graziella does not even glance at her.

"Clearly, Martial, you cannot be left in charge of a child. Didn't Alex's death teach you anything?"

Martial does not have the time to respond. Graziella's finger suddenly squeezes the trigger. Aiming for the heart, standing less than one meter from Sopha's body.

Three gunshots explode, but are drowned out by the sound of the waves.

Three bullets rip open the blanket. Almost instantaneously, the cloth becomes soaked with blood.

Martial's fingers, wrists and sleeves are stained red. In the next second, the blood beads in the corners of his eyes, flooding a myriad of scarlet veins.

A demented look in his eyes.

Fury that is absolute.

Martial, stunned, presses the little corpse against his chest.

Graziella remains impassive, continuing to aim the revolver at the blanket.

"So Josapha has joined Alex. One life for another, Martial. The debt has been paid. She had to be sacrificed so you would understand. So you understand what it is to go mad with pain and be intoxicated by vengeance."

4:23 P.M.

The man from the ITC Tropicar agency looks like a wedding guest who has been summoned to work in an emergency. Crumpled shirt, floppy tie, and sweat stains under his armpits.

"Good thing the customer called me about his air conditioning . . ."

Christos isn't listening. This guy is a word machine, a businessman who thinks he's on some kind of social bonding mission. Christos moves towards the grey Clio without any idea of what he is supposed to find in this car that Bellion abandoned. There is a ball of acid stuck in his throat. Some guy stabbed three innocent people, and that guy is not Martial Bellion. He is sure of it now.

"And it's also a good thing that I know how to count to seven," continues Monsieur Tropicar. "It's not something you see every day, you know, a car coming home on its own. Particularly when the car's been driven by a killer."

He almost chokes in a fit of coarse laughter.

The sun has modestly hidden itself behind the only cloud above the lagoon and the murky darkness makes the place look even more squalid: the washed-out mauve building, the sliding metal gate, the rows of identical cars.

Monsieur Tropicar won't shut up. He analyses the tyres of the station's Mazda pickup, which is parked diagonally across the untarmacked car park. The ochre earth still bears the skid marks of sudden braking.

"It's also a good thing that your brakes worked on the descent here, Captain. You could have killed yourself. I once knew a guy who rented a Laguna to drive up to Salazie, and after the fiftieth bend, he—'

Christos grabs the agency man by his tie.

"Will you just shut up! Got it? Open the Clio for me and give me the rental contracts, everything you have on Bellion. But, most importantly, keep your big fat mouth shut."

"O.K., O.K.," stammers Monsieur Tropicar, his mouth gaping open like a grouper fish.

Finally, he trots away towards the mauve building.

4:27 P.M.

Christos searches in the glove compartment, between the seats, under the carpet.

Nothing. No clues at all. Only an assortment of Réunion's finest sand in every shade, from white to black.

Well, what was he expecting? He could come back, or someone else could, equipped with a Polilight and some test tubes, but what could the analysts possibly reveal except for the fact that Martial Bellion and his daughter had left their fingerprints here, that they had sand on their flip-flops, and that this could be used to reconstruct a detailed map of their peregrinations on the island. But how would that help the investigation?

Monsieur Tropicar returns holding a bundle of green and blue papers. He watches Christos examine the car, intrigued and admiring.

"Don't touch anything," the second lieutenant tells him as he gets out of the Clio. "My colleagues will come by later to take care of the sand and the fingerprints."

"Good thing, too. It's in the contract. It has to be in tip-top condition when it's returned to us!"

More loud laughter.

Although he knows that it would be a stupid gesture that would not further the investigation one iota, Christos would like to smash his fist in the rental guy's face. Instead he just lets his arms hang by his sides. There's a killer on the loose. There are no clues. He has to tell five kids that their mother is dead. And none of the gods of any of the religions practised on the island could even give a shit. They . . .

Suddenly the sun appears, making the constellation of cars sparkle and gleam. Monsieur Tropicar swells with pride beside his polished galaxy of vehicles. The only blot on this pristine picture is Bellion's Clio. Drab. Dusty. Especially the doors and the windows. The rays of sunlight illuminate the traces of hands, fingers.

Christos stands motionless, paralysed with shock.

It's as if one of those gods, stung into action high above them, has suddenly made the truth burst forth from his index finger, just to convince the miserable louse below who insulted him.

On the window of the passenger door, words appear in letters of fire.

Fantastical, almost unreal.

Anse dé Cascade

Tomoro

4 P.M.

Be ther

Bring the gurl

49
At the End of the Field

I run as fast as I can. In the middle of the cane field, I can see even less than I did in the fog up on the volcano, but I don't slow down. I use my arms to push away the stalks that hit my face and my legs.

I think about Papa's words again. The words he spoke when he woke me up, just before the main road.

"Run, sweetheart, run through the field, straight ahead, and try to follow the sound of traffic, but don't let anyone see you. Look out for the bell tower of the church. Don't go up or down, just try to stay at the same level so you won't get lost. The umbrella lady, Sopha, remember? You have to reach the umbrella lady. There'll be lots of people there. You'll be safe."

I cried a lot.

I knew from the beginning. Papa was lying to me.

I'll never see Maman again. And yet he told me she was waiting for me there, near the black rocks, on the other side of the road.

Papa had crouched down in front of me then. The way I like him to. And he started speaking very fast, almost without breathing.

"You're right, sweetheart, your *maman* is on the other side of the road. But there's something I haven't told you. There is another lady waiting for us there. A lady your Papa used to love a long time ago. Alex's mother—you know, your big brother who died. That made her very unhappy, when Alex died, and she's become a bad person, a very bad person. Like the witches in your books, like Grand-mère Kalle. Do you understand, Sopha? So, you have to help us. Are you my princess, sweetheart?"

My heart hurt too much for me to answer.

"Are you my princess, yes or no?"

"Y-yes . . ."

"Good. Then you have to run, Sopha, you have to run and tell the fairy with the parasol, the one who protects us. You have to run as fast as you can."

I don't believe in fairies any more, Papa.

I am running, though. I'm running as fast as my legs will carry me.

Because this time, I believe you.

4:29 P.M.

Three smashed guava branches lie on the pebbles. The murky red liquid that poured from the fruit is almost instantly washed away by the foam from the waves. Near the guavas, a beige canvas blanket has fallen, as if abandoned by a ghost, frightened away by the three gunshots. A fourth branch, thicker and covered with sugar cane and screwpine leaves to give it the shape of a young child, has rolled a few meters further away.

Graziella suppresses an explosion of hatred. The Hämmerli shakes in her hand.

"Where is the child?"

"Somewhere safe, my darling."

Graziella moves forward. The barrel of the revolver is only a few centimeters from his chest. The dark foundation on her face, streaked with tears, looks like war paint. She forces herself to lower the tension, to keep control of the situation and of herself.

"What's the point of your little ruse, exactly?"

"I had to bring something in exchange for Liane, as you told me. But did you really think I'd be stupid enough to hand Sopha over to you? She just had to stay with me as long as possible, because I knew you'd be listening to the radio, following the hunt as it happened. If I'd given Sopha to the police, you would have known immediately. It would have been all over the news."

Graziella erupts with forced laughter.

"How touching! And how ridiculous, too. She can't have got far in that case. With a bit of luck, I should have time to kill you both and then go and flush her out with my 4x4."

For a brief instant, Graziella turns away and looks over at the Zodiac. Martial doesn't hesitate this time. His arm flies forward and, with the back of his hand, he knocks the revolver out of Graziella's grip. It falls to the ground two meters away.

Lodged between two stones.

Graziella swears. Martial shoves her backwards. Spotting the Hämmerli, he rushes towards it, bridging the distance in three strides. He reaches down, and his hand closes around the revolver. He turns and aims. Finally the mad bitch is . . .

The sun disappears behind a black moon.

This is the last thing he sees. In the next second, the huge black stone that Graziella has picked up with two hands smashes against his temple.

4:31 P.M.

The fairy with the parasol!

She's there, in front of me. I can see the big blue umbrella above the cane stalks.

I'm almost there!

It's really a parasol, Papa told me, not an umbrella!

The blue fairy hasn't seen me. Her eyes and smile are soft, like a *maman* who forgives everything.

I keep pushing through the sugar cane. The stalks hurt me. It's like swimming through a sea of sharp seaweed, but there are less of them now. I think I'm coming to the end of the field.

I can run even faster. I hear the cars on the road. I see houses in the distance. Papa told me to grab the first person I see and tell them my name is Josapha Bellion.

"Just your name," Papa told me. "The first thing the person will do is call the police."

As you wish, Papa.

If you think the police are better at fighting witches than fairies.

Sopha will never know the answer to this.

Suddenly, she bursts through the last curtain of sugar cane, her eyes fixed on the blue and gold parasol. Never did she imagine that the cane field would stop for a lava flow.

Her right foot is the first to bang against the grey scoria. Sopha loses her balance. Then her left foot trips over a block of tuff.

The little girl rolls several meters. She sees the blue fairy and the parasol spinning in the sky, like a tightrope walker defying gravity, while her whole body is scraped and torn on the sharp, serrated rock.

But she doesn't suffer for long.

Her head collides with the slender trunk of what is known in Réunion as a "rampart tree,' growing in a narrow gap between the flows of hardened lava.

4:32 P.M.

A *nse dé Cascad*
   Tomoro
   4 P.M.
Be ther
Bring the gurl

Christos turns the five lines and the eleven words over in his mind.

An anonymous hand, probably Martial Bellion's, has attempted to erase this message written on the passenger window of the grey Clio by quickly wiping the glass. But, revealed by the sunlight like this, each letter remains perfectly legible. The finger that traced them pressed down hard for each line, each curve, each point.

Rounded, nervous handwriting.

Monsieur Tropicar stands immobile, the five rental receipts in his hand. He, too, is looking at the words on the door. The cop standing before him looks so tense that he thinks he should try to lighten the mood.

"It's also a good thing I recognized the killer's car before I took it to the car wash."

The laughter dies in his throat. Christos does not react at all, as if he hasn't heard. Tropicar doesn't press the matter. He's a professional. Along with a good sense of humor, the two other qualities of a good businessman are tact and understanding.

Christos moves closer to the window, focuses on the words.

Anse dé Cascade
Tomoro
4 P.M.

Instinctively, he looks at his watch.

4:33 P.M.

Who could have arranged this meeting with Bellion?

Christos stares at the glass with the improbable hope of finding another clue. The sun, shining through the window, burns his retina. The solution is there, all the same. Those five lines should be enough for him to grasp the reason behind this wave of murders.

Bring the gurl.

Christos feels lost. All the pieces of the puzzle are here, in front of his eyes, and he is incapable of fitting them together. Imelda would have done it.

She died because of this, and he is incapable of avenging her.

Christos looks at his watch again, then gives up. Time is against him, like a game of speed in which you must not seek the solution to a problem that cannot be resolved instantly. You must simply act. Christos reads the message one last time. In the absence of anything else, he does have a meeting place, a meeting time, and a guest list. He must warn Aja. Nervously, his hand searches for his phone.

Everything was decided in the following seconds. He was not the one who made the decision, but his fingers. This is what he will always think, strangely, whenever he remembers the scene years later.

His fingers rummage around in his pocket, avoiding the pack of *zamal* and digging further down. At the moment when they close around the mobile phone, they brush against a folded sheet of paper. The middle finger and the index finger co-operate to extricate the page from Christos's pocket: the faint red-lettered printout of the email sent from Mauritius by

Graziella Doré. His gaze skims over the pale logo of the Sapphire Bay hotel, the seven barely visible names of the Creole employees, and, just below them, handwritten, the name, address, phone number and signature of Graziella Doré.

Rounded, nervous handwriting.

Graziella Doré
3526 Sapphire Bay Link Road
Mauritius
+ 230 248 1258

Christos's heartbeat accelerates.

One by one, he examines the vowels of the five lines traced on the Clio's window, then compares them to the barely readable letters spelling out the woman's first name.

Anse dé Cascade
Graziella

It's a crappy printout, and he is no graphologist, but, even so, there can be no doubt: on the Clio's window and on the printed email, the e's and the a's are exactly the same shape. An open loop traced in a spiral.

A spiral staircase descending into insanity.

Amazed, the rental guy watches as Christos moves as swiftly as a beach attendant who's just stepped on a jellyfish. He pulls out his mobile phone, types the numbers in a blur of digits, and then yells in a voice loud enough to scare all the chameleons out of the casuarina trees.

"Aja? Can you hear me? It's Christos. We've got it all wrong! Bellion's not guilty. It's his ex, Graziella Doré. She's been manipulating us all along."

"What? Christos, hang on, slow down. I thought she was in Mauritius?"

"Fucking hell, Aja. For once, just trust me. Anse des Cascades. Send everyone you can there. Maybe there's a small chance we can still save them."

"I don't understand, Christos. Save who?"

"Save Martial Bellion and his daughter! Listen to me, for fuck's sake. It was a trap! Graziella lured them to the other side of the island for one reason only. To kill them! That was what she wanted. To kill them both, just like she killed Liane Bellion."

51
The Angels

Martial curls up on the floor of the Zodiac, his head bleeding; the scattered thoughts in his head are drowned out by an unbearable buzzing. His memory crackles in flashes, reconstructing the past few minutes in strobe lighting.

His loss of consciousness was brief, just enough time for Graziella to drop the basalt rock and tie his hands and ankles with the metal wire she kept in the trunk of her 4x4. His rude awakening: his ex-wife digging the barrel of the Hämmerli into the back of his neck and ordering him to crawl over to the dinghy, without offering to help; instead, standing firmly on the stones, she watched his suffering with the sadism of a child torturing an insect. And, lastly, his head-first dive into the boat; his clothes soaked by the puddles of lukewarm seawater and blood lying in the hollows of the plastic floor.

Liane . . .

She lies next to him, wrists and ankles fettered, hands behind her back, completely naked except for the gag around her mouth.

She's badly burned. But alive . . .

While Graziella unties the boat, Liane shuffles clumsily over to Martial, her chest against his. Her eyes express the only question that matters to her:

Where is Sopha?

"Sopha's O.K., Liane. She's safe."

Graziella gets into the dinghy and starts the motor. She

stares at her prisoners, paying no attention to their weak caresses.

"I'll pay a visit to your little treasure later. Someone will have to look after her when you're gone."

Liane's eyes are filled with hatred. Martial sits up against the edge of the dinghy, as much to reassure Liane as to get Graziella's attention.

"The police will have Josapha by now. You can't win them all."

Graziella bursts out laughing then presses on the accelerator. The Zodiac leaps as it drills through the waves nearest the shore. The most violent waves. Liane and Martial lose their balance and he falls on top of her.

"Your naïvety is almost touching, Martial. You think you can get out of this that easily? Have you still not understood? You're the one the police are looking for! You're the one who murdered poor Rodin, who cut old Chantal Letellier's throat. You're also the one who stabbed that nosey black woman. You're the only one who is guilty, Martial. How many times do you need to be told? Imagine if your corpse and that of your wife are never found. What will the police think? That you killed her too then disappeared. The Creoles love this kind of murder story. You'll be famous. Like Sitarane, but without a gravestone. The serial killer whose body was never found. Is Martial Bellion really dead? You'll become a legend. Some Creoles will say they've seen your ghost in the *avoune*."

Graziella stares up at the clouds. Martial balls his fists. He rubs his head against the edge of the Zodiac to wipe away the blood that continues to ooze from his wound. The rocky coast behind them is now just a thin black line with the huge dry bulk of the volcano towering over it. They are past the strong currents, and the sea is suddenly much calmer.

"Do you understand the situation now?" Graziella asks.

She pauses for a second, then hammers in the nail:

"Poor Martial. Once again, you've made the wrong decision. Thinking about it now, killing your daughter wouldn't have brought Alex back to me. But when you're not around any more, I'll be able to visit your little Sopha. I could even offer to adopt the poor, traumatized orphan. That would be so generous of me, looking after my ex-husband's daughter. Who could possibly say a word against it?"

Martial thinks about responding with a hail of insults. But he knows that this is what Graziella is expecting. So he stares out his ex-wife, defying her with all that remains of his manly pride. Finally he turns around, carefully, and kisses Liane, with infinite tenderness, on the least blistered parts of her skin. Her eyes, her shoulders, her breastbone, the tops of her arms.

Graziella does not react. She is content to observe them furtively, her right hand tensed around the boat's rudder.

Martial does not stop. He moves further down and presses his wet lips against Liane's darkened breasts, her stomach, covered with scarlet stigmata, purple bumps and dead skin, licking her wounds like a cat tending its injuries with its rough tongue. Slowly, Liane's breathing is transformed into a hoarse gasp, muffled by the cloth gag.

"Stop that nonsense, Martial."

But he doesn't stop. He continues his exploration, even more gently. Between the thighs, Liane's skin is now just raw flesh but Martial ventures there. His wife's body shudders with every kiss.

The Zodiac stops in the middle of the sea. Graziella aims the Hämmerli.

"All right, Martial, you want to play? Come on, then! The rules are simple. I will aim at the precise part of your darling's body that you are touching. Understand? If you kiss her arm or her leg or her hand, she might survive for a few minutes longer. Anywhere else . . ."

For a second or two, Martial assesses the determination in

Graziella's eyes. He remembers the three bullets fired at point-blank range into the blanket that she thought was covering the sleeping Sopha.

He moves away from Liane.

The Zodiac's engine starts up again.

For several long, silent seconds, they move away from the coast.

4:41 P.M.

"You think you can reach Mauritius in this dinghy?"

Graziella is amused by Martial's question.

"Mauritius is just over one hundred and seventy kilometers away. It's barely a three-hour journey. The sea is calm, the weather forecast couldn't be better. It's a nice little trip. The only real constraint is petrol, which I have to take with me so I can fill up the tank *en route*. And, because of you, I've already had to make the same journey yesterday, there and back, just after you began your escape. With Operation Papangue, I realized that the police would want to interrogate me on Mauritius. Three hours in a boat . . . I arranged to meet with them late in the evening to give myself time to get back—it wouldn't have been very discreet to take the plane—and then a few hours after making my statement to a man from the consulate at the Sapphire Bay, I returned here during the night. The 4x4 was waiting for me at the Anse des Cascades. I didn't want to leave you alone for too long, with all those police chasing you. And most importantly, I had to move your wife, from my house in Saint-Pierre to a prison with a sea view, not far from here. We had a meeting. I wanted my bait to remain alive as long as possible in order to lure you here."

Martial can barely imagine the hell that Liane has been through. She is no longer pressing herself against him, and is leaning against the side of the Zodiac instead. Her blistered, brown skin, glistening with foam, looks like the patched plastic of an adult doll.

Graziella stares at the horizon, as if she can already see the coastline of Mauritius.

"Of course, the Sapphire Bay's employees don't know where I am, but they have instructions to transfer all incoming calls to my mobile. It makes no difference whether I'm in Réunion or Mauritius: a simple iPhone is all I need to send any official document. The policeman I talked to on the phone earlier seemed a bit sharper than the one from the consulate, he was certainly more curious, but I just told him what he wanted to hear. Zoreilles love hearing the sob stories of Creoles—it's their old paternalistic streak. He must have dug into poor Aloé Nativel's past . . . do you remember little Aloé, Martial? Another of your victims. If she hadn't met you, she'd have a nice husband by now, a pretty little house somewhere, half a dozen kids . . ."

Aloé?

Another victim?

Martial does not reply. He forces himself not to think about his former girlfriend.

Don't be distracted.

He has to protect Liane and Sopha.

He looks out at the horizon. They are still less than a kilometer from the coast. The curve of the Piton remains perfectly visible.

"What are you going to do with us?"

Graziella stares into the distance ahead of them.

"You remember the weeks I spent alone, Martial, when you went off deep-sea diving? You told me all about the spots you visited, those places full of fish where the seabed would slope down so dramatically, sometimes more than a hundred meters in depth only twenty or thirty meters from the coast. I listened to you,

Martial. I made a mental note. I'm going to wait a bit longer, until we're over the deep-sea plain. I can't take any risks if I'm going to look after little Sopha. Your bodies must never be found."

Graziella pretends to look sorrowfully at Martial's bleeding head and the open wounds covering Liane's body.

"At least the descent won't be as long as you think. The sharks' judicial system moves much faster than their human counterpart."

Martial forces himself to control every movement of his body so that he does not betray his fear. He won't give Graziella that pleasure. He moves closer to Liane, leaving only a few centimeters between her bare skin and his soaked clothes. They obey Graziella's orders—they do not touch each other—but they stare into each other's eyes, their irises mixing like the colors on a painter's palette, fusing their souls more intensely than any caress could.

As long as they are alive, Graziella cannot break the connection between them.

The Zodiac flies over the sea and the island recedes into the distance.

It's over. They are completely alone now.

4:44 P.M.

The seconds tick by, punctuated only by the noisy thrumming of the Zodiac's motor. Slowly, Liane changes position. She makes a few painful contractions and manages to sit up, her back against the inflatable's side, as if she could no longer bear lying down.

Graziella gives the smile of a tolerant jailor and looks back at the ocean.

One quick glance, and Martial understands. He lowers his eyes to Liane's hands, tied behind her back, held slightly apart.

He conceals his amazement.

Her fingers are gripping a sharp spike of basalt about ten centimeters long.

Once again, Liane seeks Martial's agreement with her eyes. A silent marriage vow.

Till death do us part.

For worse. Only for worse.

He checks behind them—the volcano has disappeared behind the line of mist—then nods. Liane grimaces. Her arm muscles tense. The wounds open, blood flows. It doesn't matter any more.

Graziella immediately notices that something is wrong.

Too late.

In the next moment, the sound of the motor is drowned out by the noise of an explosion, followed by an interminable sharp whistling as the dinghy deflates.

Graziella screams, stops the motor, aims her Hämmerli and violently pushes Liane out of the way.

The rip in the plastic is about ten centimeters long and is growing quickly with the pressure from the escaping air. In a few seconds, the Zodiac will be nothing but a flabby plastic envelope sinking to the bottom of the ocean, dragged there by the heavy motor and almost sixty litres of petrol.

"You crazy bastards!" Graziella spits.

Standing upright in the Zodiac, she estimates the distance to the coast.

Not much more than a kilometer.

A scowl distorts her face. She forces herself to regain control of the situation.

"You really love making my job easier, don't you? After all, it hardly matters whether you die here or a little further on."

The rip continues to blow hot air over their skin. Liane rolls onto Martial and the boat tilts under their weight. Graziella, impassive, maintains her balance.

"I seriously doubt you'll be able to swim all the way to shore with your hands and feet tied together. As for me, I'm not in any great danger. Never mind the crossing, I'll just have to take the plane back to Mauritius."

She stares at the turquoise water.

"I'll give Sopha a kiss from you both."

As the water begins to lick at the Zodiac's drooping plastic, Graziella tears open her *kurta*, revealing the two lifejackets she is wearing: the final detail of her disguise as a fat Malbar.

In the next moment, she is nothing but a red dot floating on the ocean.

4:46 P.M.

Martial is suffocating. Already, the water is entering his mouth. He spits it out. The Zodiac has vanished beneath them like a huge translucent jellyfish drifting along with the underwater currents. Liane clings to him. He feels her naked crotch against his, but they are incapable of helping each other. Without the use of their hands, they are both drawn down irremediably into the depths, but they continue to struggle against their fate, desperately moving their joined legs like two weak flippers.

Their bodies touch, crash into each other.

He can kiss Liane, one last time.

Just above the waterline, Martial's lips touch Liane's cheek. His teeth bite into the plastic sticking tape that is holding the gag in place and tear it off in one sudden movement.

Liane screams, at the top of her voice, with pure, animal pain.

One brief moment.

Then they sink together, their mouths joined.

The ocean cannot separate them. They kiss for an eternity,

sharing their oxygen. This is the only air they will ever breathe again before they asphyxiate. This is how they will die. The most beautiful death that two lovers could imagine.

They no longer think about reaching the surface.

Martial can already see the lights of the next world, a funeral chapel with fluorescent coral walls.

As he lets himself sink, he is surprised to feel Liane biting him. He stares into her eyes one last time. Liane looks up. One meter of water above them.

Martial feels the water infiltrating his brain, flooding it, feeding his hallucinations. He is surrounded by coral now, not only below him but above too. Unbelievable colors: orange, red, blue.

Liane bites him again, on the chin this time, hard enough to draw blood. Her eyes beg him. She wants to fight, to kick herself back up to the surface one last time.

Body against body, back muscles straining as they flap like two exhausted mermaids, they manage to force their heads above the water for one final breath.

Together.

Liane explodes with laughter and kisses him again.

He looks up, not understanding.

Around them, angels are descending from the sky.

Silent angels, flying with the aid of immense, rectangular, multicolored wings.

52
WATERFALL

A long plastic orange ribbon separates the hundred or so onlookers—who rush forward from picnic huts, from the village of Piton Sainte-Rose, from the coastal road where they have parked their cars on the hard shoulder—and the corner of the grassy area enclosed by the elephant-foot trunks of four Barbel palms. The space is occupied by only three people.

Martial and Liane Bellion, and Aja Purvi.

The police captain has ordered the other cops to move away, including those who agreed to throw themselves from the Enclos Fouqué, two thousand meters above, and swoop down like eagles towards the little black dot moving out to sea that they could only distinguish through their binoculars.

There will be time, later, for acknowledgements, effusions, decorations and honors.

Liane is wrapped in a survival blanket, but is shivering all the same. Martial, who insisted on keeping his wet clothes on, hugs her tight.

"You will be transferred as quickly as possible to the Félix-Guyon hospital in Saint-Denis," Aja says in a gentle voice. "The helicopter is landing now. It won't be . . ."

Liane doesn't seem to be listening.

"Where is Sopha? Have you found Sopha?"

Aja stands up, her neoprene wetsuit open over her bikini. She replies quickly, almost tripping over her words.

"We'll find her, don't worry. It's all over. It'll only be a matter of minutes now."

Her answer is evasive. It sounds as if she's guessing. Aja has done the best she could. Martial places a comforting hand on his wife's shoulder.

"You don't know anything, Captain, do you? You don't have any more information than we do."

He is silent for a moment, as if searching for the right words to express the mixture of relief and anxiety he feels.

"You've already performed a miracle, descending from the sky like that. I'm not going to ask you to go back up there."

Aja smiles. Liane's long blonde hair drips onto the blanket. She listens to the roar of the waterfall behind them. Farther off, the sounds of activity under the tropical almond trees. Car doors slamming, barked orders, men laughing, children shouting. An unforgettable Easter Monday for everyone who is here.

"Do you have children, Captain?"

Aja is surprised by Liane's question.

"Well . . . yes."

"You can't have seen much of them these last few days. How old are they?"

"Five and seven."

Liane forces herself to smile. Martial puts his hand in front of his eyes.

"That's good. They must be proud of you."

Aja bites her lips. She is moved but also disturbed by this private moment. What the hell is Jipé doing with that helicopter?

5:31 P.M.

Suddenly there is a movement in the crowd. Four officers clear a meter-wide path through the ranks of gawpers. Cameras are pulled from pockets. Fingers are tensed in readiness. Aja expects to see Jipé appear, flanked by two stretcher-bearers.

Guess again.

Laroche!

The colonel has somehow found the time to change his outfit. He is now wearing a linen jacket, beige canvas trousers, and moccasins. He's probably already done three radio interviews and two TV shows.

He steps aside.

All smiles.

An arrow appears behind him. A little blonde arrow with a large bowl-shaped bandage on her head. She shoots straight at Liane's heart.

"Maman!"

Sopha runs, holding a bouquet of hibiscus in her hand. The mauve petals are crushed and tumble all over the blanket, between Liane's chest and that of her daughter. A miraculous herbarium they will keep for the rest of their lives.

"We found her on the lava flow above Piton Sainte-Rose," Laroche explains. "She'd banged her head against a tree. Nothing serious. We could have come sooner, but she insisted on picking a bouquet of flowers before she saw you."

Liane bursts into nervous laughter.

Sopha manages to articulate a few words, in spite of her chest being held in a vice-like grip:

"It's for the fairy with the parasol, Maman. She's the one who saved us."

Martial tousles the few short hairs on his daughter's head not covered by the bandage.

"Good thinking, sweetheart. A promise is a promise."

Cameras flash. Aja slips away, leaving the spotlight on Laroche. The pictures will be posted on Facebook and dozens of blogs within minutes; the story will join the ranks of other local miracles, hurricanes, lava flows, sea rescues, accompanied by ex-voto flowers for the island's saintly protectors: the priests, the firemen, the police . . .

Very few for her . . .

Aja moves towards the waterfall. Suddenly it occurs to her that it has been years since she has come here, to this little corner of paradise, that Jade and Lola have never been, that her two little she-devils don't really know the island; that she and Tom no longer find the time to have picnics, or go swimming, to park their car by the side of the road, any of that . . . Also that time is passing so quickly.

Most of all, she realizes she wants to see them, here, now, to hug them tightly, for an eternity, and then to leave them at her mother's place in Fleurimont, in her ceramic palace, and to run away with Tom and make love for three days and nights.

53
GOODBYE, ZAMAL

5:33 P.M.

The current has carried Graziella to the Cap Méchant, almost on the southern tip of the island, between Saint-Philippe and Saint-Joseph. Her feet press down on a mixture of grass, sand and pebbles as she wearily throws aside the two soaking life jackets, which seem as heavy as lead.

She collapses on the tiny beach under the basalt cliffs. Exhausted.

She mustn't rest for more than a few seconds. She can't gather dust here. If Bellion and his slut have survived, she's going to have every cop on the island searching for her.

She looks up at the sky and thinks she can see, again, that rainbow of hang gliders whirling down towards the two bodies, like tropicbirds around a dead fish thrown from a trawler.

Come on, get out of here. Don't take any risks.

Above her, a few stones roll down the cliffs. She curses: she had forgotten those bloody *kafs* and their barbecues. Cap Méchant, Anse des Cascades, Pas de Bellecombe. She can't wait to get back to Mauritius. How could she have lived all those years on this underdeveloped island that stinks of curry and skewered beef?

Other stones fall, more of them now, until suddenly she hears a voice, above the noise of the little avalanche.

"I've got quite a few friends here who are windsurfers. To start with, I was like the girls, impressed by all the risks they took. And then they explained to me that if you studied the ocean's currents a bit, if you knew the starting point for a body that dives into the ocean, it's fairly easy to predict the exact spot where it will turn up."

Christos moves to the edge of the cliff, five meters above the beach and Graziella. He keeps his service revolver aimed at the woman.

"I had a head start on all the other cops."

Graziella has turned pale. She cranes her neck up at the cliff and sees only a huge, backlit shadow, but she recognizes the voice of the cop from Saint-Gilles. What does he know? She realizes that there is nothing now to connect her to the Malbar who murdered Rodin, the blue-haired Zoreille and the black woman: no baseball cap or *kurta*, no artificial fat, no dark foundation, which dissolved long ago in the sea.

"Bellion lured me to the Anse des Cascades. He told me that . . ."

The sudden noise of a gunshot. The bullet skims Graziella's ear and explodes three pebbles behind her.

She jumps.

"You're cra—"

Christos interrupts her, yelling:

"There's no point giving me a string of alibis, Madame Doré. I think there's been a . . . shall we say, a misunderstanding. I have the feeling that you've got me mixed up with someone else. A cop from Saint-Gilles. You remember, the one you treated like a fucking idiot? I do look like him, it's true, but as you already know, appearances can be deceptive."

Christos crouches and then sits on the edge of the cliff overlooking the beach, seemingly relaxed, his Sig-Sauer still trained on Graziella.

She steps back. A prisoner.

The grey, vertical cliff is like a prison wall, with this cop observing her from his watchtower.

"But I haven't introduced myself. I am Imelda Cadjee's

husband. You remember, Ligne Paradis, the Cafrine you dumped in a public sewer after stabbing her in the chest."

"You're crazy, you're . . ."

Graziella walks resolutely towards the little patch of beach cabbage that skirts the foot of the cliff.

Another gunshot, a few meters from her foot, orders her not to move again.

"You could have been caught by a cop, Madame Doré. He would have taken you into custody and ensured you had a fair trial. Some poor guy who's just lost the woman he loves, on the other hand . . ."

He aims pointedly at the woman's forehead. Graziella is immobile, petrified. She cannot read any emotion in Christos's expression: not fear, or hatred, or determination, only emptiness. She realizes she has no hold over him, that no attempt at blackmail or manipulation will have any effect.

He doesn't care. He has nothing left to lose.

He is going to shoot.

"I'm going to do you a favor, Madame Doré. I think Imelda wouldn't really have liked it if I'd shot you like this. She was incredibly intelligent, but like the inhabitants of this island, she had an unwavering belief in all those superstitions, offerings, prayers, respect for the dead, all that stuff, you know? Do you know any *kaf* prayers, Madame Doré?"

Graziella remains silent, but shakes her head slightly. His eyes never leaving the woman, Christos puts down the revolver and pulls the packet of *zamal* from his pocket. He takes his time, rolling a joint and lighting it, before he starts to speak again:

"No? You've never had to ask the *kaf* gods for anything? I'll try to recite one for you, then. From memory. I can't make any promises, but I've heard little Dorian, Joly and Amic repeating it almost every night by their beds. Those three kids are Imelda Cadjee's children. You can thank those little *kafs* for this brief reprieve, Madame Doré. To give you an idea, it will end with something like '*Me tir anou dann malizé,*' which means, 'but deliver us from evil.'"

Christos picks up the revolver again and aims it at Graziella's feverish eyes, then slowly begins to recite:

Aou, nout Papa dann syèl
Amont vréman kisa ou lé,
Fé kler bard'zout out royom,
Fé viv out volonté.

The prayer punctuates Christos's thoughts.

How many years in prison can a cop get for shooting an unarmed criminal at point-blank range? The worst kind of criminal? A few years? Maybe less with a suspended sentence and early release . . .

Partou toultant parèy dann syèl.
Donn anou zordi zourpouzour
Nout manzé pou la vi.

He takes a drag on his joint. Being in prison would be the best excuse he could find not to be there on the day when the island's social services evacuate the house in Saint-Louis and take the five kids to the orphanage in Tampon.

With a bit of luck, Nazir will be eighteen by the time Christos gets out. Maybe he'll even go to prison in Domenjod for theft or dealing just as Christos is being released. Maybe the house will be resold. Maybe he'll never have to hear about those kids again.

Pardonn anou le tor nou la fé
Kom nou osi ni pardon lézot.

Tears run from the corners of his eyes. He rubs them away, as if the smoke from his joint has been blown into his eyes by the trade winds, stinging them. Graziella stands motionless two meters below, awaiting her sentence; perhaps reciting the same verse in Latin or Mauritian. The children's laughter echoes in his head, blending with the Creole prayer that they recite every night.

Aren't you working today, Jesus?
Hey, stop looking at Maman's arse!
Can I sleep with you two in your bed?

The *zamal* acts as a veil. It helps to repel the ghosts of those kids when they cling to him, begging for a hug or a wrestling match; it gives him hallucinations too, and starts talking all by itself, up there, in his hazy head.

No, Imelda, no! You must be dreaming! I'm just a cynical old bastard who spends his days getting drunk in the port.

Imelda, seriously? Do you even believe what you're saying? Can you imagine me as a father?

Five kids all at once?

The *zamal* smoke takes on strange forms: faces, odours, voices.

You should have thought about this before, Imelda. I'm not even their father. What am I, for those kids, when it comes down to it? Nothing. You were clever, Imelda, the cleverest Cafre of them all, but you chose the wrong guy on that score . . . A guy who drinks punch like water and smokes *zamal*.

Bad choice.

Lès pa nou anmay anou dann tantasyon
Mé tir anou dann malizé.

But deliver us from evil.

Now put an end to it. Fire.

Christos, can you tell me a story about a bad guy?
A really bad guy.

Christos's hand suddenly grabs the packet of *zamal* that he was holding between his legs and, like a resigned fisherman, he throws it out as far as he can into the ocean.

He aims his gun at Graziella. She closes her eyes, hands held together.

It's over.

"Graziella Doré, you are under arrest for the murders of Amaury Hoarau, Chantal Letellier and Imelda Cadjee. You must answer for these crimes before the courts of this island."

He falls silent and takes an interminably long drag of *zamal*, before flicking the butt onto the beach.

The last cigarette.

Like a prisoner, condemned. To look after five children.

He can hear Imelda's laughter bellowing inside his head.

Michel Bussi is a professor of geopolitics and one of France's bestselling authors. His novels have been published in 35 different countries. He is also the author of *After the Crash* (Hachette, 2016), *Black Water Lilies* (Hachette, 2017), and *Time Is a Killer* (Europa, 2018).